EXIT 13A

A Control Tower Diary

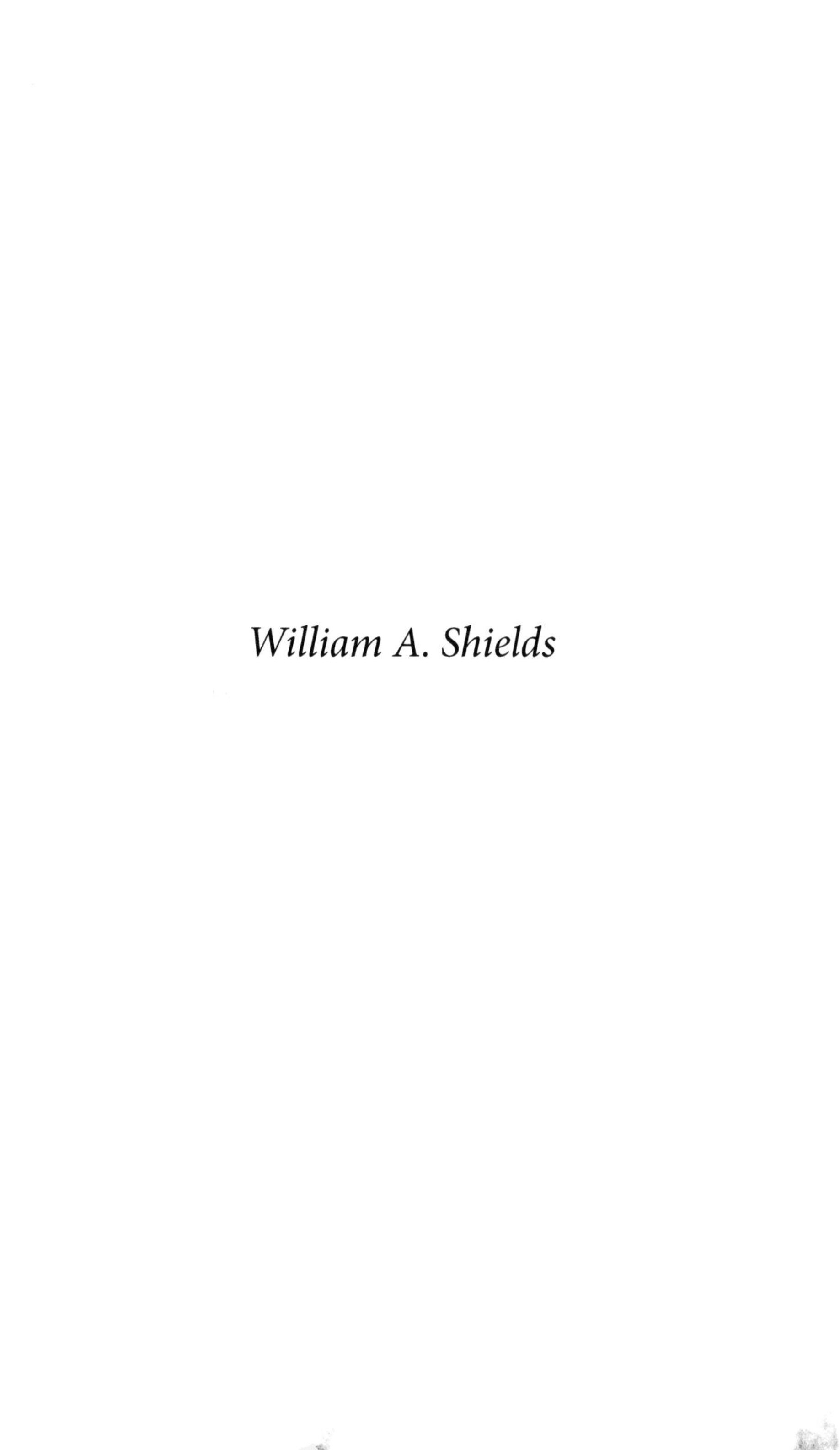

William A. Shields

EXIT 13A A Control Tower Diary

ISBN: 9781478341093

This is a work of fiction. Names, characters, places incidents are products of the author's imagination or are u tiously. Any resemblance to actual events, locales or perso or dead, is entirely coincidental. There is one exception. Va is a real person who has graciously granted permission for to be used in this story without conditions. Val is the worl ing authority on vintage recordings and the Doo Wop genr can be found in his store at 49 Garrett Road in Upper Darb surrounded by four million 45rpm records. Phone Val (at y risk) 610-352-2320.

DEDICATION

For the dedicated, courageous and faithful
air traffic controllers I have known - both of them.

PROLOGUE

A Marine drill instructor paces a Third Battalion squad bay. Sixty new recruits toe the painted line in front of their bunks, thirty a side, facing inboard. For five long minutes the recruits have been standing straight, with arms outstretched to the front at shoulder height, palms down, M-14 rifles held suspended in space, parallel to the deck.

The D.I. needs a squad leader from his new platoon and he knows almost nothing about them, except that they come from hometowns east of the Mississippi river. As teenage arms backs and shoulders begin tiring, most of the rifles start to waver, dipping toward the concrete deck.

In a process of simple attrition, the weaker recruits are eliminating themselves from consideration. Presenting eleven pounds of steel and walnut at arms length, and holding it motionless, is a twisted, Parris Island version of the common job interview. Opportunities for advancement can come suddenly in the Marine Corps, in basic training as in combat.

The Gunnery Sergeant stops in front of one recruit whose rifle butt hangs lower than the muzzle. His composure lost, the private's face is contorted, eyes pinched tight against the stinging sweat. A sloppy and wrinkled utility cap, larger than it needs to be, rests on the recruit's large ears, giving a comical appearance to the aspiring Leatherneck. The D.I. steps between weapons and invades the recruit's personal space, the brim of his campaign hat nearly touching the side of the private's head.

By this time, the entire platoon is struggling. Arms are sagging; some rifles are dropping down altogether for a momentary rest, and then quickly brought back to the parallel.

"What's your name, Private?"

"Sir, Jablonski, Sir."

"You look like one tired polack to me, Jablonski. Are you tired?"

"Sir, no Sir!"

"I'll bet if those were Suzy's titties you were holding, you wouldn't drop them now, would you?"

"Sir, no Sir!"

"Lock your body."

Private Jablonski quickly assumes a position of attention, the steel butt of his rifle coming to rest on the deck near his right foot. The D.I steps back to gaze down the length of the squad bay. Two rows of rifles are pitching and bouncing, as if the weapons were floating on an invisible ocean of troubled waves.

Suddenly, something catches the drill instructor's eye. Striding quickly to the other end he stops between two recruits whose bodies and rifles are holding motionless, as if stone-struck, or cast into bronze bookends. A port side Private from Rhode Island and a starboard side recruit from Delaware seem to be taking their orders seriously. A mirror image, they stare across at each other like two boxers at a pre-fight press conference, each waiting for the other to blink. The D.I looks at each, but says nothing. With a step and a pivot he marches away smartly, giving individual orders to "lock it up," and "lock your body" to the rest of his weary charges. One at a time, like falling dominoes, the recruits snap into a military position of attention, each welcoming the chance to rest and recover.

Finally, only two rifles remain aloft. Locked together in a silent war of determination, neither Private shows any sign of wavering. Both are standing fast, without so much as an eyelash in motion.

They are Parris Island still life, like Spanish moss hanging in the silent, stagnant South Carolina air. A housefly lands on Rhode Island and feasts unmolested on salty face and neck perspiration. The D.I. removes his hat and wipes the sweatband with a handkerchief; checking his watch, he's concerned that the training schedule is about to be compromised.

Almost unnoticed, one of the rifles drops a fraction of an inch. A minute later, it drops a full two inches. The Drill Instructor's eyes narrow. Bent at the waist, he closely follows the slow descent of the rifle. Feigning surprise, he glances from the now undisciplined rifle to the offending Private and back again. All at once, the recruit falters, his arms and shoulders giving visible notice that they are no longer taking orders from his brain. His back arches in a futile attempt to elevate the rifle to its last assigned altitude.

That quickly, one recruit's fleeting flirtation with excellence is over. His bid for exalted status among his peers, cancelled. The would-be standout is now but an "also ran," one of sixty raggedy-assed recruits. He will now try to disappear into the platoon. His high water mark will be to simply graduate recruit training with everyone else, and leave Parris Island in uniform.

Throughout the entire exercise, the Drill Instructor did not seriously belittle or admonish anyone. He ignored the weaker recruits and those who bailed out very early in the game, those who became willing spectators for the two more serious gladiators. The D.I. saved his vast reservoir of vicious ridicule for the Private who settled for second place, heaping unrestrained verbal abuse on him. He would hound and harass that recruit unmercifully until graduation day, reminding him daily, that when the opportunity presented itself, when called upon to step into a leadership role, he lacked the mental discipline required. By being unfaithful to himself, he was the type of individual that would let others down in times of trouble.

Chapter One

High above Newark Airport, the crisp November night air is saturated with jet engine noise and a curiously rank mixture of burning jet fuel and beer. Not many airport control towers smell of beer, but this one stands less than a quarter mile from the Anheuser Busch Brewery, known by the controllers as the "Bud Plant."

On a concrete catwalk an air traffic controller surveys the airport movement area below. The smell of brewing beer reminds him of the hops plants that had migrated across the highway to grow wild near the highway approach ramps on the airport property. Propping a shoe up on the aluminum pipe railing, he inspects the shine and tightens the laces. A large, animated neon eagle spreads its wings and illuminates the steam escaping from the roof of the famous beer factory, the last of the large breweries that once made Newark a beer-producing giant among American cities. A reflection of the neon sign appears in the glossy toe of the controller's shoe.

Liam A. Doherty is still buzzing from the previous two hours on local control, the busiest, most intense position in the tower. A hectic session transpired as the final approach radar controller attempted to cram more airplanes into the airspace leading into Newark International Airport, than the available space permits.

Doherty breathes deeply. Inhaling through his nose, he fills his lungs to the bursting point, then steadily exhales through the mouth, hoping to bring his blood pressure down a few points.

"Less than standard separation" is FAA jargon. It means closer than the law allows. By law, rule and regulation, anytime two airplanes get closer than permitted, a controller must file a report; an investigation must follow. Almost no FAA controller or manager applies these rules diligently. Cover-ups are so routine, that a violation or a "deal" actually acknowledged by the FAA is more rare than a spacewalk. So the public is force-fed a running newsreel that shows a nearly flawless air traffic control system, "the safest in the world." Consequently, unwitting airline customers continue to march like zombies directly into the largest game of Russian roulette ever played.

Another tower controller might accommodate such an illegal and unsafe operation, and then quickly pretend it didn't happen. Many controllers do this, to prove that they are team players. They need to show the FAA supervisors they can be counted on to play ball, and bend the rules for them, even lie for them if necessary. Lying and covering up are basic skills that an FAA controller must master prior to any promotional consideration. The management scaffolding process, constructed on rungs of mendacity, is anchored in a foundation of falsity harder than bedrock. Even so, controllers are expected to know the rules, the law and the consequences of violating the law. Should his superiors get caught trying to hold back the floodwaters, say, after an event that has drawn too much publicity, they will blame it on the controller who lied – not FOR them but TO them. Suddenly, the manager-controller relationship takes on a less than cooperative, downright unfriendly tone. *"Hey, you knew the rules. Look right here in your training folder; you signed off on it. Nobody told you it was okay to break the rules. Nobody ever asked you to lie."*

Operating on this dangerous edge has become the norm as the FAA tries to hide a dysfunctional air traffic control system. It is a system with severe problems, exacerbated by the firing of the

PATCO controllers during the summer of 1981. One of the primary goals of the PATCO strike was to bring attention to many of the safety issues plaguing the air traffic control system.

Doherty is anything but a team player. He is the FAA's biggest pain in the ass. A stern and strident perfectionist, Doherty's air traffic control world is black and white like the black letters on white paper in the rulebook, or the big white numbers painted on their corresponding black asphalt runways. He sees these things for the noble and valid purpose they hold–to safeguard human life. Unlike his FAA supervisors and many of his co-workers, he has chosen to take this responsibility seriously. Strictly applying the rules, disregarding peer pressure, and directly confronting the employer, is an agenda that dovetails smartly with his libertarian lifestyle of fierce independence and an inbred resentment of authority.

Doherty is prolific at ordering a "go around", sometimes called "the long ride", or the "air show". With their landing clearance revoked, pilots are made to over-fly the airport for re-sequencing. They are sent back to the radar approach controller for another try at the runway. This usually adds 45 minutes to a flight. Pilots who thought they were about to land find themselves in a big right turn over Piscataway, Passaic, River Edge, Hackensack and Kearny before getting back to the airport. A "go around" also impacts the departures, adding to delays as a slot is wasted while the aircraft clears the departure corridor.

Doherty ponders the two-word phrase "go around" that packs so much power over the system:

Funny, when they come back to land the second time, after a go around, they always seem to have a nice, safe, legal separation on the aircraft ahead. Wonderful thing, a go around...makes everyone a better controller- instantly. I key the mike and put two magic words in a pilot's ear, and he firewalls the throttles and sucks the wheels up. Then, controllers start jumping, and not just here in the tower, but in the TRACON, the Terminal Radar Control Facility on Long Island. It's like kicking the system in the ass. This is real power. Massive flying machines are circling around me. Pilots await my next directive. They depend on my skill, my knowledge of this airport, the local area, the rules, and their aircraft's capabilities and characteristics. They are nearly helpless without me. This air traffic control game is better than any toy I ever got for Christmas. And, when it's done right, it's better than sex. A man who can do this and do it well...and doesn't love it... well, he's not alive, or he's not a man.

Doherty changes into some fresh clothes and shines his shoes before reporting to the Manager's office on the ninth floor.

You could cut yourself on the crease in his heavily starched khaki trousers. A second pair of trousers and a shirt is brought to work for every watch except the midnight shift. The tin man's personal uniform never varies. Black military style dress oxfords, khaki trousers, black belt with a highly polished brass buckle and a short-sleeved white dress shirt, summer and winter. The watch supervisor, Frank Hamblin, had requested a meeting. Hamblin is not happy about the recent number of airliners that got the long ride, courtesy of Doherty, and his insistence on adhering to the rules. While loosening and re-tightening the laces on his shoes, Doherty thinks about the state of controller-management relations in the FAA.

It's an upside down world in the FAA these days. The managers love weaklings that will run a dangerous operation for them. They favor the meek and compliant, the pushovers who lack any sense of integrity. They prefer candy-asses that can be counted on for nothing except backing down and hesitating, stammering and drooling, horrified to the point of incontinence at the thought of standing up to the employer, even when that employer asks them to do something illegal.

The FAA will not hesitate to discipline or try to intimidate anyone who adheres to the rulebook, takes the rules seriously, or simply looks and acts like a competent, professional control tower operator. Loyalty to the employer and loyalty to public safety are mutually exclusive virtues for an FAA controller. The worst sin that an employee can commit is to try to hold FAA management accountable for their actions.

Doherty steps from the catwalk into the controller ready room. A conversation is halted in mid sentence. While passing two female controllers, he let's them know that it is safe to continue their talk. "As you were, ladies."

Doherty is used to hearing conversations stopped in mid sentence. A girlfriend once remarked that he instills a low, constant, simmering level of fear in everyone he meets. Intimidating strangers and co-workers is not something Liam Doherty tries to do, though it is certainly an overt attribute of his personality. Checking his shirt, belt buckle and zipper seam for alignment, he strides into the tower administrative offices – pogue country.

FAA supervisor Francis (Frank) Hamblin is a portly, balding man. His large head is splotchy and red, like a well- slapped ass. His lumpy face could be mistaken for a bag of bullfrogs.

A career FAA bureaucrat and a paper pushing chair-borne ranger, Hamblin represents many other FAA managers and supervisors. They make their living sucking the giant U.S. government tit, abusing their authority over air traffic controllers whenever they get the chance.

Stepping into the office, Doherty reports to Hamblin who is sitting behind the absent, air traffic manager's big desk. An unwritten law in the FAA states that the facility air traffic manager should have the biggest desk and the most expensive chair in the building. If for nothing else, the air traffic manager could have his picture taken while seated at his big desk, flanked by the U.S. and FAA flags to engender a feeling of government credibility and government security, to any who should glance upon his likeness. Appearance and style trumps substance and reality in the modern FAA. They want Americans to see a nice, big, button tufted, executive style leather chair and an expansive, impressive desk. They want the public to think: *"Hey, these government guys are important; they must KNOW something. They LOOK very professional!* And, for that one transitory moment, the flying public stops thinking about themselves or their loved ones slamming into a tobacco field and dying in some smoking crater halfway between here and Disneyworld.

Walking up as close to the big desk as possible, Doherty removes the home court advantage forcing Hamblin to conduct the entire counseling session while looking up at his subordinate. The odor of cheap cologne and perspiration makes Doherty long for the outdoor odor of jet fuel, Budweiser hops, and the occasional benzene and sulphur smell from the oil refineries of nearby Linden, New Jersey. Doherty makes a mental note to call Hamblin "Francis" at some point; he knows that the FAA supervisor gets annoyed when anyone calls him by his given name.

Hamblin appears to be reading from the contents of a manila folder. Pausing for effect, he tosses the folder aside, leaving a scrawny hairless forearm hanging in mid air for a moment. The FAA supervisor leans back in the big reclining leather chair and glances up. Liam being short for William, Hamblin like most others, uses Doherty's nickname.

"Sit down, Willie."

"No thanks, Frank. I'm not tired. I'm fine right here."

"Willie, I got a call from Continental's chief pilot. He says you cost them a lot of money tonight in fuel alone. You saw fit to send two of their flights around, and I expect to hear from Delta and TWA as well."

"Did you get his name?"

A long pause, then,

"Whose name?"

"Continental's chief pilot."

Another pause.

"I have it here somewhere. What difference does it make?"

"I'd like to put him on the record."

Hamblin leans forward in the leather chair and scratches his scaly cocoanut causing flakes of dead epidermal matter to fall onto his knit polo shirt. His beady, rodent-like eyes start darting left and right as he seemingly digests the meaning of Doherty's question. The sound of a departure spooling up engines for takeoff on nearby Runway Two Two Right precludes any conversation, so Hamblin gains extra time trying to figure out where Doherty is heading. Doherty notes the particularly high-pitched whine of the jet engines and audio-identifies the departing flight as an Airbus A300 probably Continental.

"Willie, just what the hell are you talking about?"

"Let me ask you this, Frank. Did you speak to Continental on a recorded telephone line?"

"That's none of your business, Willie. Now where are you going with this?"

Hamblin, clearly agitated, shifts his weight in the manager's reclining leather chair causing it to groan and squeak. In poker parlance this body language is a "tell." Doherty now knows that a voice tape recording exists. That quickly, he has taken control of the meeting, putting Hamblin on the defensive. Now he will push a giant pile of chips into the middle of the table.

"Here's where I'm going, Frank and you're coming with me. I believe that a Continental Airlines employee may have committed a crime, and I intend to report that crime to the FBI. I believe, from what you just told me, that someone at Continental Airlines tried to coerce an FAA employee or employees into violating published standards and regulations endangering the flying public. I would hate to think that YOU might be an accomplice to this unlawful activity. Now, I want a union representative at this meeting right now to get this on the record, and the first thing I want you to tell him is the exact reason that you called me here to this official counseling session. So be prepared to answer that question when he gets here. Now I'm not saying another word unless a union rep is present."

The sound of Hamblin's teeth grinding could be heard if not for another jet airliner departing on Runway Two Two Right near the base of the tower. His eyes darting more furiously, they would occasionally stop to meet Doherty's, searching for some sign of weakness, an opening, maybe a blink. It would not be forthcoming. With fists on hips, Doherty stares steely-eyed right through Hamblin, through the shabby curtains and dusty flags behind him, out across US Routes 1 and 9 toward the apartment buildings in Hillside, New Jersey.

Frank Hamblin remembers being warned about Doherty. Supervisors, the manager, and more than a few controllers agree that Doherty has an uncanny ability to turn the tables on authority figures, and he is always ready to go on the offensive. They say he resents authority and that he's a troublemaker. He's no dummy and he intimidates everyone he meets and seems to enjoy it. He knows the rulebook and the union contract as if he wrote them himself. The "book" on Liam A. Doherty is accurate on all of these counts.

Hamblin's Adam's apple stops bobbing. Doherty knows he is about to speak.

"Are you trying to intimidate me?"

Hamblin's attempt to sound like a tough guy, fails miserably when his voice cracks and he squeaks out the word "intimidate."

Doherty says nothing, but continues to stare down at Hamblin.

No, I'm not trying to intimidate you, you pathetic pus bag. I am intimidating you and we both know it. You brought me here to scare me into submission and now it's you with your tail between your legs.

Hamblin has clearly lost control of the meeting. His intent was to admonish an employee and put him in his place. Instead, the employee took control of the agenda, and all that Hamblin can do now is play by Doherty's rules or call for an adjournment.

"Willie, get the hell out of here."

"Sure Francis, except I'm too upset now to work an air traffic control position. It wouldn't be safe. I'm requesting sick leave for the rest of the watch for safety reasons."

"Approved. Go home."

"Aye, Aye, Sir."

Doherty turns about smartly and walks away getting another blast of Skin Bracer and body odor in the process. He makes a mental note to have the union make a formal request for a copy of the taped telephone conversation. A telegram will be sent to Hamblin memorializing the official counseling session they just had together, and what was discussed. Telegrams are more official than a certified letter and the supervisors can not claim they never received one. Plus, it pisses management off when Western Union shows up at the tower to hand deliver a love letter from Doherty.

Doherty wonders what Hamblin will do. Will he back off and pretend that nothing happened? Will he wait and see if any phone calls were made? One thing is certain when it comes to guys like Hamblin. He would call the Tower Manager at home and brief him about what happened and ask for guidance. Pussies like Hamblin can't allow themselves an independent thought or any unilateral action. Unlike supervisors and managers, working air traffic controllers have to think on their feet. Supervisors have already proven themselves incapable of such talent; that's why they are FAA supervisors. So there they are and there they go. The incompetent, the criminal, and the criminally incompetent- they all have careers in the FAA. Working air traffic controllers, tin men like Doherty, have a job.

In his car, Doherty seeks a diversion, an escape. Prying airplanes apart and returning order to busy airspace plagued by chronic chaos and rampant incompetence can wear a man out. The anxiety is heightened by then having to defend those skillful and prudent actions against inept overbearing FAA supervisors and occasionally a coworker. Doherty presses a cassette tape home and cranks up a sufficient level of volume to drown out the sound of nearby trucks on the New Jersey Turnpike. The Bop Chords get the nod, vocalizing a New York mid-tempo doo-wop classic from 1957 originally on the great Holiday label. In his mind, Doherty can see the record spinning on a turntable at 45 revolutions per minute.

Bom...Bom....Bom.
I've got a castle
Castle in the sky-eye
Built for you, dear
Bom - Bom
Just for you and I-I

Flying towards Manhattan, Doherty ponders the Doo Wop genre. It's his personal ear candy and recreational drug of choice. Except for the horizontal refreshment that female flesh yields, nothing helps take the hard edge off like Doo Wop. With its intricate harmonies and innocent lyrics, Doo Wop is that special brand of urban Rhythm and Blues. It flashed like a shooting star for a short period in American history, putting an exclamation point on a time when life and love in the USA was special, and Americans still trusted their government. The dance ended on November 22, 1963 with an Italian rifle salute in Dallas. And like the JFK conspiracy theories that will never die, Doo Wop lives, mostly in the hearts and homes of dedicated record collectors and Doo-wop fanatics like Doherty. The tri-state area of New York, Connecticut and New Jersey is the place where the sound achieved its greatest notoriety. It is in New York City, where vocal group harmony will surely make its last stand- Doo Wop's Little Big Horn.

With the Empire State Building and a full moon looming large over Jersey City, Doherty imagines himself entering a time tunnel and upon arrival in New York, it would be 1957 again. His reverie features himself on Fulton Street in Brooklyn singing with the Jive Five- the last of the great groups, or hanging out on Belmont Avenue in the Bronx with the Del-Satins and the Five Discs. The ultimate- Irving "Slim" Rose's Time Square Record Shop in the IRT subway arcade. Although long gone, it's where Doo Wop record collecting was actually born.

Man, if I could go there, then, I could die. Imagine what records I might see hanging on the wall- The Castelles on Grand, from Philly. The Flamingoes and the Moonglows on Chance from Chicago. The Orioles on It's A Natural or Jubilee. And, the records still in good shape, the wax with a nice glossy sheen, the labels bright, clean and colorful...and the prices! Are you kidding me? The Diamonds or the Cardinals on Atlantic...for what? A few bucks each?

For Doherty the Doo Wop genre is personal and meaningful. Doo Wop is Doherty's significant other, and they are mutually faithful.

A castle in the sky-eye
I wonder, wonder why
That you're my love to be
And you will always be
In my heart

Chapter 2

Gordon Russo, a journeyman tower controller with U.S Navy experience is operating the local control position. He's tall and dark haired with a large nose that makes a left turn on his face, bent in the middle from some long ago fist-fight. Russo's face is a clock that reads 12:25. Like Doherty, he was trained at the Naval Air Technical Training Center, Naval Air Station, Glynco, Georgia. And like Doherty, he skipped the FAA academy in Oklahoma City, and started on the job training in the tower at Newark International, one of the FAA's busiest facilities. Russo is a skilled tower operator, and he slings the big tin with the best. He frequently quotes the rulebook, called the Seventy One Ten Point Sixty Five. Along with Doherty and a few other talented and cocky white male controllers, Russo, known as the "G man" anchors the "crew within a crew". These guys keep the airport from locking up like a rusty chastity belt whenever the demand runs high. When the supervisors need to flush out a backlog of departures and simultaneously catch every last slam dunked arrival, they call for a tin man. Curiously, the ones the supervisors need and rely on most are also the ones they despise. FAA supervisor's hate tin men because tin men do what supervisors cannot. Tin men push the big tin and supervisors push paper. It's all about accountability. Controllers have real accountability haunting them every second they are on position. If they are lucky, they'll only be embarrassed by a scary "deal," a loss of separation. These errors are normally followed by a reprimand or a suspension and a period of remedial training. With a lesson learned, They quickly get back in the saddle. If they are scarily unlucky, five hundred persons could burn to death or die of blunt trauma in an aircraft collision.

Supervisors are mostly spared this possibility. Paperwork errors are corrected on a word processor, or a liberal dose of White-out. Then they return to despising their betters, the people they supervise.

If the American public ever came to understand that the safety and efficacy of the nation's air traffic control system, depended on such a curious and tenuous love-hate relationship, they might demand a change. The public might start to withhold their participation in the airline business.

The general population knows nothing of tin men. But the tin men know who they are, and so does the FAA. What makes someone a tin man varies from case to case, but they have a few things in common.

They want ***all*** of the tin they can get. This means, that guys like Russo and Doherty WANT to be on position during the very busiest times imaginable, daring the system to test their skills. This craving for heavy traffic is understood to be a common attribute among the tin men. It is joked about, and talked about. "Any tin around here?" or, "scare up some tin for me, will you?" These are common sayings once these guys show up in the tower cab. They allow themselves to be exploited by the supervisors who are more than willing to turn them loose on an extremely busy airport traffic area. This allows the non-talented "weak sticks" and "pogues" to hide in the break room until the heat subsides. Then, when the skies are less crowded, and the operating positions are less demanding, they safely return from the tall grass they sought when the enemy appeared. The "weak sticks" don't mind, and neither do the FAA supervisors. Everyone's happy and the agency stays out of the newspapers- usually. At least that's the plan.

The tin men are white boys. Your basic operational tin man is whiter than a glass of milk on a paper plate in the blizzard of '88. Being a white male in the FAA makes one more than just an employee. Mostly you are a target for racial and gender based discrimination. Many of the tin men recognize this, and most of them stopped fighting it. This means they stopped caring about promotions and transfers to dream facilities. In this new and improved, politically correct FAA, promotion into supervisory slots and favored facilities is reserved for affirmative action losers, or winners, depending on your point of view. FAA managers get points for giving promotions to the least talented and the least deserving at the expense of highly skilled and motivated, straight, white male controllers. It is that simple, and couldn't be more apparent unless it was chiseled in marble above the door at 800 Independence Avenue, FAA Headquarters. A career is something that someone else gets from the government for being deemed underprivileged. White males who are adept at pushing the big tin are forbidden careers; they have jobs. They also get the soggy cloak of accountability that others may shed, but white males must constantly shoulder for the original sin of being born pale, penised and uniquely talented.

The tin men are Roman Catholic. Why this is so, is anyone's guess. It's like a holdover from the old days when air traffic controllers were white, male, and 90% Catholic. Back then, when the word "merit" actually meant something, a good job was expected, demanded. Poorly skilled air traffic controllers were simply not tolerated. In a hack-it-or-pack-it world, white male Catholics gravitated to the top, because simply stated- they could be trusted to do a good job. Guilt plays an important role. When a Catholic does a poor job, he probably feels self-conscious, guilty about it. To accept compensation for less than one's best effort, to be inadequate, to malinger, is a venial sin. Striving for excellence helps to stave off Catholic pangs of guilt. Knowing that you're doing a good job in a very unique profession is a feeling like being in a state of grace. For a tin man, the feeling is God-like. An air traffic controller never needs to hear anyone tell him that he's doing a good job- he knows it before anyone else does.

In Liam Doherty's mind, one should never feel guilty about being superior at something. "Superior" is not a title to be shunned, it is an adjective and a virtue he craves.

And so what if white male Catholics do a good job? If hillbillies are uniquely suited to, and are known to have an aptitude for safely separating and expediting airplanes, then bring me the Hatfields and the McCoys.

Just as the Mohawk Indians work the high steel, and the Amish make good buttermilk, Doherty knows and believes in his heart of hearts that Roman Catholic males should be dominating the control towers of the nation, playing the role they were born to play. Just like they did when Doo Wop ruled the radio airwaves and dominated the recording industry. But just like with his beloved Doo-Wop tunes, he gave up trying to convince anyone to listen. You're a believer already, or you are not, and never will be… and there it is. Beside that, it is dangerous to utter these concepts around a government installation. Should one be heard gushing racist, sexist or antique notions that contradict Department of Transportation dogma, one could find himself severed from his livelihood.

Now, like Atlas shouldering a globe that gets heavier every day, the tin men are holding up their end. They are keeping their unspoken promise to the flying public and the people who live beneath the criss-crossing, winged sardine cans of human flesh and jet fuel. They carry on their backs a herd of third world losers, man-hating feminists, broken down fat-assed housewives, and rubber-wristed ass bandits. The unfit and the unsat…forced on the tin men and the unsuspecting public by an ungrateful and sinister FAA. Guys like Liam A. Doherty and Gordon "G Man" Russo know that this pandering policy of political correctness and social engineering at the expense of proficiency, merit and safety, will one day bite everyone in the ass. "It's like twisting a rubber band" said Russo to a trainee. "The rubber will eventually throw off the stored energy, and people will burn to death or have their bodies ripped apart violently. The objects we are wheeling and dealing with are giant aluminum cigar tubes, hurtling through space at break-neck speeds with living, breathing persons crammed inside. And even if the FAA likes to forget this sobering fact, don't expect me to. I'm not made that way."

A voice barks out on the overhead speaker in the tower cab. "Hey tower, you got a frequency for Marine One? He can't raise you on the assigned frequency." Doherty picks up the handset hanging from its cradle on an overhead console. "Eighteen three" he replies. Doherty can feel the Secret Service agent and the tower supervisor as they both close in on the action to get a better look. The Presidential helicopter, now inbound from Manhattan is indicating that something is wrong. If the pilots have to ask for the frequency, somebody screwed up. What everyone involved would soon find out is how badly this operation was bungled by FAA management, and how tin men can keep a bad situation from becoming a significant historical moment.

Doherty had been watching Marine One "tag up" on the radar as it left Manhattan under control of the LaGuardia Tower TCA controller. This means that the secondary radar detects the transponder on the aircraft and displays a data block of information, a "tag" that shows the aircraft identification, type, speed and altitude. He also saw that the approach controller in the New York TRACON had left one Newark arrival on a collision course with Marine One, inbound on the ILS approach to Runway 22 Left. Normally these conflicts are routine and rectified by the tower local controller, but since communication could not be established with Marine One, or the Twin Beech, Russo could not advise either of the intentions of the other traffic. The tin men could only watch helplessly as two aircraft converged in airspace normally under their control. Pilots, especially Marines hauling the President of the United States around, don't like surprises.

Doherty, working the Cab Coordinator position, has overall operational authority and he's not taking any chances. Stepping up alongside his friend and fellow tin man, he puts his finger directly on the BRITE radar display and said, "G Man, if this guy gets on your frequency turn him westbound, climb him to five thousand and ship him back to approach, one twenty eight seven."

"Check."

Thankfully, the Twin Beech checks in on the frequency and Russo turns the offender out and away from any conflict. Marine One finally calls.

"Tower, Marine One is with you, on VHF, one one eight point three." The Marine aviator's voice is devoid of any urgency or annoyance.

"Marine One, Newark Tower, cleared to land at the designated pad just north of the control tower, wind two six zero at one five. Traffic, two o'clock and two miles, a twin Beech at two thousand turning westbound."

"Roger, traffic in sight, cleared to land. We tried you on the assigned UHF frequency, no joy." Again, the voice is absent any hint of concern.

Just then Doherty glances at the console and realizes what happened. The toggle switch for the UHF frequency was not set to receive. Whoever gave Marine One a discreet frequency assignment, and that would be an FAA manager or supervisor, neglected to tell the controllers – so they could set the equipment to receive, on a frequency normally un-monitored.

Doherty makes a suggestion. "Gordon, tell him it's not working."

"Uh, Roger… Marine One, we're having some...uh... technical malfunctions, apparently that frequency is not working."

It's not really a lie. The frequency is not working because it is not set to receive. Doherty knows that one look at the dilapidated rat's nest of wires under the operating console and any concerned investigator would be shocked, probably literally, at the condition of this equipment.

With the tension subsided momentarily, Doherty mulled it over for a second.

Here we go again. The management team got together with the Secret Service a few days ago and stroked each other stiff while they worked out a plan of action for a presidential movement at Newark Airport. Only they intentionally disinvited the very people who would actually EXECUTE that plan- the working air traffic controllers. What's more inexcusable is that they neglected to brief the controllers about anything associated with something as important as a Marine One arrival to an Air Force One departure at Newark Airport. What good is a plan if you keep it a goddamned secret? Why does FAA management trust us to do important work, like actually keeping airplanes from smacking up, but they keep secrets from us like we're enemies of the state?

Doherty keeps alert for any other contingencies that may suddenly occur. His eyes stay glued to the two helicopters approaching, one a decoy. He is thinking they may do something unusual, like make a landing on the roof of the Queen Elizabeth Diner.

The tower supervisor and the Secret Service agent remain uncomfortably close to Doherty and Russo. Doherty knows they are concerned at how close the conflict was, and how the radio discrepancy factored into the whole scenario. Doherty also knows the FAA will make some lame excuse and say that safety was never compromised. He also knows that the White House, eager to show that Ronnie Ray-Gun was right to fire all those bad PATCO controllers, is more than willing to go along with any plausible excuse the FAA can conjure. In Doherty's mind, this kind of cover-up presents a set of problems. The FAA managers wiggle off another hook. The tin men who pulled their superior's chestnuts out of the fire will get no credit for doing so. Lastly, the PATCO controllers were correct when they said that shoddy equipment and poor communication will surely create a news worthy event. Nothing has changed in the FAA world since the strike of 1981. Doherty starts thinking about the pay phone at the Diner on Spring Street. Then, something really weird happens.

A parrot appears, making an unscheduled landing at the control tower. The wayward tropical bird takes a perch on the aluminum pipe railing directly in front of the working controllers. It's a small green parrot, about the size of a magpie, not one of those elaborately colored giant birds. But it's a parrot as sure as hell. The parrot seems to be curious about the strange looking humans inside the glass house with wires connected to their heads and ears, and microphone booms in front of their mouths. The parrot rocks from side to side, alternately transferring weight from one foot to the other, causing its head to bob as if dancing to a Caribbean steel drum beat. The bird dance causes two female controllers to squeal with delight. The control team knows they are witnessing something strange, because parrots are not native to Newark, New Jersey. Oil refineries, ghettos, open-air drug markets and landfills are not their natural habitat. A live parrot perching on the Newark Tower catwalk railing is so rare an event, it defies explanation. Even so, the tall sandy haired Secret Service agent steps up to the front line with a question:

"Whose parrot is that?"

No one, not even an FAA supervisor, knows how to answer that question. While the tin men and the rest of the crew look at each other dumbfounded, the Secret Service agent starts talking into his lapel.

CHAPTER 3

Our dear martyr and protector, Saint Expedite,

You who know what is necessary and what is urgently needed.

I beg you to intercede before the Holy Trinity,

That by your grace my request will be granted.

May I receive your blessings and favors,

In the name of our Lord Jesus Christ, Amen.

Tommy Wisnak owns a mojo. He keeps it in his ditty bag close to his controller's headset. In fact, his headset is festooned with lucky mojo items including a rabbit's foot and a pair of metal dice on a chain along with a tiny plastic vial of holy water and a scapular from a chapel in New Orleans. Occasionally, when the mood strikes or circumstances prompt him, Tommy changes his mojo hand. That means he goes into the ditty bag and surveys the contents. He may add some lucky items, like a black cat bone or a treasured old photograph, and extract something else, perhaps a baseball card or the old blues harmonica he always keeps close. His tiny wall locker on the eighth floor, just outside of the controller ready room, is a veritable voodoo shrine complete with votive candles of various sizes and colors, and incense. The central figure of Tommy's wall locker shrine is Saint Expedite, a souvenir plastic statuette obtained directly from the Chapel of Our Lady of Guadalupe in New Orleans. The legend of Saint Expedite is one of the more curious tales in Catholic folklore. It is said that one day a crate arrived at the little chapel containing a statue of an unknown, unidentified person. The figure was dressed in the garb of a Roman soldier, squashing a crow under one foot and holding a cross, marked: HODIE – Latin for "today." Since the crate was marked only "Expedite," a saint was born. Tommy has proclaimed Saint Expedite to be the patron saint of air traffic controllers, as well as sailors and whores. Unless one asks Saint Expedite for safety, prior to working any live air traffic, that controller is likely to have a "deal," a problem, a loss of separation. Worse than that, a controller could be responsible for a multi-fatal aviation disaster, the kind that leaves hair, teeth and eyeballs smeared all over the runways or the turnpike. According to Tommy Wiznak, only Saint Expedite stands in the gap between an air traffic controller's sanity, and a news leading, career ending, airport disaster.

Another important detail to know is that Saint Expedite likes pound cake. Whenever a wish is granted, or a "deal" is averted, or especially after a near mid-air collision, a runway incursion, or some other event that scared the shit out of someone, a gift of a slice of pound cake must be offered to the saint that watches over air traffic controllers. Other controllers have bought into Tommy Wiznak's dubious and quaint semi-religious protocol, and pound cake appears on the break room table frequently- usually following a close call. Only Tommy Wisnak owns the key that can open the locker that holds the shrine, and only Tommy can truly intercede by offering a slice of your pound cake to Saint Expedite, and lighting a votive candle to keep you safe from yourself.

A newly hired controller, upon hearing of the legend and protocols of Saint Expedite, called the custom "bullshit." Tommy never spoke to him or about him again, not even after the new guy failed the training program and was transferred to Teterboro Tower where he was partially implicated in a horrifying mid-air collision that rained airplane parts and five bodies down upon Cliffside Park, New Jersey. Apparently, the new guy's mojo wasn't working- and Saint Expedite was off watch that night.

Once a month each crew meets around the large conference table in a half moon shaped room near the ninth floor administrative offices. Like all of the rooms and offices in the building, the conference room is as shabby as it gets. A tacky drop ceiling hangs overhead and a stained, worn and torn, lime green carpet covers the deck. There is no view from this room as the windows were painted in an attempt to deaden the noise from the airliners operating at the base of the tower. Heavy drab dark green curtains hang in front of the windows to add to the overall depressing décor.

Training day is a chance to air petty grievances, or to review procedures and talk about the progress of any trainees. The Tower Manager would take five minutes from his busy, paper-pushing schedule to grace the crew with his presence, and to pass along important news from headquarters, or to give an award to someone who is not a white male. In fact, an award is in order just by virtue of not being a white male.

Before the meeting, Doherty stops at the management coffee pot and while pouring he notices Frank Hamblin working the combination lock to the supervisor's file cabinet. Timing his glance for maximum effect, he looks over Hamblin's shoulder while pouring fresh coffee into an oversized white ceramic mug. The coffee mug is adorned with a gold eagle, a globe and a foul anchor. *Left...twenty five, right to zero. Damn, missed the first number!*

Doherty walks into the conference room and takes a seat at the long table in preparation for the monthly bullshit session and freak show that FAA management was about to commence. Two guys from the crew, Mitch and Tony, degenerate gamblers both, were talking about the past weekend's NFL results. Mitch starts:

"Who'd ya take, Eagles-Jets?"

"I took the chalk. You?"

"I had the dog. Made two bills on the Iggles. 'Sides, the wind took the kicking game away and the birds got the stronger D. No way the Jets cover three and a half. It was a mortal lock, a lead pipe cinch." Tony nods.

"How'd you do for the week?"

"Lost six hundred. You?"

"Down fifty."

The Assistant Manager at Newark Tower is a black man or a black female –always and without exception. Unless the Manager is black, then the assistant manager can be white but someone other than a white male is always preferred. Although not written, an agreement between the FAA and the city of Newark, New Jersey whose southwestern boundary bisects Newark Airport, mandates that the manager or assistant manager at Newark Tower will always be a black-skinned person.

Dante Moore has all the qualifications needed to be the Assistant manager at Newark Tower. Along with all the professional considerations, he is well dressed and well spoken with an impressive vocabulary. He's extremely personable with a great sense of humor. Most importantly, to the FAA's way of thinking, his primary qualifying attribute is that he's as black as a mud flap laying on New Jersey Turnpike asphalt. The FAA doesn't really need Moore, and they don't really care about any of the virtues or talents that would otherwise make Dante Moore a valuable member of their team. They just need a black man with an air traffic background, and Moore was in the right places at the right times and got his ticket punched. Because the FAA doesn't really trust a black man, Moore has no real duties and no responsibilities, except on paper in his phony job description. Some of the tin men refer to him as "The Lawn Jockey."

Moore's resume includes stops at all of the big facilities where they signed his card and he moved on. Cleveland Center; Atlanta Center; New York Tracon. But, to the trained eye, a pattern emerges. As a young controller he never stays long at any one facility.

That's because he's like many career management wannabes, he's always running. As soon as he gets qualified to work live air traffic, the moment he is called upon to actually separate airplanes, he becomes accountable for his own actions. He can no longer hide behind his trainee status. So he starts running…not to something, or someone or even some place, but *from* something. Something he dares not name; a pack he refuses to shoulder. A post he can no longer guard. Then, he finds the best place for a non-hacker to hide – in plain sight, on the FAA management team. Now he is accountable to no one. Now he can direct his hatred at the competent by abusing his authority over them every chance he gets.

Guys like Doherty and Russo and the other tin men loathe a malingering fraud like Dante Moore- not for being black; hell, he can't change that. No, they hate him for being a millstone around their necks, and for going out of his way to make the controller's lives miserable, punishing tin men for the sin of being confident, for being excellent, for being what Dante Moore can never be.

Said by tin man Ray Martino with his salty, cliché laced language and a thick, Red Hook, Brooklyn accent:

"You'd think they would just say, *thank you*, and stay the fuck out of the way, let us drive the tin, but no, they have to shit in the punch bowl every chance they get, killing the goose that's laying 'em their golden fucking eggs. They're biting the hand that feeds them, just like they did in '81 with the PATCO guys. They hate themselves for what they are, and see in us what they wish they could be, but they can't. Funny thing is, the only thing stoppin' 'em…is their own state of mind. They can't think…you know…they can't see it happening, so they can never be…a tin man. Know what I'm saying?" Martino whips out a comb and runs it back through his thick black hair. The hair shines from Brylcreem. He smiles and offers an addendum: "A curse on them and their ugly mothers."

As Dante Moore walks in to address the crew on training day, the union rep, Paul Veale, pulls out a supermarket tabloid and pretends to ignore the assistant manager, burying his face and reading the paper held high so that the roomful of working controllers can see the ridiculous headline:

JERSEY DEVIL SPOTTED IN ATLANTIC CITY – PLAYING BLACKJACK!

Veale's pretense causes the room to chuckle and Moore to raise his voice for a second request for the room's attention. When Veale finally puts the paper down, Moore starts:

"As you know, work on the new break room and kitchenette is completed and the FAA spared no expense to make you guys comfortable, and give you a clean and quiet place to relax on your breaks. I know that Saint Expedite was annoyed about moving, but now he's in a bigger and better locker, so he should be happy in his new digs."

The room giggles but for a stone-faced Tommy Wiznak who strokes his rabbit's foot stoically, making Dante Moore somewhat nervous. Moore fumbles with the middle button of his three-piece suit, unbuttoning it, and fastening it again before continuing.

"I went down to the eighth floor this morning to inspect the new ready room. I opened the door to your brand new freezer. Can anyone guess what I found in there? Moore gives the team a few seconds to venture a guess and a controller pipes up. "Uhh…cold air?" Moore responds. "Anyone else care to guess?" The assistant manager pulls an expensive Cross pen from his pocket and twirls it in one hand. An uncomfortable silence ensues but for the jet noise heard from outside. A cockroach scurries along the floor at the base of the curtain. The silence is broken by Moore. "No! I found a BRICK!" Moore surveys the room, expecting a reaction to his curious revelation. When he sees none, he continues: "That's right. The first thing one of you did with your new break room was to put a goddamned brick in the freezer!" Suddenly Moore's eyes were glazing over with rage and a vein was throbbing over his left temple. He was talking to the assembled crew as if they were redheaded stepchildren, and he was about to administer a whipping. A lesbian speaks. "Umm, Dante, do you mean a common red brick, like in a sidewalk or like in a brick wall…not a brick of ice cream…or something…but a brick?" Ray Martino adds a city touch. "Yea…a big ol' alley apple!". Moore's rant continues.

"For the life of me, I can't understand why anyone would put a **goddamned** brick in the freezer!"

Moore likes saying "goddamned," and he enunciates each syllable perfectly, as if he is voicing a radio commercial. The lawn jockey scans the room contemptuously, stopping to make eye contact with each individual seated at the long conference table to assure himself that no one remains un-intimidated. An uncomfortable silence descends on the conference room. A helicopter can be heard passing overhead on its way to Manhattan. Paul Veale looks around, then he rolls his chair back and spins it slightly to face his nemesis. The NATCA rep speaks.

"Dante, if you don't mind, did YOU put anything in the freezer?"

"No, Paul. And I certainly wouldn't put a **goddamned** brick in the freezer."

The NATCA Rep leans back in his chair; glancing once around the room, after a long pause he sighs and continues:

"Cause it occurred to me, and I'm sure you know this Dante, that a freezer runs more efficiently when there is something in it, as opposed to…a totally empty freezer."

Moore, nostrils flaring, glares and says nothing.

Veale, folding his tabloid in newsboy fashion, continues:

"So, perhaps you should be commending the unsung hero among us, who saved the government money by making the new freezer run more efficiently! Instead of coming in here and showing your ass, you should get back on your trusty word processor and start writing TWO letters." Veale holds up an index and a pinkie finger, like a shortstop indicating the number two. "One letter, commending that thoughtful, bricklaying, energy saving, WORKING air traffic controller, whose actions saved taxpayer money, and a second letter condemning the STUPID SON OF A BITCH THAT OPENED THE FREEZER DOOR FOR NO GOOD REASON, WASTING ALL OF THE ENERGY SAVED BY THE UNION CONTROLLER!"

The room is shocked into silence by the outburst of profanity directed at the assistant manager, and then a few giggles are heard as the clever reasoning behind the defense of the mysterious bricklayer is realized. Most of the controllers try hard not to laugh out loud. A lesbian stares across at her girlfriend. With mouth agape, the Revlon Very New Chocolate lipstick makes her facial orifice resemble a prairie dog hole.

Assistant manager Moore strides quickly toward Veale and the union rep gets up to meet him. Standing nose to nose like an umpire and a baseball manager, Moore barks into Veale's face:

"I'm the Assistant Manager of this facility and YOU are not going to talk to me like that!" Veale, unconcerned about the possibility of a fistfight with Moore, looks down at the smaller, well-dressed man with a look of amused contempt.

"You don't like it? File a grievance against the union!" The staredown continues until the crew supervisor calls for everyone to be back in fifteen minutes. Moore turns and strides out into pogue country, and Veale returns to his "news" paper.

The G-man, Gordon Russo, says to his Union Rep:

"Man, you got some brass avocados!"

"They clang when I walk…and fuck him! He comes in here to pump up management and knock the working guys? Not on my union watch."

Russo changes the subject:

"How'd the Jersey Devil make out at the blackjack tables?"

"Won two grand, even paid the IRS the taxes." Russo grins.

"He's a good one, that Jersey Devil."

CHAPTER 4

The Monday morning push is starting, and a new guy just got introduced to ground control while it was still slow. But now the real heavy stuff was coming and with a primary taxiway closed for construction and the overflow runway Two Nine closed for electrical work, the call went to Liam Doherty. Although Doherty is recognized as the best ground controller at Newark, and excels at training others, he is not permitted to train. The facility manager does not allow it, thus depriving the tin man of training differential pay. This practice does not stop any trainees from asking Doherty for help, and many a ground control trainee would ask to monitor Doherty during a heavy push. Today a second trainee was standing in the back, pretending not to, but watching the action on ground control, trying to gain a few clues.

Newark Ground, Continental Three Twenty Six, taxi.

Continental Three Twenty Six, Newark Ground, Taxi, Runway Two Two right, Outer, Romeo, follow the TWA Seven Twenty Seven, number five, monitor Tower.

Continental Three Twenty Six, roger, TWA is in sight, switching, good day.

Doherty's technique differs from other ground controllers, which explains the reason a heavy session would draw a few observers in the tower. Doherty puts ALL of the departure traffic in a straight line, properly sequenced on the parallel taxiway. Others routinely break the line into two or three streams on different taxiways, creating a herd of turtles that mostly look alike. This causes them to make copious notes on the flight progress strips, while retaining twenty or more flights on the frequency, waiting to break ties at the runway. The pilots, who see airplanes on their flanks, and while they are waiting, forget who it is they are following in the sequence. This clutters the frequency and causes unnecessary distractions for most ground controllers.

Doherty makes the *pilots* work, assigning taxi routes that initially seem convoluted, until the pilot finds himself directly behind the airplane he will follow in the departure sequence. The arrivals have to work also, getting routed and cleverly woven through the departures on their way to their gates. It was all about controlling the frequency. Doherty usually gets his traffic all the way home or all the way to the runway with one transmission, and few distractions. Thus, with twenty airplanes moving about his area of responsibility, Doherty looks bored, leisurely sipping his morning coffee, and engaging the other controllers in casual banter.

Only a controller with the big picture, and one that is totally confident in his ability could do this. Plus, since his traffic was under control, he could look out for mistakes and problems caused by the affirmative action darlings working around him, eliminating possible conflicts before they happen. Doherty, a ten year veteran of Newark Tower, has taken Ground Control to a higher level. This is generally understood by most observers, and especially Doherty's fellow tin men. For this reason, among others, he is admired by some, yet hated by many of his coworkers, and the entire management team.

The flight data strip printer, called an FDEP (eff-dep) goes down, causing the flight data controller to go "down the pipes." A trainee is handwriting abbreviated flight plans on one inch by six inch strips of paper. Each strip is then slid into a plastic holder and posted at the proper position for use by the other controllers. As the individual flights start their engines outbound or come within sixty miles of the airport inbound, the strips of paper, mounted in their plastic "bones," start moving to their assigned places in the tower cab. Legible printing being important, Doherty decides to press the point, and at the same time, terrorize a brand new guy training on the Flight Data position. He searches his console for a poorly hand-written strip and quickly jerks the selection from the bay.

"Hey you, with the FACE!"

"Me?"

"No. Rumple-Fucking-Stiltskin. Are you handwriting these strips?"

"Yea?"

Doherty fires the strip in its plastic holder across the tower cab and hits the new guy in the solar plexus. If it was a knife, it would have stuck in the trainee's chest.

"Well, what's that? 'Cause it sure as hell ain't no abbreviated flight plan. It looks to me like hieroglyphics or some kind of Chinese fuck story! Try legible block letters please, and lose that candy-assed purple felt-tipped pen. We use number two pencils for this operation. Didn't they teach you anything in that classroom downstairs? Jesus N-M-I Christ!"

Doherty turns around and winks at Russo who tries to keep a straight face. The new guy opens the pencil drawer and selects a stubby one, tossing the felt tip away. He re-writes the truncated flight plan and asks his trainer for approval, getting a nod in response. Russo turns away from his traffic and takes up the new guy's case.

"Don't take that shit from him! Shove that strip up his big, fat, Irish ass!"

Doherty takes a bite of pound cake and washes it down with a slug of tepid, black coffee. The coffee is so thick you could trot a mouse on it.

" Forget it, G-man, he's a pussy. I pulled his punk card and he appled up. He choked like a sick whore. I could bend him over right now and pin tits on his back if I wanted."

The new guy finally responds.

"Fuck you!"

A collective "Oooooh!" resonates off the glass inside the tower cab. The new guy has just been introduced to the wacky, testosterone filled world of tinmanship. You don't get asked to join this club, you must demand entry at some point.

Later, Russo slides up next to Doherty.

" Willie, what the hell is N-M-I??"

"No Middle Initial, G-man. No…Middle…Initial."

CHAPTER 5

It used to be that Newark International Airport was the "Sleepy Hollow" of the New York airports. One day, the airlines started looking at Newark as a place to expand their New York operations, and Newark Airport never looked back. A no frills start-up called People Express cut a deal with the Port Authority, using an old terminal building and gates on Newark Airport's 's north side. For less than taxi fare to Manhattan, you could get a seat on People Express to Florida. Soon, brown and tan jets with a "mating worms" logo would cover the operating area at EWR, doubling, then tripling the traffic count in less than a year. Delays have become routine, and the Air Transport Association grumbles about it daily, and the FAA is feeling the heat.

A capacity enhancement task force is convened to brainstorm ways to increase capacity and reduce delays. Out of this task force came an idea to hire a computer modeling consultant to determine, with the help of the latest software available, how to most efficiently utilize the runways at Newark to reduce delays. The Tower Manager, John Biderman, asked the controller's union to supply a volunteer to help the computer consultant with some airport details. It seems they needed to know where the little "targets" parked and which airlines used each particular ramp exit to taxi to and from the runways. This prompted the union Rep Paul Veale to call Liam Doherty at home.

"Willie?"

"Yea?"

"If you help us with the computer guy, I can get you a day off, and it's easy shit for an hour or two on Monday."

"You know I'm a non-member, right?"

"Yea, no one else wants it, so I don't care. I gave it to Wisnak but he heard about the parrot landing on the catwalk and he swears it's a bad omen.....took the week off...says if it was a raven, he'd take the whole month."

"Okay, what do they want?"

"Just show 'em where to park their friggin' computer bugs, so they can put on a nice dog and pony show for the Air Transport Association...make 'em think the FAA and the Port Authority are actually doing something about delays, besides asking congress for more money."

"What time?"

"Zero eight hundred. You're out by ten, home by eleven, with a day off coming."

"Great. When's your chicken-shit union gonna file a ULP complaint on the queers?"

"Willie, we've been over this. The FAA meets with the gay and lesbian coalition, but they know not to discuss working conditions, so there is no unfair labor practice. NATCA is still the exclusive bargaining agent at this airport."

"Bullshit, Paul. They're making deals about hiring and promotions and all that shit. That's working conditions and you guys know it. Plus, they meet on government time, on government property and on the taxpayer's dime. I was the rep, I'd get some major ink or some TV face time over this issue, but you guys act like a bunch of pussies. You want me in your fucking union, get a goddamned backbone and stop running scared from faggots and rug munchers. It's embarrassing."

"Okay Willie, I'm a pussy. Everybody's a pussy...everybody but YOU, how come?"

"Good question, Paul. Sometimes I look around, and I feel like an island in a sea of shit."

"You need help, Willie. Have you looked into the Employee Assistance Program?"

"Yea. They told me I'm surrounded by a bunch of pussies. I could shoot in any direction and hit one."

"Right…zero eight hundred…see you at the office."

It's busy at the Flamingo Diner. The Flamingo is one of those old-school New Jersey eateries where fast food was invented, and they know what "scrambled soft" means. The Dragon Lady, a slim, mature Greek woman with jet black hair, dark eyes and hairy forearms is loading paper coffee cups with sugar and stacking them high on the counter in preparation for the morning rush. Many commuters on the PATH train will sip Flamingo coffee under the Hudson River on their way to the World Trade Center. Quickly and efficiently table-spooning sugar from a large stainless steel mixing bowl into the cups, the dragon lady shouts orders to the kitchen as regular customers amble in from Montgomery Street, anticipating their usual preferences with seemingly total recall. The Dragon Lady's job is secure because a machine could not be invented that could clear tables, take and relay orders, handle the cash register and generally run a busy diner like the Flamingo, single-handed, and not go "down the pipes." Gordon Russo admires her efficiency as he toast-mops egg yolk from a thick oval dinner plate.

"Look at her move, man. She's always doing three things at once, staying ahead of the action. She could be a tin man, no doubt. I'd have her checked out through Local in no time flat. 'Sides, she's ugly, just like the rest of them FAA hose-bags, so nobody gets distracted. No safety hazard there! And, she can cook."

"You think of everything, don't you, G-man?" Russo grins and nods, unable to speak, his cheeks bloated from stuffing egged, buttered and jellied toast into his cavernous pie hole, pushing the last bit in with the tip of his index finger. Doherty picks up the check and stuffs it into Russo's shirt pocket, then heads out to the street.

The wind is starting to whip off the Hudson River, whistling through the tall office buildings on Grand Street. The brisk wind reminds Doherty of something he first heard from a favorite old controller, long since retired: "Bad weather comes from the west; really bad weather comes from the east". Control tower operators, like sailors, are always keenly aware of the weather, especially the wind strength and direction.

On the road to Newark Airport, Doherty cranks up the volume and pumps the car full of his favorite music. A vent window is cracked open to let some of the music stream out onto US 1&9. The legendary New York group The Channels, are laying down their five-part vocal group harmony masterpiece: *The Closer You Are.*

My heart skips a beat
Every time you and I meet
My life ,my love, my dear
I can't defeat
That yearning deep in my heart
To have only you

The vocals start with the second tenor and baritone handling things while the boss, Earl Lewis, takes off with a high floating falsetto, dipping in and out and swooping up and down like a barn swallow gleefully chasing gnats on some high, open meadow. For the "hook," Mr. Lewis comes back to earth and resumes the lead on the classic, New York City favorite.

When I first saw you,
I did adore you,
And your loving ways
And then you went away,
But now you're back to stay,
And my love for you grows stronger every
Day-ahhh way-ahhh way

Even though overplayed in Doo Wop circles and on oldies formatted radio, "*The Closer You Are*" is firmly established in Liam Doherty's all time top ten. He never tires of hearing it, which could be said about only a moderate stack of his many records. Doo Wop being perfect music – "The Closer You Are" is perfect Doo Wop. Thinking about his 45rpm copy at home and the distinctive black and silver Whirlin' Disc label, Doherty decides to upgrade to a better condition copy. Later that day, he calls Val Shively in Upper Darby, Pa.

Shively is the world's most respected and enigmatic record dealer. His opinion about any particular 45rpm record is the last word and Val sets the price of old 45 rpm records. A visit to Val's Upper Darby store usually sets Doherty back a few hundred bucks. Val Shively, a tough talking eccentric, can be difficult to deal with at times. Phone conversations between Doherty and Shively usually end when Val hangs up abruptly. This time Val doesn't hang up on Doherty, but tosses the telephone receiver into the waste basket. The noise spooks Tiger, and the store's cat scampers away. In-store customers can hear "Hey Val?...Val?...Val!!" echoing from within the circular file. When Tiger wanders back, he paws the rim of the wastebasket, investigating the strange voice from inside. Doherty finally gives up, and threatens to kick Val Shively's ass before hanging up. He will eventually pay Val's price of three hundred dollars for a mint condition, first press copy of "The Closer You Are" on Whirlin' Disc. The purchase will temporarily slake Doherty's thirst for expensive 45RPM vinyl, but the tin man will be back to deal with Shively. Their relationship is not unlike that of a junkie and his drug pusher.

The Port Authority Operations building at Newark Airport houses the emergency response vehicles, the airport police department and other offices supporting the operation of a major airport. The second floor office assigned to the computer consulting company is adorned with large charts of the airport layout, or the operating area as it is sometimes called. Three computer monitors are running a program simulating live traffic and timing the delays caused by recently landed aircraft waiting to cross an active runway, and conversely, departing aircraft holding in position, while taxiing aircraft cross the departure runway downrange. It's as if there was a giant traffic signal on the airport that every landing and departing airplane must deal with.

At a busy airport like Newark International, wasted seconds quickly add up to lost minutes, and minutes to hours. Before anyone can see it happening, the airport is firmly mired in a serious departure delay program. Aircraft are held at their gates, causing the airlines to scramble for gate space, which generally cancels the plans of airlines and passengers. This causes severe discontent that reaches the higher offices of airline executives and politicians. Then, the shit starts to roll downhill, creating ad hoc committees of FAA managers and Port Authority managers and airline operations officers meeting to pretend they are doing something. The last people invited to any important meetings are the controllers, and then only because the union demands a seat at the table, to protect their member's working conditions, or to give such an appearance.

No one expects or anticipates that a lowly working stiff, like an air traffic controller, could actually contribute any meaningful ideas or offer any valuable alternatives or solutions to a problem as complex as airport delays. After all, what do controllers know? They just come in every day and actually expedite and separate the air traffic that is coming and going. How would they know what works and what doesn't? And, Doherty is only here in Building Ten to help the computer geeks set up the programs by showing them where each airline parks at which gates, and which taxiway ramps they use to get there.

Doherty walks in to see a skinny black haired man sitting at the computer monitors wearing a Hawaiian shirt and it's not even Friday. Doherty is impressed already- not by the style of shirt, but the rebel attitude it represents. As soon as he sees the man's face, he recognizes him as being Japanese, having seen many like him during a tour of duty in Japan.

Thinking back to those younger days, he recalls a litany of stereotypical racial insults his fellow Marines would recite occasionally: *slant-eyed, slope-headed, rice propelled, ocean cruising, war losing, fish head eating, chopstick licking, pajama wearing bicycle driving, retired kamikazi pilots-with 50 missions!* The point of the exercise was to see how many insults one could remember, or if one could add another colorful slur to the list. Doherty knows of one salty Lance Corporal who taught a Japanese prostitute to speak English by making her recite a long stream of racial slurs aimed at her own people.

The war losing, rice burner, turns around and introduces himself.

"Hi, I'm Dan. They call me "Stick." I don't know why." Doherty extends his hand.

"Liam Doherty. Call me Willie."

"How do you get Willie from Liam?"

Liam is short for William. It's Irish."

"Ahh, I get it."

After Doherty takes all of twenty minutes showing Stick where the airport airline tenants park and which taxiway ramps they use, Stick makes the keystroke entries into the database. He complains that finding minutes that can be shaved from delays at the airport, was proving to be harder on him, than the sixth grade was on Mike Tyson.

It is generally understood that any delay reducing scenario would involve using all three runways simultaneously, "maximizing the concrete" as they say. This means using runway Two Nine for small prop departures, and the parallel runways for jets landing and departing. That leaves two possibilities. Either a runway Two Two, southwest departure flow, or a runway Four, northeast flow, and naturally, the wind would dictate which way the airplanes landed and departed, just like it does at every airport. No matter how Stick ran the scenarios, no significant minutes can be trimmed from delays, due mostly to crossing traffic on the parallel runway operation. The arrivals have to stop short of the inboard runway to wait for two or three departures, depending on the demand at any given time. The southwest flow was slightly more efficient, but any problem, like a blown tire or an aborted take off, and it's a wash. Sometimes a passenger is not seated in time for take-off. This can send the airport into delays. This is especially true if the flight needs to be re-sequenced. Stick laments that after all the work is done, he will simply report the disappointing findings to the Port Authority and the capacity enhancement team. There is nothing else he can do. Doherty feels him out:

"So what, Stick? Do you care?"

"Not really. I still get paid."

"You should be a government employee. You've got the attitude down cold. I'll tell you what- for a typhoon fifth of saki, and one of those Hawaiian shirts in a man's size, I'll solve your problem for you."

Stick turns back toward his keyboard and makes a few entries. While typing, Doherty's words are echoing in his head. *"I'll solve your problem for you."*

After a few seconds he swivels back around and challenges the tin man.

"How're YOU gonna solve delays at Newark? The computers don't lie, and what's a typhoon fifth?"

Doherty props a shoe up on a table edge and shines the glossy tip with a Kleenex tissue. He jerks a thumb in the direction of the tower.

"Whaddya think I've been doin' in that glass cage for ten years…playin' pick-up-sticks with my ass cheeks? You think I don't know a good operation from a bad one? You think I don't know what works, and what doesn't? I'm the ace of the base. Besides, if you put garbage into computers, you'll get garbage out. I'm sure you've heard that before." Stick leans back in the swivel chair. He picks up a tiny toy airplane and spins its wheels with an index finger.

"Okay, okay, tell me something I don't know."

Doherty has a hunch about Stick. He senses that the computer geek is smart enough to quickly comprehend some air traffic realities, and independent enough to stand up to an employer if the situation calls for it. In short, brains and balls are the qualities needed to impress the tin man. However, even if Stick is lacking in these virtues, it doesn't matter. He's the right man in the right place at the right time. Stick's employer needs the information that Doherty is about to disclose. It is not in the cards that either Stick or his bosses will disregard what Doherty is about to let them in on. FAA managers have a tin ear and a blind eye when it comes to suggestions or innovation. That's why the FAA is mired in mediocrity and incompetence. The FAA has that luxury; it's a government agency staffed by government employees. The status quo is their plan of the day.

Stick and his computer consultants are private sector contractors. They depend on new ideas and innovations that produce results and translate into profits, both for them, and for their clients.

Doherty smiles. He knows that the information he is about to divulge is certain to cause a reaction of sorts. He wonders how high Stick will jump in the air.

Lock and load.

"You see Stick, in order to solve THIS problem you have to think outside the box. The key lies in not focusing so much on FLYING airplanes, but eliminating conflicting taxi routes. The bottleneck is on the ground, so the ground control position is the key. Take care of ground control; eliminate conflicting ground traffic; then make the arrivals conform to what is happening on the ground. That's really all there is to it. Then, pull down the shade – you got it made."

Stick cleans his thick eyeglasses with a handkerchief. His eyes narrow even more than usual. You could blindfold him with catgut.

"I....I don't get it."

"Not many do. That's because most Newark Tower controllers and ALL of the FAA supervisors and managers worship at the same altar. They believe that the ground traffic has to bow to the arrivals; anything else is heresy. Because they work and think on a lower level of consciousness than I do, they can't see what I see. However, after I explain it to you, you'll be born again, I promise. What's more, you can check it on those fancy computers. A huge chunk of delays are about to disappear, Stick. And if I'm lyin', I'm dyin'."

Stick squirms in anticipation and spins the wheels faster on his toy airplane.

"So tell me."

"Typhoon Fifth?"

"What IS that?"

"It's a giant bottle of Japanese saki. And I want one of those shirts."

"You got a deal, Willie, but only if it works."

The two men stare at each other like poker players vying for a jackpot pile of blue chips. Only Doherty isn't thinking about Stick and his computer problems. He knows that what he is about to tell his new friend is bound to produce a reaction from the users, especially the airlines, and not only at Newark Airport, but nationwide.

Hesitating for a few seconds, Doherty's mind flashes back to combat training and the moment he pulled the pin on a live hand grenade. When ordered, he threw the grenade, imagining that it wiped out an enemy machine gun crew. He enjoyed the exercise almost as much as losing his virginity.

Take grenade...

Pull the pin...

Look downrange...

THROW GRENADE!

"Okay, pay attention. It only works on a runway Two-Two operation, but fortunately, when the wind picks up it comes from the west, so we can stay on a southwest flow most of the time, even in calm wind. We shoot the ILS to Runway Two Two Left, but CIRCLE TO LAND ON RUNWAY TWO NINE. All Departures, props AND jets, taxi to Runway Two-Two Right at Mike. Props take off on the right and turn directly westbound. Jets cross the right *behind the departing* props and depart on Two-Two Left, eighty-one-seventy-five." Stick's oriental eyes narrow further. He could be blindfolded with a Japanese soba noodle or a shoelace.

"Eighty one seventy...?"

"Eight thousand one hundred seventy five feet remaining, it's an intersection departure and there is plenty of runway for jets departing, normally. Now look at the taxiways." Doherty points at an airport layout chart on the wall. "Departures taxi outbound on the outer taxiway and arrivals taxi inbound on the inner perimeter taxiway."

The tin man lets it sink in for a few seconds, intently watching the Jap computer geek's eyes. When he knows it is time, Doherty asks:

"What do you see now, Stick?"

Stick leans back in his chair and blinks. Then his eyes get as wide as Flamingo Diner pie plates. He leaps to his feet and faces the wall sized airport layout chart. In his mind's eye, he sees airplanes moving along the taxiways and runways. Some are coming and some are going, but incredibly, NONE stopping. The plan doesn't reduce crossing traffic, it ELIMINATES it! Departures taxi out and take off without stopping. Arrivals land and taxi back to their gates without crossing any runways or waiting for any departures to take off. The plan is ingenious on one hand, yet so incredibly simple, it begs the question that Doherty knows is coming.

Still on his feet and whirling about like a slant-eyed Dervish, Stick asks incredulously:

"Why don't they do this…NOW?"

"I told you, Stick. The FAA managers in charge of this pie wagon are a gang of knuckle dragging goons. Their brains are bouncing around inside their heads like a BB in a box car."

"I'm gonna run with this! I'll set it up and run it through the software program!"

"Sure, go ahead, but you already know it works. It's obvious to the casual observer."

"This is…incredible!"

"Domo harigato."

"I don't speak Japanese, but thank YOU!

Stick is back on the keyboard furiously typing away. Without looking up, he asks:

"What should we call this operation? Does it have a name?"

Doherty pauses. Taking a tissue, he wipes his shoes even though the shoes don't need wiping.

A Name. Everything and everyone needs a name.

"Let's call it the Veale Initiative. He's the tower union rep and he loves having his name bandied about."

Doherty smiles to himself. He knows that the FAA is going to have a major problem with this, and that naming it after the union rep would be more than a minor source of tension for them. However, the missiles have left their silos; the Veale Initiative is no longer a secret, and airport capacity and delay impacted parties will soon be asking the FAA some embarrassing questions. It couldn't happen to a nicer bunch.

CHAPTER 6

Paul Veale waits for Doherty in the control tower parking lot. As they ride the elevator to the ninth floor and the Air Traffic Manager's office, Veale gives him the bad news:

"Ten days on the beach."

"What? You can't be serious. What's the charge?"

"Charges…plural. I'm not sure, but threatening a supervisor is one of them. We'll find out more at the meeting."

The two tin men stop in the file cabinet room to boost a free cup of FAA coffee. As Veale is pouring, Doherty tries the combination padlock on the supervisor's file cabinets. *Left twenty five, right zero.* The lock springs open like the legs on a Rutgers cheerleader. Veale blinks as if he just saw a magic trick.

"Hey! How'd you do that?"

"Left twenty five, right zero."

"No shit? Two numbers?"

"Apparently so. I guess management can't memorize three or more."

"I'll bet there's some interesting reading in *there.*"

"Yeah. Let me know what you find."

"Join the union and I'll tell you."

The two men are invited to enter the manager's office where the manager, the assistant manager and Supervisor Frank Hamblin are seated. Doherty walks up to the manager's big desk and stands in front of it, looking down at the air traffic manager as he always does on such occasions. Doherty doesn't look at Hamblin seated to his right, but he can smell the cheap cologne being used to mask the body odor. Frank Hamblin is seated with his arms crossed, smiling like a Buddha, content that he is about to receive his pound of flesh. Smelling something it likes, a housefly leaves the ceiling and lands on Hamblin's forehead. Veale starts:

"You know the union doesn't get outnumbered, John, so we get another controller in here at my choosing, or you lose a man. Either that, or we postpone this meeting until the sides get evened up."

Cocking his head to one side John Biderman offers an excuse:

"This meeting is only going to last five minutes, Paul. So let's stop stalling."

Veale turns and gestures to Doherty, jerking a thumb in the direction of Hoboken.

"Let's go, Willie. We're blowing this popsicle stand."

Dante Moore speaks up:

"You know, I don't need to be here, and I have another meeting to go to, so why don't you guys have all the fun."

When Moore walks out Veale turns back and takes a seat on the shabby lime green sofa to the manager's right. Biderman speaks:

"Sit down, Willie."

Veale springs up immediately.

"You can't order an employee to sit if he wants to stand, and we've already covered this! We know Willie prefers to stand, and if you don't like it, YOU can stand and so can your management team for that matter! Now let's get to the business at hand." Biderman looks down at his desk blotter and slowly shakes his head. Doherty looks over at Frank Hamblin. He can tell that Hamblin's excitement is peaking, not because he's grinning wider, but because the room is starting to reek of perspiration and bacteria, as if Hamblin's body was a giant, frothy yeast infection. Doherty briefly considers vomiting on Biderman's big desk.

The manager continues: "That was an invitation, Willie, not an order."

"I know, John. You have a reputation for being magnanimous." A chuckle can be heard from the secretary's desk in the adjacent office.

"Willie, when you leave this meeting, you are on administrative leave for the remainder of the day. Tomorrow you start a ten day suspension, and you are to return, ready to work, on the Fifteenth. The reasons for the adverse action are set forth in this letter, and your rights of appeal are clearly stated therein. I'm sure your union representative will have some advice for you as well. It's not my style to lecture employees, but you need to know that I will not tolerate anyone threatening my supervisors, or any FAA employees for that matter. You will have time to make a verbal response at a later date, but if you feel compelled to say anything now, you have the floor. However, I advise you to wait until you have composed your response and you are better prepared to make a presentation."

Veale leaps to his feet again.

"We don't need your fucking advice you sniveling prick! And I promise you I'll have this bullshit suspension in front of an arbitrator within 21 days. You just gave one of my guys a paid vacation! And just for that, guess what? Get used to seeing your name in the newspaper, Swee' Pea. If one of your supervisors craps out of turn, you'll get ink from both sides of the river, I promise. The Air Transport Association already wants your scalp on their doorpost, and I'm here to make sure they get it!"

Biderman chews his gum with his eyes closed, looking bored. Without looking up at the NATCA Rep, he responds:

"Are you finished?"

"No. Fuck.....YOU!" Veale punctuates the profanity, leaning across the manager's desk with his index finger pointed at Biderman's face, an inch from his nose.

Biderman ignores Veale and turns to the guest of honor:

"Willie?"

Doherty nods toward his union rep and deadpans:

"What he says goes for me too."

Biderman hands a manila envelope to Doherty:

"Very well, here's the letter. There's a copy for the union in there, also. Enjoy the day gentlemen, you're dismissed."

The tin men walk through the outer office toward the elevator. Betty Jackson, a tall black office secretary with stunning, fashion model looks gives Paul Veale a silent standing ovation, lightly tapping the tips of her long fingers into the palm of her left hand. Betty loathes the air traffic manager and routinely tips off the union about management's plans. Since she is the one who types the letters, and sits in on the staff meetings, she's always among the first to know what's coming down.

On the elevator, Paul Veale confesses a "jungle fever" attraction for Betty, expecting Doherty to recoil in shock and surprise.

"You know, if I was gonna actually "do" a black girl…I think Betty…" To which Doherty quips:

"They're ALL black with the lights out."

CHAPTER 7

Tommy Wiznak, now back at work, changes his mojo hand. Introducing a little chrome top hat from a Monopoly game into his ditty bag, along with some John the Conqueror root purchased from a mail order house in New Orleans. Then he lights two candles and places a tiny wedge of pound cake in front of Saint Expedite, along with a shot glass of water to wash it down. Then, Tommy pulls the harmonica from his ditty bag and plays a few "blue" notes in a command performance for the patron Saint of air traffic controllers.

Tommy is convinced that the parrot landing was an omen, maybe even a harbinger of death, and that something bad was sure to happen. One of the tower lesbians, a stocky, man hating bull dyke named "virgin" Mary threatens to beat Tommy's ass if he doesn't "*shut the fuck up about that spooky voodoo shit*". Mary's problem is more about Tommy's Catholicism then it is about his voodoo-like practices and superstitions.

On the control positions, Tommy avoids any casual banter and concentrates on pushing the tin with an extra emphasis on neatness, stacking his old flight progress strips neatly like a deck of playing cards and sharpening his pencil every two minutes until only a stub remains. His crew is growing weary of Tommy's antics. Some openly wish that a bird, especially a big, black, nasty crow, would land on the railing in front of Tommy. Tommy is afraid of crows. He has been known to call in sick after spotting a crow on the way to work. Among other things, crows represent procrastination, Saint Expedite's nemesis. Tommy believes that if something tragic happens at the airport, the event will be preceded by a crow suddenly appearing. It is widely believed that Tommy might give birth to a Cadillac right there in the tower cab, should a crow take a perch on the catwalk railing. Should that crow land and start *talking*, Thomas Aquinas Wiznak, the former altar boy, and a Knight of Columbus, would surely turn to stone, right there on position.

These days Tommy is in a heightened state of Grace, having received absolution four times in the last three days. The Benedictine priest at Saint Elizabeth's in Linden must have known something was amiss when he heard Tommy whisper through the confessional screen, "Bless me Father, for I have sinned. It's been four hours since my last confession."

Meanwhile, a tin man named Jimmy "Beans" Larkin from Boston is training a new girl on Local Control, explaining some finer points about a night operation at Newark International Airport.

"Airplanes are like boats. They have the same navigation lights. Look down at the end of the runway. What color is the light that you see crossing the runway?"

"Uh, green?"

"That's right. That light is on the right wing tip. There is a red one on the left. So which way is the airplane moving?"

"Um, from left to right?"

"Yes. That means he's crossing the runway like you told him to. Even though you can't see him two miles downrange, in the dark, the lights tell the story. Now- what if you look down there right now and you see red AND green?"

"Um, I don't know, he's turning around?"

"No. He's turned onto the runway and he's taxiing head on to an airplane in position. And, if you don't catch it, and clear Continental for takeoff, guess what?"

"A problem?"

"No. No problem. You come back and train on Local Control tomorrow and I get life in prison with weekends in the electric chair…or I get sued – long, deep, wide and consecutive. By the time the lawyers are finished with me, I'm living in the bushes behind the 7-Eleven. Always, always, always…make sure the airplanes actually DO what you tell them to do. That's why we use glass in these big windows – so we can actually see and verify that the airplanes are cooperating."

Beans Larkin has a good feeling about this particular trainee. He knows she will eventually be certified through to the full performance level. No female with breasts as large as hers has ever failed the training program, and she's got a set of "tickets", without a doubt.

CHAPTER 8

After ordering the chicken salad club and a cup of coffee at the Queen Elizabeth Diner, Liam Doherty drops a quarter in the pay phone near the front door. While waiting for a connection, he spies a waitress taking an order and pays particular attention to her hands. The hands are nice looking, with nails that are short, clean and unpainted, perfectly suited for slinging hash and dishing biscuits in a New Jersey diner.

"Newark Star-Ledger, how may I direct your call?"

"Hi. I'm an air traffic controller at Newark Airport. I'd like to speak to a reporter who's interested in hearing about safety problems at the airport."

"One moment, Sir.....I'll connect you with our transportation reporter, Mr. Donald Schwab."

"Thank you."

Doherty beckons the waitress, and asks for French fries with brown gravy to be added to his sandwich order at he counter. When she turns, he checks her "six."

"Don Schwab."

"Mr. Schwab, my name is Liam Doherty, my friends call me Willie. I'm a controller in the tower at Newark Airport."

"What's up?"

"A few things…too much to talk in detail about now. Let's just say it involves air safety lapses and criminal negligence by the FAA. I was hoping to meet with someone."

"Not a problem, Willie. I've been meaning to get in touch with the controller's union."

"They're part of the problem."

"When would you like to meet?"

"Is Friday night in Jersey City okay?"

"Sure"

"Great. There's a restaurant on Warren street, downtown by the river, called the Lisbon. It's Portuguese. I'll meet you at the bar around Eight."

"What do I look for?'

"White shirt, khaki trousers, black shoes."

When Doherty returns to the lunch counter, a petite brunette in a sharp looking business suit is in the adjacent seat. As far as Doherty can tell, she looks to be his type, only more so. He waits to get a good look at her hands. Meanwhile she speaks to the tin man.

"Those fries look good, I mean with the gravy and all. I've never seen that before."

"It's a Baltimore thing." Doherty slides the plate in her direction.

"Here, try some. I can't eat that much."

"You're from Baltimore?"

"Wilmington Delaware. We're equally influenced by Baltimore and Philly...kind of pulled between the two."

"Well, be careful not to trip on the Mason-Dixon Line."

"You know your geography."

"I know your voice too, and now that you've mentioned Baltimore, I recognize the dialect. I'll bet I know what you do."

Doherty, intrigued, places a forkful of cole slaw back down on the heavy, oval, china plate. He turns a full ninety degrees toward his new lunch counter friend and makes eye contact. Her face is pretty with smooth olive toned skin, brown eyes and nice cheekbones. A gold cross dangles from her necklace and Doherty guesses she is part Italian or Hispanic, maybe Greek. Whatever else she is, she's beautiful.

Normally the tin man dreads identifying his occupation to persons he meets. It always starts a steady stream of tedious and predictable questions usually beginning with: "*Isn't that job STRESSFULL?*" Sometimes he lies about what he does just to avoid going down the well-worn path. Doherty has claimed at various times to be an auto mechanic and an ice cream distributor. Sometimes he makes a big joke of it, telling the questioner that he works in Northern Ireland as a tail gunner on a bread truck, or that he is employed at the hospital putting wheels on miscarriages. But when the subject is broached by a female of this caliber, the conversation goes wherever she wants it to. And, she didn't ask him what he did for a living, *she claims to already know.*

"They call you Willie, don't they?"

"This is getting scary, how do you know that?"

"You have a very distinctive voice and I recognize it from hearing it on the frequency. I used to work for Port Authority Operations at the airport. In fact, you saved my life one time, I wonder if you remember?"

"Wow. I haven't had a conversation this interesting since I called one of those 900 numbers. What happened?"

"I think you were training someone. She cleared me to cross Runway Two Nine. I started to go and you stopped me. It was raining and a Gulfstream was touching down on One One. I was standing on the brakes and the car went sideways and slid across the hold bars and the white line. The airplane's wing went right over the car."

"I remember; I got a reprimand. She got promoted to program specialist; now she's a supervisor at Teterboro. She's on her way- straight to the top."

"Good for her."

"Yea, and good for us, too. But really, it was my fault, not hers. I was in charge of the position. I'm surprised to hear my name gets mentioned in Port Authority circles." Doherty sips his coffee and let's the lady talk.

"They know who's good and who isn't. You listen to the voice and you know it's going to be a long night sometimes. Same with the tower supervisor- we would call up at the start of every watch. If Frank Hamblin answers, we know the airlines will be calling us, pissed off about delays. We refer them to the FAA region at Kennedy, but it doesn't seem to make any difference." Doherty nods and adds:

"The higher you go, the less they know, or care for that matter." You mentioned dialect; you know about that stuff?"

"I'm studying linguistics. It's really your accent, dialect is something different, but most people use the terms interchangeably."

"Hmmm. I'm not sure what linguistics is, but I like the sound of it. You used to work in operations. What now?"

"Port Authority Police, at the World Trade Center."

"That's a nice looking police uniform. And you wear it so well."

"I'm actually undercover, working plain clothes, but thank you."

Liam Doherty's imagination was working on three different levels at once, spinning like the wheels on a slot machine in Atlantic City. He dislikes the idea of female cops and female firefighters. He hates seeing female lifeguards, even female letter carriers. A mailman should be just that – a MALE MAN. In Doherty's mind, females holding traditionally male jobs are the most visible symbols of a declining civilization, a nation on the ebb. But somehow, this is different. This is curiously comfortable, and Doherty is willing to forgive the assault on tradition and western civilization for the moment.

She's perfect, everything about her. She talks to me as if we were old friends and I've known her for five minutes. She looks great; she smells great; and nice hands, too. I can't let this one get away.

With the next bite of his club sandwich, Doherty was wondering what hit him.

I need to go into the head and throw some cold water on my face. This kind of thing doesn't happen to me.

The tin man speaks.

"So, wait a minute. Are you investigating me?"

"Do you need investigating?"

"I might. Maybe you should see about me."

"Isn't that a song?"

"You probably mean *Come See About Me*, Supremes on Motown, 1964."

"You know your oldies. I like that, and I LOVE Motown."

When the checks come, Doherty thinks about picking up both, then, he decides not to. *She might not appreciate the chivalry, and no move is better than the wrong move.*

As they reach the cashier, it's now or never.

"Can I call you?"

"How can you call me if you don't know my name?"

"I'm sorry. Allow me to introduce myself. I'm Liam Doherty; they call me Willie. What's your name?"

"Maria."

Maria hands a business card to the tin man. His heart is pounding as if it would jackhammer a hole through his heavily starched shirt pocket.

"You can call me at work."

Just then, Doherty's hopes crash like the Hindenburg.

"You're married?"

"Yes, I am."

"That's not fair. You're not wearing a ring."

"I told you I was undercover."

"Okay…so…you're married, but I can call you….at work?"

Maria's brown eyes flash with annoyance and she moves in close to make a point.

"You're a quick study aren't you? Why don't you announce this to the whole diner, so *everyone* knows what's happening here."

The cashier snaps her gum. Looking over the top of her reading glasses, she gives Doherty his change along with a raised eyebrow, "*boy, are YOU dumb*" look.

Stepping into the parking lot on North Avenue, Maria turns to Doherty and lays down further terms as if she was reading his mind.

"Don't follow me to my car. We'll talk later."

"But I want to kiss you."

"And I want you to…but not here…not now…so call me." Maria wheels through the light, turning onto US 1&9, traveling north, toward Newark and the Holland Tunnel. The tin man watches her car until it drives out of sight.

Without thinking about it, Doherty pulls a boxed, white dress shirt from the back seat of his car and changes in the parking lot. His starch habit is costing him a hundred dollars a week.

CHAPTER 9

Feeling like a bundle of nerves, and hornier than a Texas marching band, Doherty leaves his car and walks three blocks to Ben's Tavern, a watering hole for airport and airline workers and a favorite among the tower controllers. Slowly sipping a Jameson's he thinks of his father. In fact, Doherty cannot enjoy Irish whiskey without remembering his father's advice:

"If you're gonna drink whiskey, drink Irish whiskey. The Irish invented whiskey and everything else is just a poor imitation. Scotch is a cheap mixture of piss and turpentine, pressed through an Englishman's dirty jock strap...and inside every Scotch drinker- there's an Irish whiskey man trying to get out."

Occasionally derailed, his mind would jump back on the Maria track. He can still smell her. Looking at his hands, he wonders how long it will be before he actually touches her for the first time. Doherty drops a quarter into the vintage jukebox at the end of Ben's horse-shoe shaped bar. Even though juke boxes are notorious for destroying 45 rpm records, Doherty loves hearing a great Doo Wop record on a good old juke box. The twin pilasters on the old Seeburg slowly turned like multi-colored barber poles, decorating the otherwise dark corner of the bar. He selects the Blue Notes 1960 version of a song originally from a 1909 operetta, entitled, My Hero:

Come, come, I love you only
My heart is true
Come, come, my life is lonely
I long for you

The beautiful rendition by this fine Philly group is momentarily interrupted by the sound of a cue ball smashing into a tight rack of fifteen. The white ball hesitates, cartoon fashion, then drives through the meat of the rack, sinking two balls and scattering the rest. Doherty knows that placing high driving english on a hard, well aimed, break stroke requires a skill that few novice pool players possess. Glancing at the tall player with the excellent stroke, he knows that the shooter is looking for a pricier game. *He's already shown me too much*, thought Doherty, and he turns back to his whiskey. The Blue Notes continue, putting a harmonious Doo Wop spin on some antique lyrics that seemingly equate love with religion.

Come, come, naught can efface you
My arms are aching
Long to embrace you
Thou art Devine

Doherty checks off his cue stick nomenclature, committed to memory, much like the parts of his M14 rifle at Parris Island. Tip.... ferrule.....shaft....joint ....wrap.....butt. He remembers what materials go into making the finest examples: a leather tip, shaped and roughed to hold the chalk...ivory ferrule, rarely seen these days.... bird's eye maple shaft....Irish linen wrap over rubbed walnut. He thinks of Cadillac Joe, the man who made custom cues one at a time in his basement, and how the best players in the world would travel to Wilmington, Delaware to obtain a Cadillac Joe cue. One such cue was made for a pool shark named "Mope" McNamara. It had a compartment in the butt end to hold the player's cuff links. Doherty contemplates pool cues and the people who use them and know about them.

How many guys can shoot well, yet cannot name the component parts of a cue? Can they excel, if they really don't know what they are doing, don't know what it's all about? Can a butcher tell a good boning knife from a poor one? Can he tell it by its heft, its grip, the shape and length of the blade? Does a mechanic feel the difference between a quality combination wrench and some cheap Chinese knock-off?

Doherty thought briefly about challenging the table, maybe even playing for money. He just wouldn't feel right pulling a cheap house cue from the rickety wall rack and trying to gauge the dead bumpers on the over-used, and smaller than tournament size, bar-room table. The green felt layout, worn thin, and ground with chalk and talcum, has all of the nap of a ceramic tile floor. Like many other things in America, shooting pool just ain't what it used to be, and Doherty will have it his way, or he will let it go.

Competing on a table like this, would be, like, Willie Shoemaker mounting a coin operated drug store pony, or Arnold Palmer playing Miniature golf. Although a better pool player than most, the tin man rarely chalks up anymore. The sorry state of pocket billiards in America is another sure indication of the nation's cultural decline. Liam A. Doherty is determined to keep from walking gently into that good night, preferring a "keeper of the flame" role to being just another palooka in a boring sea of mediocrity. On the right table, and stepping up in class, or at least with serious competition, he might chalk up again.

Sipping the last dram of Irish, Doherty drops the empty shot glass down on a five dollar bill and heads out toward his car and home.

Lying back at home, the tin man pulls the business card from his shirt pocket:

Lt. Maria Cappaccio
Port Authority Police #177
One World Trade Center

With the scent of Maria still on his mind he puts the business card to his nose, hoping to get another hint of her. The tin man drifts into a peaceful sleep. The phone rings at 0800 and the tin man jumps up, finds the card, and snatches the telephone handset from its cradle. He answers by stating his last name:

"Doherty."

"Willie! Paul Veale. You're on speaker phone and John Biderman is on the call, from the manager's office."

Doherty says with some annoyance:

"I'm two days into a paid vacation. If I need conversation I'll get married."

"Willie, this is John. Your suspension is cancelled. Your time off has been converted to administrative leave, and you and Paul are to report to Building Ten at Thirteen Hundred hours to brief the capacity team on the "Veale Initiative."

Doherty replies in tin man style:

"Hey, I've made plans! I'm going to the nude beach at Sandy Hook today. They need me in the volleyball game."

Biderman continues:

"Willie, this is your doing. I don't know what you told the Port Authority's computer consultant, but you got everyone's attention. The story went straight to Washington, and I'm getting calls from the regional office. And, since Paul doesn't have a clue about a plan that's named after him, you can explain it all to the capacity enhancement team. I promise you it will be a packed house and you'll have the floor. You like to get attention? You like being the center of controversy? Well, you got your wish. If you purposely jerked these folks around with this cockamamie *initiative*, well guess what? Everyone's responsible for their own actions."

Doherty states:

"I want an apology."

Biderman replies:

"I didn't call you to apologize, I called to order you to appear at the capacity enhancement meeting today at thirteen hundred, building ten, and you are so ordered. Your union representative is a witness, and this call is recorded." Doherty replies:

"I didn't mean you; I want an apology from that walking waste dump, Frank Hamblin."

"Willie, this call is over. Paul, I'll see both of you gentlemen at the meeting."

After Biderman leaves the call and the office, Paul Veale says to his fellow tin man:

"Willie, this union spends more time and money on you than any other individual controller, and that's *nationwide*. And, you ain't even a dues paying union member! Then, you go and name some bullshit operation after me, and I don't even know about it. You're making me look bad. Do you want to at least brief me on this initiative before we get to the meeting, so I don't come off looking like some giant hard-on?"

Doherty retorts:

"You're gonna love this, Paul, I promise you. Meet me at the Flamingo Diner at Eleven today."

Paul Veale settles into a lower tone:

"Okay, okay, I'm there. By the way, Betty Jackson clued me in on something. She heard the region talking to the staff at the tower about airline yearly fuel savings expected with your plan – excuse me, MY plan. Would you like to take a wild guess at the number being thrown around?"

Doherty: "Gallons or dollars?"

Veale: "Either way it's in the millions. That's MILLIONS!"

Doherty: "Yea, and all we get is a bottle of saki and a Hawaiian shirt."

CHAPTER 10

In the tower cab it's a busy afternoon and Judy Episcopo is training on the Cab Coordinator position. Taking nearly two full years to progress through the training program, Judy is just about ready to reach full performance level. Along the way, she hooked up with more than one tin man. Right now she seems to favor Dennis Walling. When Judy thinks no one is watching, she will occasionally back into Walling, bumping his shoulder with her plump and shapely Italian derriere. Her latest boyfriend is seated at one of the tower radar displays, clearing helicopters through the tower airspace on their way to and from Manhattan. Once, she pretended to trip and fell into Walling's lap, grinding her buttocks on him before quickly regaining her feet. This caused tin man Walling to momentarily lose his concentration. One such episode drew the wrath of the tower lesbians, and they filed a sexual harassment complaint, demanding that the FAA place the couple on different teams to spare the faggots and lesbians and other sexually confused controllers such offensive displays of disgusting heterosexual hi-jinks.

Along with being a very attractive, voluptuous young lady, with pleasingly oversized breasts and shapely buttocks, Judy's prolific and inventive profanity is large and legendary. Even Gordon Russo, an expert cursing man by Navy standards, admits that the heavyweight swearing title belongs to Judy. She can curse better, louder and longer than any female and most males on the planet and she is the undisputed cursing champion of Newark Tower. Not a shy girl, Judy is unafraid to let someone know what time it is.

Once, while reaching for a handset, Judy mistakenly calls it a "phone." When her OJT instructor tries to put a finer point on her radio equipment nomenclature, Judy angrily responds:

"IT'S A MOTHERFUCKING PHONE GODAMMIT! NOW STOP BUSTING MY FUCKING BALLS!"

Roy tends bar at the Lisbon Restaurant. Roy likes the Newark Tower tin men because they tip well, usually a hundred dollars and always in advance. Then, upon leaving, they all throw another five or ten on the bar. Roy especially appreciates that Doherty is the youngest Doo Wop fanatic that he has ever met, and likes to trade trivia questions about the "sound." Roy likes to tell folks who express an interest in "oldies" that he is friends with Johnny Maestro, the fabulous lead singer on all of the great Crests records on the Coed label, and later with The Brooklyn Bridge. An incredible, under-rated talent, and one of the founders of the Doo Wop genre, Mr. Maestro occasionally drops in at the Lisbon for a late night cognac with his friend Roy the bartender.

As Doherty enters, Roy nods and starts a pitcher of white sangria for his favorite tin man. The dark paneled bar smells of sautéed shrimp and garlic, and the juke box, at a volume that facilitates conversation, is playing "Welcome Me Love" by the Brooklyn Bridge, featuring former members of the Del-Satins, with Roy's good friend, Johnny Maestro on lead. The melancholy, love yearning lyrics prompt Doherty to think of Maria. Drawing her business card from his wallet, he reads it again and holds it to his nostrils for a moment before putting it away.

In the hours before the morning
Walking home, I pass her door
And I send a special prayer
Up to the room on the second floor

Doherty spies a diminutive, dark haired young man in glasses and a villager sweater and walks over to extend his hand toward Donald Schwab, transportation reporter for the Newark Star-Ledger.

"Liam Doherty. Call me Willie."

"Don Schwab.'

"Is Roy taking care of you, Don?"

"He sure is. What's good to order here?"

"It's all good. Try the shrimp in garlic sauce appetizer and a steak. You can't miss."

Roy brings the pitcher of sangria and two glasses. Mr. Maestro is wrapping up his tune with a vow of fidelity.

I'll try to make her happy
And I promise I'll be good
I'll play it by the rules
Just like every lover should

Doherty forgets the music and gets to the business at hand:

"Don, your paper's been screwing the controllers and the flying public for years, now what about that?"

"I don't know what you mean, how so?"

"You print the FAA's tired bullshit tag line every time. Safety was never compromised Everything *they* say gets ink. The controller's opinions about safety events get lost and never see the light of day. I mean, C'mon- the radar shits the bed during a busy period, or we experience a total power failure, radar, radios, toaster, and you tell your readers that *"Safety was never compromised"* "What will you tell them when two flights connect in mid air, and bodies start dropping onto the turnpike during rush hour?"

Surprised by such blunt criticism so early in the conversation, Schwab stops and blinks.

"Hey, I just work there. I'm not allowed to write whatever I want, you know. I answer to editors." Doherty takes a healthy slug of white sangria and responds sarcastically.

"Oh. I'm sorry. I thought the stories said, by - Donald Schwab."

"Yea, yea, okay, but someone signs my paycheck, too. You know I run into people all the time who think that the paper is owned by the reporters. They always get that notion just after reading a news story they don't like."

Doherty believes you can test people by quickly putting them on the defensive to see how they react. Schwab wasn't exactly counter punching like Jake LaMotta or Joe Frazier, but Doherty still gets a gut feeling about Schwab, that maybe the scribe could be trusted. Besides, the Newark Star-Ledger was the only game in town, at least on this side of the river, and any newsworthy story that Doherty or the tin men funneled to the paper would fall on Schwab by default. To a large degree, Don Schwab would have to be trusted, trustworthy or not.

Roy the bartender saunters over toward the two men at the end of the bar. Damming the sliced fruit in the spout of the glass pitcher with the wooden mixing spoon, he tops off the two wine glasses and attempts to stump Doherty with some fifties vocal group trivia:

"Your refill is free if you can name the lead singers of three groups." Doherty is up to the challenge.

"Go ahead."

"Dubs."

"Richard Blandon."

"Chanters."

"Bud Johnson."

"Harptones."

"Willie Winfield."

Roy shakes his head and mutters "Amazing" and snatching the empty pitcher he moves away to slice more apples for the refill.

Schwab quizzes his new friend. "How do you know that stuff? Were you a disc jockey in a previous life?"

"Nah. Record collector. Collectors know more about the sound than the DJ's ever did."

"How many records do you have?"

"WHAT you have is more important than how many. I only have three thousand 45 RPM records."

"Okay, what's the most valuable 45 rpm record to collectors?"

That's easy. "Stormy Weather by the Five Sharps on Jubilee. It's believed to exist, but has never been seen. It's the Holy Grail of record collecting." Doherty changes the subject.

"Listen Don, what's the usual story about Newark Airport?"

"I don't know, from what perspective? On what level?" Doherty narrows it down:

"What is the biggest complaint you hear about Newark Airport?"

"That's easy- delays, no question about it."

"And who do the complaints come from?"

"You name it, passengers, airlines, Air Transport Association, travel agents….everybody involved. Nobody likes it. It costs everyone money. The North Jersey area is a heavily populated market. The airlines are trying to milk it for all its worth, but the airport is not cooperating. I've talked with many airline folks and they think the airport can handle more traffic…they think the FAA is dragging their feet, or not trying hard enough."

The tin man nods.

"David, what if I told you that the controllers know how to eliminate most delays at Newark Airport? Suppose they have known this for years, and that the FAA knows it too, but refuses to do anything about it? What if I told you that the solution costs nothing to implement, requires fewer controllers than normal, no new equipment, and actually increases safety? And what if I told you it requires no new training and is readily understood by pilots and controllers alike? And, what if I told you that a runway incursion becomes damn near impossible under this plan?" Donald Schwab stabs a shrimp and looks at Doherty for a second, then answers the questions:

"I'd say that sounds incredible. Something like that would certainly interest my editors. How do I know it works?"

"It's being tested right now by the Port Authority. They hired a fancy computer consultant to test a number of scenarios to see which runway flow can save the most minutes- hourly, daily, weekly and annually. The union and the FAA assigned a renegade controller to assist the computer geeks and he spilled the beans about this incredible operation. They're running it through their software program now, but they already know it works. In fact, I can explain it to you in fifteen minutes, and YOU will know it works. It doesn't take a genius or an aeronautical engineer to figure it out." Doherty uses knives, spoons and drawings on cocktail napkins to make a presentation to Schwab about the Veale initiative. When he is finished, the reporter is astounded, and intrigued. He stares at Doherty until the eye contact makes both men uncomfortable. Shaking his head the scribe laments:

"How much money…fuel…time has been wasted? How much aggravation has been caused, unnecessarily?" Doherty responds pithily:

"Oceans."

After working on his meal for a minute, Doherty thinks about the safety angle. "You know, Don, safety IS being compromised. Because what the FAA is doing now is UNSAFE! I know you don't like to hear that word, nobody really does, but I can prove it to anyone willing to listen."

Don Schwab promises to put the Veale plan on the agenda, and Doherty lets it all sink in while the two men enjoy the steak and sangria. Doherty waits for a lull in the conversation. Then, with perfect timing, worthy of Jack Benny or Ted Williams, the tin man drops a bomb on the Star-Ledger's transportation reporter.

"So Don, did you hear about the close call that Ronald Reagan had at Newark Airport the other day?"

"WHAT?!!"

Schwab jerks a small folding notebook from his prat pocket, flips it open and slaps it down on the bar. Doherty spends the next 45 minutes answering journalism 101 questions: Who, what, when, where, why and how.

CHAPTER 11

At the Flamingo Diner, prior to the big meeting at Building Ten, Doherty briefs his union rep, Paul Veale on the "initiative" that now bears Veal's name. Nothing in the plan is a surprise to Veale. Like Doherty, he first heard about a traffic operation like this from the old tin men, now retired. And also, like Doherty, he knows the plan will be met with some resistance from some of the controllers, because they think it means they will have to work harder. What's more, he knows the FAA will exploit the weak controller's discontent, and use it as a wedge issue to damage the union's credibility. Veale plays the Devil's advocate:

"Christ, Willie, you know that a lot of guys don't like to circle off the ILS and land on Two-Nine. It gets out of hand, because the pilots take it out too wide toward the Statue of Liberty. Especially those bone-headed People Express drivers trying to give their passengers their thirty-nine dollar's worth. It ends up being a fucking air show over the Hudson River, with all that VFR sightseeing traffic at eleven hundred and below. You can't have 747's trolling for Cherokees and Skyhawks out there." Veale watches Doherty's eyes narrow, and a grin is causing a dimple to appear on his cheek.

"What?"

"You can't come out against a plan that bears your name." Veale shakes his head.

"You're a sinister, conniving bastard, Willie."

Doherty lays out the players for Veale, appealing to his union rep and fellow tin man to focus on the big picture and to avoid getting bogged down in small details.

"Paul, the tin men will go for it because it's a slick operation, and they don't shit their pants when the unusual occurs. They will accept the challenge because that's the kind of guys they are. Besides, we do this all the time when one of the parallel runways is closed for construction. And when we do it, the FAA calls it an operational necessity. Well, let them tell the aviation community that delays do not constitute an operational necessity."

Veale makes long eye contact with Doherty, something few FAA employees like to do.

"You thought this thing out, didn't you?"

"You know I did."

"Did you stop to think that the FAA would resent being ambushed by this? Do you think that they are just going to genuflect like flower girls at the May Procession, and admit that Liam Aloysius Doherty saved the commercial aviation industry by solving that annoying delay problem at Newark Airport? 'Cause if you think they're about to do that, you're pissing in the fan. Christ! They're gonna look like the most incompetent buffoons since the Keystone Cops! They won't go along with this. They will circle the wagons, you can bet your ass on it."

Doherty responds:

"First of all, the missiles have already left their silos. This thing is a done deal. Once the airlines, the Air Transport Association and the Port Authority decide they want this, the FAA will be shoveling shit against the tide, trying to stop it. Now you can handle it any way you like, but here's what I think you should do. Call Biderman right now and tell him that NATCA is willing to give the FAA credit for creating this exciting new proposal, and that NATCA is willing to work the plan on a trial basis to see if any minutes can be shaved from delays without sacrificing safety, etc. Make it look like they thought of it first. My name doesn't have to be attached to it, and you can say the "Veale" name was the FAA's idea, or, change the name to whatever they like. What I'm telling you Paul, is just get it done. It's the right thing to do. The tin men will never get credit for anything, so forget about the glory. Besides, glory is over-rated."

Veale's eyes narrow as he digests Doherty's strategy.

"Who else is with us?"

"The Newark Star-Ledger. Don Schwab is prepared to do a feature article, Your FAA at work or some such government promoting drivel. Says he'll play up the union–management cooperation since the strike. It's enough to make you sick." Veale stares at the heavy white ceramic coffee mug on the counter. While he is pondering his options, the Dragon Lady refills the mug on her way to the kitchen. Finally, Veale sides with Doherty.

"I'll call Biderman right now, feel him out. At the capacity meeting, I'll toss the grenade to you and you can brief the members. Be ready for the FAA to have a list of problems with this thing that they hope you can't address." Doherty mimics a young girl with his voice and responds sarcastically:

"Daddy, I'm *scared.*"

Yea. I just hope I'm not getting blindsided by some angle you're not telling me about, something that's sure to make me look stupid, or subject me to charges or some such shit, 'cause I have a hard time believing that all you care about is the safe, orderly and expeditious flow of air traffic."

"Paul, my motives are as pure as the driven snow." As the Dragon Lady walks by with a fresh pot of coffee looking for empty cups to refill, Veale looks at Doherty and nods his head in her direction.

"Would ya?"

"Why Not? Would YOU?"

"I'd have to be hornier than a herd of cattle, but yea, I guess."

"Then it's settled."

The two tin men laugh and head out onto Montgomery Street in the shadow of the World Trade Towers across the river. They drive toward Newark Airport and Building Ten, heading straight into one of the wildest meetings of the Newark Airport Capacity Enhancement Team ever held.

CHAPTER 12

Because it is Paul Veale's policy to avoid fraternizing or engaging in casual conversation with FAA management, the two tin men wait until 1300 straight up, to walk into the meeting on the second floor of Building Ten. The chairman of the Capacity Enhancement Team is the assistant director of the FAA's Eastern Region, James Brickle and he sits at the north end of a long, highly polished conference table. The room's walls are adorned with large airport layout diagrams of Newark, LaGuardia and JFK airports. A glass trophy case along the short wall near the door contains various awards that Port Authority employees have given to themselves to stroke each other for imaginary accomplishments. Veale had been to many of these capacity enhancement meetings, so he knew something was up when he saw that the room was packed. Along with the usual attendees, twenty or so suits and pilots in uniform are standing around the table. There are two empty places reserved with paper pup tents marked "NATCA" on the clear-coated walnut table. Only one female is present, a Port Authority secretary, to record the minutes of the meeting.

Doherty and Veale walk in as James Brickle is gaveling the meeting to order. Pandemonium follows, as Brickle is immediately assaulted with questions about the "Veale Initiative," from airline executives, chief pilots, and ATA suits. The FAA managers, all three of them, clearly don't know what hit them. They cannot get a word out, without being shouted down and ridiculed from all quarters. Doherty looks over and winks at Stick, resplendent in another brightly flowered Hawaiian shirt, grinning like a slant-eyed, slope-headed fool. Doherty thinks to himself that he and Stick have something in common – they both wear uniforms of a sort. A suit yells out:

"Let Veale talk!" Brickle pompously responds by asserting that the Veale initiative is the last item on the agenda, not the first. This is greeted with hoots and catcalls and one profane suggestion about what Brickle should do with Robert's Rules of Order. The suggested action is not a physically attractive proposition, for either Brickle or Sir Robert. Veale rises to speak, out of order. In a few seconds, the room quiets.

"NATCA appreciates this opportunity, and the working air traffic controllers at Newark Airport believe we have a plan that can significantly reduce delays at this airport." Veale glances deliberately at Brickle. "At this time, *if it pleases the chair,* I would like to introduce journeyman controller Liam Doherty to brief the meeting and answer any questions you may have."

Doherty stands and glances at the FAA team, noting the three tight faces on Brickle, Biderman, and Frank Hamblin. The hatred for Doherty radiating from these three is palpable. Although Doherty is far enough away to escape the body odor, he knows that Hamblin is stinking like the shithouse floor on a tuna boat.

For the next twenty five minutes Doherty explains the plan, occasionally slapping the Newark Airport layout diagram with a yardstick, pointing out areas of reference. When he is satisfied that the suits can see the traffic moving in what he describes as a "pinwheel" effect, he concludes the briefing by citing a little Newark Airport history.

"For many years the focus and emphasis in the tower has been on the Local Control position. That means that all other positions in the tower existed to support what was happening in the air. However, delays are primarily caused by what is happening on the ground, causing us to create longer than necessary spacing between airplanes trying to land, impacting the departures. Because an airplane waiting to depart is generally considered to be in a safe position, Controllers are content to let it happen. What the Veale Initiative does best is put the ground traffic in constant motion, eliminating runway crossing ground traffic delays. It is a flexible operation. When the departure demand is high, they get two runways, no waiting. When the arrivals greatly outnumber the departures, we go right back to straight in approaches and land on two runways, visibility permitting. Questions?"

An ATA suit speaks:

"What's the downside, the negatives? Is it new equipment, airport construction, signage, what?"

Doherty replies:

"There is nothing needed to start the Veale Initiative. No expensive equipment like a new ILS; nothing to construct; nothing to publish, no new personnel…nothing." Doherty points the yardstick in the direction of the control tower.

"In fact, I can walk into that tower and cut a new ATIS broadcast and the delays will disappear within an hour, never to return, barring bad weather." Then Doherty, sensing a need to preemptively guard against the FAA hatchet job he knows is coming, points his yardstick directly at Biderman, causing the tower manager's face to tighten further.

"The only negatives you will hear about this plan will come from THAT end of the table. I only ask that you look at any negative input you receive with a critical eye, and keep in mind that some folks in this room have an agenda that is counterproductive, and that agenda has already brought air commerce to a halt, not just at this airport, but nationwide. I'm sure you guys remember the summer of 1981."

Doherty's reference to 1981 causes Veale to send a warning glance to Doherty. Doherty is dangerously close to using the "S" word, STRIKE. Banned by the U.S. government, the word *strike*, when used by the controller's union is deemed a threat to strike. A threat to strike is unlawful, and is cause for decertifying the union.

One of the ATA suits directs a question at the FAA team:

"What's wrong with the plan and why are you NOT doing this now?"

Biderman stands and clears his throat, nervously straightening the FAA tie clasp on his outdated, overly wide, polyester tie. Beads of sweat appear on his forehead.

"We haven't had a whole lot of time to evaluate a plan like this, and NATCA hasn't seen fit to brief us before publicizing this thing." Hamblin tugs on Biderman's jacket and the manager leans down to get a whispered opinion along with a nasty blast of halitosis. When Biderman comes back to vertical, he adds:

"Oh yea, heavy jets won't circle and land on runway Two Nine, so the plan will not work."

The suit from the ATA and all others glance as one toward Doherty. They are starting to follow the verbal back and forth like tennis spectators. Doherty easily deflects Biderman's lame assertion about heavy jets.

"Mr. Biderman is correct. Many heavy jet drivers do not like to circle and land on runway Two Nine. However, one monkey don't stop no show. Approach control simply spaces the heavy jet correctly for a non-standard, straight in approach. The heavy jet lands, crosses and waits in the run-up block of Runway Four Left until the ground controller can sequence him into the inbound taxiing traffic. Non standard, non conforming traffic can always expect some delay at Newark Airport, so this is no change to any existing policy."

The FAA management team is now apparently out of ammunition, but they still advise the committee that they are unwilling to make a major change like this without some serious testing. This comment, exemplifying FAA stubbornness, draws a few chuckles and snorts from the room. A Continental "four striper" asks the Port Authority Operations Manager about the computer modeling test results and Stick springs from his chair like a rice propelled, slant eyed, jack-in-the-box:

"We can find significant delay reductions in only one scenario that we tested. That is the so called, "Veale Initiative."

The Continental driver asks:

"How much delay was saved on the Veale plan?" Stick breaks into a large grin:

"Total." The chief pilot looks at Stick and then glances around the room.

"Total? What does that mean?"

Stick, still smiling continues. "It means that ALL delays are eliminated. That is, as long as the airport stays on the Veal...*plan*."

The pilots and other airline executives look around at each other in disbelief. After a short pause, the room erupts into pandemonium. Invectives are hurled at the FAA team almost without restraint. Order is called for and finally received. The chair suggests a short break but the room ignores him. One airline suit demands a quick answer to a question about fuel savings and as Stick starts, the room quiets to allow the skinny, black haired computer geek to answer.

"Hard to tell at this point, because we don't know how long weather conditions will permit us to stay on *Veale*. Even the most conservative scenario we have run through the computer modeling software indicates MILLIONS in fuel saved per year." Pandemonium ensues once more. Veale motions to Doherty that he intends to leave, but Doherty is having too much fun watching the FAA get their asses handed to them from all quarters. Every time one of the FAA managers opens his mouth, he gets bombarded with a new wave of hoots and profanity from the assembled aviation executives and airport tenants. Doherty tries to make eye contact with Frank Hamblin, but the portly FAA supervisor is staring at his shoes, his face is ashen and contorted as if he was scared to the point of incontinence. Tower manager Biderman has all of his inane statements punctuated with "BULLSHIT!" shouted into his face from the Vice President of the Air Transport Association directly across the table. Finally, Doherty follows Veale toward the door. As if things couldn't get any stranger, the room erupts into spontaneous applause for the two Newark Tower tin men. Doherty looks over at Stick who is clapping vigorously, and bows at his oriental friend and co-conspirator. Stick returns the gesture in exaggerated Japanese fashion by bowing even lower without losing eye contact. A few uniformed pilots step up to intercept the two control tower operators before they can exit, so they can shake hands and offer kudos. The words, "good job!" were still ringing in their ears as they made their way toward their cars. Not even the sound of jet engines spooling up on a nearby blast fence could drown it out.

The two tin men are now higher than the Good Year blimp and their heads are just as big. Tired but wired, they are in no mood to go home. The afternoon events at Building Ten were more exciting than a serious runway incursion or a near mid air collision. Recognizing the need for both men to debrief, Veale calls for a union meeting sometimes called a Midnight Mass. The two control tower operators head toward McSorely's Old Ale House in the East Village. The union local president and his non-member coworker laugh up the day's events.

Many mugs of ale are downed in the ancient tap room. They say that Abe Lincoln once bellied up to the bar there. That was before the Great Emancipator freed the slaves in the southern states, and left the ones in the north in their shackles. Doherty and Veale would be at the bar until last call and beyond, then asleep in the car until three hours later, when Veale wakes up, sober enough to drive Doherty's car back to New Jersey. Speeding through the Holland Tunnel Veale ponders his fellow tin man and he remembers something that Doherty once told an FAA supervisor who was flexing his authority, asserting his right to be "in charge."

"You may have the authority, but brains trumps authority. And therefore, the smartest man in the room is really the one in charge."

Until the big capacity meeting earlier in the day, Veale never fully understood the meaning of Doherty's words. But it is certainly clear to Veale that Doherty had taken charge and implemented a dramatic change to the way business will be conducted at the airport and not by force or coercion but with brains and balls. It fascinates Veale to consider, that by merely planting an idea into one man's head, at the right moment, Doherty had turned the entire aviation industry in the region into an ally of the controller's union, and an adversary of the FAA. The FAA management team is still wondering what hit them. They're still in charge, but only for as long, and as far as Doherty allowed them to be. Veale smiles and shakes his head slowly from side to side.

Send up the white smoke. Liam A. Doherty is the Pope of Newark Tower.

CHAPTER 13

On a slow Sunday morning a tin man jacks his headset in to the ground control position and signs the tower position log with his operating initials and noting the four digit Zulu time. Ray Martino has a serious hangover from shots of tequila at an Upper East Side watering hole. He sets a quart of buttermilk down on the console. Buttermilk is a folklore cure for a bad head passed on to Martino and his six brothers by their Irish mother.

"Newark ground, TWA Four Fifteen, taxi, information Juliet received.

In no mood for wordiness, and other traffic not a factor, Martino specifies no particular taxi route. This allows the pilot to get his airplane to the duty runway using whatever taxiways he chooses, either from his own knowledge of the airport, or from the published airport layout chart.

"TWA Four Fifteen, Newark Ground, taxi to Runway Four Left."

A pause, then a different voice, probably the Captain:

"Any particular way you want us to get there, Ground?"

Martino, his elbow on the console, and his right hand cradling his forehead, keys the mike with his left hand.

"Affirmative…in silence."

Feeling he can wait no longer, Doherty calls the number on the Port Authority business card he's been carrying since the sweet encounter with Maria at the Queen Elizabeth Diner. As the number is ringing he looks at the World Trade towers, large and looming when viewed from his slip on the Hudson River. He is wondering if Maria is looking out from one of the thousands of windows. With the early morning sun still in the lower east, the buildings are dark in contrast to the colors the towers take on in the late afternoons and just before sunset. A sunset, reflected from the facade of the World Trade Towers, while relaxing and enjoying an adult beverage, was one of the tin man's favorite moments. He was looking forward to sharing this little pleasure with Maria.

"Lieutenant Cappaccio speaking."

"Maria, it's Willie, how are you?"

"I'm doing fine. It's nice to hear your distinctive voice again. How are things in the tower?"

"Things are getting real interesting these days. I may even need some police backup, or the witness protection program. Can you help me out?'

"I'll see what I can do."

Doherty comes right to the point.

"I want to see you Maria, and soon. Can we make that happen?"

Maria laughs sexily, and sets Doherty's mind at ease very quickly:

"How about today, Willie? I go to lunch at eleven, and I can arrange to take the rest of the day off."

"Great. I can take the PATH train and meet you at eleven. Where would you like us to hook up?"

"On the corner of Fulton and Church streets, right by the subway station next to the old church cemetery, Saint Paul's Chapel. Do you know where that is?"

"I know it well. Eleven-fifteen okay?"

"Perfect."

Some time is killed over a cup of Flamingo Diner coffee, and then Doherty jumps on the PATH train at Exchange Place for the ride under the Hudson River to the World Trade Center. Crossing Church Street he reaches the designated corner about ten minutes early. A street vendor supplies the tin man with a pack of breath mints and while Doherty opens his purchase, he glances down at a stack of New York Post newspapers held down against the light breeze by a brick. The headline reads:

PREZ IN NEAR MISS

Doherty drops two quarters on the counter and pulls the top copy out from under the paperweight.

Christ, I'm really kicking Biderman's ass, first the Veale thing and now this.

Doherty pictures the tower manager on the phone, getting his ass chewed like it was cotton candy. The thought brings a smile to his face.

A combination like this could send Biderman AND his boss to the showers. Oh well, like the man says, "Everyone's responsible for their OWN actions."

For one fleeting, transitory moment, the tin man almost feels sorry for the tower manager – almost.

While reading the story, Doherty glances up to see Maria in a black trench coat approaching. She extends her hand toward him, and Doherty takes that as a signal that they should not embrace. After the handshake, Maria points to the Post and asks:

"Did you almost kill my president, Willie?" Doherty smiles and replies:

"In fact, you and Reagan have something in common. I saved BOTH of your lives."

"Really? You must tell me all about it." Doherty, thrilled at the sight of her, wonders if his nervousness shows.

"Do you like boats?"

"I love boats."

"Why don't we walk over to the Seaport and get something to eat there? Are you hungry?"

"I'm starving, you?"

"I'm hungry enough to eat the grapes off the wallpaper."

They walk on Fulton Street toward the East River, and Maria suggests they try the August Destiny, an Irish pub on Pearl Street. As they settle into a booth, Doherty is glad he can get some direct face time with her at last. On one wall is a large mural depicting the Irish Proclamation of 1916.

Poblacht na h-Éireann

The Provisional Government of the Irish Republic to the People of Ireland, Irishmen and Irishwomen: In the name of God and of the dead generations from which she receives her old tradition of nationhood, Ireland, through us, summons her children to her flag and strikes for her freedom. Having organised and trained her manhood through her secret revolutionary organisation, the Irish Republican Brotherhood, and through her open military organisations, the Irish Volunteers, and the Irish Citizen Army, having patiently perfected her discipline, having resolutely waited for the right moment to reveal itself, she now seizes that moment, and, supported by her exiled children in America and by gallant allies in Europe, but relying in the first on her own strength, she strikes in full confidence of victory.

We declare the right of the people of Ireland to the ownership of Ireland, and to the unfettered control of Irish destinies, to be sovereign and indefeasible. The long usurpation of that right by a foreign people and government has not extinguished the right, nor can it ever be extinguished except by the destruction of the Irish people. In every generation the Irish people have asserted their right to national freedom and sovereignty; six times during the past three hundred years they have asserted it in arms. Standing on that fundamental right and again asserting it in arms in the face of the world, we hereby proclaim the Irish republic as a sovereign independent state, and we pledge our lives and the lives of our comrades-in-arms to the cause of its freedom, of its welfare, and of its exaltation among the nations.

The Irish republic is entitled to, and hereby claims, the allegiance of every Irishman and Irishwoman. The republic guarantees religious and civil liberty, equal rights and equal opportunities to all its citizens, and declares its resolve to pursue the happiness and prosperity of the whole nation and of all its parts, cherishing all the children of the nation equally, and oblivious of the differences carefully fostered by an alien government, which have divided a minority from the majority in the past.

Until our arms have brought the opportune moment for the establishment of a permanent national government, representative of the whole people of Ireland, and elected by the suffrages of all her men and women, the Provisional Government, hereby constituted, will adminis-

ter the civil and military affairs of the republic in trust for the people. We place the cause of the Irish republic under the protection of the Most High God, whose blessing we invoke upon our arms, and we pray that no one who serves that cause will dishonour it by cowardice, inhumanity, or rapine. In this supreme hour the Irish nation must, by its valour and discipline, and by the readiness of its children to sacrifice themselves for the common good, prove itself worthy of the august destiny to which it is called.

Maria examines the large portrait of Thomas Clarke hanging nearby, overlooking the booth. The picture portrays a frail, balding, bespectacled old man with a bushy mustache. A Dublin poet and bookmonger, Clarke is a famous figure in Irish history for having signed the Irish Proclamation and facing a British firing squad in 1916.

"He looks very kind."

The tin man smiles and wipes the residual Guinness froth from his upper lip. The irony is too much for him and he chuckles.

Maria cocks her head slightly in curiosity.

"What?"

"You would think a cop might be able to recognize a stone cold gunman, an assassin."

"You're joking!"

"I'm not joking, and neither was he." Maria looks back at the portrait.

"How many?"

"Hard to say, a baker's dozen is a safe minimum. And that's not including the political assassinations he ordered, carried out by others." Sandwiches appear on the table and Doherty orders another Guinness. Maria makes eye contact for the next question:

"You like him, don't you?"

"The waiter?"

"No, silly, the IRA gunslinger watching over us from the wall… Mr. Clarke, up there." Maria points her right thumb at the famous Irish rebel. Doherty realizes he may be treading on thin ice, here. However, his policy is to be brutally honest and only slightly less so where women are concerned.

"No less than I like George Washington or Patrick Henry."

Maria digests the answer and formulates her next question as she chews on pastrami and Russian dressing.

"Okay, Mr. Doherty. Tell the court how, an emaciated jail bird, like Mr. Thomas Clarke, and George Washington, the Father of Our Country, are remotely alike…in your mind."

The question comes right into Doherty's wheelhouse.

"Certainly, Counselor. They fought for the same cause, against the exact same enemy. The only difference being, the Irish war for independence is six hundred years old, and counting."

Maria smiles. Her teeth are movie star perfect.

"Don't you think it's time they gave up?"

"If you mean the British, yes."

On a plaque behind the bar:

The great Gaels of Ireland
Are the men that God made mad
For all their wars are merry
And all their songs are sad.
- *G.K. Chesterton*

After lunch they opt for some boat watching on the East River. Doherty retrieves Maria's trench coat and helps her into it, using the opportunity to hold her captive in his arms for a moment. Maria turns and presents her face and gets kissed long and deep by the tin man. She playfully bites the tip of his tongue in a promise of more and better things to come. The sexy gesture changes the flow of his blood, making it rip like the flood tide under the Hell Gate Railroad Bridge. Before stepping into Pearl Street, Doherty turns toward the bartender, who is gathering coasters and wiping down the corner of the bar near the front door.

"Up the rebels!" The bartender looks up. Bored, he's heard it before.

"Aye, up the rebels," he replies, and then tosses the wet bar rag into the sink.

The couple cross the cobblestones of South Street near the fish market and take a position on the railing overlooking the river. A white tug passes, towing an empty barge on a short hawser. Doherty smiles at the whimsical name painted on the stern bulwark: *Terror of New York.*

Maria wonders aloud about the tug's business. "I see these boats all the time, and I wonder where they are going and what they are doing. Do you know?"

"Sure. That one is towing a fuel barge. Since it is sitting high in the water, the barge is empty, probably coming back from a delivery in New Haven or Providence. They fill up at the refineries in New Jersey and tow the product up north to Boston and Maine, places like that." A seagull walks up to the boat watchers, looking for a handout. The tin man decides to let Maria do some of the talking.

"That badge number of yours- 177. That's a low number for such a young police...person. How do you rate it?"

"It was my father's shield. He's retired Port Authority. He started with Bridges and Tunnels. They let you pass the number on to your kids if they come in. It's kind of neat. Some of the older guys see the number and they know who I am before we are introduced. They ask, "How's your dad?" It's a nice tradition." Doherty leans against the rail and takes a moment to watch Maria's facial profile as she looks east toward Brooklyn and the old buildings at the base of the Brooklyn Bridge. He can't remember falling this fast or this hard. He hates himself for the weakness. He knows already that he can fight it, but can't defeat it. Like the British with their "Irish" problem, Liam A. Doherty has Maria fever.

"I know another good boat place, two stops on the PATH train. Do you have time for it, Maria?" Maria looks at the tin man and smiles.

"Sure. Let's go."

At Pavonia/Newport in Jersey City, they stop at a lunch truck for coffee and walk a half block to Newport Marina, an old tug boat repair facility converted to an upscale marina with an eclectic collection of sailing yachts, trawlers and sport-fishers. Doherty, ignoring a "Boat Owners Only" sign, opens an iron gate to allow entry to the south finger dock stretching east to the Hudson River. They stroll down the floating dock, stopping to admire some of the more interesting vessels. They pass the *Easton Assassin*, a fishing boat belonging to Larry Holmes, the former heavyweight boxing champion, and King Loon, a gorgeous sailing ketch of Taiwanese heritage. The wake from a passing ferry boat rolls under the floating dock, testing their sea legs. Coming to the last slip on the south side, they stop at *Tipitina*, a thirty-foot masthead sailing sloop with traditional lines and oversized fenders to thwart the wake from the ferry boats. The view of the World Trade Towers is breathtaking from here, and the Statue of Liberty can be seen two miles directly south. Doherty places one foot on *Tipitina's* port toe rail and unsnaps the pelican hook on the lifeline. Offering a hand to Maria, he keeps one on the lifeline stanchion.

"Welcome Aboard." Maria hesitates.

"That's breaking and entering, Willie."

"It's okay; I have a close relationship with the captain."

Maria steps aboard and Doherty follows her into the aft cockpit and opens the companionway, dropping the hatch boards onto the pilot berth below. Doherty enters first and offers some safety instructions. "Face aft, Maria, and come down the ladder with two hands on the rails. It's easy to lose your balance. Give me your coat first." Doherty stands rear guard at the base of the ladder and gets a close up view of Maria's exquisite "six", delightfully stretching the fabric of her pants, and seeming to come down on the tin man like a total eclipse. Upon reaching the cabin sole, Maria stops in place and Doherty holds her close burying his face into her neck below the ear. When Maria keeps her hands firmly grasped on the companionway ladder, the tin man takes the opportunity to reach under and test the weight of her breasts. After nibbling her ear lobe, he whispers: "I think you're listing slightly to starboard, ma'am."

CHAPTER 14

The news story about the strange encounter by Marine One with the Twin Beech at Newark Airport had the FAA's Eastern Region bewildered. No less than the White House chief of staff and Reagan's communications director had requested a meeting with all of the Newark Tower controllers and FAA managers involved. Not on the invited list was Liam A. Doherty; even though he was operationally in charge at the time of the event, and played a crucial role in unscrewing the screw-up. Because he was not actually working a "talking" position, the FAA fooled the White House into leaving him off the list. Everyone else could be trusted to toe the party line and they practiced until they could repeat it in their sleep. They were pleased to find out at the meeting, that the only concern of the White House was how much "juice" the story had, and who may have been responsible for "leaking" it.

The other major issue of the day was the Veale Initiative, and Doherty was the straw that stirred both drinks, the eye of a perfect storm of controversy. Many of the NATCA controllers, mostly the "weak sticks" were beside themselves with anger that a non-union member was positioned to dictate what type of operation would be become the norm, and that they would have to work this plan day in and day out, should the plan test positive for delay reduction. As the union rep, Veale was catching hell for appointing a non- member to meet with the computer geeks and give input, even though the detail was offered to them and they turned it down to a man. Now, they had to either eat it or possibly sabotage it, and some were openly talking of doing just that. And not just controllers, but supervisors were conspiring to "tank" the test of the Veale Initiative, to make sure that delays actually *increased* on the Veale

Plan. The union can't mention the word *strike*, but here's management openly talking of delaying flights on *purpose!* A management instigated SLOWDOWN! Apparently, subverting the FAA's stated mission, and thwarting the will of the flying public and the aviation community in an attempt to embarrass ONE renegade controller, is a valid agenda in today's FAA. Doherty was sure that such a tank job would carry the Region AND FAA Headquarters' Good Housekeeping Seal of Approval. Even so, he was still astonished at this blind lust for power by the FAA. They value power over all else, the safety of the public does not even finish in the money.

Doherty made a mental note to brief Donald Schwab and thank him for passing the Reagan "near miss" story to the New York Post. Apparently the story was too controversial for New Jersey's daily fish wrapper, the Star-Ledger. While breaking open the heavily starched legs on a fresh pair of khaki trousers, Doherty thought to himself:

Something is going on at that newspaper. You can't tell me that they don't know a news story when they see one. I know the Post leans more toward the sensational, but headline news becomes a NON-story once it hits New Jersey? And Schwab knew it was solid news; he passed it on to someone who gives a damn. His editors must have spiked it. Money, follow the money. Who is in their pockets? Schwab mentioned the editors before. Why are they filtering bad news about Newark Airport? Whose water are they carrying?

Since things at the tower were relatively routine as far as "deals" were concerned, Tommy Wiznak has settled back into a normal simmering neurotic mode, and his crew stopped threatening to call the FAA hotline on him. One member of Tommy's crew, a born again Christian, was concerned that Tommy might cast some kind of Catholic spell on him. The "born again" guy found a picture of the Pope in his mail slot, prompting a shouting match between the two that required management intervention, before it came to blows. Overall, it took Tommy nearly two months and an entire box of votive candles since the parrot landing, to return to "normal." Said Gordon Russo of Tommy's extreme, superstitious behavior during the 'parrot" episode:

"I should have shoved a lump of coal up his ass. I'd have a god-damned diamond by now!"

Later that night in the tower cab, Gordon Russo is coordinating, and standing behind "virgin" Mary, the militant bull dyke with linebacker shoulders and lumberjack forearms. The "G" man is scanning the stars in the unusually clear New Jersey night sky with a brand new pair of binoculars. "Which one is the North Star?" Then he trains the binoculars on the moon. "Wow, you can really see some of the moon's features with these glasses." Mary clears a Continental jet for takeoff on Runway Two Two Right.

Continental One Thirty Three, caution wake turbulence, five miles in trail of a heavy Boeing Seven Forty Seven wind two three zero at one five, cleared for takeoff. Then Russo, with the glasses still stuck on his face and pointed toward the stars, exclaims, "Hey Mary! I can see YOURANUS from here!" Mary's head cooks off like a paint can on a Bunsen burner. She turns to slap Russo's face, but her hand catches nothing but binoculars. The binoculars sail across the cab and land on the windowsill knocking over a cup of coffee. A shouting match ensues, and the air traffic is neglected for a full three minutes. A TWA jet executes a go around when "virgin" Mary ignores his requests for a landing clearance. The big lesbian is too busy screaming at Russo and threatening to knock the "G" man's teeth out of his head. For his clever and crude double entendre, Russo draws ten days on the beach, a letter of reprimand and legend status among his fellow tin men.

There are stars darling, in your eyes
They make me realize
That our love was meant to be
Take a look and you will see
-Chanters, 1958 DeLuxe Records

CHAPTER 15

One very annoying thing about working a night operation at Newark Tower is the lighting. Control towers use special ceiling lights that are deeply recessed into the ceiling and shrouded by cover panels that focus needed lighting on the consoles and work spaces and prevent the large windows from reflecting that light back into the controller's eyes. One day the Port Authority found that the suspended drop ceiling panels in the tower cab contained asbestos. It was decided to send a crew to the tower to paint the dangerous ceiling panels with a special paint that would prevent the carcinogen from contaminating the atmosphere in the enclosed working space. To accomplish this, the work crew removed the steel light shielding panels and stacked them in the stairwell leading to the tower cab. The panels subsequently went missing, perhaps thrown out with the trash. Months passed until the NATCA rep, Paul Veale noticed that the lights were being reflected, and not just once, but into and around the adjacent twelve huge windows causing a mirror effect that, if the windows could "spin," would resemble a revolving disco ball. Veale filed a grievance over the unsafe working condition, claiming that a misidentification of an aircraft could occur, and that the controllers could not see the traffic clearly. After all, an aircraft on final approach at night, appears as a "light" for all intents and purposes, and "false" lights appearing in the windows could cause a serious problem, even a multi-fatal accident. It takes Manager Biderman all of three seconds to deny the grievance, branding it "frivolous." Veale was turning to leave when Biderman made the mistake of adding a comment:

"Nobody else is complaining."

This remark sets the NATCA rep off like a volcano.

"Now hear THIS, you pompous jackass! I represent this ENTIRE bargaining unit! That means that when I talk, I'm speaking for every swinging dick controller at this facility! That means that EVERYONE is complaining, and I am delivering THEIR complaint! So take that stupid "nobody else" bullshit, and stick it in your pantry with your fucking cupcakes!"

Veale does not pursue the grievance further, but opts to send a certified letter to Biderman. The letter states that any error by a controller at night, wherein a misidentification of an aircraft occurred, would be deemed the responsibility of FAA management, until the ceiling lights were brought back to standards. A copy of the letter and a memo outlining what happened at the meeting is placed in every controller's mail slot. It is Veale's policy to keep the members informed about events as soon as possible. Because of this policy, the tin men and the other controllers get far more timely and accurate information from the union, then from the employer. Veale makes a mental note to ask Liam Doherty to feed the story about the unsafe tower cab lighting to Donald Schwab at the Star-Ledger.

On a typical Monday morning a program specialist or some other office pogue would start to wander into the tower cab shortly after 0900, bringing some sort of memo or update to insert into the "read and initial" folder for general information purposes. This Monday, a particularly toady fellow named Alan Mealey appears on the control deck, inserting more worthless information for the controllers to "read and ignore." Wearing the coat and tie uniform that designates him as a management team member, Mealey is a notorious brown-nosing "yes" man. His willingness to fawn over the air traffic manager and kowtow to anyone in a position of authority was without shame or any discernable limits. Even more than any effeminate, flaming faggot in the FAA, the sight of Alan Mealey makes Liam Doherty's stomach yaw.

After elevating the useless piece of paper from the ninth floor offices to the tower cab, Mealey ambles over to the coffee pot and pauses to engage the controllers in small talk. Controller Judy Episcopo notices that Mealey is wearing a particularly loud, paisley necktie, and another, more conservative solid blue tie is protruding from his prat pocket. "Hey, Alan! Why the two ties?" Mealey pulls the blue tie from his pocket and explains simply: "In case John Biderman doesn't like the one I'm wearing, I have another one ready to go." With jaw dropped and nearly at a loss for words, all that Judy Episcopo can think to say is "HO-LEE SHIT!!" Alan Mealy looks bewildered at the stunned, then amused reaction that his explanation receives from the controllers in the tower cab. Mealey has no idea why anyone would consider his "dress for suck-cess" wardrobe planning a source of amusement or derision. Alan Mealey leaves, descending back into pogue country. Beans Larkin remarks: "If you can't decide which tie to put on, you don't belong anywhere near a control tower." What Larkin doesn't know is that Alan Mealey's name is on a very short list for a supervisor's position at LaGuardia Tower.

CHAPTER 16

The Veale Initiative Plan, now common knowledge, is also the central issue of discussion at the tower union meetings held every training day. As a non-member, Liam Doherty is not allowed to attend meetings, so any questions about the plan go to Veale by default. Some controllers openly oppose it, claiming they shouldn't have to work harder, simply because ONE non-member convinced a computer consulting geek that he knew more than the entire Eastern Region about what works at Newark International Airport. Since the plan had not been tested for even five minutes, no one should assume that the Veale plan would work, regardless of what the computers may have indicated. When one union member flat out promises to ensure the plan would fail by staging a one-man "slowdown," Paul Veale calls his bluff. Veale asks him to put his promise in writing, or "shut the fuck up."

Doherty is quickly losing any remaining friends he has at the tower. It is common knowledge that he is the source of negative news stories appearing with more frequency in the papers. Worse than that, whenever the FAA tries to cover up an operational error, or a serious safety lapse, it somehow gets reported to the National Transportation Safety Board, and then it ultimately gets into the newspapers. Doherty's timing is impeccable and he never tips his hand. He allows three or four days to pass, when the FAA could not claim a routine delay in reporting the serious event. Then, when the NTSB starts the investigation, the Star-Ledger or the New York Post, or both, get a telephone tip. The NTSB confirms to reporters that an investigation is in progress, and that confirmation never fails to get a story printed. And Doherty carefully grooms his credibility with the reporters. He never passes a tip about a minor incident, or tries to exaggerate a minor event into headline news. Although the FAA constantly lies to reporters, and their false statements get printed, Doherty knows the same rules don't apply to a controller. Should Doherty get caught telling a lie to the Star-Ledger, he knows that Donald Schwab will cut him loose like a burning barge.

A newly certified controller named Greg Reed approaches Doherty in the break room. "Can I talk to you?"

"Why not, you've only been here almost two years. Now is as good a time as any to start talking. Here, have some pound cake." Doherty slides the Tupperware cake saver toward Reed.

"Willie, my wife's upset about something that happened at the airport."

"Listen Greg, can I call you Greg? I don't know what you've heard about me, but if People Express lost your luggage, there's not much I can do about it."

"I'm serious man, listen...I'm a non-member…like you."

"You know what, Greg? I don't feature collectivism. So if there gets to be too many non-members, I'm joining the union."

"Can we talk or not?"

"Go ahead. I'm listening."

Greg Reed then relates an incredible story about an incident in "C" Terminal occupied by Continental Airlines, and inside one of Continental's Boeings 737's parked at the gate prior to departure. It seems that a crew of flight attendants had gathered aboard the aircraft in the early morning and they were having coffee and conversation. A young, black mechanic appeared on board and with very poor and broken English started asking a question about the fire extinguishers. The flight attendants offered that he was probably on the wrong aircraft, because his presence was not requested, and there was no problem with the cabin safety equipment on board.

The mechanic left, and the ladies returned to their talk. Less than a minute later, Greg's wife, one of the flight attendants, realizes her purse is gone from the seat where she had rested it. Remembering that the company had warned their employees that personal property, especially handbags had gone missing recently and to be alert for such an occurrence, she quickly notified the airline and a search ensued. The thief was found hiding in a janitor's closet. Further investigation revealed that the "mechanic" was not a Continental employee, but was a janitor hired by a cleaning contractor.

This particular cleaning business had been infiltrated and eventually taken over, by a dangerous Haitian street gang. They were sending young recruits, illegal aliens the lot, to the airport to grab anything that was not red hot or nailed down. Handbags were a favorite target for the cash and drugs they frequently hold. The criminal enterprise had become surprisingly sophisticated, stealing airline mechanic's coveralls and reproducing airline employee identification cards.

Doherty closes the door to the break room and opens the door to the catwalk to see if anyone is taking the air, and could walk in unexpectedly. Finding no one, he closes the door and returns to the table.

"So the story you are telling me seems to indicate that illegal aliens, with criminal intent, have had nearly unfettered access, not only to terminal and ramp areas, but also to AIRCRAFT at this airport?"

Greg Reed, looking as serious as a bail bondsman, nods in agreement. "Scratch the word "nearly" and what you said is true."

"Shit, Greg, it sounds like those witch doctors did everything except jump in the left seat and take a Boeing seven-three for a joy ride around the airport perimeter! Only they couldn't get the landing gear tucked up inside the wheel wells to make it look cool!"

Greg Reed chuckles. "Yea, like a '64 Chevy. But really, it's no joke. My wife and her friends are pissed about this. It's a *serious* security risk. Someone could plant a weapon, even a gun on an aircraft…and those flimsy cockpit doors never got upgraded like they were supposed to. The flight attendants have some genuine safety concerns, and they can't get the airlines or the FAA to even admit there's a problem." Doherty looks hard at Reed.

"Let me guess. The entire thing got buried…by the Port Authority AND by Continental?"

Reed nods again. "Yep, like it never happened. They said to keep it hushed up; it could hurt business at the airport."

"And…..you want ME to tell someone…someone who could *print* the story?"

"Could you?"

"Yes. But so can you. Pick up the phone, and call a reporter. It's as easy as pissing off Pier Six." Another sliver of pound cake goes down with a coffee chaser.

"Listen Willie, this is my first facility. I haven't been in the FAA that long, and I was still training a few weeks ago. Plus, I got a wife and kid to think about, you…you're single and…

"Greg, I didn't come here to grow a pair of balls, I walked in the door with them. I'll make the call, but you still have to talk, maybe your wife, too. Reporters want TWO sources. They learn that in journalism school. They're not like FAA managers; they're taught ethics and sometimes they even try to apply it to their circumstances. If you won't talk, fine. I'll still tell Schwab the story, but it will never see ink, I promise you."

"Okay, Willie. Let me know when you talk to him. Tell him I'll call him. Thanks, man…and my wife thanks you too."

"Can she cook?"

"Yea, the best, you want to come over?"

"No."

"I'll bring something in, home cooked. What do you want?"

"A pound cake."

CHAPTER 17

Seated at the north end of the conference room table, Doherty can see Hamblin in the copy machine room, squatting in front of the supervisory file cabinet. From an expanding folder Hamblin draws out a small green bottle of Polo, by Ralph Lauren, and splashes a liberal dose into his left hand and quickly rubs it into the back of his neck. Taking a little more he pats both cheeks of his face with his fingertips, gently, as if he were afraid he might break something, like a pimple, maybe. Satisfied that his body odor has been chemically camouflaged, he stands up and locks the vertical stack of file drawers, spinning the dial on the lock that holds the secret, Left 25, Right Zero, combination. Hamblin turns and draws a cup of stale coffee from the executive pot and heads toward the tower cab to start an eve watch. Since Doherty is due back in eight hours to work the midnight watch, he gets up to leave. Waiting for Hamblin to clear the elevator, the tin man decides to take the stairs to avoid the lingering stench in the enclosed space of the elevator.

Driving home, Doherty is thinking about Hamblin and his cologne. Since the cologne's security is now compromised, a devious and wicked idea comes to mind. The tin man laughs. Deciding to put his plan in motion, his mood changes.

The Manhattan skyline, viewed from the Pulaski Skyway is fabulous and beckoning. The cool night air is uncharacteristically clear. The radio is playing some weepy Bob Dylan drivel- bad poetry put to an incessant, repetitive riff. Doherty decides to upgrade to something that matches the speed of the car and the quality of his mood.

This calls for some serious, old school, up-tempo, original, good time, vocal group harmony..

A quickly selected cassette is pushed home with an index finger. The Del-Vikings start their fabulous 1957 side, Whispering Bells, with Clarence Quick handling the lead:

Whispering bells
Ooh, so low
Whispering bells
Love you so

When the tune reaches its "bridge" with its an incredible saxophone solo, Doherty speeds up so that the *thump-thump* of the tires hitting the expansion joints, matches the hand-clapping tempo of the vocal group. For a few moments, everything is clicking. The automobile, the night, the view and the music – they all combine to take the tin man to a place that few would understand.

Whispering bells
Loud and clear
Your sweet chimes
Love to hear

On the tower mid watch at 0430, Doherty is the lavatory on the ninth floor laughing and pissing into a bottle of cologne. When the mixture and level is correct, the bottle goes back into Hamblin's expandable folder in the supervisory file cabinet.

CHAPTER 18

The biggest enemy of the Veale Initiative at the tower is Francis Hamblin. As Biderman's long time buddy, from the days when they were junior controllers at LaGuardia tower, Hamblin was brought to Newark when Biderman was selected to replace a retiring tower manager. Since delays were becoming Newark's most pressing problem, Hamblin was given the project of developing a plan to reduce delays at Newark and silence the FAA's critics that keep popping up like pimples on prom night.

Hamblin jumped into the task with two feet and no brain. Recognizing the need to maximize the concrete, his plan relied heavily on using runway Two Nine, but only for departing slower flying, prop departures. The problem with Hamblin's plan is that it creates a nightmare for the ground controller, and the ground control position is well known as the training "hump" at Newark. To make the position extremely difficult for a seasoned ground controller was to make it virtually impossible for a trainee to comprehend. Also, to allow aircraft, especially smaller ones to taxi into the areas directly behind jets departing on the parallel runways was dangerous and violated existing operating procedures. The plan also robbed the local controller of any flexibility needed to counter a go-around. Runway Two Two Right was unusable for sidestepping an arrival, as the clear area near the landing threshold was constantly occupied by turboprop departures taxiing or awaiting takeoff clearance on Runway Two Nine. This is a direct violation of standard operating procedures, or the SOP manual. In order for Hamblin's plan to work, the FAA must pretend that the SOP does not exist.

Once the Hamblin Runway Two Nine plan starts, the problems become painfully obvious. Operational errors and near collisions became epidemic, and the resulting cover ups follow like day follows night. Ground control training failures double instantly, and those trainees that do certify are taking all of the allotted hours of the program to do so. If the trainee holds membership in the Black and Hispanic Coalition, or one of the gay and lesbian organizations, serious pressure is brought to bear on FAA management. A viable excuse is found to violate the rules and extend the allowable training hours for any well- connected, affirmative action protected trainee. There might be turmoil in his or her family situation. A family member might be sick, or a kid is autistic, or the controller may have been a victim of some crime, a stolen car or a purse snatching. Any unusual event can be used as justification to lengthen the certification process. Then the trainee's hours get extended and he or she usually certifies. Straight white males, when they get to the end of their allowable hours, are shown the door, and are usually last seen doing the "sea bag drag" toward Morristown or maybe Teterboro, where the traffic is just as intense, but the airplanes are smaller.

On top of all of the safety and training problems associated with Hamblin's "ingenious" plan to reduce delays was one glaring and nagging factor that became impossible to cover up. Hamblin's plan did NOT reduce any delays. In fact, the plan actually increased delays, although the FAA was quick to point to other factors, and not Hamblin's ill- conceived plan, as the culprit for a coincidental spike in delay periods at Newark Airport.

At some point, the FAA needed to show that the plan was a success, and that Hamblin's work was not the botched abortion that Doherty and the tin men knew it was. However, when the minutes were calculated, the figures showed a disturbing trend. Delays were not disappearing, in fact, the delays were getting longer and more frequent. An annoying finger of blame is being pointed directly at Hamblin's "Rube Goldberg" method of airport traffic management.

So Hamblin and Biderman hold a top secret meeting in the manager's office and they crunch the numbers over the manager's big desk. The head scratching by Hamblin left a carpet of snow that Biderman had to "plow" from his blotter into the wastebasket using a steel edged ruler. The two conspirators determined that by subtracting ten minutes from each departure's delay and calling it "taxi" time, they could reduce the number of minutes calculated as a delay. A call and a follow up memo was sent to the FAA bosses at the Regional office and they quickly gave their stamp of approval and returned a memo to make the official change. When Alan "two ties" Mealey posts a copy of the Memo in the "Read and Ignore" binder, the tin men pass it around and get a few laughs. The change to the method of calculating delays is seen as the pencil-whipping ploy that it is. It's an attempt to fool the airlines and the aviation community into believing that Hamblin's plan is working for them.

Three months later, when delays are still climbing, Hamblin and Biderman cook the books again. They increase the "taxi" time to fifteen minutes, and one month later it is increased to twenty minutes. Newark Airport becomes the only airport of its size to lead the nation in delays, every year since the Hamblin plan was put into practice.

Francis Hamblin is thoroughly commended by the FAA, receiving numerous awards, including cash, a polished walnut and brass plaque and other kudos for his "innovative" and "ingenious" plan of delay reduction and airport capacity enhancement. In reality, Hamblin's system dramatically increases delays; increases the likelihood of a serious accident, violates standing operating procedures and makes training failure at Newark Tower more common than not. When Judy Episcopo reads another bullshit memo commending Hamblin, she shakes her head slowly and laments: "This place is fucked up like a soup sandwich."

The next night a Federal Express jet makes a landing on Runway Four Left and rolls out to turn off at taxiway "Mike" near the base of the tower. The Local controller, Ray Martino sounds uncharacteristically hesitant, even shaky.

"Express uh Twenty One Twenty Five...turn left uh...on ... Mike....standby one.".

"Standing by with you, Tower."

"Express Twenty One Twenty Five, hold there and contact ground point eight...you need to call the tower when you get back to the gate. Get the number from ground, point eight."

"Okay, Tower. Switching to ground."

Martino turns to the lesbian-in-charge. "Get me the hell out of here! I just had a goddamned deal!"

Shortly later Paul Veale gets a telephone call at home.

"Paul, it's Ray; I just had a goddamned deal."

Tin man Ray Martino relates the details of the near collision to his union rep. It seems that FEX2125, a Boeing 727 landed on the wrong runway. Normally, in such a circumstance, a controller could pretend that nothing unusual happened, and absent any other factors, if the controller was discreet, the episode could pass. The voice tapes would not show which runway the airplane actually landed on. No harm, no foul, as they say around pick up basketball games. The problem with this particular "deal," was that there was another Federal Express jet in position, on the same runway, waiting for a take-off clearance from Ray Martino. An airplane landing over another one on the same runway is a serious mishap that cannot be easily explained away, and this incident would need investigating, especially since Ray reported the mishap to a supervisor, a requirement of the regulations. Martino's other option was to play stupid and hope that neither FEDEX crew would say anything about the incident, which was likely, or that no controller present would report a loss of separation, which was also likely. At that point, the fifteen day waiting period for the voice tapes to be erased, would start. Once tape number Fifteen becomes tape number One, it is taped over, erasing any voice data from the previous period of use. The controller is then off the hook as no investigation can ensue. If however, the controller was found to have intentionally NOT reported an incident known to him, he was looking at ten days on the beach. If a troublemaker like Liam Doherty could be shown to be with such sin, he would be summarily fired.

Ray Martino is relieved from position and finds himself at the conference room table staring at a blank form. The form awaits his written narrative controller statement, describing what happened for the record. Remembering his union rep's advice about such incidents, he calls him prior to writing anything. Veale had been waiting for such a call for some time now, ever since he filed a "frivolous" grievance concerning night operations and missing light ceiling panels.

"Listen closely, Ray. It's a giant shit sandwich. If you cleared Fedex on Four Right and he landed on the left, then the Fedex driver is eating this one. Now here's how the FAA will try to make ***you*** take a bite. First, they will pretend to be concerned for your well being. They will ask you if you feel okay, and don't make a statement until you hear the tapes, make sure you confer with the union, all that happy horseshit. Then, when they think you're sufficiently softened up and not ready, they will try to blindside you with the sixty four thousand dollar question: *Why didn't you see that Fedex was lined up on the WRONG runway?* Or, Why did you fail to ensure that Fedex was landing on the proper runway? Do you know how to answer those questions, Ray?

"I guess so. I'll just say everything looked okay to me."

"Wrong answer, Ray!" Martino says nothing and allows Veale to finish explaining.

"Your answer should sound something like this: I TRIED, BUT THE AIRCRAFT WAS MIS-IDENTIFIED DUE TO THE REFLECTED LIGHTS ON THE WINDOWS CAUSED BY MISSING EQUIPMENT IN THE TOWER CAB! Write it down, Ray. Make sure you include the "false lights" in your narrative statement, and I will call the NTSB tomorrow and let them know about the unsafe condition that just caused a serious loss of separation and a near collision. And Ray, don't go back on watch. Take a few days off for safety reasons. You'll get paid, I promise you."

Aboard *Tipitina* the phone rings.

"Doherty."

"Willie. Call your guy at the Star-Ledger. Tell him the union wants to talk to him about a near collision caused by faulty and missing equipment in the tower cab."

"Sounds like you're taking the apron off, Paul. Did you get a kitchen clearance from the faggots?"

"Funny, Willie. You oughta be on TV. Then I could turn the channel and watch something else."

"Okay Paul, I'll call the Star-Ledger. He'll want to talk to you also. I'll introduce you as my sister. Now what happened at my control tower?"

"Fedex landed on the wrong runway, right over the top of a company jet holding in position."

"Nice."

"Yea."

"Who ate it?"

"Ray Martino."

"He report it?"

"Oh yea. He's taking time off, the whole works. I told him I'm going all the way with this one…NTSB, newspapers, the whole enchilada." Doherty replies.

"Ray's a good man, but will he stay on board? Cause when it comes to talking to the press, or going over management's head, some of these tough guy's balls shrivel up like little chick peas and run up inside their asses to hide."

Doherty can't see it, but Veale is shaking his head, looking down with his eyes closed.

"I know, Willie. There's a candy-assed coward hiding behind every rock. There's probably one under your bed."

"You're learning."

"Willie, Ray's given me his word. He's writing the statement now. I'll have a copy of it in the morning. He's on board."

"Sounds good, Paul, but let me warn you. You'll get a week's worth of buzz from it, and then we'll go back to business as usual. They won't fix the problem unless the unthinkable happens. That's why they call the FAA the "tombstone" agency. Every important safety milestone or rulebook change is preceded by a multi-fatal aviation disaster- enough to fill a graveyard. You can look it up. That's how it has always been, and that is how it will always be. The way it was is the way it is. I hate to say it, but we'd make more real progress if Fedex had pancaked his buddies on the runway, and then cart-wheeled through terminal B setting tourists and their kids on fire." Veale chuckles.

"You always get your point across with such subtle tact and sensitivity."

"I don't kid myself about the danger, Paul. Other controllers want to stick their heads in the sand, that's their choice. Me? I never want to lose that heightened sense of awareness. It gives me the edge I need…and controllers need an edge, Paul, even if they won't admit it. Lose the edge, and you'll find yourself hanging in a giant hurt-locker. I don't believe in luck except for bad luck, and I don't subscribe to the "big sky" theory of aircraft separation. Airplanes are like magnets, they attract each other. They require human intervention to keep them apart. If we fall asleep on the job, it's no different then a sentry falling asleep on his post- people will die." Veale digests what Doherty has said and a smile creeps onto his lips.

"So Willie, how do you sleep at night, knowing that some of your coworkers, you know – the incompetent types and the cowards and the faggots, are working the air traffic that is flying over your head?" I mean with all those airplanes criss-crossing around, trying to smack into each other, that heightened sense of awareness must keep you wide awake".

Doherty chuckles. "I sleep with one eye open, Paul- at a military position of attention…and I keep a baseball bat next to the commode, in case I shit a bobcat… and have to beat it to death."

CHAPTER 19

At Saint Elizabeth's Roman Catholic Church in Linden, a priest answers the rectory door. "Evening, Father. Could you bless these things for me?" Tommy Wiznak extends a cigar box toward the elderly Benedictine priest, and pulls the hinged lid open at the same time. Inside the box is a pair of vintage cuff links shaped like little telephones, a bow tie, a shot glass with a gold fleur-de-lis emblem, and a controller's headset with hand painted hot rod pin stripes, adorned with lucky stars and a rabbit's foot. The tiny priest, slightly bent, nods at Tommy and pulls a purple stole from the pouch on his belt and presses its embroidered cross to his lips before draping it over his neck to make the act official. "May Almighty God bless these items, and you, Thomas Aquinas Wiznak, in the name of The Father, and of The Son and The Holy Spirit, Amen." The two men simultaneously make the sign of the cross; Tommy on himself, and the priest waving his right hand over the cigar box. An envelope appears and is snapped up quickly. Tommy departs, taking his freshly blessed, lucky mojo stuff with him. The priest returns to his room, thankful that Tommy did not ask him for absolution again.

At the Newport Marina in Jersey City, the late afternoon sun is starting to reflect off the World Trade Towers, giving them an orange hue. They remind Doherty of two giant cigarette cartons standing on end.

"Who or what, is *Tipitina*?" Maria inquires of Doherty. The tin man smiles.

"I was wondering when you'd ask me that." He hands Maria a rum and Coke and pours two fingers of Irish over rocks. "As far as I can tell, she's a gin swilling New Orleans whore. *Tipitina* is the title of a song by Professor Longhair, a blues legend, piano master. The song doesn't easily fit into any category. It's kind of a crossover between Blues, Jazz, Rock and Roll, even old time "stride" piano, like ragtime. "Fess" was his own genre."

"I thought Doo-Wop was your thing."

"Absolutely. Doo Wop is my betrothed…'til death do us part. Blues and Soul are just old girlfriends. I saw that *Tipitina* was a good name for a boat. It was the first thing I thought of when I saw the title, and heard the song."

"Let me hear it." Doherty looks at Maria and smiles. Her face shows the look of a child who is about to open a birthday present.

"Be careful, Maria. The song has magical powers. One is changed forever when they first hear it."

"Now I'm really intrigued. How are these people changed? Do they grow tails or what?"

"They fall in love."

"With the music?"

"With a tin man."

Doherty presses Maria hard against the navigation table, kissing her deeply while reaching toward the cassette deck. Without interrupting the kiss, he presses the tape home starting the rollicking, bluesy, semi-famous New Orleans anthem.

Tipitina, tra la la la
Girl, you tell me where you been
When you come home this mornin'
You had your belly full of gin

The roller-coasting piano and wailing moans of the "Fess" fill the cabin and bring a delighted chuckle to Maria.

"I love it. And suddenly I have an urge for something." Doherty's green eyes dance with Maria's brown ones.

"Anything you want, Maria, just tell me, and I'll bring it to you and lay it at your feet."

"French fries with brown gravy."

CHAPTER 20

Danny Walling, working the TCA radar position, rises quickly from his chair and turns toward the Local Controller to hand off control of a helicopter landing at Newark Airport. As he turns he bumps into Judy's breasts again. A minute later, Judy leans over the back of Walling's chair and reaches toward the radar with the eraser end of a number two pencil to point out a non standard fixed wing departure requiring a piece of Danny's airspace. With her left hand she pulls her latest boyfriend's head back and tries to bury it in her cleavage. Gordon Russo is standing in the back drinking coffee and watching the cavorting misbehavior. A smile creeps onto his face when suddenly "virgin" Mary bumps him rudely on her way to the coffee pot. The collision knocks him back a step.

"Enjoying the show, G-Man? You gettin' WOOD?" Russo, annoyed at having his personal space invaded and his reverie interrupted, looks hard at the stocky, short-haired lesbian. Dressed in a man's navy blue work shirt with cuffed trousers and soiled suede chukka boots, she looks like a gas station attendant.

"I'm a tin man, Mary. I don't get wood, I get ALUMINUM!"

"Ha-ha." Mary waddles over to Ground Control, jacks into the console, and jots her operating initials down on the position log. Prompting the ground controller to brief her on the traffic, she advises: "When you stop talking, you can start walking." Despite being a militant, nasty, man hating bull dyke, "virgin" Mary has a reputation for being a crackerjack controller, and a first rate trainer. She is the only female at the tower to rate such lofty kudos. Said Beans

Larkin; "It must be the testosterone." Truly, "virgin" Mary could be a tin man – if she only owned a real penis and not one of those, plastic, strap-on, Greenwich Village kickstands.

Doherty flashes back to his first day at Naval Air Technical Training Center, NAS Glynco, Georgia. A Marine E-7, a Gunnery Sergeant, addresses the class.

"Every controller believes he is the single, best air traffic controller in the world. Naval air traffic controllers are cocky and, confident- even arrogant. Air traffic controllers are conceited and they have every right to be. Now you Marines in this class have already claimed the proudest title in the world, United States Marine. If you graduate from this course of study and earn your controller wings, you will become the best of the best, an elite member of the Marine aviation team, and an individual that commands respect. You will be the ones that Marine and Navy pilots depend on to keep them safe. I promise you Marines that your heads will be so big, we might have to take the door off the hinges to get you guys out of here and on to your next duty station. You Navy types, well, when this is over, you'll still be in the Navy, so… sorry about that!

Doherty's thoughts are interrupted when he spies Maria walking toward *Tipitina* on the floating dock. Beholding her easy motion, he smiles, contemplating a noticeable difference between the sexes.

A man lumbers, mechanically, and one movement is not smoothly connected to the next, almost as if he might lose his balance, or he is about to come to a sudden halt at any moment along the way, crashing into himself. A woman glides, fluid and ghostlike, as if she is a part of the ambient elements, and a man can't help but watch, fascinated and fearful…that she may suddenly vanish into thin air.

"I brought some wine and a loaf of bread." Maria hands the package to Doherty and he helps her aboard. In the cabin they feast on chicken from the crock pot, a favorite of Doherty's for convenience and easy cleanup. While the two start a second bottle of wine, Maria is introduced to some evocative and beautiful vocal group harmony from 1956, The Schoolboys' fabulous and tender hearted declaration of teenage love, "Please Say You Want Me."

Please say you want me to (to be your love)
I have always wanted you (to be my love)
With those stars up in the sky (you'll realize)
Then you will realize (that you belong to me)

During cleanup, Doherty traps Maria at the galley sink. Turning, she runs her soapy fingers through his hair. Their faces lose separation and their mouths have a "deal."

I have cried so much for you (for you, my dear)
I have almost died for you (for you, my dear)
I hope you do decide (to be my love)
Then you will realize (that you belong to me)

Tipitina is rocked by the wake from a passing Ferry boat, causing the vessel to pitch and yaw violently and the dock lines to slacken, then fetch up hard. The motion matches the movements of the lovers, and boat, river, bodies and music become one, all parts of the same.

Please say that you love me
Oh-oooooooh, please be mine
Please say that you care for me
Then I'll stop this crying over you

Later that evening, and alone, Doherty pulls Maria's business card from his wallet and examines it. Focusing on the last name, he suddenly remembers where he saw it before, and gets a sinking feeling. Jerking the phone from its cradle, he calls one of his few

FAA friends, an old Marine Corps buddy who works at JFK Tower in Queens, New York. In their usual routine, they start by trading crude insults, and the conversation is peppered with Marine slang:

"Hello."

"You know you could be the poster boy for birth control.

"Oh. It's you. Did your mom have any kids that lived?"

"Ha. Speaking of that – how's your wife and my kids?"

"That's a riot, Willie. I don't know what's older, your jokes or the brown racing stripes in your skivvies. I hear you're doing a bang up job at Newark. They tell me you couldn't separate mayonnaise, forget airplanes."

"How would THEY know? They're assassins, the lot.

"Yea, Yea, I know. Did you have something to talk about? Or, do you want me to put my German Shepard on the line so you two can have phone sex?" Doherty chuckles, then gets to the point.

"Listen, I seem to remember a JFK guy named Pinnochio or can-of-peas-io, something like that. Ring a bell?"

"You mean Cappaccio, Jimmy "Zeke" Cappaccio. He's running for NATCA President."

"That might be him. What's his wife's name?"

"Maria."

"Nah. Must be somebody else."

"Hey jarhead, you in any trouble?"

"Why, you got bail money?"

"No. but Zeke doesn't like non-members, so I know you two ain't old drinking buddies, now what's up?"

"Nothing, just a coincidence, and Cappaccio's not the one I was thinking of, so forget it. It's nothing."

"Okay, by the way… his wife? She's hotter than a freshly fucked fox in a forest fire."

Doherty tries to steer the conversation away from Maria.

"Why do they call him Zeke?"

"Zeke Bonura…played first base for the old Washington Senators in the thirties. Jimmy is related to him, his uncle I think."

"Thanks, and listen, you didn't hear me asking about Zeke, okay?"

"Sure, Willie, and I can't tell when you're lying to me, either. You met Maria, didn't you?" Now tell it to the Marines, 'cause if you half-masted HER skivvies, I want to hear all of the juicy details.

"I don't know what you're talking about. Now that's my story and I'm sticking to it. And don't go spreading any scuttlebutt, that's how people get hurt."

"Okay, Willie. My lips are sealed."

"Yea. Right on the leading edge of some faggot's joy stick."

"Hey, you can't blame a guy for one crazy night!" They both laugh.

After Doherty hangs up, he thinks about the confrontation he is about to have with Maria. She didn't lie to him, but she didn't tell the whole truth, either. Being married is bad enough. Being married to another tin man, especially a NATCA officer is dangerous.

Then again, she's cheating on her husband, and I'm helping her do it. What claim could either of us have to the truth? And if she's lying to him…she'll lie to me. Maybe she's lying to me now. This thing is sure to turn into a giant game of musical chairs. The last one to get lied to, well, he loses. The right thing to do is to call this off. But I'm in…way too deep.

CHAPTER 21

The next day Donald Schwab of the Star-Ledger met with Veale and Doherty to discuss the "false lights" and the serious near miss that occurred the other night. With two sources, plus an NTSB investigation in progress, it was certain that the story would be printed. These days, hardly a week goes by without Newark Airport making the news in a negative way. Even stories that get spiked are still investigated by Schwab, and when Biderman's bosses at the Region get questioned by the press about Newark, they assume a story will be printed. Then, the shit rolls downhill and Biderman gets an earful. Doherty and Veale are wearing Biderman out like a whorehouse rug. The tin men know that sooner or later, Biderman is bound to lash out in true, trapped rat fashion.

On training day, Doherty and Russo are having an early coffee at the conference table when Frank Hamblin waddles in to the copy room and fumbles with the lock on the supervisor's file cabinets. Doherty motions to Russo to come toward the head of the table so that both men can get a view of Hamblin through the adjacent office. Doherty gives Russo a heads up:

"G-Man, you see Hamblin?"

"Yea?"

"Keep watching and tell me what you see."

"He's into the file cabinets."

"Keep watching."

"Okay…he's taking some cologne or after shave…rubbing it into his neck…now he's patting it on his cheeks...like some goddamn pansy."

Right. Only its not cologne.....it's piss!!!"

Russo looks directly at Doherty. Astonished, he gasps twice then breaks out in laughter.

"What do you mean?" Doherty lays it out clearly for his fellow tin man.

"I mean its NOT "Polo", its Ralph Lauren- URINE! I pissed in the bottle and right now I'm pissing in Hamblin's face and HE'S doing all the work." Russo takes another look at Hamblin and doubles over in uncontrollable laughter, spilling coffee on the conference room table and a chair. As more controllers come in, they find the two tin men laughing uproariously. Throughout the training day, one or both of them periodically break out, unable to control themselves. Said Russo later: "I laughed until the tears rolled down my legs."

When the story about the Fedex deal at Newark Airport appeared in the Star-Ledger, the union's concern about the false lights did not get a spot of ink. None of Paul Veale's quotes concerning the cause of the mishap are printed. To anyone not close to the event and getting his information from the newspaper, the episode looks like a giant screw-up by an incompetent controller, with a little help from Fedex. Donald Schwab gets an earful from Doherty and Veale who are livid, and left to wonder why the controller's viewpoint was discarded. Doherty knows that Schwab is lying to him about the reason for deleting the union's version. It was good information, from two or three independent sources, and it was verifiable by written documentation easily obtained by Schwab. There was no legitimate reason for not printing it. There was only one conclusion to draw. On the phone with Paul Veale, Doherty lets him know what is going on:

"Schwab's cheating on us."

A ground control trainee appears in the ready room. Doherty is reading Leatherneck Magazine and does not look up or acknowledge the young controller.

"Hey Willie, I heard you helped some guys get through ground and…" Doherty stops him.

"You know they don't let me train, right?" He tosses the magazine onto a coffee table.

"Yea, I know. Man, I got six hours left. Every morning I'm getting hammered on ground. I can't get a good departure sequence to the runway to save my ass. I need to show some real progress soon, or...well, you know.

"Yea, I know. Where did you work before, Bryan?"

"Poughkeepsie Tower."

"No shit? What time does *"the airplane"* show up at Poughkeepsie?" Both men laugh.

"Listen, Bryan, who's your supervisor?"

"Hamblin. He doesn't like me. If I don't show some real improvement, I'm out of here like a big assed bird, and Hamblin can't wait. He's a real horse's ass."

"That's just his breath. Go to the training room, get me a box with twenty five strip holders and some old flight progress strips and bring them here."

For the next thirty minutes Doherty plays a game of departure sequencing and strip board management with Bryan, showing him how to sequence the airplanes as they taxi, sprinkling a few Chicago and Denver bound flights between the Florida departures, easing the pressure on the radar departure controller. The game is played with the airport layout memorized, and Doherty, acting as the pilots calling for taxi, prompts Bryan to switch departures from the Ground Control frequency and onto the Tower frequency as quickly as possible. When that happens, he slides the strip from the table and into the empty box. After three "training" sessions with Doherty, Bryan is shoving the strips from the table himself, beating Doherty to the punch, and grinning like a man who has just seen the light; the great light; the white light, the guiding light. The next time he plugs in to train on ground control, Bryan is born again hard- a junior tin man.

A week later, trainee Bryan is an hour into his check ride on Ground Control and he turns to Hamblin who is typing a log entry at the supervisor's desk.

"What do I have to do to get certified, Frank… work this position standing on my head?" Bryan's team members all laugh. Twenty two departures are at the runway, all expertly sequenced, all on the tower frequency, and all in one straight, single file line on the parallel taxiway. It is an unmistakable sign that Liam A. Doherty has been tutoring Bryan. Bryan now knows he is over the hump. He's going to make it, because if one can get through Ground Control at Newark, that controller is almost certain to reach full performance status.

So Bryan feels somewhat cocky, and his phraseology gets a bit salty.

"Delta Four Forty Two, Newark Ground, Taxi to Runway Four Left. Turn right on the Outer, tighten it up on the Boeing seven-three ahead, number twenty three, monitor tower, happy motoring."

"Okay, Ground, We'll follow the seven thirty seven on the Outer Taxiway, switching to Tower, good day.

Having run out of work, Bryan looks around for something to do; he sharpens his number two pencil. Bryan's trainer signs off on the position log and unplugs his headset from the console, leaving the newly certified ground controller to work the position with the training wheels off. A wave of satisfaction and relief sweeps through Bryan. It is a feeling unlike any he has had before.

CHAPTER 22

On board *Tipitina*, Doherty repairs a torn sail, working the leather palm and needle, drawing waxed sail thread through the Dacron jib, stitching it like a baseball, as sailors have done for centuries. Maria watching intently sips an iced tea. Doherty draws an old baseball card from his sail maker's ditty bag, and tosses it on her lap.

Maria looks at the card, then at Doherty. "I was going to tell you."

"Yea? I don't doubt that. But I have some other questions if you don't mind."

"I don't mind."

"That first meeting we had at the Queen Elizabeth Diner, that wasn't just a chance encounter, was it?"

"No…and yes…not exactly."

"And you knew who I was before you sat down at that lunch counter, didn't you."

"Yes, I did." Doherty stuffs the jib into a sail bag and tosses it into the cabin. Maria continues. "I saw you one time at Building Ten. You came over with some other controllers for a briefing on snow removal at the airport. You asked my Watch Captain about body bags…how many we keep on hand. When he told you fifty, you said we need more. By the way, that pissed him off. I saw you again at a regional NATCA convention in Manhattan. I was there with Jimmy….Zeke. That was the time you told the NATCA President that you're quitting and you called the executive board a bunch of faggots."

"And you're attracted to angry homophobes?" Maria ignores the question. "I saw you leaving the airport and I was going the same way. When you pulled into the diner, I waited a few minutes and went in." A sailing ketch motors by on its way to a slip. Doherty waves to the skipper.

"So, why all the games? Why didn't you simply introduce yourself?"

"I guess… I just wanted to get you interested...but I didn't want to lie about being married. I knew you wouldn't like it that my...that he's a controller." Maria pauses and stirs her ice cubes with a finger. "I was wondering when you would ask me about him."

"Okay, what about him? What's his story?"

"What do you want to know?"

"Is he a good husband?" Maria looks down, then at Doherty.

"Would I be sitting here if he was?" The tin man thinks.

"She wanted to get me interested. And it worked…instantly. Christ, she didn't even have to try hard. I wonder if she knows what kind of power she wields. Does she know how dangerous she is? She can get a man interested…and more. She can make a man turn his back on his religion, his sense of morality, his duty to society. She can cause a man to burn in hell and think it was well worth it, thanking her for the opportunity. All she need do is sit down next to a man, and strike up a conversation. In fact, she can do it without talking… with just a look, a little eye contact. That kind of power should be held in reserve, used only in extreme circumstances. Thank god so few women posses the ability. "Right through this door, Mister Moth…the flame awaits.

The test of the "Veal Initiative" is started at the tower. An ad hoc team of veteran controllers is assembled to work the plan during every morning departure "push." An unforeseen benefit of the plan is realized. Instead of twenty minute breaks, the controllers find themselves getting a forty five minute break and a luxurious, hour long lunch period. The plan requires less controllers and eliminates the two extra positions created by Hamblin's unwieldy plan. Pilots are delighted when they find that they can simply start engines on time and call Ground Control for taxi, without having to wait at the gate for a specified time period. The flexibility that is gained by the Local Controller is another pleasant surprise. If an airplane gets to the runway and is not ready, the offender gets taxied across and the controller clears the next departure for takeoff. The delinquent flight is re-sequenced as needed, without wasting a departure slot or causing departure delays

Beans Larkin grins the first time he gets the opportunity to work the "new" local control position. He says to no one in particular: "Two runways – no waiting." Tommy Wiznak proclaims that Saint Expedite is "pleased" with the Veal Initiative, because Saint Expedite hates procrastination. Procrastination is another word for "delay." Tommy reminds his crew that the patron saint of air traffic controllers, sailors and whores is normally depicted holding a cross bearing the word "hodie", which is Latin for "today."

The FAA managers have serious doubts about the "Veal Initiative." None of those concerns are safety or delay considerations. They are concerned because the new plan drives a stake through the heart of their empire building schemes. Eliminating useless positions and reductions in the table of organization are not concepts that government money wasters welcome. Ten-minute breaks and twenty-minute lunch periods are "proof" that more people are needed for the FAA to manage. It is also "proof" that more expensive equipment, and a new and bigger control tower is necessary. Indeed, the only answer that the FAA has to any problem is to throw more money at it, and simultaneously expand the FAA's authority over people, places and things. Because the Veale plan threatens to scale back their Newark Airport empire, the FAA has put Doherty and Veale squarely in the crosshairs.

CHAPTER 23

As a Jewish controller, Bruce Shapiro is the only employee permitted to wear a hat of any type in the tower cab. At first, he insisted on a black fedora but compromised with management and now sports a yarmulke. The compromise came shortly after the union declined to take Shapiro's "fedora" grievance to arbitration. It was a rare instance of union pragmatism in the face of minority group pressure. When Judy Episcopo called Shapiro's religious head cover a "beanie" she was awarded a letter of reprimand. Had the "beanie" remark come from a tin man, the punishment would certainly have been a suspension. Shapiro hates working with so many Catholics and he blames religious intolerance for every mistake, mishap, error or slight, real or perceived. Bruce Shapiro exploits his minority status and management's fear of him, to maintain his name on the roster of controllers at Newark Tower. He is such a terribly inept controller that he cannot be trusted to work a position without constant vigilance and scrutiny from those around him. Watching Shapiro work a live air traffic control position, is like watching a blacksmith trying to repair a Rolex watch.

Shapiro has a quirky hobby that involves the New York Post. Because New York has such a large Jewish population, the Post frequently runs stories about Nazis. Neo-Nazis, retired Nazis, suspected Nazis, dead Nazis, whatever. Whenever a story appears in the New York Post about the Nazis or the Holocaust, Shapiro clips the story and pastes it into a scrapbook. He now owns two full scrapbooks and is into his third.

As Beans Larkin is working the Clearance Delivery position, he spies Shapiro at the water cooler drawing a large tumbler full and gulping it down. Larkin decides to let Shapiro in on something.

"You know you're drinking Holy Water?"

"Oh, Yea? How's that?"

"Tommy had it blessed. A priest was up here with some students on a field trip. Tommy asked him to bless some things, like the radar, and stuff...and the water cooler."

Shapiro disappears down the stairwell as if dropped through a trap door. He takes sick leave and upon returning files an EEOC complaint and a grievance against the FAA. As a result of Shapiro's complaint, Beans Larkin and Tommy Wiznak both draw ten days on the beach. Tommy is also warned that "blessing" any FAA equipment or property will be considered an act of ethnic and religious intimidation and could result in his removal from government service. Only union intervention keeps the FAA from evicting Saint Expedite from Tommy's wall locker, causing a collective sigh of relief to echo around the tower. An act like that could have brought a serious curse on the facility. And as Tommy points out, when the curse comes directly from an angry Saint Expedite, there is nothing Tommy or anyone can do to stop it.

At the Lisbon, Donald Schwab gets an earful from Veale and Doherty. The two controllers are incensed that the "false lights" angle was not mentioned in the story about the Fedex "deal." The FAA was forced by circumstances to admit that the mishap was "technically a violation." Even so, the seriousness of the event was downplayed, and the FAA spokesperson still had the audacity to include the agency's favorite phrase- "Safety was never compromised." Veale starts in on Schwab:

"You know you can't have it both ways, Don. You want valid information from the controllers. When we give it, you print the FAA's lies instead. I'm losing respect for you. You know they're lying to you, and you print those lies. You know the controllers are telling you the truth, and our message gets shut out. It makes no sense. Maybe the union should take their business elsewhere, like to the New York Post, where they know what news looks like. 'Cause I gotta tell you, I don't think you would know a real news story if one sat on your face. Either that, or you screwed us on purpose, now which is it?" A plate of shrimp in a garlic and brandy sauce is placed in front of Donald Schwab and he starts by buttering a generous rip of Portuguese bread.

"I don't blame you guys for being pissed. But Paul, I'll tell you what I've already told Willie. I work for a boss. He's called an editor. The editors decide what gets printed, and how it reads. I made the case for you guys, and I pressed it hard. Unfortunately, I was overruled, and you saw the results." A shrimp goes down, followed by a slug of white sangria. Doherty, working on a thick, medium rare steak, has a question for Schwab.

"Okay, Don, but what reason would your editor have, for knowingly printing a lie, after you tell him what you know about the facts? Why would the editors care about rubbing the FAA's nose in a steaming pile of shit, especially when they deserve it?" Schwab pauses and looks at Doherty, then at Veale and back to Doherty.

"What I'm going to tell you, you didn't hear from me. But I can't expect you guys to be honest with me, if I don't level with you, so here goes." Schwab leans in close, like he's afraid of being overheard.

"Continental Airlines is a big advertiser in our newspaper. They don't like to see stories about safety problems at Newark Airport, and they've got the editors under their thumb. I'm not happy about it, but those are the facts. A newspaper is a business. Like any business their primary concern is making money, and advertising is where the money comes from." Roy the bartender stops by to top off glasses and refill the empty pitcher of white sangria. The two tin men look at each other, but say nothing. The moment reminds Doherty of the pause that occurs in the confessional booth, just before the priest realizes you are finished confessing and he starts dishing out the penance and the absolution. Schwab gets up to use the men's room, and stops long enough to deliver an addendum:

"There's a lot to learn about this business they don't teach you in journalism school."

Since the Lisbon is only blocks away, Doherty walks back to the marina and reflects on what he heard from Donald Schwab. It's hard to ruin a steak dinner at the Lisbon, but Donald Schwab spoiled the meal for Doherty as if he had pissed in the soup tureen.

Whores, the lot...the airlines are whores, the newspaper editors are whores and they've turned Schwab into a whore. Hell, he's not a reporter, he's a goddamned typist! He's taking dictation, like somebody's loyal secretary. No wonder the story about foreigners gaining access to airplanes at Terminal "C" never saw the light of day. You can't put any positive spin on a scary story like that one...all you can do is bury it. Hell, I've got a better chance of meeting Oswald's lawyer than seeing a story like that in print!

The next day a Trenton woman returning from a business trip is brutally beaten and raped. It happened in the airport parking lot adjacent to terminal "C" in broad daylight. A Haitian illegal is arrested, but his nationality and illegal status is withheld from the story by the Newark Star-Ledger. Also not mentioned in the story is the suspect's employment status at the airport. The fact that Newark Airport is a dangerous house of mirrors remains a story untold. A person's chances of losing life or limb increase dramatically by setting foot in one of Newark airport's terminals. This is where you enter the system. This is where you agree to play the game. You take the revolver into your own hand. You board the plane and find your seat. You chamber a round, one bullet. As the aircraft rolls down the runway and reaches the point of fly or die, you can almost feel an audible "click." But the ordeal, the game, is not nearly over. It continues until your feet reach terra firma once again. You are not really an airline customer or a user of FAA services. You are a survivor, an almost-victim that got away.

CHAPTER 24

Early on a Thursday morning, Charles Clemons is plugged into Local Control. He intentionally flexed in early to take his turn on Local before the position got busy and required a real tin man to keep the traffic moving at the speed of interstate commerce. Even though Charles had flunked the training program at a smaller, less busy tower, the Black and Hispanic Coalition demanded and received a slot for Charles at Newark Tower. In the process, they slandered and defamed a white male supervisor who had bent over backwards to try to help Charles qualify. Well connected, and well versed in the victim game, Charles is one of those employees that FAA management fears. Any attempt to impose discipline on Charles Clemons becomes an exercise in futility, usually resulting in a stretch at sensitivity training along with a demotion for any manager so inclined.

On one occasion, Charles Clemons called in from Toronto claiming he could not get to work due to a lack of flights from Toronto to Newark. Toronto and Montreal are favorite meeting places for black FAA employees who fly there for free to have sex with white women. Apparently, there are more opportunities for that brand of recreation in Canada than there is in the United States.

The call from Canada came in to FAA supervisor, Richard Bell, otherwise known as "Ding-dong Dick". Bell retrieved a tray of time stamped flight progress strips from the previous two days and extracts fifteen flights from Toronto and attaches them to a clipboard holding a large yellow legal pad. On this pad, Richard Bell starts writing a draft of Charles's letter of reprimand for lying to a supervisor and failing to report to work. By FAA standards, it was a good piece of management work. More than that, it was actually substantiated by a genuine work rule infraction that was not caused by anyone in management, but was Charles's fault entirely and without question.

The letter went nowhere except into Richard Bell's file cabinet for future reference. Tower manager Biderman and his cronies at the Eastern Region decided that a confrontation with the Black and Hispanic Coalition was not healthy for his or Bell's career. In a meeting at the manager's big desk, Biderman waxes Shakespearian about the reason for backing down by telling Richard Bell that, "discretion is the better part of valor."

A friendly, articulate and gregarious young man, Charles likes to banter and tell off color jokes while he is working, even though his skills on the operating positions do not lend themselves well to that activity. Therefore, while Charles is telling jokes, his audience is usually scanning the radar and the airport movement area, looking for airplanes that may be in need of Charles's immediate attention. Just as Charles delivers another well-worn punch line, Alan Mealey pops up from pogue country. His head is bouncing around on his shoulders like a grinning bobble-head doll. He gleefully informs the controllers on position that they may have to submit evidence of their continued abstinence from controlled substances.

"Hey, guys! The piss testers are here."

Charles's mood does a "one eighty," turning from jocular and talkative to concerned and somber. No longer the jokester, now he's suddenly as serious as the officer that offers you the blindfold on the firing squad. Charles turns away from his traffic. "Get me out of here!" The controller in charge is holding over from the mid watch and working until the day watch supervisor shows up. He questions Charles.

"What for, Charles?" "You just got on there."

"Just get me off of this position. It's an emergency!"

Since no other qualified controller is available, the controller in charge takes the position. As soon as Charles unplugs he bolts from the tower building. In his car he heads south on US 1&9 leaving Elizabeth, Linden, Rahway and New Brunswick in his wake. The next time anyone hears from Charles Clemons he is somewhere in the pinelands of South Jersey calling the tower and talking to the watch supervisor, requesting sick leave for the day. The controllers on duty, having witnessed Charles's suspicious behavior are concerned and they listen to the half of the conversation they can hear without engaging in electronic eavesdropping.

"Charles, I can't approve that leave..."

"Charles, you know I can't approve that leave, it is against standing orders. Charles..."

"Unable..."

"No...it's not possible..."

"Charles, listen closely. You are NOT on sick leave, you are AWOL. You know that no sick leave is permitted once the drug testers are in the building..."

"You were notified..."

"No, Charles...No...I can't."

Charles's actions this day cause a flurry of controller complaints to the FAA hotline in Washington, D.C. The calls come from not just the usual complainers but included even some of the shrinking violets of the tower, so strong is the resentment and concern about a controller's bizarre behavior when faced with a surprise drug test.

In an instance of incredible open-ass luck, Charles's name did not appear on the list of controllers selected for random drug testing that day. So, despite his bizarre actions, no investigation ensues. Running from the premises, in an obvious act of drug test avoidance, is somehow not a cause for an investigation by FAA management.

The entire episode only works to further convince the tin men at Newark Tower that the drug-screening program is a management weapon- a well-calibrated tool that management uses to selectively target persons they don't like, and spare the ones they favor. And the FAA favorites are females, minorities and the organized sodomy mob.

The resentment factor spikes at the tower, causing the chasm to widen between the controllers and management. Some are now openly wishing that Liam Doherty would join the union and run for local president. Not that Veale's performance as president is bad, or that the controllers like Doherty. The controllers know that Biderman hates Doherty and they want to send the manager a message he can't help but recognize. They want to give the tower manager someone so difficult to deal with, and so offensive to Biderman, that he might take an early retirement to let the cup pass. Discussing the proposition with a fellow union member, Ray Martino assesses the tower manager's preference when it comes to dealing with controllers or union officials. "Biderman would rather jerk off a bobcat in a phone booth, than deal with a union rep like Liam Doherty."

In a response to a request that he should throw his hat in the ring, Doherty reminds a fellow controller why he is not a member:

"I joined the Marines because the Marine Corps doesn't suffer faggots. I quit the union because the FAA illegally panders to homosexuals and NATCA refuses to complain about it or file an unfair labor practice complaint with the Department of Labor. I don't enlist in chicken-shit outfits like NATCA."

CHAPTER 25

Doherty and Veale decide to punish Donald Schwab for his paper's policy of spiking safety related stories about Newark Airport and the tower. From now on, they will work with the New York post, and try to embarrass the Star-Ledger by getting the paper "scooped" on stories about Newark Airport, which is right in the Star-Ledger's back yard. The tin men are not sure if their strategy will work or even have any effect on Schwab or his editors, but there is nothing much else they can do about the situation. Donald Schwab gets his first taste of the new policy when the tin men shut him out on a big story involving a serious airliner crash in queens, New York. Paul Veale gets a call from Schwab.

"Paul, I need your opinion and some background on the Columbian airliner that crashed in New York."

"You mean the one that ran out of gas and killed half of the one hundred and fifty on board? That one?"

"Yes Paul, that one." Schwab tries, but fails to deliver the line without too much sarcasm.

"Sorry, Don. I'm working with Jim Sanderson at the New York Post on this. We're giving him exclusive rights to our opinions."

"You're serious."

"You're fuckin'-A-straight I'm serious. And don't try to go over my head, it won't work. The Region and the National office are on notice not to work with the Star-Ledger. You're dead to us."

"Listen, I leveled with you guys. I told you what the deal is. I've been fair to you."

"We don't need you to be fair, Don. We need you and your paper to do the right thing. Maybe it's not your fault, but when the soup lacks a theme, the waiter is the one that gets stiffed. It may not be fair, but what else can we do? I will give you one quote you can use for your *seventy five dead, airliner ran out of gas and crashed* story."

"Okay, what's that?"

"Safety was never compromised."

The crash of Avianca Zero Five Two Heavy was an event that would further drive a wedge between Liam Doherty and Paul Veale's union, the National Air Traffic Controllers Association. The union's job is to put the best slant on any negative air safety event that involves air traffic control. Controller error is not something the union likes to see in print, and the FAA likes it even less. Avianca Zero Five Two Heavy informed air traffic controllers that they were running out of fuel. The New York Air Traffic Control Center was advised by the pilot that their remaining fuel did not allow Avianca Zero Five Two Heavy to reach their alternate airport, Boston. Approach control at the New York TRACON was told by the pilot of Avianca Zero Five Two Heavy that ***"We are running out of fuel and we need priority."*** The controllers on duty responded by keeping the inbound Boeing 707 in their normal slot, and not providing priority or expediting the Avianca flight to any degree. After a missed approach at JFK due to the bad weather and cross winds, all four of the Boeing's engines flamed out and the aircraft crashed in a wooded area of Queens, New York. Seventy-three of the one hundred fifty eight on board died as a result.

The FAA and the union seized upon the fact that the pilot did not use the word *"emergency."* Therefore, the existence of an emergency situation was not expressed to air traffic controllers, so how could they do anything about it? There was a "language barrier," in that the pilot could not express himself well enough to convey the proper urgency. It was the pilot's fault.

The story was a day and a half old, and all of the news organizations were parroting the FAA's version of events. Even the National Transportation Safety Board seemed to be pointing to the "language barrier" as a peg to hang their hat on. Jim Sanderson at the New York Post had written two stories on the sensational crash, but something about the FAA's version of the event was bothering him. When he places a call to someone he knows that may speak candidly about the event, the phone rings aboard *Tipitina*.

"Doherty."

"Willie, Jim Sanderson. How are you?"

"Fine, Jim. What's up?"

"I want to know what you think about the crash...Avianca."

"I read your story, Jim. You know what happened as well as I do. I wasn't working the flight- it's an airtight alibi."

"Listen, Willie. Something doesn't add up. I get the feeling that the FAA is lying again."

"You must have seen their lips moving."

"Does the pilot really have to say the word "emergency," before an emergency exists? Shouldn't some common sense come into play? I mean the pilot did say he was running out of fuel. Isn't that enough?" Doherty is impressed.

"You're a rare one, Jim…a reporter who can actually apply some critical thinking to a set of facts. Normally you guys just regurgitate the FAA's spin and report it as gospel. You should get the Pulitzer Prize for investigative journalism if there is such a thing."

"Thanks, Willie. Tell me about this language difference…barrier thing."

"Okay, Jim. You've seen the transcript of the voice tapes, right?"

"Just what they've released so far."

"Okay, the tapes are transcribed verbatim. So, when you read the transcript…was everything in English?

"Uh…yes."

"Plainly understood?"

"Yes."

"Of course it was, Jim, otherwise they couldn't transcribe it. So, if the investigators could understand the pilot well enough to write his words down for legal purposes, where's this giant language barrier?"

"Good point. What about the word *"emergency"* not being heard on the tapes?"

"Yeah, I laughed when I read that. It would be funnier if it wasn't so tragic. You see Jim, the FAA is not lying, they're just not telling the WHOLE truth. They rely very heavily on ignorance about the rules, especially among journalists. So call them back and ask them this question: Can the CONTROLLER declare an emergency, and if so, WHY DIDN'T SHE?"

"A controller can declare an emergency?"

"Yes, Jim. The rules say that THREE persons can declare an emergency- the pilot, the controller, or the aircraft owner or airline. What's more, the rules specifically say that whenever a controller is in doubt about a situation being an emergency, he or she should handle it as if it were in fact, an emergency. When the pilot says, WE ARE RUNNING OUT OF FUEL! WE NEED PRIORITY! What does that mean to the controller? I'll tell you what it means to me. If a pilot puts the word "fuel" on the frequency, I'm going to at least question him about it. Then, I'm writing a big red "E" on his flight strip, and he's going directly to the nearest useable runway. If the FAA employees had followed their own rules, Avianca lands safely. Then, you're writing some boring story about crime in the subway, or cops sleeping on duty. The bottom line is this: Those poor people are dead due to FAA negligence, and that is an incontrovertible fact, a lead pipe cinch. A pause ensues, and Doherty assumes that the scribe is taking notes.

"Incredible. Where are these rules found?"

"They're in the handbook…FAA order 7110.65, Chapter Ten, Emergencies. I'll fax you a copy."

"Thanks, and one more thing, Willie."

"Go ahead."

"You said, why didn't *she* declare an emergency? Do you know the controller involved?"

"No, Jim…just a hunch."

CHAPTER 26

Since Zeke was leaving for Las Vegas for a few days, Maria decides to treat Doherty to an oldies show and dance at a pipe-fitters union hall in Hoboken. The highlight of the show is an appearance by the fabulous Five Keys and their incredible silky smooth lead tenor, Rudy West. They dine on roast beef sandwiches and beer. While waiting for the headliners to appear the master of ceremonies conducts a trivia contest and starts by asking anyone to name the group that originally recorded "The Twist" in 1959. While the crowd is shouting: "Chubby Checker!" Doherty whispers the correct answer in Maria's ear. Springing to her feet as if shot from a cannon, Maria shouts: "Hank Ballard and the Midnighters!! As the crowd parts like the red sea, Maria walks to the bandstand and retrieves her prize: An album of Doo Wop Christmas songs by various artists. For the next trivia question, the audience is asked to name the soul songstress that recorded *Time is on My Side* before the Rolling Stones butchered it. Maria leans in to the tin man for the information and claims another prize by yelling: "Irma Thomas!" Before the night is over, prizes cover the table. Included are a giant lollipop and a magnetic Madonna, the type that used to sit on a dashboard…when dashboards were made of steel.

When the Five Keys appear, they look and sound as great as ever. Doherty is pleasantly surprised at how polished and professional their show is, and he joins in the standing ovation at the conclusion of their finale, The Glory of Love. Val Shively once related to Doherty that many old Doo Wop groups were frequently overcome with emotion when they are received with enthusiasm at revival shows. Backstage tears are commonplace, especially when a group re-unites after a long layoff.

As the group sings, Doherty thinks about the stage performance.

No laser light show, no pyrotechnics, no costume changes or background video, no bullshit, just five guys in suits standing around three microphones and some simple instrumentation to back them up; sometimes, no band at all- real voices, real singing, real harmony. Maybe some dance moves during the bridge. What passes for entertainment today is an embarrassment. What's happened to my country, our culture?

The final dance of the night starts and the Miracles get the nod with their slow drag classic, "Ooh Baby, Baby" from 1965. Smokey Robinson is out in front on the recording.

I did you wrong
My heart went out to play
But in the game I lost you
What a price to pay

Doherty pulls Maria in close and thanks her for the special and thoughtful treat. The slow dance reminds him of Friday night record hops from his high school days. A fleeting tinge of guilt arrives, from some far away time and place. The feeling takes him back to a gymnasium where sawdust has been spread to protect the hardwood floor. Doherty looks up suddenly, expecting an Oblate to pull him away and slap his face for the sin of clinging too tightly to teenage female flesh. Some questions flash through his mind about his own past.

Why was it that the boys got slapped, but never the girls? The girls are the ones with the attractive bodies. Isn't temptation just the devil in a dress? What am I...Evil? I'm just another guy, doing what guys do. Why must I be made to feel guilty about this?

Smokey Robinson doesn't answer the tin man's question; he's got his own problems.

I'm just about at
The end of my rope
But I can't stop trying
I can't give up hope

Later that night, Doherty's mind wanders toward the crash of Avianca Zero Five Two Heavy. The Boeing 707 is one of the most beautiful airplanes ever designed. To waste one in such an easily preventable accident is a shameful crime, not to mention the loss of all those perfectly serviceable Columbians. In fact, the Avianca accident was so preventable it doesn't rate being termed an "accident." It was more like purposely…criminally…negligent homicide. The pilot asked air traffic control for help and his urgent request fell on cold, deaf, government ears.

Avianca Zero Five Two Heavy is running out of fuel! We need priority! Help us! We are almost out of fuel! Help us! Please help us! Flameout! Numbers Two and Three!

Madre de Dios!!

Doherty bolts up suddenly from the pilot berth aboard *Tipitina*. Finding beads of sweat on his hands and forearms, he reaches for a towel. The vessel's lack of motion tells him that the river is dead calm and the digital clock at the navigation table reads 0417. The tin man throws open the sliding hatch and pops his head up in the companionway to get a look at the nightscape. The calm river is showing a mirror image of the Manhattan skyline. A tug is pushing a loaded fuel barge toward Albany. A "bone in her teeth," she breaks the still water and the drone from her twin diesel engines fades as the tug and barge push further north, passing the Holland Tunnel ventilators, and disappearing from sight.

Jesus...seventy three dead! How many wives, husbands, friends, and relatives are planning funerals and suffering...and why? What's worse we're going to blame it all on the pilot. Why do we even have rules if we don't follow them and then we pretend they don't exist when the facts get sorted out in a crash investigation? The lies...the constant lies. Am I the only one who is sick of all the lying?

The tin man climbs back into his berth and quickly falls asleep.

The next day a Star-Ledger reporter places a call to Doherty to get some help writing a story about the crash of Avianca Zero Five Two Heavy.

"I know you guys said you're not talking to Schwab, but I called to see if you'll help me with the Avianca crash on Long Island." Doherty thinks about telling the scribe off, but changes his mind.

"I'll give you one question so make it a good one." The reporter is annoyed at the petty rules directed at him and his newspaper.

"One? One question?" Doherty is about to hang up.

"That's it. So don't waste it." The scribbler pauses, and then gives it his best shot:

"In your opinion, what was the biggest contributing factor that caused the Avianca jet to crash?" Doherty's answer is pithy and condescending:

"Gravity."

He drops the telephone receiver onto its cradle.

The National Transportation Safety Board, normally one of the most independent government agencies, has lately started to lose that distinction. No longer the brave little agency that can be counted on to make accurate reports about airplane crashes, the NTSB is losing its edge. In years past they would have ripped the FAA long and deep for trying to escape responsibility for a failure like the Avianca crash. They would simply cite the orders that covered the event, how those orders were violated, and the result. Then, they would make a recommendation to preclude a future occurrence. Sadly, the NTSB went into the tank on Avianca Zero Five Two Heavy, and the record would only hint that the FAA was responsible for seventy three deaths on Long Island. They would sum it up so:

[The aircraft was put in a series of extended holding patterns as it approached New York. The crew informed Air Traffic Control they were running out of fuel but did not declare an emergency and were cleared to land. After a missed approach and during a go-around, the plane ran out of fuel and crashed in a wooded area killing 73 of 158 aboard. The captain, speaking very little English and communicating through the first officer, at no time declared an emergency. The first officer used the term "we need priority" several times, rather than declaring an emergency. The Air Traffic Controller did not realize the peril of the aircraft.]

Most of the controllers in the New York facilities stopped talking about the accident shortly after the facts about the fuel situation became known. Few controllers are comfortable criticizing another controller's actions, especially following a multi-fatal aviation disaster. Liam A. Doherty holds no compunction about chastising a fellow controller, or bad mouthing the FAA, especially where air safety is concerned. When an office pogue starts regurgitating the official story that the Avianca pilot should have declared an emergency, Beans Larkin offers a curt observation: "We can do better." Doherty nods, but decides that Larkin's comment needs no embellishment. Stretching his headset cord to reach the northwest corner of the tower cab, the tin man slices off a wedge of pound cake big enough to chock the wheels on a Lockheed Tristar.

CHAPTER 27

At a junk yard in Sayerville, a Newark Tower controller steps onto an industrial metals scale. Since a typical medical scale will normally accommodate up to 300 pounds, Mark Cushing, at three hundred seventy five and a half, weighs more than a steel drum full of old car batteries. Since starting the training program at Newark Tower, Mark's weight has steadily climbed from his normal one hundred eighty five. Every position in the tower training program has been a supreme challenge for Mark, and his doctor blames his obesity on an eating disorder brought on by the severe stress of Mark's unique and demanding occupation.

Cushing's eating habits are certifiably Homeric. He once entered a not guilty plea, to the charge of devouring an entire casserole while he was on a twenty-minute break. A trainer once chastised him for being slow to handwrite flight progress strips at the terminal control radar position, saying: "It's hard to write when you've got a can of Pepsi in one hand and a Snickers bar in the other." Mark Cushing is rumored to be the innovator of the famous "donut sandwich." That Newark Tower delicacy is made by slicing a bagel and placing a Bavarian cream or a jelly donut between the bagel halves.

The TCA radar position has been Cushing's biggest challenge to date. Not because of any air traffic considerations, but because TCA has to be worked while the controller is seated at a radar display, while all other front line positions are usually worked standing. So every time that Cushing starts to train on TCA, the struggle with the chair commences. Until that battle is won, no training session can ensue. Once, while watching Cushing slowly wedge his mammoth ass cheeks into the space between the chair's arms with a deliberate, rocking side to side motion, Ray Martino remarks: "We need a giant shoe horn!" Cushing's skin is constantly leaking, and his pock marked face resembles a plump, freshly misted cauliflower like those found on the produce shelf at the supermarket. Stepping from the scrap metals scale and leaving the loading platform, Mark waves to the junkyard worker, an older black man. The junk man turns off his acetylene torch and yells at Cushing: "How'd you make out?"

"I lost ten pounds."

"Alright!"

The old black man smiles and resists the urge to vocalize a tired cliché that features a deck chair and the Titanic.

The Dragon Lady wipes a table clean and positions placemats; utensils; napkins and two water tumblers with ice. With no wasted motion, she prompts the two diners for their orders before the "set-up" is complete. Drawing a pad from a black and white apron she jots down the information and starts toward the kitchen to relay the order. Two mugs of Flamingo Diner coffee appear in front of the hungry tin men. Paul Veale stirs his coffee while Doherty is reading Pat Buchanan's column in the New York Post. Veal interrupts him.

"Willie, you need to watch your ass. Every supervisor in the tower has a folder on you. They're trying to make a case for firing you."

Doherty folds the paper and picks up his coffee.

"I think Pat Buchanan is about to run for President."

"Willie, get serious. I said they want to FIRE you.

"Okay, but they need a case. So what is it? What do you know?"

Paul Veale leans in close and lowers his voice.

"Willie, they called the FBI on you. You were investigated. I have the whole report. I copied it from the file."

Doherty looks at Veale for a long three seconds. His eyes narrow as he digests the new information. Veale continues.

"You made some political remarks that got management's attention. They're calling it un-American and subversive. They think you may be an IRA supporter, maybe even a card-carrying member. They tried to make a federal case out of it."

Doherty chuckles.

"The IRA doesn't issue ID cards. And, I do support the cause of Irish independence, so what? I'm not allowed to have an opinion about international affairs? What did I say that sounded so…subversive to them?"

"Let's see. You said the Queen of England is the biggest drug dealer in the world." A plate of steak and eggs arrives and Veale drops down and works on his meal while Doherty replies:

"I did say that. And I'll put it in writing, if they need it. Maybe you heard about the BCCI banking scandal? International drug money was laundered through a bank owned by…guess who? The Queen…case closed. Besides, I don't remember taking an oath to support and defend England. What else has gotten their panties in a bunch?"

Veale slides his mug toward the aisle side of the table, in position to be topped off.

"Okay. Shamrock took off once, real slow and heavy like they always are. They used every bit of concrete on Runway Four Right. The main wheels were still on the ground when they crossed Runway Two Nine. They scared the shit out of everyone and set off car alarms in the north parking lot, they were so low. You said something like: "It must be the extra rifles and hand grenades on board."

"I remember." Veale has more:

"On Saint Patrick's Day you called the Queen a pig. That pissed the girls off, big time. Virgin Mary blew a head gasket when she heard about it.

"And they called the FBI, for that? So I don't like the British, or the Queen or the fucking Beatles. That makes me what? A traitor? Maybe they ought to read a little history, 'cause I seem to remember that it was the British that burned the White House, and an Irishman that kicked their asses out of here in 1814." Veale nods.

"Yea, Yea… I've heard it all before, Willie. I'm just telling you what's in the file. I boosted a copy from the tower. I'll show it to you, but I can't let you copy it. You just need to know that management is putting the full court press on your young Irish ass. They want you fired, and they want it really bad. Remember last summer when you commuted to work on your bicycle?"

Doherty cocks his head and the dimple appears under his left eye.

"Yea? So I rode a bicycle; now what…they think I'm a chink?" Veale swallows and takes a sip of coffee. "They tried to pull your medical, and fire you for falsifying the record. The theory was that you lost your driver's license for drunk driving, and didn't report it on your annual physical. They called Security and Compliance to do an investigation into your driving record and medical history. Doherty laughs.

"I'll bet they were disappointed when that didn't pan out."

"Yea, no joke. Listen Willie, everything you say in that tower is being noted and scrutinized. Usually when they go after someone like this, they end up getting him. You need to cover your six and tone down the rhetoric. That's my advice. Oh yea, and join the union. You should be paying for all this protection."

Sorry, Paul. I appreciate the effort, but I won't subsidize faggotry and organized sodomy. Veale smiles at his non-union friend.

"Did you say *faggotry?* Is that a real word? Or did you just make it up?"

The two men laugh and the Dragon Lady stops by to drop the check on the table. She knows the tin men will be in a hurry to leave as soon as they finish.

"You guys need ketchup?" Doherty answers for himself.

"Only to induce vomiting."

CHAPTER 28

Newark Airport, ATIS Information Bravo. One Niner Zero Zero Zulu Weather. Indefinite ceiling, sky obscured, fog, heavy rain. Wind- Zero Eight Zero at One Five, Altimeter- Two Niner Eight Five. ILS Runway Four Right approach in use, departing Runway Four Left. Runway Four Right Braking action good, reported by a Boeing Seven Twenty Seven. Advise the controller on initial contact, that you have Information Bravo.

On an afternoon of Zero–Zero weather, Gordon Russo walks up into the tower cab to start an eve watch. The fog is so thick it appears to be painted on the windows. While loading his coffee with heavy cream, he is startled when the tower cab is rattled by the noise of a departure. Russo can tell by the volume of the engines and the vibration of the tower windows that the aircraft, though unseen, came uncomfortably close to the tower cab. A quick flash of light illuminates the consoles momentarily. While most of the crew believes the illuminating flash to be lightning, Russo suspects something else. Leaving his coffee he strides toward the front line to get a glimpse of the flight progress strips in the departure bay at the Local Control position. Each strip in the departure lineup shows a big "360" handwritten in red. Inside the zero of the big red "360" is a black pencil check mark indicating that the pilot acknowledged receipt of the non-standard departure heading. Alan "Two Ties" Mealey is the Controller in Charge, working to maintain currency on the operating positions. A "Remington Raider," he normally toils behind a typewriter, downstairs in pogue country.

Russo addresses Mealey.

"Alan, three-sixty headings? Right off the runway?

"Yep, that's what they want at the TRACON." Mealey nods and adjusts his FAA tie clasp. Another departure is rolling on Runway Four Left and Russo looks down at the Local Controller's Simplex time stamp machine to read the strip. He notes that a Continental 747 is about to rotate. Russo looks around at the crew assembled, and realizes he is the lone tin man. Along with the toady Alan "Two Ties" Mealey, are two affirmative action selections and three females, one a confirmed lesbian and another who is suspect. Beside Mealey, Gordon "G-Man" Russo is the only FAA employee on the control deck who does not hold dual membership in the union and a militant group that puts their social engineering agenda above air safety. Taking a quick glance at the ASDE surface detection radar, Russo notes that the large, heavy jet is taking most of the runway, to a point near the control tower before rotating, which is what he expected. He voices a serious concern about the operation.

"Alan, a 360 heading turns the departures right at the tower! Tell me you are NOT launching these guys on three-sixty headings without ensuring that they pass the tower before turning!" Mealey looks confused and stares at Russo for a moment, then speaks.

"The TRACON ordered it."

The next words exit Russo's mouth as if they were tracer rounds aimed at Mealey's head.

"No shit? The TRACON themselves? Did you bother to tell them that a 360 heading puts every departure on a bee-line for the biggest obstruction on the airport – the CONTROL TOWER? - the same cozy spot that you and I are presently occupying? Do you think if they knew that little fact, they might change their minds? Did you think to exercise some authority and OVERRULE their stupid 360 headings?"

Mealey, looking confused and embarrassed looks around for some help.

"What do you want me to do?" Russo, reaching past Mealey, snatches a handset from an overhead console and punches the direct line to the departure radar controller.

"Departure, Tower, we're going to runway headings, your control on contact."

"We asked for three sixty."

"I know. But there's an obstruction in the way; it's called the control tower." The departure controller laughs.

"We've been doing it for an hour and forty five minutes." Russo replies:

"Yea, well, you missed us. Try again tomorrow." Russo replaces the handset and turns to Mealey.

"I got this, Alan. Take a break." Addressing the rest of the front line team, he changes the departure protocol.

"Go to runway headings. Local, make sure they pass the boundary before you switch 'em."

As Mealey descends the tower steps, Russo thinks about the "lightning" that lit up the tower cab and a shiver runs up his spine. The tin man knows that what they saw was the anti collision strobe light on the wing tip of a departing MD80. If the strobe light was close enough to light up the tower cab, through the heavy fog, the MD80 missed the tower by feet-maybe INCHES. Russo wonders if anyone else knows how close they all came to dying that very minute.

This place is flush with stark raving idiots. For Christ's sake, how embarrassing would it be...to die like that? You clear an MD80 for takeoff and turn him right at...YOURSELF! How would that play in the papers? ***AIR TRAFFIC CONTROLLERS KILL TWO HUNDRED- AND THEMSELVES!*** *If I didn't show up here today...maybe it would have happened. God help me, but I'm starting to wish that something bad WOULD happen. Get it over with, so this tired and broken system can get back on track. This industry can only absorb so* *much incompetence. Something really terrible is coming. I can feel it in my bones. It's just a matter of when...and where...and how many-dear Christ, how many?*

Russo's evening watch is only five minutes old. Already he has prevented a major air disaster and saved untold lives. This latest contribution to the general welfare by a tin man will go unsung, known but to Russo and God. There will be no medal draped around his neck, and no ceremony at the White House. In fact, if his words and actions this day are deemed insensitive or lacking tact toward the other members of his team, a letter of reprimand will go into his file. The work "record" of the average tin man shows that they are troublemakers, not heroes. In today's FAA, no good deed goes unpunished.

Gordon Russo's coffee has gone cold. He pours another and looks around for something to eat. He has an urge for pound cake.

Watching the action from his outside perch on the catwalk, the devil curses and scratches his balls.

CHAPTER 29

At the ACME restaurant on Great Jones Street in the East Village, Maria and her favorite tin man order blackened catfish and fried okra. Maria relates a frustrating story of Port Authority Police apathy and nonfeasance.

"I was working at Terminal B. Uniformed walking patrol duty. I liked it there; you get to meet a lot of people…help them out…get them on their way. It was okay. There was this Skycap, Loney they called him…short for Thelonius. He's a big black man…real nice, you know. He's got a big smile, always helping people check their bags at the curb. I would bring him coffee and we'd take a break together." Doherty listens intently, while buttering a thick slice of cornbread.

"I started to notice a pattern. Loney would tell people where to park for fast access to the shuttle and return to the terminal after checking their bags. Sometimes he would get real specific, even suggesting they back in against the fence in lot "D" for instance." A Cajun Zydeco tune is playing in the background and the waiter delivers salads. Maria pauses momentarily. After a sip of water, she continues.

"I noticed that the extra help was only going to drivers of nice, expensive cars, Mercedes sedans and Lincoln Continentals, Cadillacs and the like. Those cars all turned up stolen." Doherty smiles at the craftiness of the criminal, and the instincts of his law enforcing dinner partner. Maria offers more insight.

"You see, Loney knew they were out of town, and for how long, and he knew where their cars were parked. He was tipping off the pros and getting a slice of the action. Who knows, a hundred a car, maybe more. All he had to do was make a phone call." Doherty replies:

"So, it sounds like Thelonius was felonious, and you made your first big felony arrest?" Maria flashes her brown eyes at Doherty.

"Not even. Loney's still there. Still steering the car thieves to expensive cars and still getting away with it."

"You're serious!"

"Yep. I started taking down tag numbers and cross-referenced them with the stolen car reports. When I was sure I had a case, I took the information to the Auto Theft Task Force. Six detectives had set up shop in the north terminal, right under the old original control tower. The Port Authority got a nice big federal subsidy to fight car theft at the airports, so they started the A.T.T.F. When I walked in there, they were playing poker. I told them what I had. They didn't even look up, except to leer at my tits. One guy took the folder and said, "Listen sweetest, why don't you leave the detective work to the real detectives and go back to your beat at the terminal…and thanks for comin' in."

Maria takes a sip of iced tea and dabs her lower lip with her napkin. "They're real arrogant bastards, doing nothing and getting paid well for it." Doherty offers his opinion.

"If they weren't lazy, they wouldn't be cops; they'd get a job like everyone else. I never met a cop that wasn't lazy…present company excepted." Maria smiles.

Doherty is discovering something about Maria that he knows to be rare in a female, and he's pleasantly surprised. Watching Maria chew on mashed potatoes, he thinks about her work ethic and attitude.

Most females show up and put their time in. Then, they go home and deposit their paychecks and do it all over again. Rare is the working female who is motivated to do a good job for its own sake, and even more rare is one with the courage to act independently when circumstances call for it. Asking one to blow the whistle, or upset the status quo is like asking a nun to shoplift. Women are not freedom loving individuals, they are security-worshiping dependents. The employer is just another husband to them. And the radical lesbians and feminists? When they file charges against the employer, they are simply abandoning one husband for another one with deeper pockets- the federal government.

The tin man waits for his dinner date to make eye contact with him. "You know that one day I'm going to ask you to leave him."

Maria looks down at her plate, then at Doherty. "I know. I'm not ready for that…not now…not yet."

"I can't stand the thought of you going home to him…sleeping with him."

"Stop it Willie. It's no good to talk about that. Let's enjoy the dinner." The tin man searches Maria's brown eyes for a sign, an indication, as a ship's captain searches for a lighthouse, seeking the entrance to a safe, welcome harbor.

How many men have searched eyes like these? Seeing what they want to see, fooling themselves time and again. It's a sick joke that God has played on us, planting fool's gold deep in the eyes of every woman, to trick us; to make us trick ourselves. Then one day you wake up, and it's just you…and the pain…that goddamned pain. And you think that someone else did it to you. But it wasn't her…the pain is self inflicted. That's why it hurts so deeply.

Back aboard *Tipitina*, Doherty forces himself to stop thinking about Maria. When he does, his thoughts drift back to the airport.

Nothing is what it seems to be. It's a giant masquerade ball, with Haitians dressing up as airline employees and gaining access to airplanes. Skycaps are checking your bags, but they're also stealing your car. Women are getting raped in broad daylight. The airport is a giant roach motel. Then, when one police officer attempts to clean up her little corner of the place, what does she get? She gets ridiculed by her "partners." She's told to get back in line; put your mask back on like everyone else. Maybe I'm too idealistic, but I'm thinking that cops should be collaring bad guys. Reporters should be writing the news. Controllers should be separating and expediting airplanes. And the FAA? Except for the tin men, everyone else in the FAA is a fraud, a pretender. They're fugitives from accountability hiding in plain sight. And they come in two different styles. Some put on a convincing, blustering show like the fiery fucking head of Oz, and some take a more subdued role, quietly posing and passing as competent, serious safety professionals. Deep down inside they know all about themselves. They want to be a tin man, but there is something lacking... something they should've picked up long ago but didn't. You can check their gear- something's missing...you can't really name it. It's like courage, but not exactly. It's like integrity, but not so fucking noble. Confidence? Independence? A tin man doesn't have it all, but maybe just enough of each. But who are these others? The yes men, the butt boys, the pogues, the paper pushing managers and supervisors. What do they see when they look in the mirror? Do they die a little? Or maybe they're already dead...as dead as the Bishop's dick. They're just too lazy to keel over.

Doherty ponders the airport terminals, the places where people come and go.

If airport terminal security is weakened to a serious degree, than forget about the air traffic element. Someone or some organization with evil intent could put a serious hurt on the airline industry, even the American economy. If Newark Airport is the security sieve that it seems to be, well, Chicken Little couldn't overstate the gravity of the situation.

Two tin men discuss the severely strained state of aviation safety during "midnight mass" at Karl's Tavern in Elizabeth. Beans Larkin says to Gordon Russo:

"It's the people, G-Man. I hate to sound like a democrat, but damn it, they deserve better. They're the only innocent ones, here. They come and go, strolling right through airports they believe are safe, boarding airplanes they think are working properly and trusting that the pilots and controllers are on top of their game. Like the casino gambling industry, the airlines depend on a steady stream of fools. And you know what? Fools don't seem to be in short supply these days."

While the tin men are talking, Apple Two Fourteen, a New York Air DC9 is on final approach to Runway Two Two Left. Inside the cockpit, the Flight Engineer answers the secret, two knocks and a pause, then a third knock on the cockpit door. The senior flight attendant appears on the flight deck. "Can we like, circle once before we land, because we don't have all the dinner stuff stowed away yet." The Captain, turning his head from the instruments, does not actually approve or deny the request, but asks the flight attendant for more information.

"What do you think we're running here, a fucking soup kitchen?"

The flight attendant disappears, slamming the cockpit door behind her.

CHAPTER 30

You know, like, anything can be great. I don't care, BRICKLAYING can be great, if a guy knows- if he knows what he's doing and why and if he can make it come off. When I'm goin', I mean, when I'm REALLY goin' I feel like a... like a jockey must feel. He's sittin' on his horse, he's got all that speed and that power underneath him... he's comin' into the stretch, the pressure's on 'im, and he KNOWS... just feels... when to let it go and how much. Cause he's got everything working' for him: timing, touch. It's a great feeling.

- "Fast" Eddie Felson, The Hustler, 1961

On a clear, sunny Sunday morning, Charles Clemons is working the Local Control position, anticipating that the traffic will be slow in the early morning hours. In fact, the traffic is slow enough that Charles is working with a hand mike and listening to the pilot's transmissions on speaker, giving him more freedom to roam around the control deck un-tethered by a headset cord. Supervisor Jim Milner, one of the last of the "old school" supervisors, is seated behind the typewriter, making a log entry while having his coffee and a bagel. Between air traffic transmissions, Charles is telling a well-worn joke about a white guy and his black friend pissing from a bridge into a river.

In the northeast corner of the tower cab, Mark Cushing is trying to get the chair at the TCA radar display to accommodate his titanic ass once again. Ray Martino watches the assault on the chair from the back line. He wants to turn away, but he can't. It's like witnessing a car accident; Martino feels guilty about watching, but he can't avert his eyes. He's waiting for the day he knows is coming; when Cushing's ass will be so large, the chair will stop accommodating the buttocks, and the buttocks will start engulfing the chair. As it is now, the scene reminds Martino of a baby black snake trying to get its jaws around a giant dinosaur egg. When Mark Cushing finally stands up, the chair remains firmly clamped on his ass and all of the chairs wheels hover momentarily, until gravity returns the armchair to the deck. Ray Martino thinks about the emergency fire axe affixed to the wall in the stairwell below the tower cab. He may need it someday to remove the furniture from Cushing's ass, should the tower cab need to be quickly evacuated.

Meanwhile the traffic volume, as it has a habit of doing, has dramatically increased, and without warning. Suddenly Charles Clemons finds himself in over his head, and seconds later, he is hanging on for dear life. Since he's on speaker, the whole team can hear everything, pilots and controller. Jim Milner takes notice, and rises from his seat at the supervisor's desk to watch. When Charles fails to answer two transmissions in a row, it is apparent that he has gone "down the pipes." His brain has shut down, and he no longer has the picture. A People Express jet executes a "go around" when the landing aircraft in front fails to clear the runway in time. Astonishingly, Charles is watching the action, but he's not seeing anything. As if frozen in a block of ice, he stands there, a vertical cadaver, oblivious to the shouted suggestions from the cab coordinator behind him, and the ground controller to his right. Supervisor Milner calmly walks up next to Charles and snatches the hand mike from him. Before issuing any control instructions to airplanes that desperately need them, he looks right at Charles for a few seconds. In a sort of self-induced hypnotic trance, the local controller's eyes are glazed over and his lips are trembling. Milner barks at him.

"If I asked you for your name right now, you couldn't tell me who's who!"

Then without looking for any visual clues from the printed flight strips, Jim Milner with seemingly total recall, quickly and expertly brings the airport traffic back under control.

Continental Four Twenty Two, start a left turn, enter a left base for Runway Two Nine, wind two four zero at one one, traffic, a TWA seven twenty seven on a five mile final landing Runway Two Two Left, report that traffic in sight.

Continanantal Four Twenty Two, Roger.

Delta Four Twelve Heavy, cross runway Two Two Right, traffic holding in position, contact ground point eight on the other side.

Roger, Delta Four Twelve Heavy.

TWA Five Oh One, Cleared to land runway Two Two Left, wind two four zero at eight, traffic, a Continental Boeing Seven Thirty Seven, southeast of the airport, entering a left base for runway Two Nine.

TWA Five Oh One, roger, cleared to land, traffic in sight.

Charles Clemons, now back among the living, returns to Milner's side with a freshly donned headset and jacks into the console. Milner unceremoniously jerks the cord from the position, telling Charles to "take a break. I'll see you downstairs." Milner slides over to retrieve his coffee and bagel, and works the hand mike for another hour, putting on a virtual clinic for control tower operators. Applying rhythm to the runways, as a drummer sets the tempo for a jazz band, Milner is a master of airport ceremonies. Addressing the pilots as "partner" or "skipper," his folksy style engenders confidence, and occasionally a pilot will call him by name, saying "Good job as always, Jim." or something similar.

Liam Doherty is watching Milner from the northwest corner of the tower cab. A controller on top of his own game, The tin man never tires of watching a good man work, and while Milner is expertly whipping and driving the big airport tin, an admiring smile creeps onto Doherty's face, causing a dimple to show under his left eye.

"You feel it, don't you, Jimbo? Yea, I know all about it. It's the juice, the power, that bulletproof feeling, like you're suddenly electric. You're a plugged in paragon of air traffic excellence, a one-off piece of work, dipped in gold and showcased for all to admire, a tin man for all seasons. I've been there, and I like it. I like it a lot. If it was a drug it would be on the controlled substances list. Do you ever feel guilty about it, Jim? You know, having a talent that few others possess, being really good at something, something very unique, like this air traffic control game? Let me tell you about guilt. It is the lasso thrown from the hapless, forlorn fold below to try to topple you and me and guys like us. The pogues, the weak sticks and the miserable, luckless bastards, shit-birds, the lot. They desperately want you numbered among them, tired and mediocre as they are, even on their best day. You've shed that sad, shabby hair shirt long ago, so rave on, Jim – rave on. Keep showin' 'em what they need to see.

Jim Milner is a rarity. He's an FAA supervisor and a confident, highly skilled tin slinger. A throwback to the days when there was no such animal as an Air Traffic Manager. There were only Chief Controllers who could do the job as well as any of their charges. In today's chicken-shit FAA, if you can manage a hamburger stand, you qualify to take the helm at a major control facility. When Milner retires, the tower is not likely to see his ilk again. The affirmative action gang has arrived, and they are riding herd over today's air traffic controllers. They have outlawed skilled and competent professionalism and replaced it with social engineering and multiculturalism. When Milner's gone, the airport will become a slightly more dangerous place. The rubber band gets twisted that much more. The war on merit and competent, straight, white males came to the air traffic control occupation long before it showed up in other sectors; it is now firmly bunkered in the FAA.

CHAPTER 31

Despite objections from the Air Transport Association, and the Port Authority, the FAA Eastern Region has quietly strangled the Veale Initiative. Claiming that the plan is unworkable and unsafe, the FAA orders a halt to further testing of the plan at the tower. The peg that the FAA has hung their hat on was the "unmanageable" circling of airliners, which, if allowed to get out of hand, could encroach on LaGuardia airspace, or conflict with sightseeing traffic flying uncontrolled up and down the Hudson River. Paul Veale fires off a letter to the FAA and the Capacity Enhancement team members, pointing out that the FAA still routinely circles air traffic in the same manner whenever one of the parallel runways is closed; they call it an "operational necessity." How they can justify ordering ANY unsafe operation to counter construction delays, but prohibit that same operation for everyday, routine delays is inexplicable. Discussion of the matter is shut down by the FAA at the Capacity Enhancement meetings. The Air Transport Association, flabbergasted at the arrogance of the FAA, is left to pull political strings to try to force new management into the Eastern Region. Privately, Paul Veale meets with the ATA President and gives his opinion about the FAA and their agenda: "This is the same bunch that brought you the controller's strike in 1981. Do you really need to know anything more about them?"

Veale and Doherty's efforts concerning the Veal Initiative are seen as noble and courageous by most of the tin men. The weak sticks, the pogues and the affirmative action types saw it as a direct attack on them, forcing them to learn new tricks when they have yet to fully grasp the routine. The FAA, after suspecting the plan for reasons they were not sure about at first, came to see the Veale

Initiative as an assault on their empire building schemes. The airport delay straw man is one they need desperately. Without a major problem to solve, they cannot justify their existence or get congress to throw more money at them.

Like cops need crime and doctors need disease, the FAA needs airline delays and accidents. Any streamlining or downsizing of air traffic operations threatens to put managers out of work, or put them back in front of a radar display where their incompetence magnifies, becoming as obvious as a hard-on at a nudist colony, and only slightly less embarrassing, and certainly more dangerous.

A suit appears on the control deck. It is the same Secret Service agent that faced down the visiting parrot. Tall, sandy haired and dark suited, he takes his normal position at the top of the stairs in the southwest corner of the tower cab. Frank Hamblin goes over to greet him, and the two engage in some small talk. The treasury agent's nose wrinkles and he steps back noticeably. Apparently, a blast of halitosis from Francis Hamblin has subjected another visitor to the "breath penalty."

Liam Doherty is working Local Control and John Lundy, a newly hired Air Force veteran has plugged in next to the tin man to monitor the position, trying to collect a few clues about the operation. President Ronnie Ray-gun is due today and Doherty will not be on position when he arrives. The traffic is extremely light in the early morning and the weather is clear. Instead of picking Doherty's brain, Lundy tries to impress the tin man with his own ideas, all of which are wrong.

"You know *he's* in charge now."

"Who's in charge?"

"The Secret Service guy." Lundy nods toward the rear and Doherty turns around and sees the agent standing with Hamblin in the back. The tower manager has also joined the group, presenting the Treasury agent with an official Newark Tower coffee mug emblazoned with the phrase, "I like your approach - now let's see your departure." Doherty turns back to Lundy. "Why do you think *he* is in charge?"

"Well, because the President is coming. If he tells you to send someone around, you've got to do it, man. It's Air Force One!" Doherty is amused and surprised, especially when he realizes that Lundy is not pulling his leg; the Texas fly-boy believes that what he is saying reflects an official policy.

"You're serious?"

"Yes. That's what they taught us in the Air Force." Doherty resists the urge to laugh out loud, and stabs his thumb rearward in the direction of the Treasury's finest.

"Lundy, let me tell you something. That guy doesn't know what the words *go around* mean. He's vaguely aware that there is an airport nearby. He doesn't know the leading edge of an airfoil from the trailing end of the Mummer's parade. So how could he tell me what to do?" Lundy looks surprised in a serious sort of way.

"I'm just telling you what I was told in the service."

"Yea, I know. They told me I was getting a square needle in the balls, and that turned out to be false too. Now let me ask you this: If the President was in the hospital having brain surgery, would the Secret Service agent give orders to the doctor about how to proceed?"

"Well, no…but…"

"Look Lundy, this job will present its own problems to you, and plenty of them. If you're going to do this shit, learn your job and have confidence in yourself. Stop looking for problems from people who show up here from time to time wearing dark suits and tasseled loafers. The Secret Service guy is just here to relay information, not to exercise any authority." Lundy posts a flight strip in the arrival bay with the identification, A1 underlined in red. Air Force One is sixty minutes out. Doherty lightens things up a little.

"Of course if you want to get that guy's attention, tell him you like to print fifties in your basement to supplement your income."

The Secret Service suit is walking around the cab with his new coffee mug, peering over the consoles to the catwalk, apparently searching for his old nemesis, the parrot.

The wayward parrot hasn't shown up again, but one day a huge flock of seagulls came to visit on a sunny afternoon. It was popcorn they were after, and it took almost fifteen minutes for the nasty sky rats to devour the treat and move on. Meanwhile, they caused a hazardous visibility obstruction that impacted the operation and prompted an official FAA investigation. It seems that a prankster had implemented a well thought out and clever plan to attract the birds to the tower. He or she had spread a thick carpet of popcorn all over the eighth and ninth floor catwalks. The prankster had patiently waited for an extended period of calm wind, so that the bait would not blow away. One can only speculate as to how long a period elapsed from the time that the popcorn was spread, and the arrival of the first seagull. Once the feeding frenzy was underway, nothing could be seen except seagulls in any direction. On a clear summer day, in calm wind, and without a cloud in the sky, a call went to the weather center from the cab coordinator, tin man Beans Larkin:

"Hey weather, tower visibility restricted, seagulls."

"Really? What are you calling it?"

"Zero." A pause.

"Are you serious, 'cause I got no time for fools."

"Yea. We think it's real temporary but we can't see shit. Wait a minute, we CAN see shit. It's all over the windows." As quickly as they arrived, the seagulls vanished, leaving behind thick grey lumpy streaks of seagull droppings that spangled the large windows, causing one female controller to gag. When Beans Larkin opens a plastic tub of yogurt with blueberries and offers her some, the young lady signs out sick and goes home. The popcorn prank has now cost the government money, impacted safety and the "efficiency of the service." An official investigation ensues, conducted by the tower manager and he appointed Francis Hamblin to be the chief investigator.

Although many persons have access to the tower, including Port Authority engineers, FAA equipment maintenance specialists and building cleaning contractors, the FAA directed its investigation at the controller workforce only. Paul Veale objected on behalf of the union and quickly pointed out that along with the unfair targeting of controllers, the FAA had no evidence to show that the seagulls were attracted by popcorn, or "bait" of any kind. They could have been after the June bugs known to swarm on the tower every summer. Since the scavenging birds devoured every morsel of whatever it was they were feeding on, nothing remained to show anyone exactly what it was. After digesting this legal maneuver by the union, Hamblin counters with his own carefully crafted chess move. Two days later, he calls Paul Veale into the manager's office for a "one on one."

"What's up, Frank?"

"I have something to show you." Hamblin is leaning far back in the manager's big swivel chair with the fingers of his hands interlaced behind his large melon, grinning like the honoree at a retard's birthday party. His sweat stained armpits are serving as port and starboard running lights for his shabby and wilted knit Polo shirt. Hamblin is enjoying his "Columbo" moment, and milking it for maximum effect. Finally, Francis Hamblin sits up and carefully maintaining eye contact with Veale, he slides open the center drawer of the manager's big desk. Slowly and dramatically, he pulls out a folded, monogrammed linen handkerchief with a lump in it, and ceremoniously lays it on the desk blotter in front of Veale.

"Go ahead, open it." The union rep looks at the handkerchief, then at Hamblin. The drama is almost too much for Hamblin and a bead of drool appears on his lower lip. Veale ponders the strange behavior and tries not to laugh.

This is too comical to be real. It's like I walked into a cartoon and I'm being forced to take on a role as one of the characters. I guess Hamblin is Wile E. Coyote and I'm the fucking Road Runner. Now he's going to show me a kernel of popcorn. Maybe I'm supposed to pull a stick of dynamite from my back pocket and roll it under his chair. Isn't that how it works in the cartoons?

Veale slowly pulls back the folds of the handkerchief to reveal a large, plump, buttery flavored kernel of recently popped, popcorn. The NATCA rep can tell it is fresh because the smell of freshly popped microwave popcorn is still in the air. Feigning surprise with his mouth agape, Veale hesitates for the required effect and says, "I don't know what to say, Frank, except thanks, and…you got any more?" Veale then tosses the popcorn into his mouth and devours it.

Hamblin, now enraged, accuses Veale of destroying evidence of a crime, and interfering with an "official" investigation. He threatens the union rep with charges. Veale laughs at Hamblin and taunts him, saying, "Some detective you are, Frank…a real Sherlock-fucking-Holmes. You couldn't find a Jew in Williamsburg." Turning toward the door, the NATCA rep stops momentarily to loudly break wind in Hamblin's direction.

The "popcorn prank" investigation flounders, and management decides to place a warning in the "Read and Ignore" binder. The memo is read aloud to everyone on training day. Management stresses that actions that impact safety are not harmless pranks they are in fact, crimes that will not be tolerated, but prosecuted by the FAA.

Doherty has a nearly airtight alibi. During the popcorn incident he was enjoying a three day weekend aboard *Tipitina*, anchored at Sandy Hook, and reading *Trinity* by Leon Uris, a fellow Marine. Perhaps some of the Sandy Hook seagulls are the same unwitting accomplices in the prank that launched an "official" government investigation. In the comical and strangely fascinating world of the FAA, seagulls are not simply common, web footed, maritime shit-birds. They can also be un-indicted co-conspirators, or unwitting accomplices to a federal crime.

CHAPTER 32

Resting quietly at anchor near Sandy Hook, *Tipitina* yaws gently in the nearly calm sea, lightly tugging on her anchor rode. After 48 hours aboard, broken by two dinghy excursions to the beach, Doherty is going mad with the need of Maria. He instinctively looks north toward the World Trade Towers, but in the distant haze, can just barely make out the superstructure of the Verrazzano Narrows Bridge. In six hours, he will weigh anchor and sail under that bridge, narrowing the distance between himself and Maria. Meanwhile there is always Doo Wop, his old standby and loyal partner. Doherty drops into the companionway, finds a cassette and shoves it home, starting the music. He cranks up the volume and draws a cold beer from the galley ice box. A New Haven, Connecticut group, The Nutmegs, start their heart-rending tale of love, lost. The tin man wonders if he will be singing their tune some day soon.

Well, here in my heart
There's a story untold
Of a girl who left me standing
Standing in the cold

Examining the circumstances and his own conscience, Doherty wonders how one gets into a predicament like this. God, how could I do this to myself again? We both know this cannot turn out well. It's like a runaway train; it ends badly, but where, and when?

Well I hope and I pray
That she'll hear my plea
And maybe someday
She'll come back to me

An Amtrak Metroliner is pulling into Newark Station. The conductor announces the stop on the train's public address system. His message contains more than a hint of an existing, inner city, cultural reality.

Ladies and gentleman, our next station stop will be Noo-erk, Noo-Jer-Zee, Noo-erk, Noo-Jer-Zee. Please check to make sure you have all of your personal belongings before you leave your seating area. All passengers are reminded to keep an eye on your personal items while the train is stopped in the Noo-erk, Noo-Jer-Zee train station. Watch your step leaving the train. Noo-erk, Noo-Jer-Zee.

With the crash of Avianca Zero Five Two Heavy came a renewed focus on air traffic communications. Every time there is an aviation disaster, controllers individually examine the event and dissect it. They put themselves in the same situation and imagine themselves doing things differently, or doing something that keeps them from getting into the same dangerous predicament. In such ways, tragedy is avoided and a measure of continuity prevails. The process starts where all human events start – in the mind. Any controller claiming to have never engaged in this Walter Mitty activity, is either a liar, or he is a dangerous, malingering, meat-head. Liam Doherty did not need the Avianca crash to reinforce the importance of recognizing and declaring an emergency when confronted with such circumstances. As fate would have it, he didn't have to wait long to be tested. Also, as Doherty would find out, aviation emergencies test not only the controller involved, but the entire team, even the controller teams at adjacent facilities, and emergencies say something about the readiness of the air traffic control system. Not unlike a surprise barracks inspection, and how it says something about the readiness of an individual. Who's ready – and who's unsteady.

Newark Tower TCA, Twin Beech Five Two Two Four Tango, we're over Staten Island, two miles southwest of the Verrazzano Bridge northbound.

Twin Beech Five Two Two Four Tango, Newark Terminal Control, go ahead.

Two Four Tango is headed to Teterboro, we've got number two shut down, low oil pressure, overheated.

Doherty grabs a red pencil and writes the big red "E" on a flight progress strip. While punching the aircraft I.D. into the radar ARRTS software key-pack, he holds the strip up so that the cab coordinator can see it, while he talks to the pilot.

Two Two Four Tango, squawk seven seven zero zero, radar contact, two miles west of the Verrazzano Bridge, how can I help?

We need direct Teterboro if that's okay, Newark.

Two Two Four Tango, cleared into the New York terminal control area direct Teterboro, verify altitude two thousand.

Affirmative, Newark. two thousand, we'd like to maintain that as long as possible.

Two Two Four Tango, maintain two thousand and proceed direct.

Just then, approach calls via direct override into Doherty's headset. The emergency squawk code is causing the radar target to "blink" on every radar display in the New York area, including the three scopes in the tower.

"You need anything for your emergency, TCA?

"Direct Teterboro, Two thousand and below."

"Approved, your control."

"Aye Aye."

"Dee Cee."

The controllers end the interphone communication by putting their assigned operating initials on the audio tape. Doherty gets up and steps over to the Local Controller, a novice two-year man and long haired pretty boy named Timothy "Slim" Chance. Putting a pencil's eraser on the radar target with the blinking data information, Doherty tells the Local Controller and the Cab Coordinator what's happening.

"EMERGENCY, Direct Teterboro, Two Thousand, one engine out, number two."

Chance snaps his head left, causing his hair to bounce. When his shiny, shoulder length hair catches up with his head's new direction, it falls back into place perfectly. Chance is now facing Doherty. The two controllers make eye contact as Doherty waits to get an acknowledgement from Chance. When the pause becomes longer than normal, Doherty suspects that Chance is about to over-think the situation.

Either his wheels are turning, or he's queer for my gear.

"Take him up the Hudson."

Doherty thinks he heard something that needs clarification. Maybe it was a joke.

"Say again?"

Chance says it again, chopping his prescription into syllables for sarcastic emphasis.

"TAKE – HIM - UP - THE – HUD - SON."

By this, Chance means to treat him like a sightseer, or any other annoying, intruding puddle jumper. Keep him out of the way, make him steer clear of the Newark terminal control area and stay off the tower frequency and out of our hair, because we are too busy to allow him to come close to the big tin at the major airport. Tim

Chance is suggesting that Doherty do something illegal- something that violates the first rule of air traffic control. An aircraft in distress gets priority over ALL OTHER TRAFFIC, even the President of the United States, if necessary. Doherty responds to Chance:

"Maybe you didn't hear me, Tim, this guy is an EMERGENCY! He's going DIRECT TETERBORO at two thousand, and that's NOT a request."

Now, Tim Chance is crestfallen, confused and disillusioned. Like a prom queen that just lost her cherry, the pretty boy local controller is on the verge of tears. He continues to press a case for delaying an emergency aircraft for his own convenience, or because he can't think of a plan for accommodating the inconvenient intruder with the broken airplane.

Like most unseasoned controllers, Tim Chance likes the routine, and hates anything that causes him to think. Unusual circumstances are the bane of a weak controller's existence. They are a reason for fear and an unwelcome opportunity for professional embarrassment. Chance squeals like the community punk in Rahway State Prison.

"I've got ARRIVAL TRAFFIC on the Four Right ILS!"

Back at the radar scope, Doherty assesses the situation. He needs to coordinate with other facilities, tell them what is happening, but first he has to deal with Tim Chance. All eyes in the tower cab turn toward Doherty. The controllers smell a clash of personalities coming, and Doherty does conflict very well. He would not disappoint.

Perfect. I get an emergency, and I need to stop and train this idiot. On top of that, his eyeballs are about to squirt all over his shirt. I'm going to look like the bad guy, no matter what happens, so here goes.

"I've heard rumors to that effect, Tim, and since you mentioned it, my *emergency* may need that runway! If I were you, I would STOP departures, move the arrivals over to the inboard runway and be ready for a twin beech landing on Runway Four Right! Now my guy wants direct Teterboro, but it could become DIRECT NEWARK! And the ONE EMERGENCY on my frequency trumps every bit of tin on your fucking Four Right ILS!"

Both controllers look to the Cab Coordinator who is serving as the controller in charge. In fact, every pair of eyeballs in the tower cab are now focused on the CIC and how he will respond, and whose side he will take. Doherty's mind is made up. If ordered to turn the Twin Beech up the Hudson he will flatly refuse the order. The possibility of an aviation fatality due to gross negligence, in direct violation of basic standing orders, and common sense, is now looming large. Doherty will have no part of it. He punches up Teterboro on the direct line.

Teterboro Tower, Newark, EMERGENCY.

Teterboro.

Twin Beech Five Two Two Four Tango, landing Teterboro, #2 engine shut down, low oil pressure and overheated. ETA fifteen minutes, he's five north of the Verrazzano Bridge, direct your house.

Okay, Newark. Tell him to make a modified straight-in approach to Runway One, tower on one one niner point five when you're done with him. The equipment will be standing by.

Aye Aye.

Pee Dee.

Although Doherty believes that a prudent pilot with a malfunctioning airplane would land at the closest useable airport, controllers are forbidden to make decisions for the pilot. If the aviator wants to press on to Teterboro, Doherty's job is to provide the pilot with all of the information and assistance he needs to reach his chosen destination. If a pilot is going to die somewhere, that place is selected by the pilot, not the controller. The tin man quickly examines the pilot's options and he relays them.

Two Two Four Tango, Linden airport is nine o'clock and three miles, Newark airport is ten o'clock and six miles, landing runway Four Right, wind calm. Teterboro airport is twelve o'clock and eleven miles, landing Runway One, Newark altimeter two niner niner five.

Tim Chance looks at Doherty. Although he's already decided to back down and adapt to the exigent circumstances, Chance still thinks he's right to pretend that the emergency doesn't exist. Incredibly, he believes that because he is working the Local Control position, he is the central figure in the tower, the cock of the walk, and he can simply order problems to disappear. Chance whines at the tin man once more. This time he sparks Doherty's Irish.

"Why can't you just do what you're told?" The tin man leaps to his feet and points an index finger.

"SHUT THE FUCK UP AND KEEP YOUR NASTY ARRIVAL TRAFFIC AWAY FROM MY EMERGENCY! IF YOU SCREW THIS UP, I WILL PERSONALLY KICK YOUR ASS AROUND THE PERIMETER!"

Tim Chance looks at Doherty and blinks twice. He still doesn't get it.

Doherty thinks to himself:

Unbelievable. I'm trying to keep this Twin Beech driver alive and I have to fight everyone around me to do it. This is one for the record. Oh. It's an emergency you say? Okay, take him on a fucking safari up the North River. See how long it takes before he has to dump it in the drink, or prang into Central Park. This Chance guy? He hasn't got the brains or the balls of a bull canary. No wonder the lesbians like him so much – he's as "girl" as it gets!

The team has reluctantly taken Doherty's advice and they've gone to a temporary, one runway operation. With the departures stopped, Chance is clearly antsy and a tad melancholy. He's also upset at being severely admonished by a co-worker in front of his team. Mostly, he is unhappy because he hates having to be the bearer of bad news to pilots on his frequency. Chance does not like to tell pilots that they can't take off when they want to. He especially does not like to send them around, or cancel a pilot's approach clearance. He likes being a perky voice of pleasantry and friendliness, like the doorman at the Waldorf-Astoria or the hostess at the Sunday brunch buffet in the Oak Room. His radio lexicon is limited to *cleared for takeoff and cleared to land and have a nice day, Captain.* To Chance and guys like him, its far more important to be bubbly and nice, than it is to apply sound air traffic standards and keep the airplanes safely separated and expedited.

When Two Two Four Tango gets north of the airport, departures will stay stopped until he clears the departure corridor. Chance continues whining, like somebody's nagging, mop squeezing, mother-in-law. He looks down at the flight strip on his time stamp machine and makes a quick calculation.

"We're gonna go into *delays!*" Doherty resists the urge to slap Tim Chance in the face, not out of malice or vindictiveness, but more like a public service because Tim Chance desperately needs slapping, if for nothing else, it might knock his priorities into order.

Doherty grabs the binoculars from their pigeon hole in the console. While taking a look at Two Two Four Tango, the tin man realizes that Timmy Chance has upset him, and now he is having trouble concentrating.

Some of these guys like to operate a control tower like it's the kissing booth at the county fair. Where does the FAA find these pussies, and why do they favor them? If any one of them showed up at Parris Island, they'd dress him up like a clown and send him back to his parents on the next train smoking.

Just then, as Two Two Four Tango is abeam the airport, over Newark Bay, things change dramatically.

Hey Newark, I'm getting a strong smell of smoke, we need to land. Doherty springs from his chair. "SMOKE IN THE COCKPIT! GET THE EQUIPMENT OUT. I'M TAKING HIM TO RUNWAY TWO NINE! The cab coordinator brushes past Chance and pulls the red desk model receiver from its cradle in front of the Local controller. In less than 30 seconds some big yellow trucks and other assorted vehicles will be swarming all over the airport operating area, racing toward their standby positions along Runway Two Nine.

A week after the emergency Doherty is standing tall at the manager's desk. Another manila envelope appears, containing a letter of reprimand and a ten-day suspension for being rude, profane and insensitive toward fellow employees. The letter further states that Doherty's intimidating and strident demeanor made it difficult for team members to make prudent decisions impacting the handling of an in flight emergency. Although Doherty is well acquainted with the drill, Biderman explains the appeal process and union rights to him, again. This time, Doherty elects to speak; Paul Veale stops him.

"Willie, no…don't do it." Doherty reminds his union rep and friend that he is a non-member.

"You're here to represent the union, not me…isn't that right, Paul?" When Veale nods, Doherty turns back and looks down at the air traffic manager. Knowing the eye contact makes Biderman uncomfortable, Doherty waits a few seconds before speaking.

"I did what needed to be done, and I said what needed to be said, and I will do it again if the circumstances call for it. I'm an air traffic controller, not a goddamned assassin."

An hour later *Tipitina* slips her lines at Newport Marina and motors toward the East River and the Long Island Sound, destination: Block Island.

The emergency landing on Runway Two Nine would be the last operation for N5224T. The aircraft was damaged by fire, beyond repair. Injuries to the pilot and co-pilot were second degree burns on the arms and legs, smoke inhalation, and one broken ankle. Both are expected to recover.

It is the FAA's position that the excellent service provided to an aircraft in distress came from the professional actions of the controller team on duty, despite the disruptive, rude and uncooperative behavior of Liam A. Doherty. Overlooked was the fact that Doherty refused a clearly unlawful suggestion that he should lengthen the pilot's emergency flight rather than shorten it. By keeping the aircraft in distress close to a useable runway, Doherty clearly saved the lives of the two aviators aboard N5224T.

Soon a letter arrives at the tower, from the wife of the co-pilot, commending and thanking the controllers for saving two lives. Because the letter singled out Doherty for special recognition, Biderman files the letter away and refuses to acknowledge it or disseminate it among the controller workforce. He reasons that the excellent service was a product of teamwork. Since the letter singled out Doherty, it would be unfair to the rest of the controllers to commend him alone. Having disciplined Doherty for his actions during the emergency, he could not turn around and commend him for the same incident. An unauthorized copy of the letter appears anonymously in Paul Veale's employee mailbox. Veale reciprocates by anonymously placing an expensive box of chocolates on Betty Jackson's desk.

Veale shows Doherty the letter.

How's it feel to be a hero there, honcho?

Doherty finishes reading the letter before answering Veale.

"I guess this is where I'm supposed to say, I was just doing my job…or give the credit to my crew, or those who trained me, or to the FAA…right? Or maybe I should say something ***really*** stupid, like…oh, anyone would have done the same thing under the circumstances. Well guess what, I am a hero…because it takes a hero. It takes a hero to prevail against incompetent co-workers, abusive supervisors, faulty and unreliable equipment, and the FAA in general. Those aviators don't know how much they owe to open assed, fly-shit luck. They're lucky it was me sitting at that radar position, when they reported in with a broken airplane. They could just as easily have drawn an affirmative action darling, or some spineless limp dick that couldn't stand up for them. Am I a hero? You're fuckin' A-straight. I'm a larger than life hero, and I've got a ten day suspension and a letter of reprimand to prove it. I've been decorated by the FAA."

CHAPTER 33

Crossing through Washington Square Park on the Manhattan campus of NYU, Ray Martino is making his way toward "midnight mass" at McSoreley's Olde Ale House on East Seventh Street. He is stopped by two derelicts, street people who appear to Martino to be more of a nuisance than a threat. When they ask the tin man for a cigarette, he responds by politely advising them that smoking is bad for one's health. Then, this exchange:

"Give me the jacket."

"I'm sorry. You said…what did you say?"

"Give me the jacket."

Martino hesitates for a long moment. His hesitation is not born of concern for his safety, but because his brain does not quickly register the extremely odd circumstances. When he finally realizes that he is the target of a lame attempt at robbery, and that the robbers are two pathetic street bums, with no weapons and no realistic chance of prevailing in a contest of physical skills, even considering the numbers, he is amused. Martino makes direct eye contact and finally responds:

"Really? Give you my jacket? I'll tell you what…you give me YOUR jackets, now how about that?" When the two, wretched, would-be felons quickly turn and walk toward Fifth Avenue, the Newark Tower tin man is not finished with them. He quickly catches up and shouts:

"Maybe you didn't hear me, I said GIVE ME YOUR FUCKING JACKETS! C'MON, GET 'EM OFF, RIGHT NOW!"

The bums quicken their step and when Martino tires of chasing his new friends, he leaves them near the monument at the foot of Fifth Avenue, and turns east toward Astor Place. When he relates the story to the assembled tin men at McSoreley's, they all get a good laugh. Martino takes a long, lusty slug of dark ale and wipes his upper lip with the back of his hand. While building a cheese and cracker sandwich from a plate on the bar, the Brooklyn tough guy points a thumb toward NYU and offers a moral to the bughouse fable. "You know what we call guys like them two… in Red Hook? Fucking FLOATERS!"

Asleep in the pilot berth aboard *Tipitina*, Doherty is having another dream about the control tower. A bubbly, longhaired local controller with a pencil neck is prattling on in sing-song fashion and lisping like a fruity male flight attendant.

Hi. My name is Tim and I'll be your Local Controller this afternoon. Today we are featuring landings on Runway Four Right and departures on the left, with overflow traffic on Runway Two Nine. The weather is perfect for flying and delays are less than fifteen minutes. If you need anything, please do not hesitate to call me. Thank you for choosing Newark Tower, and have a wonderful, uneventful flight.

In his dream, Doherty's hands are around Tim Chance's neck and he is choking the life out of him. It's a death dance with Doherty leading, but for some reason, "Slim" Chance is largely unflustered by his assassin's efforts. He looks Doherty in the eye.

I'm sorry you're having this trouble, Sir. May I offer you some complimentary tickets to a Broadway show? It's a token of our appreciation, especially for you, our valued air traffic customer.

The tin man quickly surveys the area for weapons of opportunity. He will remove his hands from Chance's throat if a suitable weapon can be quickly obtained. A man can be beaten to death with any number of otherwise mundane items, such as a helmet, a canteen, an ammo can, even a hand grenade. In a civilian office setting, desktop items and furniture can be quickly used outside of their normal functions. A letter opener can open a jugular vein. A telephone or a typewriter can be called upon to dent a skull. An electrical cord from a table lamp can quickly strangle an opponent. A Marine in any social setting, may appear to be the life of the party, ever cordial and gregarious, always polite and respectful, but he has usually devised a contingency, a plan to kill everyone in the room if necessary.

Staying with the program at hand, Doherty tries to pop Chance's head off his neck so he can kick it around the area like a soccer ball. Chance's eyeballs are about to explode, but his voice and his bouncy hair remain perfect, like he's starring in a shampoo commercial targeting flamers and cross-dressers. Chance's face finally starts turning a deeper blue but the real world intervenes suddenly. Doherty wakes up before Tim "Slim" Chance expires.

Damn! I was almost there.

The tin man climbs up the companionway ladder to piss into the North River before returning to his berth, trying to fall quickly asleep, perchance to dream. He's hoping he can catch up to Timmy Chance and set his hair on fire.

In the tower, Thomas Aquinas Wiznak jacks into Local Control. When his right hand comes off the two pronged telephone style jack, it immediately goes to his forehead starting the world's most prolific religious ritual, the Roman Catholic Sign of the Cross. As he does, Ray Martino watches and prays along, in sync with Tommy's action, but the prayer is not actually authorized by the Church. *"High fastball, low sinker, fastball inside, slider on the outside corner."* Tommy's bold act of blessing himself is a defiant challenge to FAA management, as it violates their standing order to refrain from such overt religious gestures while on duty in the tower cab. Paul Veale watches the action and notices Bruce Shapiro staring "daggers" at the back of Tommy's head. The NATCA rep can see war clouds building, and he knows that disputes of this type are bound to drag him and the tower manager into the fray, and this time, neither one of them wants to be there.

These two idiots are like kids who can't play nice in the sand box. This union has far more important business on its plate than some ridiculous religious spat between head cases like these. It's not even your classic Jew versus Catholic, Bronze Age bullshit argument. Tommy's more of a witch doctor than a real Catholic and Shapiro's just mad 'cause his relatives got holocausted and he thinks the Pope authorized the whole party. I don't have time for this kind of crap.

Beans Larkin sits down next to Shapiro at the Clearance Delivery position with a fresh mug of thick tower coffee. He decides to "jack up" Shapiro a bit.

"This coffee smells absolutely HEAVENLY! Hey, Tommy! Did you make the coffee? It must be Chock Full of Nuts!" Beans Larkin sings the well-known coffee jingle to Shapiro.

"Chock Full of Nuts is a HEAVENLY coffee." Shapiro ignores Larkin, except that he pulls a small notepad out of his shirt pocket and makes an entry. No one knows what Shapiro writes in his little notepad, but it makes more than a few controllers and supervisors nervous when he does it. Because he has no personality, Shapiro has fewer friends among the controllers than Liam Doherty. Doherty intimidates folks with his bearing and demeanor, but he's a good conversationalist when he wants to be, and he's not likely to withhold his opinions for any reason. And, Doherty has a reputation for being fair, treating everyone the same, from the junior janitor to the senior Senator. Shapiro is flat out, anti-social. He normally responds to any questions that are not directly work related with a stock, one word reply: PERSONAL!

"Hello Bruce. Did you enjoy your days off?"

"PERSONAL!"

"Pardon me?"

"PERSONAL!"

CHAPTER 34

A new air traffic manager is selected to fill a vacancy at LaGuardia Tower in Queens, New York. His name is Randall Kemp and as predicted by the tin men, Mr. Kemp is a gentleman of color – black, to put a finer point on it. On the day that Kemp shows up at LaGuardia, he is given a tour of the facility by one of the office pogues, a Program Specialist. Standing in the tower cab among the working controllers, Kemp is shown some well-known New York landmarks that can easily be seen from the tower. After pointing out the Chrysler Building and the Empire State Building and the Hell Gate Railroad Bridge, the specialist directs Kemp to the tower radar display to show the new boss some landmarks and their depiction on the radar video map. Kemp smiles and listens intently while shaking hands with some of his new charges. Finally, the Program Specialist finishes the short dog and pony show, and asks Kemp if he has any questions about his new facility. Kemp looks up at the radar. Tugging on an ear lobe, he asks the question that would drop every jaw in the tower, and make Kemp a long running subject of derision and ridicule among the tin men at LaGuardia.

"Which way is north on this thing?"

Now some people like to say there is no such thing as a stupid question. There are however, questions that let people know how badly untrained you are. There are disturbing questions that let air traffic controllers know how severely unqualified you are. There are deeply troubling questions that serve as mileposts along the government road to total ineptitude. Had the question come from a fifth grade girl scout on her first field trip to the big airport control tower, no one would have blinked. That it comes from a facility Air Traffic Manager at one of the nation's busiest airports, is shocking and obscene.

In the air traffic control world, all radar displays are oriented with north at top dead center. Otherwise, aircraft vectors and hand-offs would be impossible, as the direction that airplanes are flying could not be readily determined. This radar standard is as basic and familiar to an air traffic controller as a trowel is to a stonemason.

Now most controllers already knew that the FAA's affirmative action rush to *diversity* had dented the effectiveness of the air traffic control system. Even many of the beneficiaries of the policy would admit as much – at least when talking to close friends. Kern's question was palpable proof that the standards had vanished completely. It was now possible for anyone, no matter how unskilled and unschooled, to gain the title, Air Traffic Manager, as long as that person fits the government's diversity profile. And for those naïve enough to believe that a diversity appointment like Kemp's does not impact safety, that the rubber band is not more twisted, a series of eye popping near misses and other dangerous events would occur that coincided with Ralph "Wrong Turn" Kemp's time at the LaGuardia helm.

In one incident, a G2 was cleared to land on a closed runway, demolishing a Port Authority truck. Fortunately, the electrician working on the runway saw the large business jet coming, and sprinted for the grass, clearing the impact area in the nick of time.

As a libertarian, Liam A. Doherty despises the FAA's favorite word, diversity. In the national lexicon, diversity is a word whose meaning has long passed the vanishing point. He discusses the definition of the word with tin man Gordon Russo on a midnight shift in the tower.

"Think about it, G-Man. Diversity is a code word. It means we hate straight, white males, and we're proud of it."

"Ya think?"

Both men are sitting with their shoes elevated and resting on the front line console. An inbound People Express flight is flashing "VAP" on the radar displays, signaling that the pilot is conducting a visual approach, ten miles west of the airport.

"Sure. They can't come right out and say it, so they assign the concept a positive sounding term – a feel good, catch phrase. You know...*affirmative action, diversity, pro-choice, The New Deal, Rich Chocolate Ovaltine.* Who could be against that? It sounds so good, you almost want to eat it. Russo slides a paper flight strip from its plastic holder and slips it into the electric time stamp machine.

"We are eating it, Willie. How long have you been here?"

"Ten years."

"And how many spear-chuckers and roach-ranchers have come through here and moved on to greener pastures, dream facilities like Tampa and Phoenix and Las Vegas? And guys like you and me train them. I swear Willie, we're fattening frogs for snakes...forging our own chains; digging escape tunnels for others to use, while we stay here and grease the skids for these losers. Oh. I'm sorry – winners." Doherty puts a mug of cold coffee into the microwave oven and starts the timer.

"They don't let me train."

"Yea. That's funny, Willie. You don't train, but you got more saves than John the Baptist. You turned that guy Bryan around so fast, we thought you sprinkled him with magic pixie dust. The guy's an animal on Ground Control, and guess where he's going? Nowhere- he's a tin man now, and you sealed his fate. Eventually, he'll grow to hate you like everyone else around here." Doherty checks the shine on his shoes and gives them a quick wipe with a coffee filter.

"I'll tell you a little secret, G-Man. I like it here. The tin is dependable, and I'm so used to the stench of burning rubber and jet fuel, I wouldn't know how to breathe in some sweet smelling place like Honolulu or Seattle." Russo nods.

"You know what, Willie? San Francisco – that's a good place for a big, tight-assed, homophobic ex-Marine like you. Those faggots get a hold of you and your ass will see more traffic than the old Tunnel of Love at Palisades Park!" Both men laugh, and then Russo gets serious again.

"You watch what happens. When that guy Bryan gets certified through the tower, he springs another lesbian or a porch monkey right out the back door." Russo stabs the air with his thumb pointing in the direction of Pennsylvania. "Remember, the manager making the selection as well as the manager releasing him gets diversity reward "points." Everyone wins in the FAA diversity game except the lowly tin man. He gets to stay here, push the big tin and push other people's careers.

Doherty, standing straight, sips the re-heated coffee with his forearm and elbow parallel to the deck. "There are more losers, G-Man. The flying public loses because air safety suffers. And guess what? Even the beneficiaries of affirmative action have to put themselves into the system they've helped to weaken, by boarding an airplane from time to time. So, ask yourself now – winners and losers? There are no winners in this game. A perpetual game of Russian Roulette will eventually run out of players- especially when you keep adding more bullets to the gun." Russo nods his head and then scans the runway in a deliberate, mechanical way, starting at landing threshold and ending at the roll out end near the turnpike. Finding no ground traffic or vehicles threatening to foul the runway he keys the hand mike. "People One-Oh-Five, cleared to land Runway One One, wind, one eight zero at seven; after landing, taxi to the ramp on this frequency."

People One-Oh-Five, cleared to land, thank you, Tower. Turning to Doherty he coordinates:

"I'm short for runway One One."

"Check."

CHAPTER 35

Walking toward *Tipitina* on the floating finger dock Doherty notices that the cabin lights are on. This could only mean that Maria is aboard, though she's normally home pretending to be married at this time of night. Climbing aboard Doherty finds Maria on the starboard settee and senses that she's distressed. He can tell she's been crying.

"Did he hit you Maria?"

"He called me a nigger lover."

The tin man pulls her close and Maria starts crying on his shirt. When she stops, he asks her the only question he can think to ask.

"Why would Zeke say something like that?"

"I had a boyfriend in high school; a black guy."

"Maria, I'm sorry." Maria's face tightens.

"No. You're not sorry. You're disappointed. I can see it all over your face."

Amazed at her perception, Doherty decides to postpone the conversation until he can gather his thoughts and defend his position better. She's right, however; he is disappointed. Soon he will tell her how he has a right to his disappointment. He puts Maria to bed in the forward vee berth. They agree to talk about it in the morning.

In his dream Doherty's arms and shoulders are screaming, begging him for quarter. In an exercise of mind over matter, he wills the pain to stop.

A brick wall, solid… square and plumb…at just the right height…. my rifle is resting on top of a brick wall. My rifle cannot fall; it can-

not budge. My arms are fine. They're not tired at all. Resting on this brick wall my rifle is steady and level, even as I am steady and level. A brick wall can last, what? Damn near forever. I've never been more alive than I am right now...at this very moment...in this place. I was born to keep this rifle from falling. Who's to say I won't live forever? And the people I protect? They may not live forever, but as long as I hold this rifle in place, they will live to see another day.

After a few minutes, the mortar between the bricks starts melting. The weight of the rifle, getting heavier by the second, is bearing down on the bricks causing the mortar, now the consistency of warm peanut butter, to start oozing out. The wall weakens, becoming less serviceable. Then the bricks begin to flatten, crack and split. What was sturdy and solid brick and mortar, is now runny, rancid peanut butter and crumbling graham crackers. The wall is no longer serviceable. The rifle loses altitude.

My rifle! Jesus, my rifle!

Wide-awake, the tin man goes forward to check on Maria who is sleeping peacefully. Cracking open a beer from the ice box he climbs up into the cockpit and chugs most of it down. Naked but for the sweat on his face and arms, Doherty dives from *Tipitina*'s transom into the North River.

The conversation about Maria's first love continues over breakfast at the Malibu Diner in Hoboken.

"Are you familiar with the term "libertarian", Maria?

"I think so. It's a person who dislikes government, like an anarchist, only not so extreme."

"You're close. Would you allow me to give my definition, since I claim to be a libertarian?" Maria nods, her lips forming a sly smile, anticipating the back and forth to come. Doherty glances around for a waitress, thinking the Malibu Diner needs a dragon lady to put their business on a speedier track.

"Libertarians don't like government because government is force and force needs to be limited, and used only as necessary. Police officers know this as well as anyone. I'm sure the Port Authority has trained you in the rules for using force, especially deadly force. Am I right?"

"Yes. Basically I can shoot to defend my life or someone else's life."

"That's right Maria, because government exists to protect the rights of the individual. This country was formed to protect individual rights and libertarians trace their heritage back to the architects of the Republic, especially Thomas Jefferson." Two coffees appear along with a waitress to take their orders. When the waitress leaves, Maria smiles at Doherty. "Is this lecture on American government and political science leading to something connected to my dating history?"

"Sort of…I just mean to say that you have a right to freely associate with anyone you choose to. As a libertarian, I recognize that right, and would never interfere with it."

"But you would discourage me from associating with someone based on their color, wouldn't you?"

"On their color, no, on their culture, yes; and more often than not, the two are closely intertwined; but I would never interfere in a way that would violate anyone's rights. I would simply exercise my own right to NOT associate with someone whose culture or lifestyle I strongly object to. I'd cut them loose like a burning barge."

"Does that mean you're cutting me loose?"

"Maria, if that was the case you'd be talking to an empty chair here. I'd be gone already, like a cool breeze. Your association, your marriage to Zeke is more of a deal breaker than your past dalliance with the third world, if you don't mind me being so blunt. I'm supposed to be living up to the motto *Semper Fidelis* – Always Faithful. How does that comport with breaking up your marriage?"

"You Marines- you can't let go, can you?"

"No more than I could jump out of my own skin." A devious twinkle appears in Maria's eyes.

"Who do you love more – me or the Marine Corps?" The tin man panics and tries to formulate an answer. Before he can speak, Maria pre-empts him.

"Your hesitation speaks volumes."

CHAPTER 36

Beans Larkin is navigating a shopping cart through the produce aisle of a supermarket in Red Bank. Air traffic controllers have to eat, too. At the end of the aisle he runs into a traffic jam as three shoppers wait for a senior citizen to check the integrity of individual eggs within their paper-Mache carton. With her cart blocking the entire aisle, the elderly egg inspector has traffic stalled in two directions, holding up local commerce and threatening the fiscal viability of the community. Larkin quickly formulates a traffic flow solution in his head. Not satisfied with waiting for the gridlocked supermarket aisle to unclog, Larkin pictures himself standing near the aisle end cap, on top of stacked cases of Coca Cola. From his station above the store's shopping traffic movement area, he can now direct the action.

Sir! You in the red pants! You're after chopped meat? Make a one-eighty and go to the end of Aisle Three and turn right. Pass behind the pregnant lady and approach the meat section from the west. Ma'am, you in the babushka, turn right and travel down Aisle One. You'll find the peanut butter on the shelf about a third of the way down. You can then turn right again and return for your eggs via Aisle Two. Don't forget the kielbasa and the pierogies. Use caution, braking action is poor due to a recent spill in Aisle Two. Lady, yes, you with the varicose veins and the flabby upper arms, you want the frozen food section? Give way to Red Pants and turn left into Aisle Three. Turn right at the end and go as far as you can. The frozen foods are against the west wall of the store. Caution, two kids are drag racing with shopping carts ahead. If you have them in sight, maintain visual separation and caution wake turbulence.

Satisfied that store traffic is now flowing at the speed of interstate agriculture and local retail, tin man Larkin goes about his shopping routine. Stopping by the bakery section, he cops a pound cake and heads for the front end. In the checkout lane, the action is stopped when the shopper in front of him has an item that will not scan. The clerk picks up a telephone handset and keys the public address system: Price check, number five! Annoyed, Larkin massages his temples with his thumbs, his forehead resting on the knuckles of both hands, and his forearms resting on the handlebar of the shopping cart. He says to no one in particular; "What's the use?" Adding to his angst, Carole King is heard on the store's background music, screeching her tedious ode to boredom and a love that got stuck in the mud:

But its too late, Baby, now it's too late…

Beans Larkin is staring at a frozen turkey. He's thinking of bashing someone's head in with it. Carole King has that effect on him. The tin man takes a deep breath and concentrates on relaxing. His daytime shopping experience is almost over. In three hours he will be on position in the tower; he will be back in control.

It's Monday morning and another training day for Doherty's team. A new supervisor is taking the reins and he wastes no time flexing his FAA management muscles. A tall blonde chubby faced Dutchman named Bill Van Geffen is stabbing the table with a long bony index finger and emphasizing that he is in charge at all times and will not tolerate any challenges to his authority. As the room is struck into silence, Van Geffen gives the long conference table the once around, stopping to make eye contact with each controller assembled. After a moment, and satisfied that he has everyone intimidated, he speaks.

"Does anyone have any questions about what I just said? Oh, and by the way, please call me Van." When no one speaks, he voices an addendum. "There's a new sheriff in town." After a few seconds,

Doherty rises and goes to the blackboard a few feet away and chalks a quote from an American novelist and philosopher:

"THOUGHT DOES NOT BOW TO AUTHORITY"

- *Ayn Rand*

Van Geffen purses his lips and examines the quote. His chin is poking the air like that famous photo of Benito Mussolini.

"Okay, Willie. What does that mean?"

"It means, Van, that the smartest person in the room is really the one in charge. You may have all the authority, but if you're not the smartest one here, you are not really in charge. Authority will only get a person so far. Eventually, he will find himself leaning on the smarter person or persons in the group. In any contest between brains and authority, brains will win every time." Van Geffen is annoyed and feels more than a bit threatened. Since he cannot easily comprehend the underlying philosophical premise supporting the chalked maxim, he dismisses it as simply a raw challenge to his authority. He looks hard at Doherty.

"What are you, some kind of smart ass? A wise guy?" Doherty, now seated, chuckles and responds:

"Hey, you're picking this stuff up faster than I thought you would!" The room laughs and Van Geffen's pasty Dutch face starts turning red.

"Don't screw with me Willie. I've been briefed about you. I heard all about that episode with Timmy Chance, and if it was my decision, you would have been removed from government service." Doherty comes right back.

"Yea, that's right. And if it was Tim's decision we'd be fishing two dead aviators out of the North River." Just then, Alan "two ties" Mealey sticks his head in the door. "Hey, there's bagels in the break room for you guys!" The team springs up and heads for the door, but Doherty remains seated. Once alone, he addresses the new supervisor. "Okay to take a break, Van?" Van Geffen nods his head, and the tin man leaves the room. It never occurs to the FAA supervisor, that Doherty was the only team member that actually paid any heed to what Van Geffen had to say. Nor did Van Geffen even notice that Doherty had extended an appropriate amount of respect for the supervisor's authority. Not intimidated or threatened by authority, Doherty is well suited to follow orders, as a former U.S. Marine, even more so than the other controllers subjected to FAA discipline and work rules.

A major airport like Newark is constantly experiencing some level of construction or maintenance and that activity closes runways and taxiways for long periods, especially during the summer. Rarely is the entire airport operating area and all of its related facilities fully open and useable. The air traffic control team must constantly learn to adapt, utilizing the available space as advantageously as circumstances permit.

A month after the initial meeting between Van Geffen and his new team, an airport construction issue arises, impacting the operation. A normal Northeast flow is in progress with landings on runway Four Right and departures using the parallel runway, Four Left. The Port Authority has closed the two high speed turn off taxiways on Four Right. Because of this, each landing aircraft, in order to make a ninety degree turn has to slow down on the runway to nearly a dead stop before turning off and clearing the runway for the next landing. Subsequent landings, lacking a clear runway get the "go around." To avoid a "go around" some are sidestepped over to the parallel runway, causing departure delays. Now the ground controller is getting swamped, so Van Geffen opens up Flow Control and starts a local departure delay program. Holding departures at their gates, the flow controller issues them expected engine start times. This keeps airplanes from burning up fuel while waiting on the taxiways for takeoff. Liam Doherty is standing at the Flight Data position rather than sitting to avoid wrinkling his heavily starched khaki trousers. Watching the action up front, Doherty wonders if anyone will figure out a workable air traffic solution to the airport surface problem presently challenging the team. As in a game of chess, there are many moves that are available, but only one best move. Van Geffen picks up a phone and talks to his counterpart in the radar room, the New York TRACON.

"I need to stretch out the final, John. Give me a full six miles between arrivals and seven behind the heavy jets. And John, I need a good six miles, don't cheat on me."

"Christ, Van, that's gonna put us into a serious program, we'll be into delays all night." Van Geffen makes his case, believing he is out of options.

"I can't help it John, these guys are all stopping on the runway to use the ninety degree turn offs. I can't sidestep any more; the departure demand is too high. Blame it on the Port Authority. They closed my high speed turn offs." When Van Geffen hangs up, he moves over and sits at the typewriter log to memorialize the action he just took. Doherty waits for Van to make his move official and then walks over to the new supervisor. He decides to smack some of the shelf dust from Van Geffen's ass.

"I've got an idea, Van. Why don't we advertise ILS approaches to runway Four Left, land on the *left, and depart* on Runway Four Right? Departures don't need the high speed turnoffs, and there are two, beautiful high speed turn offs on the left side. They're just sitting there, waiting for someone to ask them to dance. It seems like a shame to go into delays for lack of high speed turn offs and not utilize the two that we have." Van Geffen looks out toward the operating area as if to verify that the runways and taxiways that Doherty is referring to are actually there. His brow furrows and his face tightens except for the dark bags under his eyes. He ponders the idea for a few seconds. Like most of the supervisors, he is suspicious of any suggestion that is coming from Doherty. Instead of examining the proposal and evaluating it on its merits, prejudice toward the messenger is blinding Van Geffen. Even so, he mulls it over for a few more seconds, or about as long as it takes one to order from a Chinese take-out menu.

"No."

"No?"

"No."

"That's what I thought you said." Doherty returns to Flight Data and pulls some flight progress strips from the printer. The strips are marked, then mounted in plastic strip holders and posted at their appropriate positions. A girl named Patricia sits next to him at the Clearance Delivery position. She crosses her long shapely legs and smiles at the tin man. She's been watching the discussion with interest.

"You know what they say- you can lead a horse to water…"

Doherty smiles back. Patricia is a smart girl, and she has come on to the tin man before. He decided against starting a relationship because her hands are unattractive. He picks up the phone and calls a buddy at the New York TRACON.

"O'Brien! Joe, you busy?"

"I'm busier than a one legged midget in an ass kicking contest. What's up?"

"Do me a favor. Put a bug in your supervisor's ear. Point out that Newark can land on Four Left and depart on the right side. Bring an airport chart with you and show him that there are two high-speed turn offs on runway Four Left, and explain that departures don't need turn offs and can use the right side. This way the Port Authority's construction issues are no longer a factor. You understand?"

"Yea, Willie. I'm lookin' at the chart right here. Is the ILS useable on the left?"

"Yes, Joe, as soon as I throw the switch. Now listen, Joe. Pretend it was your idea. You didn't hear this from me, okay? Then sit back and watch the delays disappear."

"Okay, I'll call you back after I talk to him. Now tell me, is that tall one with the legs still working up there?" Doherty looks over at Patricia.

"She's sitting right next to me." Patricia, and Doherty look at each other while O'Brien continues his verbal lusting. Luckily, Patricia can only hear Doherty's side of the conversation. Tin man O'Brien continues.

"Man, she's got some set of pins; they go all the way up and make an ass out of themselves. If she had bigger tits, she could lead me around by the nose."

"I got the picture, Joe."

When Doherty hangs up Patricia asks him: "Who was that?"

"That was an admirer… he says you got brains."

Fifteen minutes later Van Geffen is deep into a conference phone call with the TRACON and the Flow Control desk in Washington. When he hangs up, Van Geffen turns to Judy Episcopo who has relieved Doherty at the Flight Data position.

"Judy, cut a new ATIS broadcast. Advertise ILS approaches to Four Left, landing Four Left and departing on the right side. Delete the info about any high speed turn offs being closed."

CHAPTER 37

Jay Sansone is Newark tower's version of the "shithouse lawyer." A libertarian like Doherty he is constantly schooling anyone who will listen about why air traffic control services should be privatized, and why the public school system is a form of socialism and child abuse. The privatization issue is strongly opposed by the controller's union, and Sansone has found himself in some very heated arguments from time to time with one or more of his union brothers. On a midnight shift he starts in on the politics and "virgin" Mary humors him by pretending to be interested in what Sansone has to say.

"Mary, do you realize that if we worked in the private sector we could take home twenty five to 30 percent more money in our paychecks?" Mary is seated at the Local Control position squeezing a rubber ball, causing her forearm muscles to flex. Her knuckles resemble large over-ripe grapes, like those on a boxer from hitting the heavy bag for an hour each day. She has no desire to engage Sansone in conversation, so she feigns interest sarcastically, hoping that the talkative tin man will take the hint.

"No shit, Jay? How come?" Jay explains.

"Because our earnings would not be subject to federal income taxes."

Mary turns from the overhead radar display to make eye contact with Sansone.

"What are you, fuckin' high? Everyone pays federal income taxes. In fact, if they didn't, we wouldn't get a federal paycheck. REMEMBER?"

"Listen, Mary…and keep an open mind here. Have you ever actually SEEN the law that makes anyone's earnings subject to the internal revenue code?"

"Of course not, Joe, but when I see trees waving back and forth, I think its safe to assume that the wind is blowing. Besides, I have a CPA that does my taxes. He went to school to learn how to do it. He doesn't tell me how to separate and expedite airplanes, and I don't tell him how to interpret the tax laws." Mary watches a TWA jet roll out to the end of runway Four Left. The Boeing Seven Twenty Seven turns off near the base of the tower. "TWA Three Twenty Three, turn left on Romeo, taxi to the ramp via Mike and the Inner, remain this frequency."

Jay Sansone waits his turn, then he starts working on "virgin" Mary again.

"Yes Mary, OUR income is subject to federal taxation because the federal government is our employer. Congress never gave the federal government jurisdiction over earnings in the private sector. The tax code is written to reflect that reality, and if someone takes the initiative and actually does some serious legal research, they will find NO LAW that makes private sector earnings taxable. In fact they will find ample evidence that the opposite is true- most earnings are NOT taxable under the IRS code."

Mary changes hands and works the rubber ball with her left. Digesting the legal theory she just heard, she takes a minute to absorb it and formulate a response.

"So let me see if got this right, Jay. You say that the federal government cannot tax the paychecks of employees in the private sector, despite the opinions of thousands of tax attorneys and accountants, academics and other professionals all across this land. And I should disregard their *professional* opinions, and heed yours?" Sansone responds.

"You don't need anyone's opinion, Mary. You can walk into a law library and pull Title 26 of the U.S. Code from the shelf and read it for yourself. I swear to Christ, it's written in English…black letters on white paper. And you know something else? The truth doesn't depend on numbers…it's the truth even if NO ONE believes it. Remember, at one time the earth was thought to be flat and resting on the back of a giant turtle. A lot of *professionals* believed that to be true, and anyone who questioned it was a heretic." Mary continues to work on her rubber ball. She looks at Sansone and ponders the veracity of his message. She knows that Sansone is smart, but smart people are fooled occasionally.

These goddamn conspiracy nuts! They've always got a convincing argument to support their bullshit ideas. You can't shut them up. I wish I had the law book right here so I could throw it on the table and say, "Go ahead, Jay. Show me the goddamned law! But that still wouldn't shut the little pis-ant up. He would just switch gears and start talking about black helicopters or JFK's brain disappearing from the FBI evidence lab.

Mary's mid watch is half over. Even though she wants to tell Sansone he's full of shit, she makes a mental note to discuss the income tax issue with one of her girlfriends, a paralegal who works for a personal injury lawyer.

A month after her midnight conversation with Jay Sansone, "virgin" Mary is reading a news story about a Federal Express pilot from Tennessee and an attorney from Louisiana. Both were acquitted of income tax evasion after testifying that no law makes their earnings taxable. Neither the Department of Justice nor the IRS could cite any statute that contradicted their defense.

CHAPTER 38

At a union meeting in the tower ready room, Paul Veale is discussing the thorny issue of sick leave. The FAA is in the habit of pressuring controllers to come in and work, even after they have reported that they are too sick to work. Supervisors have resorted to using the code phrase: "no sick leave is available" in response to a controller calling in sick. This is taken to mean that they will be marked AWOL for the shift and disciplinary action will result. Many Newark Tower controllers will back down, and decide to report for their assigned shift, rather than risk a letter of reprimand or a suspension. At a union meeting, Veale gives the union's advice on such events.

"If and when you decide to pick up the phone to call in sick, then do so, and do NOT change your mind. I don't care what an FAA supervisor says to you on the phone. You are entitled to sick leave if you need it. A supervisor that suggests that a sick person should operate a motor vehicle, and come to the tower to control live air traffic, is hanging his ass way out over the rail, from a liability standpoint. If that supervisor was to flat out ORDER a controller to do something like that, he is committing a crime." Veale pauses and looks around the room making eye contact with each of his union brothers. "Also, what message are you sending when you call in sick, and then decide to come in because a supervisor suggested it, or threatened you with discipline? I'll tell you what you're saying. You're saying you are not really sick…that you just wanted a day off…that you were *lying* about being sick. What kind of message is that? A controller asks for clarification.

"Is there anything we can do to protect ourselves from disciplinary action, or having our sick leave denied arbitrarily?" Veale responds:

Absolutely. Many of you have a three way calling option on your telephones, and if you don't have it, I do. Call me first, and I will get the supervisor on the line. I will tell him that you are on the call with union representation and the conversation is being recorded and that you are calling in sick. I promise you that under those circumstances a supervisor will not respond by pressuring you to come in and work traffic." Veale looks around the room at the ten controllers assembled. Another thought comes to mind.

"You know, a lot of people don't have the personal fortitude, the guts, whatever you want to call it, to do what you and I do for a living. If you've got the balls it takes to push the big tin at the airport, why can't you stand up for your rights with the employer? And remember, the union is here to help you. Let me slap their balls around for you, that's what you elected me do, but give me a chance. I can't help you if you're not willing to take a stand. If you pick up the phone to call in sick – you're too sick to work – end of story."

At the risk of appearing to be a tourist, Doherty is standing across the street from World Trade Center One and gazing up at the top of the towers. The awesome height and majestic appearance of the structures never fails to amaze the tin man. He remembers how badly architecture critics panned the buildings even before construction, but the towers withstood the test of time and now are favorites among the camera toting tourists and New York residents alike. Maria is walking across Church Street to meet the tin man at the designated news stand rendezvous point.

"You like the towers?"

"I like the towers a lot."

"What about the Statue of Liberty?"

"I don't like it at all. I'd dismantle it and ship it back to France, or cut it up for scrap.

"Aw, that's no way to treat a lady. I like the Chrysler building, and the Brooklyn Bridge. What other famous places do you like, Willie?"

"Well, there's one that stands out from all others in my estimation, that's Independence Hall in Philly." The two start walking down Greenwich Street toward Battery Park. Maria picks his brain.

"Because of the history?"

"Sure. It's because of what happened in that room right inside those front doors. When I walk down Chestnut Street, and I get close to that place, the hair stands up on my neck. It happens every time."

"Wow. That's something. I've heard about people getting that feeling when they view priceless works of art, things like that." Doherty continues:

"It's Providence, Maria. If you believe in Providence, than you have to know that the Declaration of Independence was written by the hand of God, through the Founding Fathers. What happened in Philadelphia was a miracle, and although it is considered a secular national monument, Independence Hall is really one of the Holiest places on earth maybe the Holiest." After a pause, Maria stops and makes eye contact.

"I've never known you to be so religious." Doherty nods at Maria.

"And that's the most religion you will hear from me. Mostly I worship at two altars-capitalism and the Constitution." Maria takes a minute to think about what she's just been told.

"I have two things to tell you, Willie."

"I'm listening."

"I love you so much it hurts."

"And I love you, Maria. What else?"

"I'm hungry."

CHAPTER 39

In the break room, Doherty is finishing his lunch period. Taking his coffee on the catwalk, he surveys the airport operating area. Across the parking lot in front of Building Ten, a Port Authority cop is pacing the sidewalk, playing the bagpipes, obviously practicing. Even though the sound of bagpipes has been known to cut through thick prison walls and time itself, Doherty cannot hear the musical notes through the wall of jet noise. When he steps back into the break room, the door closes out the noise and the tin man finds himself facing Judy Episcopo. She has something to tell him. Her tone and profanity underscore the seriousness of her message.

"Holy fucking shit, Willie! You should have the seen the mother-fucking- goddamned- deal Charles just had on Local! I've never fucking seen anything that fucking close before! Judy starts hyperventilating, causing her huge breasts to heave. "Angela ran down the stairs and tripped. I think her arm's broken. She's in the bathroom throwing up." Judy sits, plants her elbows on the table and buries her face in her hands.

"Okay, Judy. What happened?"

"I don't know. Jesus! I was working goddamned Departure Flow Control. I was up to my ass in fucking engine start times. I look up and see two Continental jets right over the fucking Runway Four numbers." Judy's hands form two moving airplanes and when they stop, a cross hangs in mid air. "Jesus Christ! Jesus Christ!"

"Judy. Calm down. Tell me how it happened."

"Willie, I swear to God. You've never seen anything this fucking close. Two Continental jets…closer than white on fucking rice. Jesus, I think I'm gonna puke." Doherty sits down across from Judy and tries to make eye contact. He notices her hands shaking. With her eyes closed, and her lips trembling, she appears to be praying. Judy finally looks up at the tin man.

"Willie, those broke-dick-mother-fuckers are up there right now doing damage control. I shit you not! They're actually trying to cover this one up. I heard Charles tell Bell he was using VISUAL separation…after Bell suggested it! Willie, that stupid fucking idiot is dangerous. They should never have checked him out. They only certified him because he's…" Judy's face goes back in her hands, leaving the word *black*, floating unspoken.

"Judy, you want some water or something?" After a minute, Judy looks up at the tin man again, making direct eye contact. Her eyeballs are wet, and her makeup is getting out of shape.

"Willie, Don't let 'em fucking do it. I know you can do something, call someone. I don't care about these assholes anymore. If they keep getting away with this shit…who knows what will happen. FUCK THEM! I'm tired of their stupid bullshit! Tears of rage start streaming from Judy's eyes.

"WHY WON'T THEY JUST LET US BE CONTROLLERS? Why do we have to play their silly games every time someone has a fucking deal?" Doherty tosses a box of tissues onto the table and heads for the stairs up to the tower cab.

In the tower cab, Charles Clemons and Richard "ding dong dick" Bell are sitting at the supervisor's desk. Bell is on the phone talking with Continental's Chief Pilot and Charles is listening on an extension, and jotting notes for Bell on a yellow legal pad. Doherty notices that Bell is speaking on a recorded line, and chalks that up to arrogance or stupidity, perhaps both.

As Doherty jacks into Local Control, Ray Martino gives him a quick position relief briefing and then asks:

"Did you hear about the deal?"

"No. Something happened?"

"Officially? No. Nothing happened. I'll tell you what didn't happen later." The mood in the tower is quiet and somber, like a Protestant wake. Charles shoots a few glances in Doherty's direction. He is clearly not comfortable with Doherty's presence in the tower cab at this crucial time. He believes that Doherty is a racist, a sexist and a homophobe, in that order. In Charles's small mind, anyone that might hold him accountable for his actions is no less a racist than David Duke or Bull Connor. Charles glances over at Doherty and the two make eye contact. Doherty considers warning Charles and Bell about the dangers of covering up their "deal." He decides against tipping them off. After all, it's just like the tower manager always says- "everyone's responsible for their own actions."

Aboard *Tipitina* the red light is blinking on the answering machine. There are three messages from Paul Veale asking for a quick return call. Doherty gets naked and climbs into the pilot berth. Thinking about the near miss at the airport, he wonders if he will need to take any action. Perhaps the incident will be fully investigated without his involvement. Maybe Bell and Clemons will realize that they can't keep the lid on this one and report it for a thorough investigation. Maybe the controllers can learn something from it. Maybe the learning experience will have a positive effect. Maybe the event will go a long way toward preventing an actual mid air collision.

Yea, sure, and maybe I'll start shitting diamond cuff links and rare postage stamps. The pilots involved will dictate the action. The FAA will almost always go for the cover-up. Supervisors, controllers, office pogues and managers...they'll all get in line, just like they usually do. But the pilots, if THEY make a big stink, the game changes... They'll have to start an NTSB investigation. And the passengers...if this one was as close as it sounds, the passengers may be heard from. On every flight there is always someone important or politically connected. In that case, phone calls will be made. You can count on it.

The phone rings.

"Doherty."

"Willie, it's Paul."

"Why are you calling me, Paul?" I had nothing to do with Charles's deal. I didn't even see it, for Christ's sake. I have nothing to tell you about it."

"I think you know why I might be calling, Willie. I just had a meeting with the people involved. They are concerned that you might make a stink about this. They know that the girls spoke to you… looking for you to call someone. Funny that the girls come to YOU…if you had your way, they'd be home cleaning the oven and ironing shirts."

"That's right, Paul. A female will recognize real balls before anyone will. And since American men have been emasculated so thoroughly over the years, it's not surprising that a hard charger like me stands out in a crowd. Maybe that's why I get more ass than a horse trailer."

"Let's get serious, Willie. The preliminary conclusion is –no violation…visual separation was being applied."

"I thought you wanted to get serious. Then you hit me with THAT punch line? Unless you mean that the PILOTS were using visual separation. Is that what you're saying?"

After a pause, Veale continues.

"No. Listen, Willie. There's another meeting scheduled for 0700 tomorrow. This thing is still in progress. But there's concern…about you, and I need to set some folks at ease. Plus, whether you believe it or not, I'm looking out for your interests here, also." Hearing that last remark, Doherty realizes that his friendship with the union rep and fellow tin man has just reached a turning point. Veale has chosen sides and Doherty's on the other team.

"You don't need to look out for me, Paul. You need to be looking out for the folks that are flying around in the airplanes and the people who live under them. You took an oath to defend the Constitution and by extension, the associated laws and regulations. And now you are telling me that your loyalty lies…where?…with those that are attempting to commit a crime?... persons who are engaged in cover up and obstruction?"

"Listen, Willie. I don't need a civics lesson from you, so save the populist, libertarian horseshit for your stump speech when you run for office. My job is to protect my union members, and unlike YOU, Charles is a dues paying member in good standing. He gets the benefit of the doubt from me. In fact, he gets more than that. He gets the best defense I am able to give him. If he says he was using visual separation, then that's the union's position. Now if that position changes, I'll let everyone know. Until then, visual separation was being applied. You were not there, so if you start telling tales out of school, prior to an investigation being completed, you're being irresponsible. Veale pauses. When Doherty says nothing, Veale continues.

"You know Willie, in the past, I defended you. I was glad to do it and it was my duty as your union rep, even though you don't pay for the privilege. But if you go where I think you're going with this Charles deal, well…

"Well what, Paul? You'll stop defending me?"

"No Willie. But I'll stop being glad to do it. Now I need some kind of assurance from you. I'd like you to give me your word."

"My word? About what?"

"Your word…that you won't talk to an outside source about this…Charles…non event."

NON EVENT!? Did you say NON EVENT? Where did you hear THAT, Paul? You went in the tank with those bastards, didn't you? They've made up their minds already, and they got the pilots and Continental Airlines on board with this bullshit, didn't they?"

"Willie, listen to me."

"No, Paul. Listen to me. You need to re-think your position on this. If you can't reconcile your duties as union rep, with the truth and with the general welfare and safety of the public, then you need to resign."

"Did you say, *resign?*"

"Yes, but not immediately. Go to Charles. Ask him to do the right thing. Tell him that as his union rep your advice is that he takes full responsibility for his error. If you have to, appeal to his collectivist, racial, class warfare instincts. Tell him if he wants to stop being viewed as a second class citizen, then start taking some first class action. Step up to the plate and act like a man. As soon as he does it, as soon as he lets FAA management know that he's not one of their boys…his chains fall. Then he steps across the line of scrimmage and stands with the tin men. He'll be proud to be in the crowd. And I'll be proud to be standing with him. A long pause ensues. Then Paul Veale replies in a softer tone.

"Willie, you're a smart guy. You're one of the smartest people I've ever met. I appreciate your advice, I really do. But let's get practical. I'm not dealing with people who are as smart as you are. I'm constantly running around plugging holes in the dike. I have to do the quick fix. I can't approach every problem as if I'm trying to win the Nobel Peace Prize. I'm trying to keep one of my members out of trouble and in the process, I have to deal with the devil. Now if you think I'm the next coming of Al Capone, or I'm some kind of traitor, I can't help it. I have to do what I have to do." Doherty answers.

"You just don't get it, Paul. You've never been able to see it. Charles is not in trouble – FAA management is in trouble! Why do you think they asked you to call me? And they DID ask you to call me, didn't they?"

Willie, it's late. I called to get some assurance from you. I need your word on this. Do I have it or not?"

"Paul, what good is my word…if you're asking me to lie?"

"I need to know whose side you're on."

"I'm on the side of truth and accountability; there's room here for both of us, and Charles too."

"Good night, Willie."

"Good luck, Paul."

Tipitina sits motionless in her slip; wind and water are dead calm. Sitting in the cockpit and sipping a Jameson's, the tin man thinks about the central figure in the controversy, Charles Clemons:

All he has to do is walk in and look them in the eye...tell them he's a man just like they are, and he made a human error. Sure, they'll hate him for it. But Charles will stop hating himself. They won't trust him again, but his loyalty will cease being misdirected. It's all up to Charles. He can walk away from this incident or he can carry it like a hunchback wherever he goes. His fetters fall or he clings more tightly to them.

CHAPTER 40

At the wall locker shrine, Tommy Wiznak lights a votive candle, and places a shot glass full of water and a tiny wedge of pound cake at the feet of Saint Expedite. He thanks the Saint for sparing the lives of the people involved in the near mid-air collision that recently occurred, and asks him to continue to keep the controllers ever vigilant, so that God's Will may be done through them. Then Tommy lifts the statuette and places a lottery ticket underneath the Saint's pedestal. Tommy blesses himself, extinguishes the candle and locks the door on the Saint's home, lest the devil enter to strangle the Patron Saint of sailors, whores, and air traffic controllers. After walking a few steps away, Tommy returns to double check that the locker door is tightly secured.

"Zeke was talking about you the other night." Maria reaches up and straightens the collar on Doherty's shirt. Without replying to what she said, his facial expression tells her he needs to know more.

"He was talking on the phone to someone at NATCA. He said as far as he knows, you're a scab and a scumbag that can't be trusted. They think you're on some kind of twisted mission to report errors by union members, trying to destroy confidence in the union." With Maria this close, Doherty is distracted. He wants to bask in her beauty, become intoxicated by it. He wonders if she really knows how attractive she is, how dangerous it is for a man to let his guard down, to hand her his heart. He quickly answers his own question.

Damned right, she knows.

"Did you tell Zeke you're rather fond of me?"

“Christ, Willie! If he had a clue about what was going on, especially with YOU…he'd go absolutely postal. I'd have to shoot him in self defense.” The tin man smiles at Maria and she returns the look in her own way.

“You have the most beautiful eyes I've ever seen on a man. I know women who wished their eyes looked like yours.” Doherty has heard about his eyes from women before.

“They're only beautiful when you are reflected in them, Maria.”

“That line sounds a little too practiced, but I like it.” The conversation turns from eyes to skies. “What happened at the tower the other night? Zeke mentioned some guy named Charles.” Doherty is surprised that the news of a deal at Newark Tower has reached other facilities. It verifies the seriousness of the event. And since Maria rarely talks about tower issues with the tin man, the fact that she would ask about this incident is even more telling. He fills her in.

“Two Continental jets nearly smacked in mid air over Exit 13A of the New Jersey Turnpike. One was departing and the other was making an overhead approach to runway Two Nine. The Local Controller didn't save any airspace between them. I didn't see it, but one of our girls got sick over it, so it must have been real close.”

She got sick? You mean physically sick?”

“Yep. She gave it up… all over the steps and the floor near the ladies room.”

“Jesus, Willie. How does something like that happen? How do two airplanes come…I mean…get that close…right in front of the tower?”

Doherty thinks about the question. It's a good question, and it deserves a thoughtful response. A pause ensues.

“Pilots and controllers are *human,* Maria, and the answer lies therein. Humans make mistakes. As a controller, you just don't want to be there when it happens." The tin man pauses again. Maria waits patiently. She knows there is more to come.

"Think about the nature of this game that controllers play. Air traffic control is the one game that no one ever wins. You can only keep from losing and losing big. You can lose your job, you can lose your freedom and possessions, but most of all you can lose your sanity. Just imagine trying to live with the kind of guilt and shame associated with causing the deaths of hundreds of innocent persons." Doherty pulls a fifth of Jameson's from a locker. Maria watches Doherty and remains silent. She wants the tin man to keep talking.

"You know, you're working that traffic in that tower, and everything is routine. But it's like the goddamn devil himself is standing in the shadows, constantly watching…waiting…looking for you to miss something…forget something, so he can pounce on you and suck the life out of you…and the game goes on…twenty four hours a day, every day…at airports all over the world. Think about it, Maria. You're like a goaltender making the routine save after routine save, but in this game you can NEVER, EVER, let one in. Sure, there's a margin for error, but you never know what it is, so you cannot make an error. Do you think Charles didn't feel the devil jump on his goddamned back and scream in his ear? If he didn't, he's more retarded than I thought he was." Maria pours two Irish over rocks and hands one to the tin man. Doherty continues. "You know…Eisenhower…before the D-Day invasion…he screwed the pooch. He had the troops make a practice run in very bad weather. Six hundred men died. We lost a bunch of ships to German U-boats. I'm sure that Ike thought about those boys every day until he died, but the dead weren't totally innocent. They knew the risks going in. They were soldiers in a war, and shit happens in war. Airline passengers are innocent persons just trying to get to some place for whatever reasons they have, business; vacation; visiting some animated rat in Florida. They don't expect to die, and they don't believe they are taking any big risk. Do you think they would wear those stupid Mickey Mouse ears if they thought they were going to die?" Maria interjects something.

"Jimmy…Zeke… thinks you're a racist, and maybe that's why you want that guy Charles to take a fall." Doherty looks directly at Maria while sipping the Irish. "That's rich! The same guy that called you a nigger lover…he's calling ME a racist? You mean *that* guy?"

Maria looks up through the companionway at the World Trade Towers. "The towers look so close on a clear night like tonight." The tin man waits for Maria to face him before speaking again. When she does, he moves in close.

"You're going home to him tonight. I'll be alone and you'll be with him, sleeping with him. You say that you love me. That means you *don't* love him. If these things are true, you will stay here with me. You don't ever have to cross the river again. There's the phone, Maria. Call him and tell him you're not coming home." A tear runs down Maria's cheek. Doherty reaches out to squeeze Maria's arms near her shoulders. "Don't do it to me, Maria. Don't do what I think you're going to do. If I lose you, I will never be the same. I'll be a dead man walking and talking." Maria looks long and hard at the tin man, then pulls away and gathers her things.

"I have to go." Doherty watches her leave, her black trench coat trailing in the wind, she disappears down the finger dock. After removing his shirt he presses a cassette home, sinks back into the starboard settee and knocks back the last of the Jameson's. The Jesters start their mournful, spooky tune of love lost and memories that return from time to time…on the wind.

Ooooohwind, wind… blow-oh-oh-oh wind, wind
When a cool summer breeze
Sends a chill down my spine
Then I long for my love deep within

I know she has gone
But my love lingers on
In a dream that the wind brings to me

Five days have passed since the Charles Clemons nearly made a connecting flight out of two Continental jets in the sky over Elizabeth. That Charles is still working, and was never decertified, even briefly, is proof that the FAA has decided to cover up the mistake. Out of respect for his friend, Doherty wants to warn Paul Veale that he is about to blow the lid off the whole thing. He decides against giving any warnings.

Veale's a big boy...and he knows my position on these things. If this deal gets reviewed by folks that draw more water than the FAA, well so be it. Somebody's going to get hurt, but Veale is fairly safe. He's just doing his union rep thing. He may end up looking stupid, but that comes with the territory...it's time to make the call.

The air traffic manager gets a call two days later at home. The tower and the Eastern Region go into a full investigation mode. Tapes are ordered to be pulled, transcribed, and saved. Narrative statements are placed under lock and key and schedules are changed to make witnesses available for as long as the National Transportation Safety Board needs them. Along with the NTSB, Doherty has notified every one of his news media contacts including a friend who does talk radio on a small station in Plainfield, New Jersey. The word *cover-up* is being heard, and that is the one word that scares the average FAA manager. Doherty knows that when the dust settles, the FAA will be coming for him. They won't really care what happened and why. They won't care to implement any changes to procedure or training methods that will prevent a future occurrence and save lives. In the end, they care only that someone threatened their authority and their ability to extract money from the public while providing nothing substantial in return. Thinking back to his Marine Corps days, he compares the two organizations in his mind. The FAA's culture of corruption and cowardice stands in stark contrast to the Marine Corps' method of operating, and the standards they instill and strive for on a daily basis. Sure, Marines are subject to human failing, but they are held accountable. Some can hide behind their rank and "skate" for a while, but the Marine Corps has a way of catching up to them. When that happens, Leatherneck slack fetches up hard. Doherty gazes at a document framed and mounted on the cabin bulkhead.

To all who shall see these presents, greeting:

Know Ye, that reposing special trust and confidence in the fidelity and abilities of LIAM ALOYSIUS DOHERTY 2747290/6712, I do appoint him a CORPORAL in the

UNITED STATES MARINE CORPS

To rank as such from the first day of February, nineteen hundred and seventy four.

This appointee will therefore carefully and diligently discharge the duties of the grade to which appointed by doing and performing all manner of things thereunto pertaining. And I do strictly charge and require all personnel of lesser grade to render obedience to appropriate orders. And this appointee is to observe and follow such orders and directions as may be given from time to time by Superiors acting according to the rules and articles governing the discipline of the Armed Forces of the United States of America.

Given under my hand at MABS-14, MAG-14, 2ndMAW, FMFLANT, MCAS Cherry Point, N.C. this sixth day of February, in the year of our Lord nineteen hundred and seventy four.

D. M. GRIFFIN, Major, USMC

Commanding

Gordon Russo is the first controller to be interviewed by the NTSB. They ask him if he knows the rules concerning the application of visual separation by controllers. Russo explains the rules nearly verbatim from the book. The crucial part of the rule, the one that Charles and FAA management failed to consider, mandates that some other standard separation must exist before visual separation can be applied. This means that if two aircraft are maintaining altitudes that preclude them from coming too close, a controller can visually reduce that separation. But, standard rule book separation must exist first.

The NTSB investigators are impressed with Russo's grasp of the order. They ask him if he had read the rule recently. He smartly and candidly replies:

"I knew you guys would be asking me about it today, so I brushed up on the rules last night."

The G-man is the only FAA employee interviewed, that is willing to tell the truth about the Charles incident. Since the FAA was caught NOT reporting an incident within the time frame allowed, they are forced to cling tightly to their story that nothing happened, lest they admit rank incompetence, or a criminal cover up. There are no other possibilities. The FAA supervisors and managers told Charles to claim the visual separation excuse, and now they desperately need him to maintain that false alibi. Should Charles get off the reservation, should he tell the truth, the FAA would take a serious hit. Managers and supervisors might even be demoted or fired. It is conceivable that someone could be charged with a crime. Shit would start rolling downhill and much needed change would occur. In three weeks not an hour has gone by that Charles has not been coached by an FAA manager about the need for him to maintain his story, to stay on board their perjury train.

In his mind, Doherty envisions Charles turning the tables on the FAA. He sees Charles testifying before the NTSB investigators. He sees Charles demanding his civil rights, not by marching or beating drums or any other comical collectivist exercise. He does it by standing there alone, with no support but his own mind, his own integrity and his willingness to tell the truth. And what better collaborator can one have but the truth? Charles tells the NTSB that FAA managers told him to lie and that he is refusing to go along with their plan. He apologizes for the momentary lack of vigilance that caused such a serious near collision and he accepts whatever corrective action is deemed necessary, because it is more important that the system be corrected, than for one controller to escape a little embarrassment. Then he walks out from the shadowed world that the FAA has created for him, and into the sunlight. Free at last. Now, when Charles sees Doherty, there is no anger, fear or hatred because Charles no longer cares for the opinions of others. All that matters is what he thinks about himself. Charles cancels his membership in the "black community." They needed him far more than Charles needed them. He has tossed that millstone away. Free at last.

But reality settles in again; Doherty stops daydreaming. Charles will not save himself, he can't see the way out. He believes himself to be inferior and therefore, he is. Doherty wonders if anyone else sees the connection between things like transportation accidents and the personal human tragedy of collectivist thinking.

When humans huddle together in fear, instead of asserting their independence and individuality, they invite their own demise, and move closer to it. History is replete with examples. That's bad enough for one person, but in the air traffic control world, others can get killed…and a lot of them.

CHAPTER 41

Two ex military controllers are talking shop during their evening meal period at the tower. Russo says to Doherty:

"Where's the pride, Willie?"

"What do you mean?"

"I mean…remember when you spent hours picking Irish pennants off your uniform with a pair of tweezers because you wanted to look sharp? Remember practicing your hand salute in a mirror, until you were satisfied that it was perfect?" Doherty nods, Russo continures. "Compare that to the culture in this horseshit FAA. What do we have to be proud about? The only time anyone hears about us is when two airplanes smack like that time at Teterboro. Most controllers I know don't even tell people what they do for a living unless they have to." Doherty draws a stale cup of coffee from the tower pot.

"I know what you mean, G-Man. Remember evening colors? Some guys hated it. They called it "getting caught in the rain." You know, having to stop and face the music and salute. I liked it. Sometimes I would get myself squared away and walk down to Headquarters just to be there for it. And you know what, G-man? I looked good in uniform- that's no shit. I was what they called a "billboard" Marine. When I walked down the street, women would stop…and drop dead. I left a trail of female bodies everywhere I went. I wore dress blues to a wedding once, and the bride got pissed because everyone was looking at me." Russo chuckles and shakes his head slowly.

"Willie, you need to do something about that low self esteem." Doherty smiles. He's exaggerating…but not much. He thinks about

Russo's remarks concerning pride and examines his personal FAA experience.

"You know what, G-Man? I can remember my proudest moment in the FAA." Doherty takes a sip of coffee and pauses for effect, causing Russo some annoyance.

"Okay, are you gonna tell me, or just sit there grinning like a goddamned chink?"

Doherty nods at his co-worker.

"One day FAA management was surveying the area, checking all their human resources like they do from time to time, looking for another supervisor to groom, someone to do their dirty work. That's when they gazed upon me. They took a good, long look and then someone said, *"He's not one of us."* Now THAT…was my proudest moment in the FAA.

Russo's eyes narrow. He nods knowingly. The same thing surely happened to him. He just doesn't remember when.

At Karl's Tavern in Elizabeth, some tin men gather for another "Midnight Mass." Karl's features some genuine German beers and cuisine, and an elderly, white haired German bartender named Werner who always wears a big smile and a black cummerbund with a white shirt and no jacket. Werner speaks with a German accent. He is jokingly rumored to be an ex-Nazi hiding from his past. In order to keep the controversy alive, Werner is intentionally vague about his past, saying that he arrived in the U.S. "after the war." He is not offended in the least by an occasional "Achtung!" from a thirsty tin man in need of a refill. Occasionally, he will pull out a copy of Mein Kampf when it is needed, and he will swear upon it, right hand raised, as if it were the bible, to prove his veracity about certain statements he may make from time to time.

This night Werner introduces the tin men to Jagermeister, a green colored German Liqueur. He sets up four ornamental shot glasses and fills each one. The drinks are on the house. As the tin men down the drinks, Werner translates the German writing on the label which features a dear carrying a Cross in its antlers.

It is the hunter's honor that he protects and preserves his game, hunts sportsmanlike, honors the Creator in his creatures.

After a second round is poured, Ray Martino of Brooklyn leans in and beckons to Werner to come and answer a question about the secret ingredients of the strange green elixir. Since Martino is drunk, he believes he is whispering, but in fact, he is speaking loud enough to wake up the dead in nearby Rosedale Cemetery.

"Hey Werner! C'mere! Listen! Shhhh! Hey! How many Jews does it take to make a bottle of this stuff?" The bartender purses his lips, raises one eyebrow and looks directly into Martino's eyes at point blank range.

"About fifty."

The next afternoon Tommy Wiznak is working Ground Control during a period of light to moderate traffic. Three taxiing airliners are making their way toward Runway Two Two Right on the parallel taxiway. Inside their cockpits, the crews are going through their pre-departure checklists. Tommy has his back to the ground traffic and he's talking to one of the girls working Flight Data at the rear console. Suddenly Tommy feels a cold chill and he shivers. He wonders about the sudden chill and thinks to check the thermostat. Then it happens. The hair stands up on Tommy's neck. A burst of panic hits him as if a bolt of lightning shot up from the floor, entered his ass and exited his throat. The tin man quickly wheels about and checks his traffic. Three outbound airliners are proceeding on the parallel taxiway with a Delta Boeing 727 in the lead followed smartly by two United 737's. A quick look at the radar shows a landing jet on a one mile final for the inboard runway. The superstitious controller checks his active strip board and counts to three. The panic has now subsided and Tommy is breathing almost normally. But he knows something is amiss, something is out of kilter…not right.

Someone or something is here that can't be seen…but I felt it. I can still feel it. It's still here! It's coming for us!

The former altar boy looks down at three flight strips in their plastic holders sitting on the console. The count is still three. Nothing complicated…in fact, it's routine…slow.

All present or accounted for…ducks in a row…but something's going on here…something is not right…

Tommy drums the console with the fingers of his left hand and scans the airport operating area. Then he checks one of the radar scopes hanging from the overhead, thinking that perhaps the final approach controller forgot to turn someone onto the localizer and left him streaking across the final and into LaGuardia's airspace. Finding nothing out of sorts, he returns his focus to the taxiing Delta jet. For some reason his eyes are drawn to the airplane and its rolling nose wheels as it approaches taxiway Golf at mid-field.

Don't do it Delta. Don't…

Suddenly the Boeing "Seven Two" turns sharply right and starts to cross the active runway at midfield with the landing jet on very short final, about to touch down. Tommy slaps the Local Controller on the arm to get his attention and points at the Delta jet. At the same instant he keys his mike hard. "DELTA ONE EIGHTY EIGHT, STOP! HOLD SHORT OF THE RUNWAY! DELTA ONE EIGHTY EIGHT, STOP! HOLD SHORT! HOLD SHORT!

Delta does stop. But he's well onto the runway and the Local Controller has already sent the landing jet around. A People Express 737 sucks up the wheels and flies over the Delta jet missing him by a few feet. Tommy's warning to the Local Controller was just in time to avert a disaster. Without thinking about it, Tommy has already blessed himself five times with the mike still keyed in his right hand. When he recovers, he gives Delta a right turn on the active runway to get back in line on the parallel taxiway. Delta is now sequenced number three behind the two United jets. It's a small penalty to pay for scaring the living shit out of everyone in the tower, not to mention the crew aboard the People Express jet now circling over Bayonne for another try at Runway Two Two Right. An unidentified voice on the tower frequency has some unsolicited friendly advice for the Delta crew: *"Hey Delta! Why don't you get your head out-a-yer- ass?"*

On his break, and for the next three days, Tommy pays homage to Saint Expedite, thanking the patron saint of air traffic controllers for sending the telepathic warning that spared the lives of the airline passengers and crews and preserved the sanity and reputations of the controller team and air crews involved. He thanks Saint "E" for foiling the devil's plans and banishing that evil, yellow-eyed bastard from the tower cab. He picks up the leather pouch holding his mojo. Tommy will not alter the contents of the pouch in any way until his luck turns. Right now, Tommy is convinced that his mojo is working.

Tommy doesn't know it, but his nemesis has been forced back into his familiar hiding place. He's hunkered down on the tower catwalk, sitting on the damp concrete. The devil smiles and nods, breathing in through his reptilian nostrils. The devil likes the cold, sulphur and benzene saturated, North Jersey, oil refinery air. It's exactly what hell would smell like, if someone turned off the pilot light.

CHAPTER 42

When Tommy finally does change his "hand," he respectfully removes Saint Expedite and all other locker contents. He carefully cuts a rectangle of red velvet material and fits it into the locker giving Saint Expedite some brand new wall-to-wall carpeting. He replaces the contents in the reverse order, ensuring that the statuette of Saint Expedite is the last to leave and the first to return. Tommy then removes the leather pouch from his ditty bag. Pouring the contents of his mojo onto the break room table, Tommy scatters the sundry items. The controller-spectators get a rare look at the contents that include antique cuff links, a joker from a worn out deck of playing cards, a broken piece of an old rosary, a lead fishing sinker, a skeleton key, a dry wishbone and a New York City subway token. After concentrating for a full thirty seconds, he removes a pair of white dice with black pips and replaces them with a red pair of dice with white pips. Tommy has now officially changed his mojo hand. Beans Larkin has been watching the tabletop ceremony, head bowed and hands clasped, extending to Tommy a measure of respect and solemn dignity. A new guy named Vinny watches Tommy's actions with curiosity and when Tommy leaves he asks for an explanation from Larkin.

"What the fuck was *that* all about?"

The tin man from Boston casually explains:

"Tommy knows what a lot of controllers know, but very few ever talk about. He understands that "deals" come in threes and he's trying to break up the karma…stop something bad from happening. I don't blame him. Many people do the same thing, just in different ways, for their own reasons. Mother Theresa prays for world peace, clicking away at her rosary beads. American Indians might do a rain dance, kicking up prairie dust with their moccasins. Cannibals in the Congo beat their drums all day to ward off the evil spirits. Tommy relies on his lucky mojo, among other things. Is he being ridiculous? I don't think so, Vinny. Around here, in this control tower, in this fucking FAA, you need to believe in something… you need to love something, or you need to hate something. If you don't, you will surely lose your mind."

Manuel Mercado is a naturalized U.S. citizen who is constantly extolling the virtues of his former home, the Dominican Republic. He will describe in glorious detail the colors and textures and the natural beauty of the fauna and flora, the white sand beaches, the beautiful palm trees and the quality of the people that inhabit his home island. And he always talks of the women, the women, the women. The most beautiful women that God ever created and they walk the luscious palm groves and beaches of God's secret paradise – the Caribbean island utopia that is the Dominican Republic. When Manny is not talking about Dominican women, he's usually talking about Dominican major league baseball players. He ticks off their batting averages and other stats as if they were all his own kids. His favorite bit of baseball lore concerns three brothers once playing in the same outfield for the San Francisco Giants: Felipe, Matty and Jesus Alou- Dominicans, the lot. Though Manny Mercado is a one man, tourism promoter for his homeland and favorite Caribbean island, he always fails to mention that one side of the same island is Haiti – the most God forsaken, destitute point on the globe, where people have been known to eat dirt. Manny also forgets to mention the abject poverty that resides just beyond the tourist dependent beaches and hotels of the Dominican Republic, where thirty percent of the people live below the poverty line.

It is early on a Monday morning watch. Manny is five minutes into his tedious and predictable Dominican Republic sales pitch. Liam Doherty, weary of the essay he has heard a hundred times, decides to jack him up a bit.

"You know, Manny, I've never been to the Dominican Republic, but my Marine Corps went down there in '65. I wasn't there, but I've heard all the sea stories, and here's the straight skinny. We drank all the beer and raped all the women. Then we took a giant shit on the place and shoved off for home."

Manny Mercado's mouth is agape as if he is presenting his gold fillings for inspection. Gasps of air escape from his rum hole, and when he recovers, it is clear that he takes umbrage with Doherty's unique historical perspective concerning his beloved birthplace. However, most of what Manny says is in Spanish and although Doherty is being cussed at, he cannot translate much of what he hears. So Doherty simply smiles and says, "Thank you Manny." And Manuel replies in English:

"F-F-F-uck you, Guillermo!"

A week later, Doherty is reaching across the air traffic manager's big desk receiving another manila envelope containing another ten-day suspension. This time for being racially insensitive toward a minority member of Newark Tower's air traffic control team. Doherty is further warned by the tower manager that another infraction of any work rule could result in his removal from government service.

Using the time off, Doherty hauls *Tipitina* to scrape and paint her bottom. While working on the sloop, he ponders taking a second job. Not because he needs the money, but because he gets so much time off from his FAA position, he could do something else in his "spare" time.

Meanwhile, Manny Mercado reports Liam A. Doherty to the Black and Hispanic Controller's coalition, and they send a letter to the Secretary of Transportation complaining about the "racist" comments and the "threatening" and "insulting" words that one of their members had been subjected to at the hands of Newark Tower management. Their letter further states that a ten-day suspension is a mere slap on the wrist and that Doherty should be fired, and for that matter, the tower manager should be removed for tacitly approving Doherty's behavior by responding in such a lenient manner. The letter also points out that Biderman has virtually guaranteed future racial incidents by demonstrating the FAA's tolerance toward such behavior.

A copy of the letter is sent to Doherty. He has it framed in a stand-up picture frame. The framed letter gets displayed at the break room table whenever he is taking a meal. No member of the Black and Hispanic Coaliton will eat at the same table with Doherty. When Doherty sits down at the break room table, black and Hispanic controllers get up and leave, preferring to take their meals in their cars or in the conference room, rather than break bread with a racist, sexist, non-union, homophobe.

One day, a lean and muscular black controller named Thaddeus Jamison confronts Doherty in the break room. Sitting across from Doherty, his intent is to intimidate the tin man, something very few ever try.

"I don't like what you said to Manny."

Doherty makes direct eye contact, but says nothing. Jamison speaks again.

"I don't like…YOU."

Jamison extends an index finger at Doherty's face. Doherty does not react. Jamison escalates the rhetoric, crossing a line.

"I ought to kick your cracker ass."

Doherty had been anticipating this. He didn't know who would do it, but he was certain it would eventually happen. Now he replies.

"What you think of me, is none of my business. I don't expect you to understand that, Thaddeus, because if you're stupid enough to threaten me while being tape recorded, you're probably incapable of grasping any basic psychological concepts."

Doherty pulls a small voice recorder from his pocket and places it on the table. Jamison is dumbstruck. He's been painted into a corner of silence. Nothing he can think to say, can be said with a tape recorder on the table. He stares at the voice-activated device with its little red blinking light. It seems to be mocking him. After a long and very awkward pause, the Pope of Newark Tower speaks.

"We wish to be alone."

Jamison gets up from the table and takes his leave.

At a "Midnight Mass," two Newark Tower tin men are schmoozing some flight attendants at the bar in Karl's Tavern. Ray Martino takes up his position at the other end of the bar as a signal to Beans Larkin to start a well practiced ruse. Larkin is telling the two amicable flight attendants about the physical attributes of a typical control tower operator.

"First, you need good lamps. I mean REALLY sharp eyes, better than twenty/twenty. You need eyes like a red-tailed hawk on steroids. Here, I'll show you. See this print? Larkin picks up a Budweiser bottle and points to the small print on the front, "ribbon" part of the beer label.

"Can you read it? The girls squint at the label.

"Well, yea…but just barely." Larkin nods, then looks down the bar at his partner in crime. "Watch this. Hey! M-O! Can you read this?" The tin man holds the bottle high in one hand, pointed toward Ray Martino about twenty five feet away. Martino squints as if actually straining to read the tiny print. In reality, he has the advertising essay memorized.

"This…is…the…famous…Budweiser beer…we know of…no brand…produced by any other brewer which…costs so much to brew and age. (Martino stops here and cocks his head as if straining to see the words.) Our…exclusive…beech-wood aging…produces a taste, a smoothness and a drinkability…you will…find…in no other…beer…at any…price."

The two flight attendants patiently wait for Martino to finish, and then, along with the other patrons at the bar, they applaud his fine acting job.

When Tommy Wiznak checks his mailbox, he finds a 45rpm record in a heavy green paper sleeve. After hearing about Tommy's incredible save and the strange circumstances that made it possible, it only seemed appropriate that Doherty should add something to Tommy's mojo. So the tin man unloaded his extra copy of "I Put a Spell on You" by Screamin' Jay Hawkins, a 1956 original on the Okeh label. A 45 rpm record is an item that has a certain "old school" character that makes it eligible for inclusion into Tommy's arsenal of mojo items. When Tommy sees Doherty in the parking lot he stops and thanks his co-worker for the thoughtful gift.

"Hey Willie, Thanks for the record, man."

"You're welcome, Tommy. Say a prayer for me, will you."

"I sure will."

The record goes into the wall locker shrine behind the statuette of Saint Expedite. Another candle is lit, a prayer is recited and a slice of pound cake is left at the feet of Saint Expedite, along with a shot glass full of water to wash it down.

CHAPTER 43

Occasionally, a tour of the control tower is granted to one of the local schools as part of a day trip, or a career information tour or some similar academic endeavor. The FAA has produced a public relations film that all facilities keep on hand to help spread the FAA's message of professionalism and the promotion of aviation and diversity, and not necessarily in that order. Since space is limited in the tower cab, and extra bodies create a visibility issue for the controllers, the school groups are divided into manageable numbers and those groups get a short visit and a quick introduction to the tower functions, after viewing the propaganda film.

On Tuesday morning, a group of girls from The Ursuline School and their basketball team are in the conference room watching the FAA movie. The students are traveling from their home in New Rochelle, New York to visit New Orleans. Liam Doherty is in the break room and Alan "two ties" Mealey enters.

"Hey Willie, can you bring some girls up to the cab and give them a tour of the facility?"

Doherty looks up at Alan Mealey. Every time he sees Mealey, Doherty gets the same queezy feeling in the pit of his gut. The glow on Mealey's face says that he is a true believer, a religious zealot, whose religion is government. He believes in the government, he believes in the FAA's mission, and he believes in the veracity of his superiors and their golden goodness. He has swallowed so much of the FAA's Kool-Aid, his head is starting to look like one of those smiley-faced pitchers of the popular sweetened and artificially flavored kiddy water. The tin man answers the "yes" man.

"Sure, Alan, why not? Any of 'em got tits yet?"

"C'mon, Willie, be nice. They're Catholics, like you. They're from New York…going to visit New Orleans. One of their teachers is friends with John Biderman." Doherty feigns surprise with his mouth wide.

"Wow. No shit? John Biderman himself? That teacher must be very proud. You want me to come get 'em?"

"In about ten minutes. They're still watching the movie. Hang out here and I'll call you when the movie's over. Doherty nods, and takes a sip of coffee; his forearm and elbow are parallel to the deck.

"Okay, Alan. You know, I never saw the movie. How does it end? Is there a surprise finish…like with the crew and passengers all screaming because the airplane is diving into a corn field like a frigging lawn dart?" Alan Mealey laughs and shakes his head from side to side while walking away.

"Funny. You're a funny guy, Willie."

In the tower cab, Doherty waits while the last of the group of girls reaches the top step before he starts his spiel. He keeps the talk very basic, elementary, and brief.

"This is a control tower. It is one of three types of facilities used in air traffic control. In the tower, the controllers are concerned with airplanes that are approaching the airport to land; are landing or taking off on the runways, or they are taxiing to and from the runways from their gates or their parking places." Doherty points to one of the three women working the front line. He notices that management has pandered to the Ursuline girls by loading the operating positions with females.

"Judy is working the TCA radar position. She is making sure that helicopters and other small aircraft that need to pass through the area around the airport do not get too close to the airplanes that are landing or departing." Pointing toward "virgin" Mary, he continues.

"Mary is the Local Controller. Nobody can use the runways without her permission. She clears the arriving airplanes to land and the departures for take off." Nodding toward the female on the right end, Doherty identifies her duties. "Susan is the Ground Controller. She controls all of the airplanes on the ground and makes sure that no vehicles or airplanes cross the runways without a clearance. All of the controllers work closely with each other and they talk to each other about the airplanes. That's called coordinating. To help them coordinate, Jimmy is standing behind Mary. He's called the Local Coordinator. Are there any questions?" A very tall girl speaks.

"Is this a good job for a girl?"

Instantly, the three females working on the front line snap rearward in unison, as if their heads are wired together like the slats on a Venetian blind. Two of the female faces show concern, bordering on panic at the thought of Liam A. Doherty answering such a question in front of a group of young impressionable females. "virgin" Mary's face has tightened into a look of anger and defiance- a sort of, *go ahead…I DARE YOU TO SAY IT,* kind of look.

For a long moment in the tower cab, time is virtually standing still. The words, *"Is this a good job for a girl?"* are hanging in mid air, and big, like the Goodyear blimp. Doherty decides to milk it. He pauses for a good three seconds and smiles at the broad-asses working the front line.

"Well, let's see…that's a very good question."

Mary, now with her back to the runways takes a step closer to Doherty. To do so she puts a hand on Jimmy's shoulder and shoves him aside like a defensive end rushing past an offensive lineman. Jimmy nearly loses his balance and gives way to the stocky bull dyke. Doherty glances from one female controller to the other. Cocking his head slightly, and grinning, causing a dimple to appear just below his left eye. For a moment, Doherty has "virgin" Mary and the other feminists over a barrel. Certainly, Doherty can offer his experienced opinion about females in traditionally male occupations. He can also opine about female controllers. As long as he identifies his answer as "opinion", he can say whatever he wishes. There is no standard operating procedure covering tours for visitors. Doherty turns to address the tall schoolgirl. The moment of truth has arrived. After teasing the female controllers long enough, he will now answer the question.

"This is a GREAT job for a female, and I'll tell you why. Air traffic control does not require any great upper body strength." Doherty makes an iron pumping motion with both arms curling imaginary dumbbells. He grabs a headset and hands it to one of the girls. "Here put this on, and key the mike …like this. You see, you already have all the tools you need. Controllers rely on their brains and their ability to communicate effectively. Big muscles are of no use in a control tower. Think about it. Not one of you girls could beat Mike Tyson in a boxing ring. But in this ring...this control tower, who has a better chance of being a successful air traffic controller…YOU or Mike Tyson? So the question is…Is this a good job for a girl? And the answer…this is a GREAT job for a girl."

After a pause, "virgin" Mary and her two girlfriends turn their attention back to their air traffic control duties, somewhat content with Doherty's reply to the students. Mary is not satisfied. She thinks Doherty's answer was sexist. Virgin Mary believes that women are as physically capable as any man, and has said so on many occasions. Doherty thinks about what he has just told the schoolgirls.

Yea, this is a good job for a girl. Now the question becomes- Is this a good job for a man? Or is it more suited to pussies? Maybe that's why this FAA attracts so many spineless jelly fish, toady yes men, conflicted cross dressers and pencil necks… cake boys who were raised by their grandmothers. Boys more suited for work as interior decorators or flight attendants. Boys who never fired a shot in anger, or pulled the pin on a live hand grenade, or shouldered a pack while humping through the boonies, or stood a guard post, or laced up a pair of boxing gloves, or slid head first into third base, or disassembled a .45 automatic and put it back together…blindfolded. Men who never mixed it up in a fist-fight where the outcome was in doubt, or worse yet, knowing you will lose.

This is the job I was born to do, and somehow, I don't belong here. I'm the squarest peg being hammered into the roundest of holes. Maybe I should have stayed in the Marine Corps and died in a combat zone surrounded by people of character. But here I am in this chicken-shit, faggot infested FAA. And as long as I'm plugged in to an operating control position, I can claim some measure of self respect… doing this job like only I know how to do it…the way it was designed to be done, and more…taking it to a higher level. But then, I look around and what do I see? Except for a few dependable tin men, I'm lashed up to a mindless herd of pathetic, comatose shit-hooks. I can't change them. Even if it was possible, the FAA wouldn't stand for it… and I certainly won't let them change me. I don't know where this is going, but it's certainly not going to end well.

CHAPTER 44

In a store on Garrett Road in Upper Darby, a legendary record collector and dealer sits behind four huge rolodex files and stacks of 45 rpm records scattered about in their paper sleeves. Behind the desk and in the floors above are four million 7 inch vinyl discs, forgotten 45's, sitting like old girlfriends, waiting for the call from someone who remembers, wallflowers waiting for another dance. It's Saturday morning and the British freaks will be arriving soon. They come from London Heathrow through Philadelphia airport and take a fifty dollar cab ride to Val Shively's record store. When they board the return flight they'll be toting copies of Joe Tex on Dial or Solomon Burke on Apollo or some unheralded Harvey Scales or Willie Tee recording, Sixties soul music obscurities long forgotten by most of the world, but now sought after voraciously by a subculture of Brits for some reason known but to them. Such is the strange world of record collecting; it's an addiction that attracts odd-ball fetishists of every conceivable stripe. Sooner or later, they all end up at Val Shively's R&B Records in Upper Darby.

Val looks up at a walk in customer. Standing in the cramped confines of Shively's store foyer, the shopper gawks at dusty posters, glossy publicity photos of old R&B vocal groups and 45 rpm records stacked long deep and wide on two by four shelves forming narrow aisles of old vinyl records from floor to ceiling. A sign posted near the door says, New Records, $2 each - Three for $7.

"Can I help you?'

The customer, a twenty something white man in a blue, button down poplin short sleeve shirt and penny loafers is looking up and around like a tourist would, in say, the Capitol Rotunda or Grand

Central Station. He looks like a student from Penn or Drexel who braved the subway ride through wild, West Philly.

"Do you sell …*oldies?*"

Apparently, the preppy walk-in customer has no genuine clue about his location. He has just wandered into a veritable shrine to vintage vinyl recordings – a vast repository of Doo Wop, Soul Music, Rockabilly and sub-genres like Carolina Beach Music. The lost yuppie is standing in the only place on the planet where one can ask for the Five Keys on Aladdin, or the Solitaires on Old Town, and not get a blank stare for his effort. Now, he's asking if anyone has seen any…*oldies.* Without hesitation, Val deadpans. "Oh, yea. I got *At the Hop and Rock Around the Clock.* Which one do you want?"

Before the customer can reply the phone rings.

"Hello, records." Tiger pads over to get some attention from the walk-in customer, but he's busy examining a political cartoon pinned up to a wooden post. In the cartoon, an 8-track tape cartridge is protruding from a slot in the side of Richard Nixon's head. The preppy tourist steps over the store's cat and walks out while Shively is checking the condition of a 45rpm record. It's the store's only copy of "Flat Foot Sam" by Oscar Wills on Argo. Holding the disc up in the air between a thumb and middle finger he looks across the surface, and then reports to the phone customer.

"It's dished and seriously juked, and it's got some writing on the A-side label. Somebody named Fenton autographed it. I'd fling it across the street, but it might come back like a fucking boomerang and damage something of value. You still want it- I'll throw it in for ten bucks."

Outside at the curb some Brits are climbing out of a taxi. When they enter, "Flat Foot Sam" is getting a test spin on the store's vintage turntable, salvaged from an old radio station in Camden.

Flat Foot Sam, got him a job
The very same day, the place got robbed
The cats got away, and couldn't be found
They fingered old Sam and they carried him down

CHAPTER 45

On the midnight shift Patricia asks Doherty about his habit of wearing the same "uniform" to work every day.

"Willie, why do you wear khaki trousers and a white shirt every day? You must know that people see that as being…well…*odd*. Don't you get the urge to wear something else once in a while. You know…variety is the spice of life…or so they say." Doherty smiles. A long awaited moment has just arrived.

"You know, Patricia, I've been here about ten years, and you are the only person to ask me that question. I've known that someone would ask me about my wardrobe eventually; I never dreamed it would take this long. Now, suddenly, YOU ask me.

Patricia is stacking plastic strip holders on the console, like a house of cards. Doherty finds Patricia's activity more like something a man would do, but he says nothing about it to her. He takes a long look at her hands. Without looking at Doherty, Patricia speaks.

"They're afraid of you."

"They're afraid of me? Is that why they don't ask me questions? They don't want to know what makes me tick? Do you think they're afraid of me…or maybe they're afraid of the answers?

"I don't know, maybe both. You seem to like the fact that management, and others, are intimidated by you. The two controllers make eye contact.

"But you're not afraid of me?"

"No. You remind me of my brothers, and you helped me a lot on Ground Control. I almost didn't make it, remember?" Doherty nods and smiles. He remembers the time that Patricia tied the ramps and taxiways up in knots, coming dangerously close to grid-locking the entire airport. Instead of taking the frequency from her, Doherty forced her to extricate herself from the messy traffic situation. Making her realize that she could overcome the problem was a real confidence booster. She never looked back after that training session.

"So what's with the… uniform?"

"It's not complicated. I like trousers that hold starch, and khaki works better than other materials. I take them to a special dry cleaner near Gramercy Park in Manhattan. They specialize in starching garments for the theatre industry. They probably think I'm queer. The white shirts I copied from a guy named "Mope" MacNamara. He was a friend of my dad's, a real pool shark. He wore long sleeves and a tie in the winter and short sleeves in the summer, but always white. So I thought, why not? It simplifies things; no wardrobe decisions to make, just put the same thing on every day. Khaki on the bottom and white on the top; if I need to dress up, I put on a blue blazer. Besides, if I tried to color coordinate my dress I'd come in here clashing like a bad trip." Patricia sweeps the stack of plastic strip holders into a cardboard box.

"So you're not trying to intimidate anyone or make some kind of an anti-establishment statement by dressing like that?"

"No, Patty, if I'm making a statement at all, it's this: I dress to please ME, not those around me. I don't care what others think about me, or what they approve of. I live my life to please myself, to make myself happy. And hopefully, when it's all over, I'll die in my own arms." Patricia raises an eyebrow.

"Well that's something to look forward to."

Most visitors to Newark Tower are surprised at the lack of modern equipment and the overall rundown look of the tower cab. The working consoles lack any sense of streamlined continuity and give the appearance of having been made in three different parts of the world, from plans that were described over the phone to persons who don't speak English, and whose previous experience was fabricating a childhood tree fort. Access panels are missing some of their fastening screws and the rat's nests of wires underneath will sometimes start smoking and arcing. The carpeting is badly frayed and some of those tripping hazards are now covered with rubber mats. A few pencils are stuck in the asbestos ceiling panels, left there by bored midnight shift controllers. 1940's era telephone operator style headsets can still be jacked into the consoles, and a controller will sometimes use one of those ancient headsets to work live traffic. A rickety steel bookshelf sits at the top of the stairwell holding binders, FAA orders, menus from neighborhood takeout restaurants, and old telephone directories from six surrounding counties and Manhattan.

Alan Mealey appears in the tower cab to supervise the installation of some important emergency equipment. In the event of a major crash at the airport, local community fire and police personnel will be needed to augment the Port Authority's equipment. After all, with only fifty body bags on hand in Building Ten, and most airliners holding hundreds of passengers, well, even the FAA can do the math.

So Mealey and the telephone company employee have staked out a vacant spot on the bulkhead to mount three trim-line style telephones; one is white; one is powder blue and one a very stylish avocado. Their purpose is to contact the Newark City Fire Department, Newark City Police, and the Elizabeth Fire Department. Ray Martino is annoyed that the workers are obstructing his view of the taxiways.

"How long you gonna be there, Alan?"

"About thirty minutes, why?"

Martino doesn't answer the "why" question. That Mealey needs to ask it, is evidence of incompetence. Martino slides back to the northwest corner of the cab. He pours a cup of stale coffee, then returns to the Cab Coordinator position directly behind the Local Controller. The Telephone Guy drops to one knee and starts drilling holes in the bulkhead. When Mealey and his new friend finish mounting the telephones, they stand back to survey their work and congratulate each other on the fine job. Three Trim-line style phones standing by like soldiers, side by side in a space no larger than a breadbox.

"Looks good."

"Yea. Not bad for a government job."

Leaning back against the center console, Martino is flipping a six inch plastic strip holder and catching it with the same hand. He asks the question that someone was bound to ask.

"Hey Alan, why are the phones three different colors?" Alan's reply would make a great punch line, but like most FAA pogues, he is far too stupid to be funny – at least not intentionally. Mealey looks directly at Martino and says flatly: "So we can tell which one is ringing."

The controllers all exchange glances before laughter breaks out. Alan Mealey has absolutely no clue about why they are laughing. Shaking his head in bewilderment, Mealey follows the Telephone Company guy down the stairs and disappears for the remainder of the watch.

On her way into the building, Patricia notices two feral cats hanging out near the back door to the tower. The next day she opens two cans of cat food and leaves them by the door. On the same day a personal ad appears in the Newark Star-Ledger:

```
To Saint Expedite:
Thank you for your
timely intercession.
I endeavor to always
exalt thy name. T.W.
```

A copy of the ad appears on the bulletin board until someone complains to management that the posting promotes religion, specifically Catholicism. Management agrees and removes the ad. Tommy Wiznak and a few others condemn FAA management for the direct insult to Saint Expedite. Although Tin Man Tommy believes that the complaint came from his Jewish nemesis, Alan Shapiro, in reality the demand came from the gay and lesbian coalition. Nobody hates Catholicism as intensely as militant homosexuals, save the devil himself.

Predictions of dangerous times start creeping into controller conversations. The Jersey Devil is back on the inside, having left his windy perch on the concrete catwalk at the northeast corner of the tower cab. Squatting on the bookshelf, the yellow-eyed bastard grooms himself, picking crab lice from his scaly tail and popping them into his mouth like Tic-Tacs. Casting his jaundiced gaze upon the tin men, he is waiting for that moment he craves, one of carelessness followed closely by sheer, heart-stopping terror. At that instance of acute panic the soul leaves the body momentarily, and may be snatched away forever, leaving the offending controller with no place to hide, no excuse to seize upon and no one else to blame. Naked, but for the straight-jacket of accountability, and as friendless and shunned as a leper, the devil's shrill laughter will ring in that controller's ear for eternity, and he will die a thousand deaths a minute. Not even his own real death will provide any escape, because the magnitude of his professional error will be recorded for posterity. It will live, numbered among the large blunders of history. The Charge of the Light Brigade, The Alamo and The Little Big Horn are all remembered with a sense of wonder at the courage and bravery associated with those events. Courage is not an attribute one thinks to attach to an air traffic controller. Risking one's sanity for his country, if considered at all, is not an act of valor. It is evidence of an intense masochism, a curious mental disorder as unique and misunderstood as air traffic control itself. Other professionals kill one or two at a time. A doctor kills one of his patients with a bad prescription or a botched surgical procedure. A client gets the gas chamber because his lawyer failed to object when hearsay evidence is introduced at trial. A cop mistakenly shoots and kills a kid or an innocent bystander.

Asked to compare these occupational hazards, tin man Beans Larkin notes: "Yea, it's a tight face, when a poor cop shoots somebody by accident or gets killed himself; but nobody comes close to us. What's the worst that can happen at the big airport? Five hundred, that's what. Five hundred formerly walking and talking human beings can burn to death or die from blunt force trauma or they get sliced up like soup chickens. Yea, society cries for cops. Their job is so hard, so dangerous. You've heard the P.R.: They put their lives on the line every day. The average cop can thank his lucky stars he's not a tin man. On the average day, only the President is responsible for more lives. Sure, a cop can accidentally kill someone, but an air traffic controller can kill hundreds with one mistake. Yea, a cop takes a bullet now and then. A controller will take the same bullet, only it will be self inflicted, and there won't be any glory, no big fancy funeral, no lying in state, no medal, no plaque and no dignitaries on hand to eulogize him. His relatives will change the family name and move to New Zealand. The brand of shame that causes a controller to end his own life will spill onto his friends and family, and they will wear that shame like a bad tattoo until their own death. Controllers never talk about this kind of shit, because it is too horrible to contemplate. But what is possible has happened before, and it will happen again. If you're a controller and you don't realize this, then you're a mildly retarded meat-head. You don't dwell on it, nobody does. But wherever you go, it's right there with you. How you deal with it is your business. Just hope it never deals with you."

Larkin thinks about what he has just said.

Where does a controller go after he fucks up big time? What happens to him when the live air traffic show, seen through the big windows, turns into a real life horror scene? Is there a special seat at the end of some dark bar, in some remote town, reserved for those who suddenly hate themselves for being born? To err is human they say, but for air traffic controllers, humanity has nothing to do with it. You're expected to rise above your human condition, and not to blame it for your own shortcomings.

Larkin knows a guy who was partially blamed for a mid air collision. That's why whenever he thinks about these things, the phrase, DM 135 pops into his head.

DM 135! Jesus! DM 135!

If one stands at the intersection of Grand and Warren Streets in downtown Jersey City and looks south, the Statue of Liberty appears to rise in the center of the Street, perfectly framed by the brick and brownstone apartment buildings on either side. Not far away, *Tipitina* lies docked in her slip, gently tugging on her spring lines, as if she wants to break free and make for some destination like Cape May or Newport, Rhode Island, and the challenge of the spray and the open water that lies betwixt. On board, a tin man tosses about in his sleep. A place is revisited.

This time two sturdy industrial steel cables extend from the overhead. The cable ends are attached to his M14 rifle. One, through the shoulder stock and the other firmly clamped to the flash suppressor at the muzzle. It is steel wire rope like the stout suspension cables on the Brooklyn Bridge.

With support like this, how can my rifle fail? How can I fail my rifle? Where can it go? I can go on like this forever. My arms and my body are simply at rest and the cables are doing all the work. My rifle is steady because I am steady. The cables are my friends and my friends are real- like Pittsburgh steel. Behold my rifle…myself… steeped in discipline…radiant in glory.

An outer strand of the starboard wire rope begins to fray, then it pops and the cable unravels like a false alibi. The port side starts to fail in the same manner. What was once sturdy, steel wire rope is now cheap, dry rotted, common cotton clothesline, unable to take the stress. As the cables fail and start to fall from the overhead, more reliance on arm strength becomes necessary to hold the rifle in place. Arm fatigue gives way to arm and shoulder pain. The rifle begins to drop. To compensate the Private steps up slightly on tip-toe to elevate the rifle to its last assigned altitude. The cables have fallen from the ceiling. Their weight is now pulling down on the rifle from below. Panic and embarrassment sets in. Failure is on display. There is no place to hide.

My rifle! Jesus, my rifle!

Now awake, Doherty draws a water jug from the galley ice box and takes a long pull. Climbing the companionway ladder, he stands in the cockpit looking south toward the Statue of Liberty. A few feet away a seagull is cooping on the floating dock. Scanning the night sky there is no air traffic visible. Doherty wonders who is on duty at the tower and if they are as wide awake as he is. After toweling the sweat from his face, the tin man climbs down into his berth. A familiar aching in his arms is subsiding, and he knows it is now safe to fall asleep.

CHAPTER 46

If an airline pilot knows what to ask for, he can sometimes shave 30 minutes or more from his flight time. In periods of good weather, if the wind is calm, or from a favorable direction, a pilot can ask for a visual approach to a non-standard runway. This means that he will be taken from the downwind, vectored directly at the airport, and once the airport is in sight, he is switched to the tower for a landing clearance. It's like sneaking in the side door of a theater, in front of those waiting in line ahead of you. The airline most adept at this maneuver is the hometown favorite, People Express. Newark Tower controllers and People Express drivers maintain a friendly, close working relationship. If a controller needs a "familiarization" flight, a People Express pilot is likely to allow that controller to occupy the jump seat without filing the FAA paperwork. If two controllers show up for the same jump seat, one is almost always directed to an empty seat in the cabin. People Express pilots bend over backward to maintain excellent relations with the tower controllers. In exchange, they frequently get approval for things like a visual approach any time they ask for one.

Occasionally a team of controllers will get in the mood for something special to eat, especially on the evening shift. It could be Chinese or Italian take-out or perhaps pizza. But, when they get the urge for Buffalo wings, nothing will do except *real* buffalo wings – from Buffalo. To make this happen, a controller solicits a People Express flight to Buffalo, usually on the clearance delivery frequency. The crew agrees to bring back two or three buckets of wings and a controller meets the flight at the gate, pays for the wings, and brings the spicy treat back to the tower. The wings are usually still warm when they arrive in the tower cab.

One such People Express flight was en-route from Buffalo to Newark with three buckets of "yard-bird" in the cockpit. A radar approach controller at the New York TRACON calls the tower.

Coordinator, Newark Approach.

Yea, Newark, what's up?

People One Seventy Seven is forty five miles northwest, looking for a visual approach to Runway One One.

The Local Coordinator mulls it over for a few seconds. Looking over at Ground Control he sees that the trainer and his trainee are "down the pipes" with heavy traffic. Something non-standard might set them back.

Tell him we're unable due to heavy ground traffic and taxiway construction in progress.

Okay tower, no problem.

A minute later, the approach controller comes back on the overhead speaker.

Hey Tower, People One Seventy Seven says he's got the Buffalo wings on board!

The Cab Coordinator jerks a handset from an overhead console and punches a button to respond to the radar controller at the TRACON.

Send him direct. When the airport is in sight, switch him to Tower, One One Eight Point Three.

The coordinator turns to the local controller.

"Mickey, your getting a VAP to One One, People One Seventy Seven. Get his gate number and I'll clear a taxi route to the ramp." Turning toward the back line, the Cab Coordinator asks: "Who wants to go over to the gate and get the wings?"

That evening the tin men chow down on Buffalo wings, complete with celery sticks and blue cheese dressing.

At the next training day, Supervisor Van Geffen plays a tape recording of the entire event for the team. Once again, Van Geffen's bony index finger is stabbing and thumping the conference table, punctuating the FAA supervisor's demand that he be in charge.

Van the supervisor is also upset that he was not consulted before asking an airline crew to do a favor for the controller team. Van Geffen claims that such consultation could have saved the team from entering into an illegal relationship with the users.

A letter of reprimand goes to every controller that participated in the Buffalo wing scandal along with a warning about any future incidents. One of the lesbians cries because her previously unblemished work record now includes a "breach of ethical standards." NATCA grieves the letter, claiming that the controller was simply ordering lunch and knew nothing about the origin of the Buffalo wings. For all she knew the wings could have come from the Queen Elizabeth Diner. She certainly was not involved in any *quid pro quo* arrangement with an airline, exchanging preferential treatment for a delivery of food for the controllers. The tin men, proud of their letters, do not file a grievance. Said Beans Larkin:

"Those were some damned good wings! I never had any *squid pro quo*, but that sounds good too!"

A misty, early morning fog descends on the tarmac at Terminal "C". A row of Continental airliners, mostly 737's and 727's sit at their gates. An FAA safety inspector is inside the terminal at Continental's flight operations desk, exchanging small talk with the Chief Pilot on duty. Since these two have been meeting regularly, they've become good friends. In fact, the FAA inspector plays golf in a foursome that includes two Continental executives and the Chief Maintenance Engineer. The Continental guys routinely lose money to the FAA inspector on every one of the golf outings. The two friends exchange greetings. "How's your game, Ed?"

"Almost broke eighty, Joe. But I took two bogies and a snowman on the last three holes."

"Keep after it, you'll get there."

"Yea, I guess."

Inspector Ed punches 2244 on the door's combination pad and walks out onto the wet tarmac. With clipboard in hand and large, white FAA letters on the back of his blue windbreaker, no one is likely to mistake him for a "friendly." Ed walks past three 737's and stops near the nose wheel of a Boeing 727. Hydraulic fluid is on the primary strut and forms a small pool, visible on the wet tarmac. Inspector Ed takes a measurement on both tires with a tread gauge, and makes a notation on the clipboard. Walking around the right wing, his head traces the leading, then trailing edges, and he heads for the rear stairs invitingly in the down position. In the cockpit, a Continental airframe mechanic sits in the flight engineer's seat. His handheld radio cackles with the sound of the chief mechanic on duty. "Twenty five twenty…Bill, he's coming up your aft stairs."

"Roger."

Bill the mechanic pulls the aircraft's service card from its envelope on the bulkhead and makes a quick notation, officially marking the aircraft out of service. After replacing the card, the mechanic heads for the rear exit and passes the FAA inspector in the aisle coming the other way.

In six years of official inspections of Continental Airlines aircraft, Ed the FAA inspector has never found a Continental jet to be in violation of Federal Air Regulations. His reports routinely note that Continental is "extremely diligent" about removing aircraft from service for minor repairs when needed.

Before leaving the airport, the two golfing pals have breakfast in one of the restaurants in the terminal. The ritual is so familiar, that Ed makes no move to pick up the check or leave a tip. While the two men are dining, Bill the mechanic is making another notation on the service card, returning Twenty Five Twenty to service. After bringing the hydraulic fluid levels back to normal, the aircraft flies to Orlando. It will leave a puddle of hydraulic fluid on the Florida tarmac before returning to Newark.

CHAPTER 47

Socrates appears this night, dressed only in plain white boxer shorts, heavily starched and creased. A tattoo on his left forearm shows a bulldog wearing a World War One "doughboy" helmet and the letters, USMC. True to his legend, the famous philosopher of ancient Greece supplies no answers and writes nothing down. He has only questions.

"Why do you stand so, holding your rifle suspended, as if it were imperative?"

"Sir, the Private is following orders."

"And, ordered as you are, you feel obligated?"

"Sir, yes Sir. I am so obligated. I must follow orders instantly, and to the best of my ability."

"You are in pain. Do you not question orders, especially those designed to visit pain and discomfort upon your being?"

"Sir, pain is weakness leaving the body. I am training for combat. My body must be conditioned…so that I may endure…so that I may prevail against the enemy. I cannot fail my country…my Marine Corps."

"How can this be that you are training for combat, as your rifle is but partially serviceable? I see no bayonet affixed to this weapon."

With that, Socrates reaches for the Private's duty belt and draws the bayonet from its scabbard. With a familiar *click*, the blade is affixed to the bayonet lug at the muzzle. The added weight causes the

Marine recruit to falter. The M-14 rifle falls below its last assigned altitude, but is brought quickly back into shape. Socrates decides to torment the young recruit. He pulls on the taut web sling as one would draw on a bow, and lets it loose to strike the magazine. Socrates repeats the action again and again until the recruit objects.

"Socrates! You stupid, senile, civilian bastard! My rifle! My rifle!"

Awake now, Doherty can hear the tell-tale slap of a loose halyard against the mast. He pulls the line taut and refastens it on the cleat. Two anglers make their way down the dock each holding an end of an oversized ice chest. As light starts to filter into the eastern morning sky, the tin man goes below and starts the coffee maker. His vessel back in order, his mind is free to wander. When his mind is free, he thinks of Maria. He hopes to see Maria today, and that's always a good thing, because Maria is one for the eyes. If not for Maria, the tin man has no need of eyes.

Judy Episcopo enters the break room and tosses a Lean Cuisine meal into the microwave. She turns her attention to Tommy who is doing another spring-cleaning of the voodoo locker shrine. Seated at the table, Tommy is wiping down a few items with a moist towel-ette. Judy decides to play some head games with Tommy.

"Whatchya doin' Thomas? Playing with your toys again?" Judy leans over the table, her hands gripping the edge with her thumbs pointing outboard. With her low cut sweater, she is giving Tommy a generous view of her ample cleavage. Judy waits until she catches Tommy looking, then she smiles at the superstitious tin man. Tommy is wiping down the blues harmonica that he calls a "harp." He can't help but glimpse at Judy's intentional flick, but he decides to ignore her and pretends to be too occupied to gawk. Besides, another look at Judy's bosom could prompt those impure thoughts that plague every devout Catholic and that would force him into the confessional immediately after work.

"I'm just cleaning up a few things, Judy."

Judy is in a playful mood and she wants more attention from Tommy. She picks up the statuette of Saint Expedite and examines it closely, turning it in her hands. Tommy stops what he is doing and watches Judy intently. He normally does not allow anyone to handle Saint "E."

"Hey, this guy's kinda cute!" With that, Judy plunges Saint Expedite head first, deep into the gap between her meaty breasts until the round green felt bottom of the statue's pedestal is all that can be seen of the now skin-diving Saint.

Expecting Tommy to freak out at such an outrageous and irreverent sacrilege, Judy is dismayed when he simply sits back in the captain's chair and cocks his head to one side. Tommy, with arms crossed on his chest, says nothing. Judy grabs the plastic pedestal with a thumb and forefinger and starts using the statuette on her breasts, plunging it in and out as if as if it were a sex toy, not allowing the Patron Saint of air traffic controllers to come up for air. Still, Tommy seems less than impressed. He watches Judy with a bored look on his chubby, baby face.

"Look at what Saint Expedite is doing, Tommy! What a naughty boy! And I thought he was a religious man!" Tommy nods slowly, patiently waiting for Judy to finish her lewd show. The former altar boy speaks:

"Saint Expedite is a man like any other…even more so, Judy. He was a Roman Centurion. Do you think he has never succumbed to temptations of the flesh? I'm sure he appreciates the generous attention you are showing him. May his blessings be upon you, and keep you safe."

With that, Judy slowly withdraws the plastic statuette and carefully places it back on the table.

"You never step out of character, do you Tommy?" Tommy does not answer, making Judy's question a rhetorical one. He wipes Saint Expedite clean and places him back among the other items on the table. Although Tommy maintains a stoic manner, he can't help but think about Judy and her sexy ways. Curvaceous, full figured and foul-mouthed, Judy cultivates and conveys a mostly unspoken message that any male employee or controller at the tower has a real opportunity to bed her. At one time or another, she has flirted outrageously with every male at the facility, not excluding visitors and the pizza delivery guy. It is a curious fact that among the employees at Newark Tower, the most egregious and serial violator of FAA sexual harassment guidelines is a female, and whoever is second to Judy Episcopo is not even close.

CHAPTER 48

The attitude toward Liam Doherty is changing, as more controllers find out about his willingness to report operational errors by controllers. Doherty's name is frequently mentioned on newfangled computer bulletin boards and his reputation is starting to spread nationwide. Many controllers are openly contemptuous of a fellow employee who would "turn them in" and report their errors. Operational errors can trigger the disciplinary process and termination could result. Even among some of his fellow tin men, Doherty is seen as a person who is actively threatening the livelihood of his co-workers.

Beans Larkin is bored. He's sitting at the TCA radar position having his coffee. Since it's early on a Sunday morning, and without any traffic to speak of, the TCA position is closed, the airspace and control duties assumed by the Local Controller. Larkin decides to call LaGuardia Tower and jack them up a bit. He reaches up and punches the direct line to the LaGuardia TCA controller.

"Hey LaGuardia, Newark."

"LaGuardia."

"You ready for the Pope?"

"What Pope?"

"The Pope-Pope. The Bishop of Rome."

"Didn't hear anything about it. What's he comin' here?"

"Apparently. Supposed to bless some Portuguese shrine in Down-Neck, then he's headin' your way for High Mass at Forest Hills…center court. Tell me you didn't get the brief."

"Nothin'. Swear to Christ. You sure? I mean…today? He's comin'?"

"Yep. Swiss Guard's here already. Standin' in the back. Nice uniforms!"

"Awesome. I'll see what I can find out…call you back."

The two controllers end the conversation by putting their operating initials on the tape.

"B.B."

"T.D."

Fifteen minutes later the Washington Center Flow Control phone rings at the supervisor's desk. Van Geffen answers.

"Hey Newark, let us know if you need a program or anything for your VIP operation."

That quickly, a rumor, purposely started as a joke, is now an FAA reality. In the blink of an eye, it went from being a prank conversation between two New York area controllers to being a problem requiring headquarters intervention and brainstorming.

Because Supervisor Van Geffen believes that he missed something, he pretends to know what Washington is talking about. When the tall, tow-headed, baggy-eyed, pasty-faced supervisor hangs up, he moves over to the Read and Initial binder to see if it contains any notice or memo about the Pope flying into Newark International Airport. Finding nothing, he slides up next to the Local Controller and scans the bay holding the inbound flight strips. Nothing is posted that would give the supervisor any clue about the Pope, or his impending arrival at Newark.

Meanwhile, Beans Larkin is standing by the coffee pot watching Van Geffen closely. What started as a simple, practical joke to see how gullible a LaGuardia Tower controller could be, the episode has morphed into a psychological experiment, and FAA management is now Larkin's subject. This time they prove to be sadly predictable, like Pavlov's dogs. Instead of simply asking a straight-forward question aloud, Van Geffen is so paranoid and so lacking in personal confidence, that he elects to sneak around looking for clues to discover on his own, hoping that no one will notice. Finding none, the supervisor re-scans the area, scratches his head and tugs on one ear lobe. His lips give the appearance that they are about to move. Tin man Larkin butters a bagel and tries to send Van Geffen a telepathic message.

Say it, you simple bastard! Speak! It's easy…just ask the question out loud...DOES ANYONE KNOW ANYTHING ABOUT THE POPE COMING HERE TODAY? You can do it. Remember what they always tell us: There's no such thing as a stupid question. C'mon, you tired, dim witted, chalky, hound dog looking, Nazi wannabe! Say it! Say it!

Just then, Richard "ding-dong-dick" Bell appears at the top of the stairs and Larkin overhears VanGeffen asking the other supervisor about a possible Papal visit to the airport. Van Geffen is off the hook. Asking a fellow supervisor for help is okay, because Ding-Dong Dick understands. He understands because he's cut from the same cookie sheet of malleable, bland, uninspired substrate that makes an FAA supervisor.

And they call this a TEAM. The sups are too afraid to ask the controllers a question for fear they might look human. The controllers are not supposed to know more than the supervisors, so the last thing that VanGeffen would do is ask a controller for help. What a bunch of sorry, pathetic, spineless idiots. In the private sector, an FAA supervisor couldn't get hired to mop up the floor at the peep shows, yet here they are, in charge of a controller team at a major air terminal...and folks wonder why so many controllers refuse to fly- not even for free.

His watch over, Larkin washes out his coffee mug in the tower sink and stuffs his headset bag along with the mug into its assigned cabinet pigeonhole. Larkin thinks long and hard about starting a business. This time, while driving home, he thinks it might be a bagel shop. He works out a business plan in his head.

CHAPTER 49

Maria and Doherty meet for dinner at a red sauce joint in Greenwich Village. Watching her sip wine, the tin man takes in her presence. The sight and scent of her are enough to drive him mad. Feeling almost unworthy, he pauses before asking her to talk.

"Tell me about linguistics."

Maria looks surprised.

"I thought it might bore you."

"Why? Is it boring?"

"Oh no, on the contrary, I find it very exciting. I just…didn't think you would"

"Then school me, Maria. Tell me about it, and see if you can get me excited. What is linguistics?"

"It is the science of language and the human mind, how language is perceived in the mind. Linguistics crosses many other disciplines such as sociology, psychology, English, even archeology. It is a very layered and involved academic subject." Maria sips her wine without losing eye contact with her dinner date. The sexy look she is giving thrills the tin man.

"The only linguist I know is that communist Chomsky." Maria smiles, replies.

"That's because to a libertarian like you, a socialist like Noam Chomsky is the anti-Christ. You know him for his politics, not for his work in linguistics." She sips the wine. "People are complex too, you know. You can't just slap a label on someone, and move on to the next victim."

The tin man keeps his thoughts about Chomsky to himself:

Fuck Noam Chomsky. If he had his way, nobody would be allowed to study anything-we'd all be in one giant prison, with him and his communist buddies in charge. If he were here right now, I'd rupture his spleen.

Doherty tries to get the conversation back on track. "Okay, let me ask you something that a linguist might know the answer to. It's about something that's been bothering me." Maria's eyes widen. "Wow, this sounds good! Tell me!"

"Okay, okay. There's some well-known record collectors and Doo-Wop enthusiasts, well-respected guys…keepers of the flame…experts like Val Shively in Philly, and Ronnie "I" in Clifton, New Jersey. They despise the term "Doo Wop." They say it's cartoonish and it cheapens the sound, the genre. They say it turns their beloved music into a joke, a bumper sticker. They prefer to say, "Rhythm and Blues" or "Vocal Group Harmony. You know, something that befits the lofty status that their preferred music deserves. The problem is, "Doo Wop" as a label, has already won this race. It is more commonly used by far, than those other terms."

Maria smiles. "This is an interesting linguistic issue. Lets examine it. First, let me ask you, how do YOU feel about it?"

Doherty leans back and puts his arm up on the adjacent chair. "I don't care, really. Doo Wop is fine with me, but if you use one of those other terms, I don't get offended. You know, a rose by any other name…"

Using a fork and a spoon, Maria twirls her linguini. "Do we know where and when the term "Doo Wop" originated?"

"Yes we do."

"Okay…so…where?"

A disc jockey named Gus Gossert started the "oldies" format by playing records from the fifties on Sunday nights, right here in New York, around 1969 or 1970. He is credited with coining the term

"Doo Wop." Some dispute this, but Gus gets the credit. But, you see the problem: The sound goes back to the late forties. It peaked from 1955 to 1964. Gossert wasn't flipping the wax biscuits until 1969. But the label he used, Doo Wop, has stuck."

Maria ponders the information for a moment.

"You know, this has happened before."

"How so?"

"What do you think World War One was called, up until 1941?" The tin man smiles and lets Maria continue.

"It wasn't until World War Two came along that we stopped calling it "The Great War." World War Two gave us a frame of reference. With historical events, we sometimes have to look back and make comparisons. Then, the right name will win out, for many reasons. Language evolves over time in many ways. This is just one example. Look at the options: rhythm and blues, vocal group harmony, rock and roll, race music. Some of these terms overlap. They cover other styles. They don't fit as perfectly as Doo Wop seems to. That's why you're comfortable with it and so are many others."

Doherty is impressed. "I didn't use the term, "race music." I'm surprised that you know about it."

"Linguists know a lot about many things. That's why linguistics is so exciting. The tin man leans in close.

"I never wanted you more… than I do right at this moment." Maria bats her brown eyes naughtily and lifts her glass. While sipping, she gazes seductively at her date. She speaks.

"See what I mean? It's exciting."

Doherty peels a fifty from his money clip and drops it on the table. The folded bill lands on its edge.

Aboard *Tipitina*, the Vanguards are reprising "Moonlight."

Whoa, oh, moonlight
Won't you hear my plea, yea, yea , mmm, hmmm
Cause my heart is beating oh repeating, hmmm
Oh shine on bright moon, oh whoa oh whoa

The telephone rings. "Doherty."

"Mr. Doherty, this is Richard Wentworth of the NTSB. We spoke last week, very briefly, about an incident at Newark.

I remember, Richard. How are you?

Fine, sir. Can I call you Liam?"

"Call me Willie."

"Okay, Willie. The reason I'm calling is to update you on the progress of our investigation."

"Thanks for calling, Richard. What's up?"

"The preliminary call is that it's an operational error by the tower. Specifically, the Local Controller failed to separate the two Continental airliners involved. He descended the landing jet to fifteen hundred and put him on the downwind, crossing directly in front of a departing MD-80 that was climbing to two thousand five hundred."

Doherty injects some levity. "Doesn't everybody?" Wentworth chuckles.

"Well, I sure hope they don't. This one was close. Exactly how close, we're not sure. They were nearly right at the main bang when they crossed, so the radar couldn't display their altitudes accurately. I'll tell you this, though. I've heard every adjective you can name that translates into close. We're estimating it was 100 feet or less."

"Jesus!"

"Yea."

Doherty offers his thoughts. "If it was less than 100 feet, and you're not sure how close it was…it could have been…*inches*."

"This is true. Listen, Willie. There's something else you need to know. The FAA really got caught with their trousers down on this one. Right from the start they tried to cover this thing up, but it didn't stay covered up. Your call got the investigation started, but something else happened."

"What was that?"

"Well, it seems that a guy who owns a tug boat company out of Baltimore was on board and he got a good look at the other airplane from his window seat on the right side of the departing MD-80. I interviewed him. He said that when he saw the other airplane, you could've put a watermelon in his mouth but couldn't get a pine needle up his ass."

"He complained?"

"Oh, yea. First, he had it out with Continental Airlines. When they brushed him off, he called his friend."

"Who's his friend?"

"Drew Lewis."

"The Secretary of Transportation?"

"Former…Secretary of Transportation…and he called HIS FRIEND...the guy who appointed him."

"By that, you mean, Ronald Reagan."

"That's right, Willie. Now listen. The last thing that President Reagan needs is a collision between airliners that gets blamed on the air traffic control system. Remember, he fired the PATCO guys. You can bet that he's not happy about this incident. My guess is that he's started a snowball rolling that's about to land on your FAA bosses at the Eastern Region." Doherty blinks.

"Couldn't happen to a nicer bunch."

"Yea, well don't get too complacent, Willie. You had better hope that the president gets to them before they get to you. Because they have said, flat out, they are after you."

"ME? They mentioned me personally?"

"No. They don't know who phoned them in. We don't reveal the names of anyone who makes a report. But they think they know, and they said they are going to get that person."

"Well, Richard, that sounds like my life's just been threatened. Did you think to inform the FBI, and tell them that someone threatened to get me?"

"If you want to call the FBI, I'll give you their number. That's up to you. They didn't threaten you personally, because officially, they don't know your name. Are they going to KILL you? I seriously doubt that. Will they try to FIRE you? You can bet on it. So take whatever steps you need to take to cover your ass. That is the primary reason I called you today." Doherty pauses, then replies.

"I hope you kept your notes, Richard, because I may be in need of a witness."

"Let's hope it doesn't get to that. And Willie, it takes balls to do what you did…to make that call…I just want to say, thanks…because I know that no one else is going to say it to you.

The tin man responds: "Don't thank me, Richard. I got paid for it."

More feral cats are hanging out near the back door to the tower. Patricia has been leaving cat food for them, and now there are six or more short-haired tabbys. Patricia is fond of a runt, a grey one with white socks and a white bib. She's been coming in early to befriend the kitten, with the intent to adopt.

On the midnight shift, the new guy named Vinny props open the door and leaves a trail of tuna to the stairwell door and up three flights of stairs. After five hours, Vinny rides the elevator to the first floor and closes the door to the stairs, trapping five cats in the stairwell. Meanwhile, Vinny's co-conspirator, Ray Martino, opens a can of tuna and spreads clumps of the cat treat around the stairwell door near the executive office door on the ninth floor. An open can of tuna is placed inside the office behind a closed door. The plan calls for the office pogues to arrive by elevator in the morning, and the cats will be waiting in the stairwell on the Ninth floor. As soon as someone opens the door to the stairwell, six cats will scurry into the office area, attracted by the smell of tuna.

The trick does not work exactly as planned. Only one cat enters the office area and only very warily. The others scamper to the bottom of the stairwell and cower under the bottom step.

When an animal control officer arrives, Patricia pleads for the life of the grey and white runt. Only after Patricia promises to take the kitten directly home, does the officer relent and violate the rules. Taking annual leave, Patricia drives straight home with her new friend, which she names "Radar."

The next training day the FAA has scheduled some diversity training for the employees. Thirty minutes is allotted for a presentation by "virgin" Mary and her subject is "The Glass Ceiling." While Mary prattles on about gender discrimination, the tin men do not interrupt or ask any questions, hoping that the boring and predictable exercise will pass more quickly. Beans Larkin throws a pencil at a real ceiling and it sticks in the foam tile next to three other pencils already present. After absorbing Mary's government sponsored attack on white males, the tin men take a coffee break. Ray Martino combs his shiny, jet-black hair and inspects the comb before sliding it into his prat pocket next to his wallet. He says to Larkin: "You believe any of that shit?" Larkin looks over the top of his coffee mug at Martino. "Nah, but who cares? They wanna crash through some stupid ceiling, let 'em. It's all imaginary, anyhow." Martino throws a bag of popcorn into the microwave and sets the timer. He turns to his fellow tin man. "I don't know about a glass ceiling, but I saw a girl crash through a glass coffee table, and I got the scars on my face to prove it!"

CHAPTER 50

"Trains are better than planes."

The statement is made by Beans Larkin to Gordon Russo. The two tin men are having lunch in the controller ready room. Russo is working on reheated lasagna, while Larkin has a ham sandwich and sips a bottle of Doctor Pepper. Larkin has an aversion to cans. He never consumes anything that is packaged in steel, aluminum or tin. He's a tin man who hates tin cans. Russo responds.

"You ever clear a train for takeoff? I swear…they take a long time to rotate." Larkin smiles, but otherwise ignores Russo's inane remark. The Boston-born tin man continues.

"Air travel doesn't really work well, except for very long distances. Even then, the drawbacks are considerable." Gordon responds.

"You serious, Beans? "Cause I don't want folks to find out. It could hurt me financially."

Larkin chuckles. "Yea. It's no joke. Think about this. You know how people get sick after flying? It's because they're stuck in those pressurized cabins for hours. They're marinating in everyone's juices up there. Suppose some idiot is sitting next to you, and he's got tuberculosis? He could give it to the whole plane. The airline is forcing his disease right down your neck."

Russo nods. He knows that Larkin is just getting started.

"Then there's the weather. Not much bad weather can stop a train. Snow, thunderstorms, high winds, ice. All the stuff that stops or delays airplanes, has no real effect on the train schedule. And, a train can safely come to a dead stop anywhere along the route. With an airplane…*dead stop* takes on a whole new meaning."

"Virgin" Mary walks in and plops down on the sofa. Propping her steel-toed engineer boots on the coffee table, she buries her face in a magazine, blocking out the view of her chubby face and her Dutch boy haircut. Russo glances over at Mary.

Jeez, what a goddamned dyke! I've never seen anyone look more like a dyke than "virgin" Mary. She looks like she stepped right out of Lesbian Central Casting. She could be the Gay Pride Parade Marshal, or the poster boy for the sexually conflicted. I don't care what anyone says...homosexuals are simply not wired right. You can tell by looking at them.

Knowing that Larkin wants some feedback, Russo resumes thinking about trains and planes.

"Yea, but Amtrak sucks." Larkin nods in agreement.

"Like a Hoover. But it doesn't have to be that way. Suppose the government supported rail travel like they support the airlines? Suppose we had a nation-wide system of high-speed rail service... like 500 MPH long distance trains? Like mag-lev trains...magnetic levitation technology. You know you can speed along at 500 and leave a full glass of wine on the table without fear of spilling a drop. You can get up and walk to the café, or the bar, or even an exercise car. And, when you arrive at your destination, you're already downtown. You don't need a $150 dollar cab ride to get to your hotel." Russo responds.

"That magnetic stuff...that works?"

Larkin: "Oh yea. It works. Why do you think it doesn't exist in this country? Because if Americans could choose between fast, safe, comfortable, super high speed trains and flying Spam cans...well, guess what wins. The airlines would virtually disappear...except for real long distances and overseas flights. They wouldn't be able to compete on routes like New York to Chicago or New York to Florida.

Russo nods in agreement. "You think there ever was a midnight train to Georgia? Or did Gladys Knight just make it all up?" Larkin laughs.

"I don't know…but she's got some nice pips!"

On the north side of Liberty Island a small anchorage is available, but most boaters are unaware of its existence. Since Maria is available for a rare overnight visit, they decide to take advantage of the spot. Doherty eases *Tipitina* as close as possible to Lady Liberty and drops the hook. It's a sunny Sunday afternoon and tourists are lining up to climb through the statue or wander on and around the massive pedestal. After coiling down lines, Doherty checks to make sure the anchor is holding fast. Maria is people watching with the binoculars. Doherty looks up at a People Express jet making a right turn toward Newark Airport a quarter mile northwest of the statue. He knows that the jet's turn is wider than it should be…typical for People Express whenever they circle to land on Runway Two Nine.

The pilot is giving the cheap-seaters a nice view of the statue and the New York skyline. If there's more traffic close in trail, it will have to go just as wide…or wider, and so on…the Local Controller could end up with a mess that is hard to straighten out. You cannot let the pilots do what they want. They will screw you every time.

The couple snack on wine and cheese in the cockpit. Doherty tries to relax, but he's concerned about the traffic pattern at Newark. The airplanes are circling wider, getting closer to the statue. It's a sign that the Local Controller is struggling, unable to keep the traffic in tight, and now the circling jets are threatening LaGuardia's airspace. Maria is enjoying the sights and has no idea that her shipmate is thinking about air traffic.

I should've cruised down to Sandy Hook…maybe checked out a few nudes on the beach. I wouldn't have this annoying Newark Airport traffic pattern to consider. But then, there's the straight line of boring JFK arrivals coming up the Jersey coast. What is it about this fucking job? Why can't I leave my work at the office like other people do? It's like I'm being followed around by airplanes. I look up and there they are. I drive down the Turnpike and here comes a Newark arrival on final and I'm thinking...he should have his wheels down by now...There's no real escape from the big tin- at least not for me. Maybe I should take up scuba diving, or spend more time in museums and theatres.

Maria finds a small gift wrapped package in the galley.

"What's this?"

"It's a gift...for you."

"Really? For me?

Doherty drops down through the companionway to watch Maria open her gift. It's a cassette tape album entitled "Motown's Best Love Songs."

"You said you like Motown."

"And you remembered. Can I play it now?"

Doherty takes the cassette tape.

"There's one on here I want you to listen to first. I think you'll like it." The tin man sends the cassette tape into the slot and cues up one of The Miracles' great love ballads. The music starts and Smokey Robinson avers:

> *I will build you a castle with a tower so high*
> *It reaches the moon*

Maria draws the tin man close by simply touching him on his shoulder. The two lovers embrace, and while *Tipitina* swings on her anchor rode, Lady Liberty looms over the open companionway, as if she is peeking in on the vessel's activity. Maria whispers in the tin man's ear.

"I remember this one. It's a beautiful song. This place is beautiful. This day is special...being here with you."

I will take you away with me as far as I can
To Venus or Mars
There we'll elope with your hand in my hand
You'll be Queen of the Stars

Doherty thinks about the things he loves. Maria…Sailing…Doo Wop…pushing the massive tin at the big airport. Which ones could he lose? Maria could pull the rug out from under him; women have a habit of doing that. The FAA could take the tin away. If they did, Doherty knows he could not afford to sail or live aboard a sailboat. That leaves Doo Wop as the only reliable constant in his life. Maria runs her fingers through the tin man's hair. She knows it drives him mad.

And every day
We can play
On the Milky Way

CHAPTER 51

A scaly, yellow-eyed bastard is squatting on the tower catwalk watching the airplanes as they come and go. Cocking his head, he's listening to the voices inside the tower cab. As he waits for an opening, a chance to deal someone a losing hand, the wind starts to pick up, forcing the airplanes to abandon the parallel runways. All traffic at Newark Airport will be landing and taking off on the short runway, into the stiff wind. The devil gets stiff, too. He loves a one-runway operation at a busy aerodrome like Newark International, because the margin for error is smaller. The chance that something very tragic will happen, is multiplied. The seagulls in the parking lot are facing west, into the wind, like a hundred tiny tetrahedrons. Likewise, the devil faces windward, folding his greasy wings back and tucked in tight. With reptilian claws gripping the edge of the concrete catwalk, he watches the Runway Two-Nine traffic with a sideways glance. His head bobs slowly in a knowing motion of patience, like a vulture, or an undertaker.

A Runway 29 operation demands the most skill from controllers and pilots. It is not unusual for the Local Controller to put a departure in position for takeoff, with a landing on a one- mile final and waiting for the previous landing to clear the runway on a high-speed turnoff. The word anticipation comes into play. The controller must anticipate that the landing will clear the runway as he or she clears the take-off for an immediate departure. As one jet is lifting off at the departure end, another is crossing landing threshold and a third is taxiing into position for take off. It is a ballet of wings, flaps and shoulder straps. Any tiny screw-up can cause a traffic separation problem that is hard to rectify. If a boneheaded pilot stops before the tail of his airplane is completely clear of the runway, the departure cannot roll and the landing jet must execute a "go around." When that happens, the go around jet is now chasing the previous departure and the Local Controller must somehow build space between the two. This could involve "S" turns or circling. But, the Local Controller must also straighten out the problem on the ground with the taxiing airplanes, and quickly, or the problem could repeat itself. Like a short order cook must clean up spilt eggs from his work surface with one hand while plating an omelet with the other, then quickly prepare the pan for the next order, be it over, up or scrambled... and new customers are constantly streaming in the door. The pressure never lets up.

A Local Control trainee is getting his first taste of the dreaded Runway 29 operation. He has already missed one departure slot when he balked at putting a Continental 737 in position on the runway, with a landing jet on a mile and a half final. Gordon Russo admonishes his charge.

"C'mon, C'mon. For Christ's sake, you can't waste a slot like that. You gotta be loading that runway after every landing." Russo snaps his fingers three times in quick succession. "In position... ready for an immediate...landing guy rolls into the high speed turnoff- cleared for take-off. C'mon...c'mon. Think about what you're gonna do next. Land...load...launch...Okay, here comes TWA...soon as he gets over the turnpike-start talking. Ready?" The trainee takes the frequency.

Continental Two Sixteen, taxi into position and hold, be ready for an immediate departure, traffic on a one mile final.

Continental Two Sixteen, position and hold.

A few seconds later, TWA is rolling into the high speed turnoff.

TWA Four Eleven, taxi ahead on the high speed, turn left on Yankee, then contact Ground Point Eight.

TWA Four Eleven.

Continental Two Sixteen, cleared for immediate take-off, wind two eight zero at three five.

The trainee is gaining invaluable experience. Very few major airports move this many air carriers on a one runway operation. There is rubber on the runway constantly except for those few seconds after a take-off, and another big jet is about to touch down. If a controller doubts his own abilities, if he loses confidence in his skills, even for a moment, it will become obvious to all concerned. An ugly air show will commence. Departure slots will be wasted; delays will result. Then the supervisor will start looking around for the only remedy there is, the only commodity that the FAA can add, that will produce positive results, the thin line of excellence that the FAA's reputation hinges on – a tin man.

A few team members and their families gather at Beans Larkin's house in Red Bank for a backyard barbecue to celebrate a July Fourth holiday. Because of the rotating shifts and schedules, it is rare for controllers to have time to get together. Most gatherings of tin men occur at a bar after an evening watch, the so-called Midnight Mass, where they drink and bad-mouth any controller or supervisor who is not present. When they run out of co-workers and supervisors, they will normally start in on pilots and airlines, then graduate to Congress and the President. Then, after drinking enough booze to float a battleship, they drive home.

In Larkin's back yard, two kids are throwing paper airplanes, trying to get the airfoils to meet in mid-air, and head-on. Larkin watches the air show and twists the cap off a Heineken. He gestures toward the kids.

"There it is, M-O, the "big sky" theory, actually being tested. You see…even if we TRIED to put two airplanes together…it *almost* can't be done. We've got the public fooled. They don't need us; they have the law of averages on their side.

Ray Martino stabs a cheese cube with a toothpick and transfers the morsel to his mouth.

"Yea. But it only works if no one's there. You know, if no one is legally responsible…the airplanes would probably miss. But, put controllers on the job, then let one drop his guard for an instant… or make some wrong traffic call…or something stupid like missing a read-back…then WHAM! Just like that mid-air smack-up at Teterboro. Did you ever hear the tape of that deal? Did you hear the cockpit voice recording?"

Larkin nods, grimaces.

"Yea, I heard it…I can still hear it. That pilot saw the ground coming up to meet him. He sounded…well…you know. It kinda made you sick."

"Yea…I hope I sound better than he did…If I know I'm about to die, and investigators will be transcribing the tapes…listening to my last words…over…and over.

Larkin takes a pull on the beer.

"Okay. Here's your chance. You've just collided in mid air. You know your last words are being recorded, and you're dropping in on the neighborhood like a fiery fucking meteor. You've only got a few seconds…what do you say?" Larkin points the beer bottle at his fellow tin man as if it were a microphone.

Ray Martino looks across the picnic table at his friend and grins.

"Hey, Tower! THANKS FOR THE SERVICE!"

CHAPTER 52

The arbitrator's decision on Liam Doherty's suspension arrives. Paul Veale calls to deliver the news.

"Willie, the arbitrator clearly does not like you. What a surprise. He said you were *strident and lacking tact.* He also said your demeanor *bordered on insolence.* Oh, and here's the part I really like:

"An intelligent young man with an impressive vocabulary, Mr. Doherty's communication skills are none the less poor, unless one gives points for being condescending, smug and conceited." "And this:

"Mr. Doherty's contempt for Supervisor Hamblin is palpable; however, that contempt is not unrequited."

Doherty gets annoyed, but he can sense that the arbitrator is starting to see things in their proper perspective.

"That's great, Paul. Does he ever get to the point or does he just ramble on incoherently?"

"Yea, yea. The union wins another one- full back pay and benefits. Here's what the arbitrator ruled:

Supervisor Hamblin clearly had discipline in mind when he called Doherty to a one on one meeting. Accordingly, management is required by the contract to offer the employee union representation. In fact, at one point during the counseling session, Doherty asked for a union representative, and instead of providing one, Hamblin promptly adjourned the meeting and subsequently ordered the ten day suspension. Even if Mr. Doherty's actions did in fact support the charge of threatening a supervisor, Hamblin's course of action violates due process and is barred by the agreement.

"Here's what the arbitrator said about you threatening a supervisor."

"A threat is defined as a vocalized intent to commit physical harm. Mr. Doherty's expressed opinion that supervisor Hamblin committed a rules infraction or even a possible crime, and Doherty's articulated readiness to report such an incident to anyone having oversight authority, does not rise to the level of a "threat." I find that the facts do not support a charge of threatening a supervisor and that charge is discarded out of hand.

Paul Veale continues: "Willie, the arbitrator stopped short of calling FAA management a bunch of lying scumbags and cover-up artists, but if you read between the lines of this decision… that's what he's saying."

Doherty responds.

"Very good, Paul. Nice job by NATCA. Maybe I'll join the union now…just kidding."

Veale answers.

"By the way, Willie, do you know the paralegal in the NATCA national office, Seth Johnson? He's the guy that did most of the leg work on your case. He's gay…and he knows you're a notorious homophobe, but he did journeyman's work anyhow. Now what do you think of a guy like that?"

Doherty chuckles.

"Wow. I'd send him a fruit basket, but that would be like bringing sand to the beach."

The NATCA Rep continues:

"You can also thank your fellow controllers. You know, the ones that pay your union dues for you. They actually paid for this victory. They paid so that YOU would not suffer financially. Do you have a fruit basket for them, or a card, or some small gesture of gratitude?"

"Stop it, Paul. You're making me feel rather melancholy. My eyeballs are about to squirt."

CHAPTER 53

Back on Local Control the next day, Doherty settles into a groove. The traffic is busy, but that's how he likes it. There's training going on all around him. There's training on Ground to his right and TCA radar to his left. Massive tin means good training opportunities and the FAA tries not to waste the valuable traffic. There are seven flight progress strips in or on top of Doherty's time stamping machine. Four flights are cleared to land on Runway Two Two Left. Another is touching down. On the inboard runway, a departure is rolling and another is taxiing into position. Ten more strips are sitting in the departure bay. They represent flights that are near the runway, waiting to depart in order. The ground controller is asking him for permission to cross one of the runways with a taxiing Boeing 737.

"Cross Two-Nine at Papa?" Doherty checks to make sure there actually is an airplane at taxiway Papa, and that the airplane is able to cross, and safely. The entire exercise takes no longer than two seconds.

"Cross Two-Nine at Papa." When the airplane crosses the yellow hold bars on the other side, all three runways belong to Doherty again. An aircraft checks in on the frequency. ***"Tower, Delta Eight Fifteen is with you, ten mile final for Runway Two Two Left."***

"Delta Eight Fifteen, Newark Tower, five miles in trail of a heavy Boeing Seven Forty Seven, caution wake turbulence. Cleared to land Runway Two Two Left, wind two four zero at eight." While he is talking, Doherty is moving Delta's flight progress strip from its plastic holder in the arrival bay into the jaws of the time stamp. The action is performed at the same time, every time. Doherty knows that to be perfect, he has to be like a machine. If he suddenly woke up at

the Local Control position, the placement of the paper strips would tell him exactly what is happening with the airplanes. A strip in or on the time stamp means one thing and nothing else. To vary the routine is to court disaster. Attention to tedious detail is obedience to God. The reward is knowing, with absolute certainty, the identity, position and intentions of all of the aircraft within Doherty's area of responsibility. As a young trainee, like any other, Doherty has experienced the feeling of "losing the picture," or "going down the pipes." Like sea sickness, it's a feeling you don't want to get again, so you do what it takes to prevent it from happening. For a tower controller, that means you become machine- like in your actions, automatic…electric.

The tin man harkens back to a time when he was still allowed to train others. Sensing that a young man lacked confidence, he urged the new guy to take stock of present company – the qualified controllers all around him.

"Look around, Bob. Take a good look at the people assembled here. Do they look special to you? Do you think they were born control tower operators? Do you think their parents willed them their skills? Do you think any one of them is smarter than you? Let me give you the straight skinny and don't forget it, because if you think for one minute that you are less able or somehow unworthy – you're finished…and you might as well pack it in. Everyone up here has had to learn this job just the way you are learning it, and they made the same boneheaded mistakes that you've been making. Nobody is born an air traffic controller; it is a learned function. Don't believe me? Ask any one of them. They'll tell you the same thing. You feel inadequate, uneasy. I know the feeling well, and so does everyone else. Just know that you're gaining experience and you're getting better every day. Then one day you'll look around, and the people you thought were so smart will suddenly remind you of the retards that rode in on the short bus. That's when you become a tin man…when you know you're better than anyone else."

"Virgin" Mary overhears the conversation and her face tightens with a look of disgust. She exchanges a knowing glance with one of her girlfriends.

"Apple One Eleven, Runway Two Two Right, taxi into position and hold."

"Apple One Eleven, position and hold."

"People Three Fourteen, cross Runway Two Two Right, traffic holding in position, contact Ground point eight on the other side."

"People Three Fourteen, crossing with you, then ground." Doherty looks at the strip bays. The traffic load is diminishing. He's already getting bored. Beans Larkin has a trivia question about a song he heard on an FM oldies radio station. "Hey Willie, I don't know the name of this one but it goes like this: (Larkin croaks out the "hook" line.) *You're not sick…your just in love…*

Doherty recognizes the long lost oldie.

"It's *Twistin' Pneumonia*, by The Genies, 1960 on Warwick. It was a Long Island group with two guys from Brooklyn." They had some local success with it." Larkin shakes his head in amazement. "How do you remember this stuff? Were you a disc jockey in a previous life? Are you Wolfman Jack? Alan Freed, reincarnated?"

Later that evening Beans Larkin is driving home. *Twistin' Pneumonia* is still in his head.

When you love me, you shatter my brain
I know I'm sick, but I'm feelin' no pain.

In the middle of the song, an intruding, unwelcome phrase keeps recurring in Larkin's head: DM 135! DM 135! Larkin punches a button on the radio, trying to get the phrase out of his head. Turning the volume up, he pushes his car into the fast lane to pass a few trucks on the turnpike. *DM 135! Jesus! One simple bit of coordination. A six syllable phrase! Six dead! And all that was needed to prevent it was DM 135! A falcon jet surprises a Local Controller in the tower at Teterboro and ends up smacking into a Piper Cherokee.* Larkin imagines the horrible scene on the ground in Fairview and Cliffside Park, New Jersey. The Local controller got no prior notice that the Falcon jet was coming to shoot the VOR approach to a full stop landing at Teterboro. Prior notice should have come in the form of a printed flight strip. Because the business jet departed earlier than planned, the computer did not recognize the beacon code assigned to the flight. When that happens an inbound strip is not generated, nor does one print at the inbound destination. *So, what? It happens all the time. DM 135!*

Larkin knows the approach controller involved in the mid-air collision. He's a guy named Steve Keeler who dropped out of Yale Law School. Larkin and Keeler attended the FAA Academy together.

Jesus Christ, Steve! DM135! All you had to do was turn around and shout it out! DM135! Then the Flight Data guy punches five keys on the FDEP! DM135! Departure Message, strip number One Thirty Five! An information strip gets generated, sent to Teterboro Tower- no surprises, no collision- no lives ended or survivor's lives ruined!

Larkin rocks back and forth in the driver's seat, then pounds his fist on the dash. His eyes well up with anger at the unkind and unlucky circumstances that turned his friend's life into a living nightmare of constant self-doubt and "what ifs." The sad truth is that Steve Keeler failed to coordinate when he had a clear duty to do so. Lawyers call that sort of thing *negligence*. The FAA calls it… routine…if they call it anything at all. And the devil? He knows all about it. Negligence is the springtide that floats his shabby raft, and if it lifts him high enough he can toll the bells of hell. The devil hates the tin men because they are guardian angels incarnate- less than a god, but certainly more than a man. The service they provide is good, noble, and righteous. The devil understands this. And so, he waits and listens…peering through the big tower windows from his perch on the catwalk…biding his time…rocking to and fro on his nasty feet, using his tail to provide the motion…waiting patiently for carelessness to open the door, and horror and death to come riding in. When death arrives, its mount will be a swaybacked nag, a pale horse named negligence.

CHAPTER 54

Driving home after a mid-watch, Doherty passes by the old north terminal. At one time, it was the home of Newark Airport, the operations center, the passenger terminal and the control tower too. You could fit the entire building into the corner of one of Newark's massive parking lots today. For all outward appearances, the building is common and insignificant, yet is one of New Jersey's most important landmarks. On a lark, Doherty decides to take a closer look.

The front doors are open and once inside Doherty can tell that the lower floors have been sectioned off into smaller offices. On the wall a sign points the direction to the office of the Auto Theft Task Force. A door on the left opens to reveal stairs and Doherty climbs two dusty flights to the ancient control tower. The glass dome of the tower cab is shaped like an upside down canoe or a long inverted relish dish. Remarkably, not one of the many, small, glass window-panes is cracked or missing. A black desk model telephone sits on a plywood console, its cord severed and neatly coiled, as if someone was about to take it away. The vinyl, tiled floor is in new condition but is dusty and lacking wax. The tin man looks around in amazement, wondering what it must have been like, working live air traffic in a facility such as this, when aviation was young, its future still very bright.

Wow. Holy shit. I'm standing in the nation's very first control tower. I'm walking in William "Whitey" Conrad's footsteps. He was the first air traffic controller and he worked right here. That was back when the runway was called the "cinder patch" and Whitey and the boys were working Ford tri-motors and snub-nosed Curtis Condors and tail-draggers like DC3's and Boeing 247's. They must have built this place when Christ was a Lance Corporal.

Doherty's mind wanders through history up to the present state of air traffic control and the FAA.

Kind of ironic they called him "Whitey." I'll bet he never worked along side a negro or a broad ass. I'll bet no one ever questioned it either. Maybe I was born in the wrong era. Maybe I should've been working in THIS tower, a member of Whitey's crew, the original tin man and his merry band of hard-chargers. Imagine. You could fart out loud if you wanted to. You could spout all the words that have been long banished from the American workplace. You could bad mouth foreigners and minorities, if you had a mind to, even Jews and Italians. And the guy next to you? It's likely he's a veteran like you, so you can trade sea stories, and there's that mutual respect among warriors. Sure, you're bound to encounter personality conflicts…but nothing like the climate of fear and loathing that permeates today's "diverse" control towers.

Doherty takes one final look around, hoping to find a genie in a bottle, or the Ghost of Aviation's Past.

If I could just click my heels three times and go back…I'd do it right now. I'd start my next shift right here, say, fifty years ago. My white shirts would go perfectly with this place. All I'd need is a bow tie.

The tin man looks at the two clocks recessed into the console. One clock is for the local time and one for Greenwich Mean, or "Zulu" time.

Why do I get these longings for the past? Why do I constantly see and hear things that no longer exist? Why do I resist conforming to current societal norms and contemporary styles? Maybe I'm the ghost…maybe I'm some sort of time traveler, a home-sick bastard living in two different dimensions.

The tin man reaches toward a console and slides a drawer open. Inside is an old World War Two-era headset with a heavy adjustable boom and a conical shaped ear and mouthpiece. Fingering the heavy, two pronged, jack-piece, he resists the urge to slip the headgear on.

In the supervisor's room adjacent to the secretary's office, Frank Hamblin is once again, applying a mixture of Polo by Ralph Lauren, and urine by Liam Doherty, to his face and neck. In a few minutes, he will be meeting with a young controller on his team to deliver some bad news. The young man has failed to certify on the Ground Control position in the allotted hours available and accordingly, his training at Newark Tower is now terminated. Hamblin pulls the letter from his file, copied from his stack of boilerplate letters that the supervisors keep on hand so that they don't have to actually compose anything, just fill in the blanks. The letter explains that the young man's status as an employee is now in a state of limbo until management decides what to do with him. It is likely that he will transfer to a less busy tower at a smaller airport, but the FAA can in fact terminate his employment if they choose to. After scaring the young controller trainee by explaining the worst-case scenario, Hamblin plays the magnanimous role by assuring his charge that he will recommend a transfer to a slower facility. Hamblin points out that there are many cases of controllers failing the training program, starting over somewhere else, and returning to succeed at Newark Tower.

At this point in these counseling sessions, Hamblin likes to add his own cute rhetorical flourish. He pauses a few seconds and makes eye contact with the employee before delivering his favorite quotation, tailor made for these occasions.

"Love is lovelier,
The second time around.
Much more beautiful,
With both feet on the ground."

The young controller is a bit scared, but mostly embarrassed and ashamed. He apologizes to Frank Hamblin and thanks him for the opportunity and for all the help he has received. When he reports for his next shift, he apologizes to the members of his team and thanks them, also. It never occurs to the young man to blame anyone but himself for the failure. When he meets with NATCA Rep Paul Veale, he tells him there will be no grievance, and he will accept whatever decision the FAA makes concerning his future.

In fact, the young trainee's failure is not his fault, but rests squarely with Supervisor Frank Hamblin. Hamblin took a smoothly operating, straightforward, relatively uncomplicated and basic ground control operation and turned it into a botched abortion, a complicated cluster-fuck, intentionally making it far more difficult than it needs to be.

Even so, the young training failure could easily make this cup pass. He could claim some sort of victim status. He could claim that his Great –Great uncle on his mother's side was Hispanic, and he overheard someone call him a "spic." He could claim that he was under marital stress or that his kid got arrested and he was having turmoil at home. If a trainee is a female, a whole new world of excuses unfolds. "My husband is pressuring me to have children." "I'm having a difficult pregnancy." "Some of the men on my team keep staring at me." "Someone said I have *piano* legs."

In the FAA's upside down world, the accountable ones are those with the least amount of authority. The trainee that Hamblin is washing out, has more integrity and guts than the FAA supervisor will ever know. It seems that wherever virtue is found in the FAA it must be eliminated, transferred, defeated. The slimy, the inept, the corrupt, they get second and third chances and prime consideration for promotion. Dependable men of character get demoralized and humiliated on their way out the door.

And now, another future tin man gets sidetracked, his career thrown into the ice box for a while. His only sin? He couldn't navigate his way out of Hamblin's House of Horrors- the new and improved Ground Control position. Even so, this young trainee who had the bad luck to sail into a foul wind named Francis Hamblin, then found his ship in irons, will be back somewhere, sometime, because he's got a few basic tools in his ditty bag. He's got a little bit of what it takes, even though no one in the FAA, except a few tin men, can even recognize it, much less name it.

Walking near Wall street, Doherty stops amid other pedestrians waiting for the light to change on Broadway. A young business type, a suit, perhaps a stockbroker, is at the curb directly in front. The tin man looks around, feeling a bit uneasy like he sometimes does in crowds. Suddenly a blast of marijuana smoke exits from the mouth of the suit, curls around his head rearward and hits Doherty full in the face. Angered, he voices his umbrage. "Hey meat-whistle! You want to blow that shit in someone else's direction?" The yuppie turns and looks at Doherty. Just then, the light turns green and the suit steps off the curb, but not without a parting response.

"Blow me."

The tin man reaches out to stop the smoker. Doherty intends to inflict pain. He spins the offender around and the yuppie pulls away, but Doherty's left hand is clenched on the fat end of a silk necktie. Still holding the tie, with the same hand he delivers a short, quick jab landing full on the chin. Like a tetherball, the yuppie's head is jerked back into Doherty's fist when the necktie fetches up. The two quick blows to the chin and face cause the suit to stumble backwards. Then, almost comically, the smoker looks quizzically at Doherty for a long moment. At first, he appears to have weathered the attack quite easily, but then the legs stop working. After a pratfall onto the crosswalk the stoner sits there with his eyes closed, one hand on the asphalt as if he's trying to stop Manhattan from spinning. A spot of blood appears, slow dripping from a nostril. Pedestrians walk around, unconcerned except that the light may change soon. A large cop appears.

"What happened here?"

A skinny, twenty-something female with stringy hair and a John Lennon tee shirt, points at Doherty and starts shrieking: "He like, hit that man in the face like ten fucking times! He just walked up to him and starting punching him for no fucking reason!" Doherty glances down at the tee shirt. John Lennon in his silly granny glasses, underscored with the word: IMAGINE. Doherty considers the one word message on the shirt.

Imagine there's no Beatles…Hell! Imagine there's no England.

The cop turns toward Doherty.

"Is that true?"

"He blew marijuana smoke in my face. That's assault." Doherty points to the marijuana joint lying on the curb.

"Then he suggested that I perform oral sex on him."

The cop nods. "And you objected, naturally."

"I'm trying to quit." Besides, I didn't want to lead him on like that."

The cop turns toward the yuppie, now back on his feet. "You okay? You want to go to the hospital, get checked out?"

"No. I'll be alright. I need to get back to my office."

"Okay. If you want to press charges, you can. But if you do, you will also be charged… for misdemeanor possession of marijuana. You got any more on you?"

The yuppie pulls out a small zip-lock plastic bag and hands it to New York's finest.

"I don't want to press charges."

More cops have arrived. Two are standing behind Doherty." Only the big cop is speaking and he turns his attention back toward Doherty.

"What about you, tough guy? You got enough satisfaction? I mean you got a little smoke in your face, and you want to start world war three. Where do you work?"

"I'm with the FAA. I'm an air traffic controller. I could lose my job if I flunk a drug test. That's why I don't like getting marijuana smoke blown in my face."

As the yuppie departs, the big cop gives Doherty a long look, stopping at his shoes.

"Were you in the service?"

"Marine Corps."

"Viet Nam?"

"Japan."

"See any action in JUH-PAN?"

"All I could afford."

The big cop exchanges glances with his partners, and Doherty evaluates his position.

If he was going to arrest me, he would have done it already.

The big cop speaks again. "You're lucky I didn't witness this incident, or you'd be locked up right now. Here's your license. Now get the hell out of here before I change my mind."

"Thank you, Sir."

Doherty takes his leave. The incident and the policeman's reaction only reinforce his beliefs about law enforcement, especially the big city variety.

You can always count on a cop to be lazy. Sometimes it works in your favor.

CHAPTER 55

A year after the Veale Initiative was cancelled and discarded by the FAA, Paul Veale gets a call from the aviation division of the Port Authority. A female assistant to the Aviation Division Manager has a few questions. It seems that someone is still pressing a case for delay reduction at Newark Airport, and the Veale plan has resurfaced. The new manager of the Port Authority's Aviation Division wants some answers, so his assistant calls NATCA.

"Mr. Veale, why do you think the Veale Initiative could actually reduce delays at Newark Airport…to any real degree?"

"Call me Paul."

"Okay, Paul."

"The plan has been tested, both by computer simulation and actual live traffic testing in the control tower. It works. The controllers know it works, and the FAA knows it works. There's no question about it. In fact, by NOT utilizing the Veale plan, the FAA is committing air traffic malpractice. They're intentionally delaying air carrier operations."

"Hmmm. I see." A pause ensues and the NATCA Rep assumes that notes are being taken.

The Port Authority secretary continues:

"But Mr. Veale, why would the FAA want to delay airplanes at Newark Airport?" Veale takes a deep breath of polluted New Jersey air and exhales before answering. Since he can smell beer brewing at the Bud plant, he knows the wind is from the west.

"It's because delays and accidents are what keeps the FAA in business. You can't be the answer to a problem if there is no problem. NATCA has shown you OUR solution to delays. It's simple. It's inexpensive. It's streamlined and effective. What does the FAA offer in contrast? They want you to believe that the problem is so complex, they will need more and better equipment, a larger table of organization, another layer of managers and bureaucrats, more controllers and more positions of operation in the tower…in fact they want a NEW control tower! Every answer they have requires MORE MONEY and a bigger empire for them. And after all that money is spent, they still can't produce any positive results."

In his mind, Veale pictures the FAA as a giant tick on the ass of the commercial aviation sector. He resists the urge to voice the metaphor. Veale continues.

"You think the FAA is in business to FIGHT delays, and to PREVENT accidents. I'm telling you they NEED these things. The Pope's nemesis is the devil. Did you ever stop to think about where the Pope would be if there was no devil?" Veale pauses here. He remembers that he's talking to a bureaucrat from a bi-state governmental agency – the Port Authority of New York and New Jersey - empire builders of the first order. After another pause, the Port Authority assistant manager questions Veale again.

"I've read the FAA's report to the Capacity Enhancement Team. Their reasons for canceling the Veale Initiative seem to make sense. They mentioned heavy jets, the weather, a lack of gate space at the airport, among other things. They also mentioned you. They said that you have an axe to grind." Veale laughs.

"Now maybe you can see the FAA's motives, and how disingenuous they are. You see, the biggest problem they have with Veale initiative is that it bears MY NAME!" That's how scarily juvenile and petty they are. Let me tell you that NATCA pleaded with FAA management. We don't care about the name. We told them they could take ALL of the credit, they could pretend the whole thing was their idea, and they could name the plan after Spiro Agnew if they so desired. NATCA's motives are pure. We simply want what's best for the flying public and the airlines. I didn't ask for any personal notoriety. You can thank a renegade, non-union controller in the tower who attached my name to the plan, without my permission. By doing so, he probably torpedoed the whole idea, because I'm telling you…that of all the problems that the FAA has with the Veale Initiative, its NAME is their primary concern." A muffled chuckle is heard on the line. Veale asks: "Are you still there?"

"Yes I'm here. I'm still digesting what you've just told me. It's kind of…bizarre. I'm not sure how I can report it to my boss, quite frankly." Veal nods to himself.

"It is what it is. Either I'm nuts, or the FAA is. Take your pick, because at this point, I don't really care. In five years I'm planning to retire…to some place where airplanes can't find me. I thought I might write a book about all of this. But then I'd have to THINK about the FAA."

"Thank you for your time, Mr. Veale." The NATCA Rep cradles the telephone receiver. He knows that the Port Authority manager thinks he is crazy, and believes everything the FAA has told her and her boss. Picking up his headset, Veale starts for the tower cab. A good long session of heavy tin slinging might actually be therapeutic.

Maria hasn't made herself available in over a week. Lately, telephone conversations have been short, with Maria claiming to be busy with police work. The tin man is worried, uneasy, but circumstances considered, if Maria wants to end the relationship, there is nothing that Doherty can do or say that will change her mind. Asking a woman to re-start a love that has ceased, or worse, one that never really existed, is like pissing in the fan.

One day Doherty calls and voices his concern that she is ending their relationship. Maria responds with words that are code for "it's over."

"I just need some time to think."

The sudden realization that their relationship has vanished, strikes fear into the tin man. It's the fear a sailor gets, when he finds his hull has been breached; his vessel is taking on water. He can bail all he wants – he'll just drown tired.

If it comes to this, Doherty decides that he will not withhold Maria's freedom from her, not even for a moment, not even long enough to ask her to change her mind. The tin man ponders the nature of freedom, the concept that underscores his libertarianism, the ideology that frees him, yet traps him at the same time.

Freedom. What greater gift can one give? A mother gives a child freedom from her womb, and endures great pain to do so. And now, Maria wants freedom from me, and runs to her abusive husband. It's her choice, her freedom of association, not mine. I can pray; I can hope, but in the end, not even Saint Expedite can deliver Maria to me. The only person that can send her into my arms is Maria herself, and I wouldn't have her any other way. I will give Maria her re-birth, as I cannot demand freedom for myself and deny it to her...but the pain...what do I do about the pain?

A week becomes two, then three. After a month, Doherty knows he is addicted, not to any controlled substance, but worse, to another person. It's worse, because a drug addict only needs money to get what he wants so badly. Money can never buy the love of a woman, despite jokes to the contrary.

The withdrawal pangs begin. Doherty tries to distract himself by working extra hours on position during the busiest times imaginable, hoping that the tin will demand all of his concentration, leaving no room for Maria. He starts reading Ayn Rand's tome, Atlas Shrugged, for the third time. He goes to movies alone. He starts an exercise program, running through the streets of Jersey City at Oh-Dark-Thirty. Nothing works; everywhere he goes, Maria is there. No greater reminder exists then the twin towers on the other side of the river, his next-state neighbors, Maria's place of employment. One day, while walking on the floating dock, a sudden weakness in the knees causes a momentary loss of balance. Leaning out against a wooden piling, the tin man vomits into the North River.

Judy Episcopo jacks into position on Local Control. Before taking a position relief briefing from Gordon Russo, she reports a concern:

"Hey G-Man, I just saw Willie in the break room. I think he's sick." Russo looks at Judy and waits for her to look away so that he can ogle her breasts.

"What'd he do, throw up down there?" Judy checks the radar. Matching an inbound radar target and data block to its flight progress strip, she pulls it from the strip bay and repositions it, now in its proper landing order.

"Nah. It wasn't what he *did*, it was more…what he *said,* that's got me really worried." The entire crew stops to wait for Judy to tell her story. Judy continues, loud enough for proper emphasis.

"Willie said, I DON'T CARE ABOUT THE TIN!" A collective gasp is heard and concerned glances are exchanged among the team.

A short while later, A Gulfstream G2 is on short final for Runway Two-Two Left. Judy is watching a Delta 737 that has just landed, but may not clear in time because the G2 is now about to land. Quickly measuring and re-measuring time and distance in her head, Judy ping-pongs between Delta and the G2, hoping for Delta to clear the runway before the G2 crosses landing threshold. When Delta rolls past the last available high speed turn off, it is clear that the operation cannot be saved. Judy starts the air show.

"Gulfstream Four Six Papa, GO AROUND, there's an airplane on the runway." The G2 pilot does not comply.

"Uh…yea, Tower, we're okay. We see the traffic, er, 737…he's clearing down there…we're fine." Now the G2 is on the runway, rolling up behind the 737. Brought quickly to taxi speed, there is no chance of a collision. There are however, two landing airplanes on the runway, and that is an air traffic no-no, a "deal", an operational error or a pilot deviation. It's a reportable incident, no matter who is at fault. Judy turns to Supervisor Jim Milner. Her left arm and index finger stab the air in the direction of the offender. While pointing at the G2, she loudly reports:

"I told that stupid sonofabitch to fucking GO AROUND, goddammit. Motherfucker! He refused to go around, Jimbo! He ate Delta's ass on final after I slowed him! He didn't listen to one fucking thing I said, and then he gives me a deal by landing without a clearance! Stupid, dick-less rat bastard!"

Jim Milner had been watching the entire operation and remained calm, but concerned, throughout. He answers Judy.

"Okay, Judy. You can stop calling him names, now. Give him the phone number and tell him to call the tower on the land-line when he gets to his parking ramp."

The G2 pilot calls. He knows he's in trouble, and his pilot's license is in jeopardy. His tone is contrite. "We're sorry, Sir. This is the last leg of a long flight, and we're very tired. We knew we had enough runway. We saw Delta clearing at the end and we just thought it was better to land than for us to go around." Supervisor Milner responds:

"I don't know where you usually operate, but at this facility, you need to comply with the controller's instructions. A "go around" is not a suggestion. It is not a request. It is a direct order for you to abandon your approach to the runway and stand by for further instructions. When you substitute your own judgment for the controller's, and land without a clearance…well, you're being…dangerous. The FAA does not license dangerous people to fly airplanes. Do I make myself clear?"

"Yes, Sir. I'm very sorry. It was a one time thing, Sir, I promise it will never happen again." The pilot is praying that Milner will cut him a huge chunk of FAA slack. Milner does.

"I'll tell you what. The record will show that the airplane ahead of you was clearing the runway, and that YOUR landing, although technically illegal, was safe. I will exercise some discretion here, and spare you a violation." The G2 driver sighs a silent sigh of relief.

"Thank you, Sir. I assure you we will use this incident as a learning experience, and please apologize to the Tower Controller for us, she did a great job." Milner responds:

"Okay. You guys have a good night and try to stay out of trouble."

"We will, Sir. Oh, and Sir, we fly to Vegas just about every weekend. You're certainly welcome to come along, any time you like." Milner chuckles.

"What? The way YOU guys fly? Thanks, but no thanks, guy. I don't want to use up all my luck just GETTING to Las Vegas!"

Milner rotates the controllers to give Judy a break from the position, and to cover everyone's ass. Should Judy subsequently have another incident or a crash, the G2 pilot deviation would become an issue, perhaps even a contributing factor. Whenever a controller gets upset on position, no matter what the circumstances, it simply makes sense to give that controller a break, and to protect everybody involved.

Downstairs in the ready room, Judy quickly forgets the G2 incident and uses the time to flirt with a new employee, a tall, handsome, flight data assistant from Cape May. Wasting no time, Judy introduces the new guy to her breasts. Bending over the table, she smiles and offers him a generous wedge of pound cake on a paper plate.

"Want some cake?"

The new guy takes what is offered: the cake, and the flick. He is now officially a part of the running freak show that is Newark Tower. It's like getting on a roller coaster. Once you're strapped in, you're there for whatever comes next.

On a 3-11 evening watch, the traffic demand is such that two controllers are needed to stay over and help the midnight crew. Around 1:00 AM, Liam Doherty and Judy Episcopo are in the elevator going home. Since the building is empty except for the controllers working in the cab, the elevator is taking a long time between door openings. Judy reaches out and hits the stop button, halting the elevator. She turns and traps Doherty against the back wall. Her breasts are touching his shirt, and her eyes look straight into his. Doherty always knew that a "Judy" moment like this would eventually happen. Judy speaks without losing eye contact.

"I have a serious question, and I want a straight answer."

"Judy, you're scaring me."

"Shut the fuck up. You're not scared, and we both know it. Now answer my question."

"Sure, Judy, what is it?"

Judy is now closer than the employee handbook allows. Her breath smells of Wrigley's Juicy Fruit chewing gum. Her eyes are searching closer, and the tip of her tongue appears momentarily to moisten her lips. Her mouth does a tiny flex thing, as if she is trying to taste Doherty's face without actually touching it.

"Why don't you ever come on to me? Don't you like me?"

Her eyes leave the tin man's to look at his lips, then, they return to his eyes. She does it again. He can feel her knee moving in, touching his leg.

"I-I don't know, Judy, I guess I, we... never had the opportunity before." Judy cocks her head slightly and moves in even closer. A Post-It note couldn't fit between their lips, but still no contact. Doherty has decided that if there's going to be a kiss, it's going to be HER idea, and her action, not his. Judy closes her eyes, and inhales deeply through her nose. When she does, her breasts heave slightly, pressing closer into Doherty's starched white shirt.

Judy turns about suddenly and pushes a button on the operating panel. A few seconds later, she steps into the first floor foyer.

"Hey Judy, where're you going?" She stops and looks back at Liam Doherty, still in the elevator.

"I'm going home, Willie. Good night." The doors start to close and Doherty slaps the "door open" button and follows Judy to the door. In the parking lot, he watches Judy get into her car and drive away. The tin man's dick is harder than Chinese arithmetic. Doherty looks up at the neon eagle flapping its wings on the roof of the Bud plant. It seems to be mocking him. In his car, Doherty grips the steering wheel tightly, trying to normalize his blood flow. He looks at his arms. Judy would have been a welcome diversion, but his arms ache with a special need.

Back on board, conditions are causing *Tipitina* to fight her lines. The vessel is twisting and jerking in the slip, like a wild filly trying to break free and run with her friend, the wind. Doherty considers taking a hotel room for the night to get some sleep. He stares at the telephone, but he knows she won't call. He picks up a paperback novel – it belongs to Maria. Touching the book like she would, he thinks about her hands. He imagines her hands holding the book, turning the pages. A dog-eared page gets special attention. Laid back on the settee he presses the book to his chest, crossing his arms over it. The tin man weeps.

CHAPTER 56

NATCA Rep Paul Veale is summoned to a meeting in the manager's office. John Biderman is seated behind the big executive desk in the big leather executive chair. The assistant manager is present and Veale has asked Beans Larkin to sit in as a witness for the union. Veale has no idea about the purpose of the meeting. Even though smoking is banned in the building, the manager's office stinks from cigarette smoke. A ceiling panel is out of place and a coil of wire is hanging down near a portrait of Ronald Reagan. Dante Moore goes to the desk and takes a piece of rock candy from a glass jar. The door remains open and Veale winks at Betty Jackson working at her desk in the adjacent foyer. Veale's mind wanders, lusting for Betty, Newark Tower's black pearl.

I'll bet she'd like some cream in her coffee.

Biderman speaks. "Paul, we want to talk about the opening for a new Program Specialist." The tower manager adjusts the position of three folders, aligning one with the left edge of his desk blotter. He looks up toward Veale. "We've narrowed the field of candidates down to two controllers: Thad Jamison and Jim Kent." Biderman pauses. Veale makes no comment, so Biderman continues. "Kent and Jamison are pretty evenly qualified, so we decided to call it a dead heat on the points, and whoever does better on the interviews will be selected for the new position. Both candidates will interview twice, once with me, and once with Dante Moore." Biderman nods toward the Assistant Manager. Veale smells a giant FAA rat.

"You said you are *calling* it a dead heat. What were the points?" Biderman probes the inside of his cheek with his tongue. He's annoyed at the question.

“It really doesn’t matter. It’s close enough to call it even, and we’ve considered other factors, favorable to both candidates. We think this is a fair way to make the selection.” Without losing eye contact, Veale repeats the question.

“What were the points?”

Biderman leans forward, now more than annoyed, especially since Veale does not seem to be intimidated by the big desk, the leather executive chair, the flags or the portrait of President Reagan.

“It doesn’t matter. We’re not going strictly on points.” Veale leans back on the sofa. With one arm on the backrest, he cocks his head to look up at the ceiling and speaks. This time the words come more slowly for emphasis.

“What… were… the… points?”

Biderman, pressed like a nearly spent tube of toothpaste, exudes a little more information.

“Thaddeus has the edge on Jimmy Kent. He’s got more radar experience, and almost two years of college.” The NATCA Rep is now fed up with the word games and the lack of candor.

“Do I have to give you a written information request to get you to answer a simple question here? What were the NUMBERS, John…the POINTS? And if I can’t put a numerical value on the next word spoken here, I am walking out that fucking door.” Veale points toward Betty Jackson’s office and the foyer. Biderman looks over at Moore. As Moore shrugs his shoulders, Biderman speaks.

“Six.”

“SIX! Jesus Christ, John! Six? You call that an edge? That’s a landslide, considering he only needs a ONE POINT advantage to win!”

Veale can’t believe what he is witnessing. Incredibly, FAA management is screwing a black controller out of a job that is rightfully his, and giving it to a white boy. He thinks:

This is totally out of character for these guys. Normally they screw the white male and pass the savings on to the affirmative action candidate. For some queer reason they want Kent to have this job, but as dumb-ass luck would have it, a more qualified black man stands in the way. How ironic. They want their golden boy in place so badly; they are willing to nullify the rules, risking an EEOC complaint and a lawsuit to get their way.

Veale speaks:

"Did you get these two mixed up? You know who's who, here, don't you? I know that Jimmy Kent is Frank Hamblin's favorite butt boy. I know that he's a fascist, management wannabe, but surely you realize that he has already lost this job on points – TO A BLACK MAN!" Veale looks at Moore. "Did YOU go along with this, Dante? I'm surprised at you!" The assistant manager speaks up:

"Hey, that's not fair, and I resent the implication! We didn't consider race at all…never…at any time during the selection process." Veale answers:

"Well, you should have. Because even giving the *appearance* of racial discrimination is unlawful, and you guys know this! Let's see…hmmm…taking three points from a black employee, and giving those points to a white guy…to keep the black employee from getting the position he deserves, and effectively handing over his well earned promotion to the white boy…I wonder if THAT will look like discrimination to the EEOC or the Merit Systems Protection Board? What do you guys think?"

Biderman and Moore exchange glances as an uncomfortable silence descends on the room. Veale again:

"So what is it that you guys need from me? Did you want me to sign something? Do you want NATCA to validate this new promotion policy?"

After a long silence, Veale takes his leave, stopping at Betty's desk. He rocks his head around on his shoulders like a proud horse. "How do you like me now?"

"I like you a lot, Paul, I always have. Here, take these." Betty hands Veale some EEOC complaint forms for Thaddeus Jamison. On top of the forms is a Hershey's Kiss. The imagery of a chocolate kiss is not lost on the NATCA Facility Rep.

Veale can't wait to meet with Thaddeus Jamison to tell him that he just hit the FAA jackpot. Jamison will likely settle for a boatload of cash, and a supervisor's slot at Philadelphia. Veale suspects that the FAA managers did it on purpose. They promoted two at once-Kent through normal promotion channels, and Jamison through the EEOC discrimination complaint process.

The NATCA Rep, Paul Veale is asked to appear on a Sunday TV news program on Channel 7 in New York. Since the show is taped a week in advance, Veale and Doherty are watching the broadcast with two other controllers in the ready room. The show is a "fluff" piece, a filler, for the local station to air on early Sunday morning when few are watching. The typical questions are asked. "How many controllers are on duty at Newark Tower?" "What is the name of your union? What is a typical work day like for an air traffic controller?" "How much training is required of a controller?" After the first break, the host actually asks an important question: Why is there a need for a union, and what are some pressing issues for air traffic controllers at Newark?

Veale highlights a laundry list of complaints: not enough fully qualified controllers; short breaks and short meal breaks, sometimes none at all. Veale points out that the equipment is outdated, unreliable, and prone to failure. This includes the radios and radar failing frequently, usually during periods of intense traffic. The NATCA Rep goes on to blame FAA management for being overbearing, incompetent and fraudulent with Congress, their employees and the flying public. Veale explains that safety incidents are ignored, covered up or downgraded deceitfully. Controllers are denied their sick leave, vacations, and are frequently left on position longer than the safety guidelines permit.

The picture that Veale is painting for the TV viewers is not a pretty one. Yet inexplicably, in answer to the host's final question about overall safety, Veal contradicts himself: "The air traffic control system is absolutely safe. It's the safest system in the world… flying is far, far safer than driving."

Liam A. Doherty leaps to his feet. "Christ, Paul! Whose side on you on here? SAFE? Did you say SAFE? You unload on the FAA with a laundry list of SAFETY items, safety violations, and then you say that this system is SAFE? Do you realize what a contradiction that is? Do you know how fucking STUPID you sounded? Veale stands up and confronts Doherty.

"I don't see any point in scaring the public. You know, if no one flies, we don't have a job. Did you ever think of that?"

"Yea, I thought of that. If people stop flying, economic pressure will be brought to bear, then, maybe the system gets fixed. Isn't that what you want, Paul?"

"Hey, I don't need this shit from you. You're not even a member, so don't concern yourself with anything the union says or any positions we take. As far as I'm concerned, you're just a fucking SCAB!"

Doherty stares at Veale. He analyzes the union Rep's attitude and motives.

Just like a collectivist. Safety in numbers, misery loves company… all those cliché's apply. Some people just cannot stand up, on their own, with no weapon but their own intellect and their own confidence. They feel empowered when surrounded by others just like themselves. Deep down inside, they really believe in their own worthlessness. They can only gain strength from others, and that's a false strength, which is really a weakness. Veale shows signs of intestinal fortitude at times, but he knows his union posse is always ready to ride to the rescue. Like the time he stood up to Dante Moore. He knew he couldn't be fired or disciplined. It wasn't him, it was the union talking. He's got the Wagner Act, The union contract and a team of lawyers backing him up. Strip him of that armor, relieve him of those reinforcements, and he's a pussy, a bed-wetter, just like the rest of these FAA punks.

The tin man responds to the union Rep.

"What you did was stupid, Paul, and you know it. That's why you're pissed. Don't take it out on me, you only have yourself to blame. You expect me to dummy up, and not criticize you? Is that what you want? Well, you'll have to get that kind of service from your fellow union brothers. They don't talk much 'cause they all got their faces buried in your ass…except the lesbians, they got each other."

The two men engage in a stare down. Their friendship has been fractured along the fault line that exists between independence and collectivism, between an objectivist attitude and the herd mentality.

Deep down somewhere in a place Paul Veale never talks about, he knows that Liam A. Doherty is right. Occasionally Veale can feel himself trying to break out, trying to free himself, from himself. As it always does, the feeling passes, and the union Rep reverts to his default position – worrying about what others think, and trying to live for other people.

Tommy Wiznak walks into the break room. He's shaking a box of Cracker Jack, trying to get the prize to float to the top. If it's something good, he may enlist it in his "hoodoo" militia. If it has some unique character, or if the trinket is perceived to be intrinsically magical or whimsical, Tommy will put it to good use. He can always use another sand bag to reinforce his mental bunker...a lucky charm to counter any bad karma. Tommy is about to report for duty in the tower cab. The weather is socked in, solid IFR, and three members of his team have called in sick. Bad weather, bad staffing, bad equipment and bad-ass traffic. It could be a long night for the home team, the kind of night that is tailor made for a deal or two. What will it be tonight? Maybe a pilot will abandon an approach without announcing that fact to the Local Controller, until a loss of IFR separation ensues. Maybe a pilot will get lost in the fog and taxi across an active runway. Maybe the radar will fail at the worst possible time. Maybe the delays will deplete the available gate space, and the Ground Controller will go "down the pipes," looking for space on the movement area to park airplanes. Whatever happens on tonight's evening watch will have to be dealt with.

Tommy is searching for help where no one else has thought to look- in a box of sugar coated popcorn and peanuts.

Somewhere outside the devil laughs. The laugh resonates on the windows of the tower cab, lost amid the sound of the wind driven raindrops against the angled glass.

On his day off, Doherty rides the PATH train to lower Manhattan. The train approaches the World Trade Center and the realization that he is geographically close to Maria causes the physiological process that is all too familiar. First, the butterflies in the gut, then, the dull ache and pangs of tightness in the chest. Then, for a long moment, the tin man feels vacant, like there is a large hole where his torso should be, and people can see through it. He feels himself slipping into irrelevance, starting to disappear. Thoughts of helping the process are entertained. Surely then, the pain would cease. The tin man surveys the commuters on the train.

What do they see, when they look at someone like me? They probably think, "there's a tough guy. He looks like a cop or a military type. He looks capable, able to handle himself." Human beings are so limited. We see almost nothing. Hell, a dog can see a thousand times more with his nose, than we can see with our eyes. That's why one shouldn't care about another's opinion. Since their opinions are always based on scant information, they are always logically and scientifically unsound. They see broad shoulders, beefy forearms and a confident posture. They draw conclusions based on the superficial. I wonder what they would think of me if they knew the sad, inescapable truth: that I've been defeated…devastated…by a weakling, a five foot two brunette, and she didn't need to lift a finger to do it.

Walking toward the seaport, the tin man retraces the route of his first date with Maria. On Pearl Street he enters the same Irish pub where they took a meal. At the bar, Doherty re-reads the Irish Proclamation posted behind the bar. He considers the significance of the document and its beautiful prose. Only the Irish could give fighting words such elegance and texture, yet retain the important element of urgency that such a statement would naturally feature. He sips a whiskey and ponders the Irish:

I'm sure they just wanted to be left alone...left alone with their fields, and their shops and their church...content to come home to a fire and enjoy a pipe, or meet at the pub and sing their songs...and not an airplane in the sky, just big white clouds rolling by. I should be there. I would be there if not for some quirk in my family history, some unfortunate circumstance that caused my grandfather to be born on a ship, halfway between Ireland and Baltimore. There's nothing holding me here. I have no wife or kids. I have no Maria. Maybe the Irish will have me, if I get into that nasty little war they've got going on. The tin man focuses on words that seem to come alive: ***The Irish republic is entitled to, and hereby claims, the allegiance of every Irishman and Irishwoman.*** *I should go there, and offer them my allegiance. Maybe I can claim to be a political refugee in search of freedom, one of the huddled masses who bounced off the golden door and wants a return to the teeming shore, no longer yearning to breathe free, now just wanting to spend himself in a worthy cause. To die of natural causes would be such a waste of life, and dishonorable.*

For the next two months Doherty readies *Tipitina* for a sea voyage. He considers a new name for the sloop, re-commissioning his vessel, with a name that reflects the spirit of her future home, like *Warrior Poet, or Fenian.*

Mark Cushing is out on extended sick leave, for elective surgery. He has decided to have his stomach stapled. At 405 pounds, his crew figured he was one Pop Tart away from exploding like a giant keg of gunpowder. The loss of another full performance level controller makes the tower seriously short of qualified personnel. In this case it means the loss of one massively rotund control tower operator, so visibility in the tower cab is increased dramatically. Cushing has been known by various monikers, one being "a total eclipse of the airport." His shadow has been known to change the official temperature in Elizabeth, New Jersey. Because of Cushing's absence, Judy Episcopo has just been notified that her annual two-week summer leave has been canceled. Judy is not happy with her overweight co-worker, and she lacks any sympathy toward his unfortunate condition. She signs in for duty in the tower cab and immediately unloads, in her comically profane way.

"The fucking CRISCO KID! Just because that FAT, GLUTTONOUS, OBESE, COCKSUCKER can't take a meal without gnawing the legs off the fucking buffet table, I have to cancel MY GOD-DAMNED PLANS!" Judy jerks her headset from its plastic, zippered bag and flings the empty bag against one of the large windows. The bag slides down the slanted pane and comes to rest on the sill. "That greasy…lard-assed…SON-OF-A-BITCH! The last time he went to the Zoo, one of the animals turned up missing. They followed the trail of bones all the way to that FAT LOSER'S house!" Throughout the rest of the evening watch, Judy stays distracted, making comments, fat jokes, and generally expressing hatred toward Mark Cushing. The only smile she could muster came later in the watch, when Ray Martino presented a homemade get-well card, and asked each member of the crew to sign it for Cushing. Judy opens the card and reads the inscription:

DIE, YOU SICK BASTARD!!

CHAPTER 57

Because of Charles' deal, the tower has been the focus of a few news stories that are embarrassing for the FAA. Rumors are flying about a renegade controller who is feeding selected news stories to the press, and then gleefully watching the FAA managers dancing through all the hoops, trying to explain how serious near collisions are being reported and investigated, but only after the newspapers start asking questions.

The FAA has decided to take action. Liam Doherty is summoned to the manager's office at the tower. Biderman is holding court and a manager from the Eastern Region named Rod Harris is present, along with two staff specialists for reinforcement. Four against one- the tin man likes the odds. Marines are happiest when they are outnumbered. He strides over to the big desk. He knows that a union rep is called for, but decides not to ask for one.

Biderman speaks: "Willie, I believe you know Rod and the rest of my staff?"

"Of course, John, thy rod and thy staff… they comfort me."

"That's very clever, Willie. Let me get to the point. I want you to know that when controllers bid on job vacancies, we managers talk to each other. I get calls nearly every day, from managers in places like Tampa, Phoenix, even Honolulu. If they ask me about a guy who is bidding on a vacancy, I tell them. What I say about a controller, goes a long way in determining the outcome of a particular vacancy selection. If a guy is not a team player, if he can't be trusted or is disloyal toward management, I tell them that. I can guarantee you, such a controller will not get selected, and he could find himself languishing at Newark Tower for quite a long time, maybe his entire career." Biderman leans back in his chair and watches Doherty, waiting for a response. Doherty snorts, then chuckles, laughing in Biderman's face.

Biderman bristles. "Something funny?"

"Yes, John. Something is very funny. It's funny that you would try to intimidate me this way. It's funny because it can't work and I'll tell you why. I like it here. I like it fine. Me and Newark Tower, it's a comfortable fit." Doherty takes a few seconds to glance around the room, taking in the shabbiness. A cockroach charges on a piece of something near the coat rack. "There's a lot to like here. I like the smell of the place, you know, the jet fuel, the diesel odor from the turnpike, the burning rubber from the heavy jets touching down on runway two-two right, the refineries and the landfill. Take a whiff, John. I'm sure you can smell it too." The manager looks around the room as if asking for help. Rod Harris flares his large nostrils, head raised slightly, trying to identify the smells that Doherty has just described.

"I belong here, John. Newark Tower is my natural home. I know the cockroaches and their children by name, the rats too. Most of all, I like the big tin around here. I mean where else can I line up twenty five commercial jets in a long straight line like they're waiting to receive Communion? C'mon, John! They don't get massive tin like this in Phoenix. What kind of a pussy would want to work in a place like that? And my skills get tested here, you know? I like that. I like having equipment that can be counted on for nothing, except to fail at the worst possible time. I love it when the radios shit the bed, at the exact moment I need to send a heavy jet around because an undisciplined pedestrian decides to jaywalk across the runway. I like it when Air Force One is on final, and the wires behind the Local Control console start arcing and smoking, and the Secret Service agent starts looking at me like I'm an immediate threat to national security. I like pretending I can see airplanes at night, through windows totally unsuited to the task, because FAA maintenance personnel tossed out some essential equipment. I really enjoy participating in the FAA's giant social engineering program called affirmative action. I mean, hey! I'm damned glad to help out. There's nothing quite like the fuzzy feeling you get, knowing that the guy on your left and the one on your right are incompetent and dangerous, but why should anyone care? They like taking warm showers together, and you get points for buggery in this man's FAA. No, John, don't you worry about me. If anyone calls, you just tell 'em, thanks but no thanks, I'm staying right here. Tell them I'm not a team player. Tell them I'm disloyal and can't be trusted. Just make sure I stay right here, because I'm the Pope of Newark Tower. This is where I belong.

CHAPTER 58

After the PATCO strike of 1981, the FAA hired a new controller work force. Wide-eyed and energetic, the new guys were mostly thrilled to be in their new situation. And what's not to like about this control tower? You come to work carrying no tools. You don't get your hands dirty. Your "office" is a clean, air conditioned tower with a great view of Manhattan and The Statue of Liberty. Or, at least it's supposed to be clean and air conditioned. Aside from the pressure of the training program, and the ever-present specter of a "deal," or some other kind of operational mishap, your life is set.

The FAA managers and supervisors, although not fired during the strike were under scrutiny by congress. They came to work with a new attitude, determined to ensure that the workplace was a happy one. They wanted their new charges to be happy and content- at least until the scrutiny subsided. There were, however, some controllers who did not go on strike, and knew the supervisors and managers before they got religion, and knew quite well, that the FAA's new act was just that – an act.

Brendan Kelly, A Citadel graduate, and an air force veteran who served in Vietnam, is one of the "old" guys. Kelly was and is, constantly passed over for promotion, probably for the sin of being a veteran, but more likely because he was willing to speak up about safety infractions. Kelly, like Liam Doherty, does not kiss the big shiny FAA ass. Because he has such a bad attitude, he is allowed to come to work and collect his pay. He will not, however, be admitted into the club. He will not be given a license to lie, nor will he be anointed in a special ceremony, when the hairy, dank cloak of accountability will be lifted from his shoulders. Kelly and Doherty have much in common, but in contrast to the brash, in-your-face style of Doherty, Brendan Kelly is quiet and unassuming. Because of his reserved style, FAA management is less threatened by Kelly, yet Kelly is not lacking in courage.

During a Midnight watch, Brendan Kelly discusses the new and improved FAA management with a new guy.

Kelly: "You like it here? Everything Okay?"

New Guy: "Sure…It's all good… Why not?"

Kelly: "You should consider the pendulum."

New Guy: "The…pendulum?"

Kelly: "Yes. The pendulum. It swings."

The new guy takes a long look at Brendan Kelly. Kelly is a walking and talking contrast. Mostly quiet, almost shy, he seems like he should be a librarian or an accountant…someone who keeps his head buried in books, someplace where conflict with real human beings never enters. Yet if you watch closely, he walks with a military bearing, the way that some have that is hard to define, yet instantly recognizable. When he does make eye contact with you, you know who is in charge.

New Guy: Oh…Kay…Tell me how it swings."

Kelly: "You'll see. And one day you will tell me I'm right. You think this is pretty good. This is a great place to work. It won't always be this way. One day, things will take a dramatic turn. It will happen so fast, you will be stunned." Kelly stops to adjust the resolution on the BRITE radar scope.

New Guy: "How come? What's going to happen?"

Kelly: "The pendulum starts to swing the other way. You see, the spotlight is now on the FAA. They're being watched and they know it. So, they stay hunkered down. They put on their masks, pretending to be good stewards of the system, good employers, good to the employees, good to the users. One day the spotlight will go out.

That's when the cockroaches come out onto the kitchen floor and dance the big ugly bug dance."

New Guy: "You mean the Jitterbug?"

Kelly: "Mark my words. Not only will they change, they will revel in their evil ways. Their eyes will turn green and their heads will do a three sixty like that exorcist thing. They will celebrate the fact that they can once again be who they really are. They will especially turn on you new guys for being new guys and so naïve. They'll laugh at you for thinking they were nice guys, thinking they were noble, forthright. Hell, they're practically laughing at you right now... laughing at you new guys for believing that it was the PATCO guys who needed firing, and not the managers who really caused the strike. One day they will start doing what they have always done…what they do best- they will make life miserable for controllers. They will make it nearly impossible for you to do your job. They will lie, and when you complain, they will call YOU the liar. You will stop looking forward to coming in to work. You will either get a bad attitude and walk around with a chip on your shoulder, or you will go about your business with eyes averted, head bowed and an apology in your mouth. They will buy most of us and intimidate a lot more. You will be able to recognize the ones who are left... the ones who cannot be bought or intimidated. They will be singled out for very special treatment. They will be targeted because they are the only real threat to FAA authority. I'm speaking of "whistleblowers." You know, the guys who talk to the press...the ones who testify before Congress. Wait till you see what happens to them."

A long silence ensues. Finally the new guy asks another question. "So, who is likely to be a…you know…one of those whistleblowers?"

Kelly keys his hand-mike to launch a jet to Detroit.

"Northwest Two Ninety Two, Runway Two Two Right, wind two zero zero at one one, cleared for takeoff."

Kelly scans the runway in front of the departing DC9. With his back to the new guy he responds. "I've seen a few of those guys. All different for the most part, different personalities, none of 'em really tough guys, not what you would think. They didn't get in your face, you know. Another pause for a transmission. "Northwest Two Ninety Two, contact Departure."

On the speaker:

"Northwest Two Ninety Two, Good night."

Kelly turns back toward the new guy. "The whistleblowers I have known? They did have something in common. Something you would never guess. Funny…but…they were all Catholic…every one."

CHAPTER 59

Due to shift swaps and other circumstances, Ray Martino noticed that for a solid two weeks he would be working with six females on his team. That would put him and Jimmy Kent in the tower cab with three or four other females at any given time during the shift. While thinking about this, Ray devised a plan for some cheap and tawdry entertainment for himself and Jimmy Kent.

Ray stops at a convenience store in Elizabeth and purchases a case of 30 ice cream push up rockets. These small ice cream treats resemble cardboard toilet paper tubes full of ice cream pushed up with a small wooden plunger as the confection is consumed. With a freezer stored full of ice cream rockets, the stage is set for an afternoon of fun with the girls in the tower. Ray appears with a half dozen ice cream treats and hands one to each person in the tower cab, then warns Jimmy Kent against making any sounds or laughing. Both men watch intently as the ladies use their hands, lips and tongues to keep the ice cream molded into shape as they consume it. Tongues swirling, lips engulfing…hands manipulating…it is almost too much for a horny tin man to take. The two men exchange knowing glances, careful not to let the girls in on the joke. Even Virgin Mary doesn't get it. But then again, she has no prior experience at that sort of thing, so she blissfully licks away at the frozen phallic symbol, giving the tin men a show they would normally never see. Though the men employed their imaginations to a large degree, the girls were actually sucking and licking, fueling the sexual fantasies of the tin men. The scene would be recounted and the story retold at many a midnight mass, according legendary status to Martino and Kent. It would become known as the day that virgin Mary went down on Ray's pocket rocket.

CHAPTER 60

One day Doherty decides to make a change. A strong premonition, a gnawing feeling that something very bad will happen, has been dwelling deep in his bones. It is not just a guess. Somehow, he knows it will happen. He has already written a few columns, published in a newsletter directed at the nation's air traffic controllers. Those writings predicted a major aviation disaster would occur in New York.

If one draws a fifteen-mile arc around the Statue of Liberty, 4 major airports are encircled. Doherty predicts that death will visit within. When asked to pin-point it further, his best guess is LaGuardia Airport, which he knows to be unequaled for danger.

The tin man has done his best to warn others. He stood his post according to standing orders and alerted the Corporal of the guard when circumstances required it. Above and beyond, he illustrated that reducing delays and increasing the margin of safety are not mutually exclusive agendas. He held his rifle aloft as long as humanly possible, and now must accept a reality, a truth that was driven home long ago. The time has come to stack arms. Having spent a career protecting others, Doherty needs to save himself.

Doherty asks, "will I miss it?" And of course, he knows he will. He will miss working with the pilots. He will miss directing the airport ballet and making safe operations out of situations that have deteriorated due to the culture of danger in the FAA. He will miss making a training success of someone otherwise destined to be bagging wood screws at his uncle's hardware store. He will miss it, but he can't stay. A person can only stay alive and independent by maintaining his sanity. A healthy mind and a rational self-interest are symbiotic virtues. Doherty's exit is a personal act of self-preservation, a gift to himself, but a necessary one. Should Doherty witness the event he knows is coming or worse, should he be unlucky enough to have contributed to it, his mental health will suffer. Suffering in such a way is no fate for a man of self-respect. No, the others can have it. Doherty can't say they deserve it, no one does. Whatever is coming will happen on someone else's watch.

Having saved a cache of gold coins over the years, Doherty has weighted *Tipitina*'s bilge with sealed plastic bins full of shiny yellow Canadian Maple Leafs and South African Kruggerands. Val Shively was visited, and Doherty dropped off three thousand 45rpm records, mostly Doo Wop groups of the fifties, but many Soul and Motown recordings. Val will hold them for 6 months, and then a decision will be made between the two record collectors about their value and ownership. Most likely, the vintage wax will be turned into gold coins and deposited in a safe box at a bank in Upper Darby. Funny and ironic, but "solid gold" is the term used by the old disc jockeys to describe such valuable recordings.

After months of preparation, on a hot august morning, *Tipitina* slips her lines in Jersey City and heads for the Verrazano Bridge and the open ocean. While passing the World Trade towers, Doherty gives the buildings a long look. Wondering if Maria is watching from her office, he busies himself stowing fenders and coiling down lines. Doherty resists the urge to wave goodbye on the slim chance that she sees and understands what is happening.

At the navigation table, Doherty takes a sip of coffee and does a quick calculation. Figuring a conservative 100 miles per day, he counts the days and circles a date on the calendar.

He will arrive on the west coast of Ireland on September 11, 2001.

Made in the USA
Middletown, DE
31 January 2019